By
Helen's
Hand

OTHER BOOKS BY AMALIA CAROSELLA

Helen of Sparta

WRITING AS AMALIA DILLIN

Honor Among Orcs

Blood of the Queen

Forged by Fate

Fate Forgotten

Beyond Fate

AMALIA CAROSELLA

BY HELEN'S HAND

LAKE UNION
PUBLISHING

Published by Lake Union Publishing, Seattle

www.apub.com

Amazon, the Amazon logo, and Lake Union Publishing are trademarks of Amazon.com, Inc., or its affiliates.

ISBN-13: 9781503933484 (paperback)
ISBN-10: 1503933482 (paperback)

Cover design by Anna Curtis

Printed in the United States of America

For Helen.
And Theseus, too.
That we might never forget the heroes of our past, no matter how far away they feel.

TABLE OF CONTENTS

And do not fear lest, if you are stolen away, fierce wars will follow after us, and mighty Greece will rouse her strength. Of so many who have been taken away before, tell me, has any one ever been sought back by arms? Believe me, that fear of yours is vain.

—Paris to Helen (Ovid, *Heroides*, 16)

.

PROLOGUE
PARIS

As a youth, Paris had dreamed of glory. He had dreamed of the day his name would be known far and wide, of the time when he might be more than just a shepherd's son, but a warrior, too, proud and strong. A dream that all boys shared, of course. He was just another fool child, not realizing what he asked for.

But when he found the girl in the woods, beautiful as a goddess, he knew his time had come. One glimpse of her golden hair and lithe body as she bathed in the river, and something deep inside him stirred. Twelve years old, and he knew his fate when she met his eyes. If she were his, he would be remembered for all time. She would bring him glory, at his side, this beautiful girl, and he would be the envy of every man, every hero, every god.

He tried to rescue her, to steal her from the man who guarded her on the opposite bank, only to find himself run down, the guard's sword at his throat instead.

"He will tell the tale, no matter what he promises," the man said, when she pleaded for his life. "You know what it will mean if word travels before we leave. Troy is not so far from Achaea that rumor will not spread."

And he realized then that he had misjudged her. She had already found her hero. She was already stolen, and desperate to remain so. Running away with her lover and wanting nothing more than peace.

If not for her kindness, her mercy, he might have died then. His name would have been forgotten, all his dreams twisted into sorrow and grief. She saved him, demanding that her guard set him free, trusting in the silence Paris had promised her in exchange for her kiss—a silence he was determined to keep, so long as it meant her safety and her freedom.

But the gods heard his prayers, smiled upon his courage, even if he had failed to make her his. For when he returned home, to the gentle slopes of Mount Ida, he found the Athenian raiders setting upon the cattle. Paris raised the alarm, shouting for the herdsmen who were farther afield, more concerned with lions and wolves than the threat of men, then took up a staff to defend the cattle himself. The thieves came at him with swords and laughter, and he braced himself, dug his heels into the rocky earth, and lifted his chin.

Perhaps he had not been able to win the girl as his prize, but he could stop this. He would stop this.

Somehow, he held them off. The gods were with him, granting him their blessing and their favor, and he survived, triumphant.

That was the day he earned his name. Songs were sung of Paris Alexandros, protector of men, and the bravery he had shown, even at so young an age. The story spread, and he no longer feared he would be forgotten. Glory had found him, at last.

But he never forgot the golden-haired beauty who had spared him with a kiss. Such was the cruelty of the gods, gifting him glory, only to steal every satisfaction from its winning.

For all Paris had dreamed of since that day was her.

PART ONE:
THE ASSEMBLY

CHAPTER ONE
PARIS

The bull charged, stygian black, with horns like crescent moons. Ekhinos cheered, his hands turned to fists in his dark curls as he urged the animal on. But Paris's bull was more nimble, turning fast and tight to meet his foe head-on with all the bruising strength of a cyclops.

The two animals crashed together again with a meaty thud. Ekhinos's bull huffed, pawing the loose earth, and Paris's prized Tauros swung his head, slashing the other beast's shoulder with the tip of one sharp horn. The black bull slipped, startled by the cut, and Tauros forced him back another step, and then two.

"No!" Ekhinos cried, all but tearing his hair from his head the way he tugged upon it. "No, no, no!"

Paris grinned, knowing already he had won. Tauros pressed the black bull until one hind hoof stumbled over the small stones that marked the edge of the ring, signaling his defeat. Tauros had not failed him yet, and today's fight was no different than the rest. Ekhinos had brought an immense beast, fit for a king, and the wagering had been fierce, favoring his greater size and strength against Tauros's known skill.

Ekhinos grumbled as he paid his debt, along with the other three herdsmen who had dared bet against Paris's bull. An amphora of wine, three rabbit furs, and an olive-wood staff that would make a fine gift for his aging father. A shame he was running out of opponents.

"Better luck next time, my friend," Paris called, clapping his hands to distract the bulls and draw their attention from one another. When that wasn't enough, he vaulted the fence, circling wide. "Tauros! Back!"

The great white bull snorted, still swinging his head, eyeing his challenger askance. Their horns clacked together, once, twice, and the black bull tossed his head, stomping. Shepherds and herdsmen could not afford to let their beasts fight to the death, the way a king might.

"Tauros!" Paris called again, slapping him upon the flank. "Enough, now, enough!"

Ekhinos moaned. "My father will spear me through when he learns I've lost Psolios."

"Then perhaps you should not have brought him to fight," Paris said, laughing. "Haven't you learned by now my Tauros always wins?"

This was the third bull he'd won, since he'd been sure enough of Tauros to bet the animal itself. Agelaus would have speared him, too, if he'd lost, though he hadn't been nearly so pleased as Paris had imagined he should be when he'd brought the first two bulls back home. Now Paris offered a golden crown for the bull who could defeat his own. No animal had yet managed to claim it.

"A full dozen fights," Oenone said, her pale hair shining in the sun. A touch of her hand upon Tauros's shoulder and the bull sighed, lifting his head proudly. "And what will you do now that Tauros has defeated all your neighbors?"

Ekhinos snorted, much like his bull. "Hasn't he told you?"

"Told me what?" Oenone asked.

"He's hoping to bring Tauros to the festival of Apollo," Ekhinos said. "To fight him against the king's bulls during the games."

Oenone scowled, and Paris carefully ignored it, busying himself by looping a length of rope around Tauros's neck.

She was beautiful and lithe, his Oenone, more than a poor shepherd's son could ever deserve, and yet, when he looked on her, he imagined another face. Hair more golden, eyes the color of grape leaves, and the petal softness of her lips. All these years later, that girl in the wood still haunted his dreams, his waking days. He didn't think Oenone was fooled, not wholly, but she hadn't abandoned him, seemingly content to herd and hunt at his side, and warm his bed at night.

"Consider me your prize," she'd told him once. "A gift from the gods for your courage to go along with your fine new name. So long as you dwell upon this mountain, herding your father's goats and sheep, and caring for the king's cattle, I'll remain at your side."

He'd never been quite sure whether she'd meant it, whether or not she was truly the nymph she claimed to be, a daughter of the river god. For surely if she were truly divine, his desires would be satisfied.

"You cannot mean to leave me behind so soon?" she asked then, one delicate hand wrapped around Taurus's long horn to keep him from lumbering away.

Paris smiled. "Only for a day or two, and you needn't remain behind. Come with me to the golden city, if you desire."

Her lips thinned, her gaze falling to the bull between them. "You won't return."

"Where else would I go?" he asked, laughing. "A shepherd's foundling son has no place inside those great walls, and Agelaus has need of me at home. A day or two, only, and I'll be back. You'll see."

But Oenone would not be consoled, turning her face away and drifting from the ring. Nor did she warm to him that night, when he drew her down to him in their bed. Stiff and silent and refusing to meet his gaze, she let him have his way, and then she rolled to her side, her cold back to him, rather than nestling close against his chest.

"You could not believe I would stay on this mountain forever," he said into the dark, the smothering silence stretching too thick between them. "I may be a shepherd's son, nothing more than a herder, but that is not all I am worth."

"Can you not be satisfied even by me? I, who would give you a long and peaceful life?" She twisted, desperation in her eyes, the caress of her fingers, and the sweetness of her breath. "Stay, Paris. Stay upon this mountain with me and think of nothing else, desire nothing else but that. Lord Apollo himself desires it, I promise you."

He wished he could say yes, could swear his heart and loyalty to her, his Oenone, his nymph, his gift from the gods, but when he closed his eyes, he still saw only one woman, barely more than a girl herself. He saw her golden hair, glowing like the sun, shining like a beacon, meant to bring him home.

"I am more than this, Oenone," he said at last. "I need more."

Her lips pinched, anger flashing across her face, impossible to miss even in the night. "You long for something you will never have. A love that will always be false."

But it was nothing he did not know already. Nothing he had not seen with his own eyes, when the woman he had hoped to claim as his own had looked to her hero, untold affection in her gaze, and the man had told her hoarsely she need not give Paris anything of herself.

So long as her hero lived, she would never love anyone but him.

It was a good thing, then, that no man lived forever, because one day, Paris promised himself, one day, love or not, she would be his.

"I've found another bull to challenge your Tauros," Oenone said, some days later while they took their turn watching his father's flock.

Since that night, all her anger had fled, replaced by soft, lingering touches and lustful glances. She took him to her heart, to her warm core, as if she might hold him, joined with her, upon the mountain for all time. He could not bring himself to dissuade her.

"The mightiest bull I've ever seen," she said, "with fire banked in his eyes. And if Tauros wins this fight, you will have all the glory you could ever desire. More than you could ever achieve at any festival, I promise you."

He laughed, pressing a kiss to her brow. "And where did you find such a magnificent bull?"

"Call it a gift from the gods, if you wish," she said, a sly smile curving her lips. "Just like me."

"The gods shower me with their favors," he said, taking her in his arms. "Shall I show you mine?"

"After you've seen the bull." She pushed him away before he could so much as kiss her. "They've named him Ares, after the god of war."

"They tempt the gods with such a name as that," Paris said. "Perhaps a sound defeat is what they deserve."

"And you are just the man to deliver it," she said, drawing him away from the flock. "Come and see if Tauros has finally met his match."

He glanced back at the sheep. "This moment?"

"He will not be kept waiting," she said. "Please, Paris? There is nothing near that will harm your father's sheep in the time it will take. You have my word, even the promise of the gods, for they've delighted in your games just as I have."

"Oenone," he chided. "You should not blaspheme."

"It is not blasphemy if it is truth, and Lord Apollo himself will guard your flock, but you must come, please, I beg of you."

He let her persuade him, sparing one last glance over his shoulder for the sheep. Even if a few were lost, he could trade one of his bulls to replace them before his father ever learned they were gone. She laced her fingers through his and pulled him along down the winding path from the pasture, breaking into a run. He chased her, so close upon her heels that her hair tickled his nose and cheeks, a caress upon his lips.

His Oenone, his gift from the gods, his nymph. In moments like these, he could not help but wonder. Any man would count himself lucky to call her his own, but the hollowness of his heart only grew, day by day, night to night. What was wrong with him that he could not shake another woman from his mind, even while he held Oenone in his arms?

It was as though the barest kiss from that strange golden goddess had bespelled him, ensorcelled him still, these years later. Perhaps she had been Aphrodite, and she had cursed him for his boldness in demanding such a boon for his silence.

But he had kept his promise, never spoken a word of the girl or the man she had named her hero. The king of Athens, he'd long suspected, after his encounter with the Athenian raiders who had meant to steal King Priam's cattle. He had held her secret locked in his heart alongside his own. Not out of fear of the gods, nor even honor, for he would have broken any vow if she had asked him to. She had desired his silence, required it for her safety, perhaps even her freedom, and he had needed no other reason but her pleasure. That she might look back upon that day and remember him, the boy who had protected her in his own small way.

And perhaps, that she might remember him when they met again, some day.

"Here!" Oenone said, slowing, her fingers still locked tight around his and forcing him to match her pace. "Here is the challenger I've found for your Tauros. And if he can keep his crown, you will have more riches than you could ever dream!"

This Ares was a burnished bronze beast, taller than Tauros at the shoulder, and broader, too, with long sickle horns, tipped with gold at the knife-sharp points. Paris stared, drinking in the sight. He'd never seen a bull so fine, so perfect in its proportions, so beautiful to behold.

"Bring Tauros, and take your prize," Oenone breathed in his ear, wrapping her arms around him and pressing her curves against his back. "Take your prize, take me, and be satisfied."

CHAPTER TWO
PARIS

More than two dozen men gathered for the fight, all herdsmen and shepherds from the surrounding lands, and two officials from the palace, who had come to check on the king's flocks. Paris walked with Ekhinos, checking the circle of stones and pebbles that marked the ring, ensuring it remained unbroken. Tauros paced the inner edge beside him, trained well to keep inside his circle, and the bronze Ares stood unconcerned, idly scratching his flank with the tip of one curved horn.

"Tauros is not favored in the wagering," Ekhinos said. "Truth be told, my friend, I do not see how he can win this fight."

Paris pressed his lips thin, but his gaze found Oenone rather than settling upon the rival bull. She sat upon the fence, neat ankles crossed, laughing with the palace men. And what would she do if he lost? He was not certain what outcome he hoped for, not truly, despite her determined words. Always, she behaved as if Tauros would win, but when she looked upon Ares, there was something strange in her eyes, as if she knew the bronze bull's mind. When he'd questioned her about the animal's owner, she'd only laughed and waved the concern away, promising him he would learn all he needed to know after the fight was won.

"The ring is ready," Ekhinos said. "The longer you delay, the more men will bet against you, thinking you have no faith in your own bull."

"Tauros will not betray me," Paris said, and he did not doubt his own words. He reached across the stones to slap the bull's white shoulder. Tauros would fight well, as he always did; he only feared that Ares would fight better still. "Defeat him, and you will be king among bulls, my friend. Men will speak of your magnificence for ages to come."

And then he stepped back, ducking beneath the fence posts and taking his place beside Oenone.

"Bring the heifer," he called.

Ekhinos's brother brought the cow into sight, then nearer, to the fence line, where the bulls might catch her scent. Unmated, but ready to be planted with her first calf. Tauros stopped his ambling, lowing long and bold, claiming her for his own. Ares snorted, his gaze hard upon Tauros as he pawed the ground. And charged.

Nimble Tauros turned easily to meet him, dropping his head and tangling their horns. They scraped and clattered, bone on bone, the sound ringing sharp and loud in the air. Silence had fallen over the men, and Paris gripped the fence, his fingers digging into the wood so hard it splintered in his hands.

The bulls broke, backing warily from one another, circling like men with swords, waiting for the other to drop his guard. Ares's tail swung, snapping against his flanks, and Tauros snorted in response, stiff-legged and proud.

This time, it was Tauros who charged. Ares moaned, eyes rolling, then ran to meet him hard. The thwack of their horns, the thud of their skulls striking. And Ares turned, catching Tauros's horns in his own with a twist of his head, lifting the white bull's forelegs off the ground and tossing him away.

The men cheered, and Paris's heart sank. Tauros scrambled, nearing the edge of the ring before he gained his feet beneath him again, steady and strong, but shaken. Paris could see it in the tremble of his hide, the whipping of his tail, and the twitching of his nose. And Ares waited, patient as Athena, his head held high. Waited for Tauros to rise and come for him again.

Slower this time, cautious after his fall, Tauros moved toward him, tossing his head. Ares pawed the earth, once, twice, almost lazy now.

"He knows he's won," one of the palace men murmured.

Paris knew the man was right. Knew it in his heart even as he shouted Tauros on. It wasn't about only strength, after all, but strategy, and Tauros had learned the game well. That, more than anything else, was why he had won so often.

"Push him back, Tauros," he urged. "You do not have to be the stronger, only the wiser. Push him back!"

Tauros knew his purpose, and Ares deigned to lower his head, watching his approach. Their horns whispered against one another like a lover's caress, their foreheads touching, barely brushing. More a question than a test. Tauros braced himself, digging his hooves into the loose earth, finding purchase before he made his move.

Their horns, four crescent moons, locked with a snap, and Tauros strained, one step forward, and then another.

And Ares gave. A hind hoof slipped, forcing him back. Just a handspan, at first, and then an arm's length, while Tauros grunted and heaved against his foe. Paris cheered. Just a little more, a little farther, and they would have the win. Oenone's hand covered his, squeezing tight, her joyous laughter singing in his heart, burbling and bright.

But Tauros stalled—they both did, horns still locked and breath coming hard.

Then Ares pushed back.

Muscles rippled beneath his bronze hide, and he surged forward again, causing Tauros to lose his hold, then his footing, too. Ares bellowed, catching him, horn to horn, twisting his head until they turned, turned, turned.

The arc was too wide, the bulls too large, and Tauros's hind hoof caught on one of the ring's stones.

Burnished Ares had won.

Paris closed his eyes, took a breath, and then nodded to Oenone. She lifted the golden crown from her neck, too large to sit upon her head, and Paris vaulted into the ring. Tauros had lost, and Ares had won, and there was no honor in delay.

He set the crown upon Ares's broad head and called out, "The winner is Ares, lord of all bulls upon the mount, bringing glory to the god of war!"

The mighty bronze bull threw back his head, gold-tipped horns flashing, and laughed.

Ares.

The bull had been the god, come to test him, and one glance at Oenone had told him she had known all along. But he had bitten his tongue and knelt before the god of war, the bronze bull melting into an armored man, breastplate embossed with a bloody battle, so real, so grim, Paris could hear the cries of the dying when he looked upon it.

And that ruthless god, friend to no one, had laughed and called him just, named him honest and fair.

"Do you not see?" Oenone said later, after all the rest had gone, and they had led Tauros back to his herd, awarding him the heifer for his work. "I did it for you! Now, all of Troy will know you for your judgment, will praise you for your nobility. You are more than just a shepherd's son, Paris, you are marked and acclaimed by the gods them-selves. Surely you must be satisfied by that."

Satisfied. He searched her face, wondering at the word. "You've done this to keep me upon the mountain, haven't you? To keep me at your side."

She smiled, taking his hands in hers, gripping them tight. "To give you what you desired, my love. As is my duty, if I am to be your wife."

"My wife?" He pulled away. "Oenone, I have told you before, I will not live a life chained to this mountain, this place. You have given me a gift, and I thank you for it, but there is more for me than a small sheepfold and a few bulls, I am certain of it."

Her eyes hardened into chips of glass, her chin rising high. "And what will I tell your son of his father, then? The man who was named by Ares himself as just and fair has left him behind, for he did not think us a worthy purpose for his life?"

His thoughts tripped and all argument fled. "My son?"

Oenone pressed a hand, fingers spread, to the place above her womb. "Even if you would abandon me, you cannot think to give him up so easily. No matter what fortune you seek."

"My son," he said again, staring at her stomach. He reached out, covering her hand with his own, hoping for some small sign of the life within. "Truly?"

"A nymph knows," she said simply. "And soon enough, you will see the proof."

They had been lovers for so long without any fruits, he'd long since forgotten to think of it at all. "Have you known all this time?"

"The month," she admitted. "But a quickening does not always bring a child, not when the father is a mortal. I waited only to be certain this one would live. And he is strong, my love. Strong as his father to cling so determinedly to my womb."

He laughed, meeting her eyes. His Oenone, his gift from the gods. And now she would give him a child, too, a son. There was no greater gift, not even the praise of a god.

"Tell me you will stay," she said. "Tell me you will be a father to your son."

"Of course," he said, drawing her close. He pressed his nose into her hair, breathing in her scent. Fern and clover and meadow grass, his nymph. "I would not ever spurn such a gift as this."

And when the boy was grown and weaned, he would show him the world beyond Mount Ida. Surely even Oenone could not object to that.

CHAPTER THREE
HELEN

The stone walls rose up to form a narrow channel, guiding us toward the immense gate, and I shivered beneath my cloak. *Mycenae.* Thank the gods I did not ride alone, for I never would have had the courage to enter otherwise, and even with my brother Pollux behind me on the horse, and his twin Castor at our side, I wanted nothing more than to throw myself off and run back the way I had come. If I could only return to Athens, and Theseus's bed, where I had known myself safe and free and loved. But my brothers had marched on Athens to bring me home, stealing me back while Theseus journeyed to the house of Hades on a fool's errand.

"Castor and I will guard you at every moment," Pollux promised, when I caught sight of the lion gate and began to tremble outright. "Menelaus will not touch you, Helen, I swear it."

Two years I had spent in safety, as Theseus's guest, and then as his wife and queen in Athens, hidden from my family by a false name. Two years believing I had foiled the gods, stolen my fate from their hands, and averted a war that would destroy us all. Two years of peace and love, lost in one moment's betrayal when Theseus's cousin, Menestheus, traded me for the kingship of Athens. And now I shrank beneath the weight of so much stone, watching it close in around me, squeezing out every breath of hope and crushing me into dust.

After I had left Sparta, arranging my own abduction by Theseus to escape the future of my nightmares, I had hoped I would never have to see Menelaus again.

"Did you send the riders?" I asked, fighting to keep my voice steady, my heart calm.

"Two dozen men," Pollux assured me. "And another dozen sent to the nearest ports, to travel by sea."

Though they'd stolen me back, my brothers were far from indifferent to my plight. Castor and Pollux had agreed to help me, to protect me from my fated marriage to Menelaus in every way they could, even if they could not return me to Theseus's arms. We would begin by spreading the word of my homecoming. Riders and runners had been sent to every palace, every king and prince from Attica to Ithaca, Thessaly to Crete. Menelaus would have more competition than he could manage, and more importantly, my father would have no choice but to entertain their offers of marriage with an assembly and games, as he'd sworn to Zeus long before. It would give me time, give Theseus time to make his way back from the Underworld, that he might retrieve me. And if for some reason he could not come—a thought I would not so much as whisper aloud, for fear the gods would hear and make it so—surely one of the many men to arrive would be better suited for me than the prince of Mycenae.

I could only pray. To my father Zeus, to Aphrodite, to Hera and Athena for his protection and safety, to Hermes and Iris, that word might travel to Theseus even below the earth among the spirits of the dead and hurry him on his way. I meant to spend every day from dawn to dusk upon my knees in supplication, begging every favor from the gods, if that was what it took to bring Theseus to my side. I would do everything in my power to keep Menelaus from winning me as his bride and the war from following. But even the war, I thought, I might suffer more easily, if only I could face it with Theseus.

The massive gate groaned open before us, and I could not keep my eyes from rising to the lions above it. Two immense beasts, carved from the stone itself, and vicious as the brothers who ruled the lands surrounding us. Agamemnon and Menelaus, the cursed sons of Atreus.

Pollux kicked our horse into a canter and we rode through, the rock swallowing us whole. But I had no intention of allowing it to bury me.

Let the lions roar at the storm, if they liked. Perhaps I was no longer queen of Athens, but I was still Helen of Sparta and a daughter of Zeus. I was wind and rain and thunder and lightning. And no matter what came, I would survive it.

We were greeted by more stone inside and an immense ramp, leading up above workshops and small houses. My sister, Clytemnestra, met us at the palace proper, atop the grand staircase with a red-haired daughter in her arms. Pollux and Castor dismounted, but I could not bring myself to drop from the horse's back. Once I set my feet upon the ground, I was no longer queen, no longer Theseus's wife, no longer safe. And my sister—the new queen of Mycenae, as Agamemnon's wife—had the power to ruin me, ruin everything, if she breathed one wrong word in her husband's ear. If Menelaus learned I had been in Athens all this time, that Theseus had stolen me two years ago—and worse, had done so in obedience to my own wishes—I did not believe for a moment he would not march against them, and queen or not, I owed the Athenians my protection still. It was the least I could do for Theseus, when he had given me so much.

"Come, Helen," Castor said, reaching up for me. I let him help me down, clinging to his strength for support. "The sooner this is done, the better. And at least it is not Agamemnon and Menelaus who greet us."

I swallowed at his name, my throat suddenly tight. Menelaus had done more than simply violate my body that night so long ago. He had betrayed me in every possible way with his lies, and the violence and threats that had followed. Once, perhaps, I might have called him my friend. I might even have believed I could love him when we were children playing together, that of all the men in Achaea, he was the one I would choose for myself as a husband. But that time had ended when he had gone to war, fighting for his brother to take back Mycenae, and had come back so changed. As I had become a woman, he had become a man obsessed, and now his name, even the thought of him, only sickened me with dread. Because according to my nightmares, our marriage would bring about the war, and my beauty had already inspired his rage.

If it had been only my suffering, my pain, I would not have fought so hard to escape. But I could not, would not, doom Sparta to such a fate. I would not betray my people the way Menelaus had betrayed me.

"Do not make me stay more than this night, Castor. Whatever excuses we must make, I cannot linger here."

He shared a glance with Pollux, who offered the barest nod, and we climbed the stairs to reach our sister, who stood tall and regal before the palace entrance. A far grander palace than Sparta's, perhaps it would be enough to satisfy her, after so many years of strife. Resentment had grown between us as thick as Mycenae's walls, nursed by Leda's jealous mothering as much as by my beauty. Nestra had never believed that I did not care for the attention it brought me, the ogling of the men, even after she had been promised to Agamemnon. And she had hated the way they could not tear their gazes from my body when she stood willing before their eyes.

"My brother-in-law will be pleased to hear the news," Nestra said, after welcoming us formally. She gave up her daughter, Iphigenia, to a servant, and sent them both back inside with a flick of her fingers. "Menelaus has done nothing but mope about since you were lost, and I cannot say I will not be happy to have him out from underfoot, now that you're returned. Mother will have you married before the new moon, I'm sure, and thank the gods for Menelaus. I don't know who else would have you now."

There was no hiding my disappearance, of course. The news of my sudden abduction two years ago had traveled throughout Achaea. But my brothers had put out the story that I had only lately been found by the Athenians. Castor and Pollux claimed that Menestheus, Theseus's trusted steward, had sent word to my family in Sparta, allowing them to retrieve me. It kept Theseus's people safe, and I could not argue with that, but I also could not escape a certain amount of shame and dishonor with such a story. My virtue as an untouched bride would be questioned after so long spent in the supposed company of unknown brutes, and it was clear my sister delighted in how far I had fallen.

Pollux's jaw clenched at her assumptions, so blithely offered as fact. "After everything our sister has suffered, even Leda cannot expect her to marry so quickly. She needs time to recover from her abduction, and the sooner she is returned home to the safety of the palace in Sparta, the better."

"There is no palace safer than mine," Nestra said primly. "Agamemnon will agree, and Menelaus will have my head if I let you go before he has a chance to see Helen."

"Where is the prince of Mycenae?" I made myself ask, for if I stood there a moment longer, exposed at the top of the staircase, unknowing, I would scream.

Nestra waved a hand. "Out hunting, of course. Mope and hunt, mope and hunt. He's worthless for anything else. My husband and his brother will return in time for the evening meal, and you'll spend the night, of course. Truly, I do not see any reason why you should be in such a hurry to leave again."

"Father will wish to see Helen with his own eyes," Castor said. "And so will Mother. To say nothing of the men who are likely to come pouring in from all corners of the earth, in pursuit of her hand."

Nestra laughed. "You cannot honestly believe that? After she was stolen away and held captive for more than two years? She could be with child, for all anyone knows, and no one wants a cuckoo in their nest."

The accusation ripped through me, and I flinched beneath her sharp-eyed gaze. Her lips curved just slightly, and I had no doubt she had meant for her words to hurt me. But she could never have known I had been pregnant, that Theseus had been forced to sacrifice our child, our living daughter, to Zeus, or that it had nearly cost us everything.

"Tyndareus made a vow to the gods that I would not be given into marriage without the proper rites and games," I said, keeping the flare of anger from my voice with no small amount of effort. "He must keep it and call an assembly of suitors. If no other man desires to win me but Menelaus, so be it, but Father will not risk Zeus's anger. Not again. And nor will I."

"The mistake you have always made, Helen, was believing you had any choice at all," Nestra snapped. "And a pretty face will hardly make up for the rest—Sparta's kingship is not so great a prize that men will flock to a woman who did not have the decency to take her own life after she was raped. Had I been you, I would have rather died than be found unmarried, to save Father the disgrace."

I narrowed my eyes. "Then perhaps it is better if Menelaus loses me in the games, that you need not be tainted by my infamy."

"You ungrateful little—"

"Nestra, she is overwrought, that is all," Pollux interrupted, stepping between us. "And if it is anyone's fault that she lives, you must blame me, for I would not let her give up her life, even for honor. Give us a room for the night, and you need not tolerate us beyond morning, I promise you."

Clytemnestra sniffed, lifting her chin even as she turned her face away. "If she is so ill at ease, as you suggest, perhaps it would be better if she remained in her room. Come to think of it, I doubt very much my husband will desire to flaunt our connection before his assembly."

"We will happily accept a meal sent to our room, if that is your wish," Castor said. "It has been a long journey, and while Pollux might have strength to spare for feasting, I confess myself exhausted. A bed, a meal, and wine will serve me very well."

She gave another flick of her fingers, and a man stepped forward from his place in the shadow of the wall. "Our steward will show you to your rooms. If you wish to wash, he'll take you to the bathing room as well. Helen, however, will have to use a basin in her quarters, for I will not have her walking the halls and distracting my husband's men."

"Of course," Pollux said. "My thanks for your kindness."

"When Menelaus arrives, I will send him to you," Nestra said to me, before dismissing us into the care of her steward.

Whether it was malice or ignorance, I could not tell, but I was beginning to wonder just what my sister knew of my relationship with Menelaus and the night he raped me. How much had he told Agamemnon, and how much had Agamemnon shared with his wife?

The steward led us through a wide, open court of painted cement and deeper into the palace. The stone was thick, and while there were windows and light wells enough, the halls felt damp and dark rather than bright and sun warmed. It did not seem as though Agamemnon was interested in prettying his walls, or perhaps he simply refused to part with the gold and goods it would require to see it done. Mycenae might have been grand once, and it was surely well fortified still, but compared to Athens, to the beauty of the palace upon the Rock, it may as well have been a cave.

"My queen suggested you would not be unhappy to share a room together, my lords," the steward said, stopping before an open door off the long sloping hallway. "And if my lady will follow me—"

"My sister will remain with us," Pollux said, his hand on the small of my back propelling me after Castor, inside the room. "I do not dare leave her alone for long, no matter how safely ensconced, for fear she might yet find a way to do herself harm."

"My queen—"

"What your queen does not know will not offend her," Pollux said, offering a far too charming smile. He slipped a gold bracelet from his arm and pressed it into the steward's hand. "With my gratitude for your assistance. Now, if you would be so kind as to escort me to the baths and have that basin brought to our room. If you like, you can claim Castor desired it . . ."

Castor shut the door on the rest of his excuses, and I repressed another shiver at the state of the room. Sparsely furnished, with two beds and plenty of furs and linens, but little else. Not even a low table at which to eat or seating of any kind.

"Is Mycenae truly so poor as this?" I asked, frowning.

"Agamemnon is too thrifty to waste his gold on comforts," Castor said. "He would rather spend it on arms and armor and ships, if he spends it at all. Most of the finest goods made here leave in trade for more of the same."

"Ships for what?"

Castor arched an eyebrow, as if I ought to have known. "Menelaus has been certain that war was coming from the moment you disappeared, and I'm certain you can imagine how happy Agamemnon was for the excuse to build his army. He promises men gold and land if they will come fight for him, and in the meantime he sends them out raiding to sharpen their skills. They bring him back even more gold and goods for his hoard, and he allows them a share of the spoils in return for risking life and limb."

The damp chill settled into my bones at his words, and I hugged myself. "He used me even while I thought myself outside of his power."

"You should consider, Helen, that it is not only Leda who has reason to desire this match. Agamemnon is too powerful to offend, and Tyndareus will play a dangerous game if he chooses any other but Menelaus for your husband. Far more dangerous than it was two years ago, when Mycenae was only just recovering from the war, and even then . . ."

"Even then, Father risked much," I finished for him. "But if marriage to Menelaus brings war, the death of thousands, it is worth the risk to thwart it, Castor."

He shook his head. "I am not so certain that it will not bring a war, regardless. No matter who you marry, there will be fighting and blood spilled. The way Menelaus has carried on these two years—you do not know how near he came to marching upon Athens after Theseus married, though we had no reason to think you had remade yourself as the Egyptian princess Meryet. He was convinced, utterly, that Theseus could not have taken another bride but you, that Theseus was as mad for you as he was. If Agamemnon had had more men or more ships then, if he had believed he could win a fight against Theseus, blood would already have drowned the fields of Attica."

I let out a breath, my chest tight. "Theseus will return. And if Agamemnon chooses to march upon the Rock after my husband reclaims me, let him. He will not win, and the gods will have the death they desire."

"And if Theseus does not return in time, Helen, what then?"

I pressed my lips together and met his eyes. Did he truly not realize how much it pained me even to think it? Every assumption they made of Theseus's doom drove another blade into my heart. He had to come for me. He had sworn as much. But if he didn't . . . "I will do what I must to protect those that I love. Even to protect myself, if it is necessary."

"Not your people?" he asked, his voice softer. "Not Sparta, too?"

"Do you not see?" I said. "It was for Sparta that I left, Castor. For Sparta that I fought against a marriage to Menelaus, from the start. But if the gods are determined that Sparta should be brought to ruin, that this nightmare of destruction should be wrought through me, what am I to do? I have tried to escape this fate and failed. I will try again, and again, and again, and I will pray to the gods for Theseus's return, but you and Pollux have brought me to this place. You brought me here, you mean to bring me home, and now you ask me what I will do to save our people? Perhaps Nestra is not so wrong, after all. Perhaps it would be better if I died and all of this was ended."

"Helen." He caught me by the shoulder, drawing me into his arms when I would have turned away. I hid my face against his chest, blinking back the tears that threatened to spill from my eyes.

"Forgive me, Helen," he murmured into my hair. "Forgive us both."

And I knew that I would. Because they had done all this for me. For the sister they loved. But it did not mean I wanted it. It did not mean they had done what was best or right. It did not mean I trusted them to keep me safe from the fate I still fought against or the will of the gods.

Not even Theseus had saved me from that.

CHAPTER FOUR
HELEN

Long days on the Isthmus road had left us all covered in dust and sweat, and I envied my brothers their baths while I struggled to wash myself properly with nothing but a basin and a rag. I did not dare to even rinse my dyed hair, for fear of the dark stains it would leave behind. Pollux stood outside the door, granting me some small measure of privacy for the task, but just being in Mycenae, knowing that Menelaus would seek me out, made me too uneasy to enjoy the solitude. And I missed Theseus's mother, Aethra, with her steady hands, her kindness. She had treated me as a daughter, even knowing the danger of my presence and my love for her son. I missed the way she had looked at me—as if I were simply a woman, and my beauty a happenstance.

Pollux had not been able to meet my gaze from the moment the small basin had arrived. As if the sight of the water conjured images of my nakedness that he could not bear. My own brother, unable to look upon me without lust. It was as Leda had said all my life. This beauty, this supposed gift of the gods, was nothing more than a curse. A tool meant to drive men into madness.

"Where is she?" a rough voice demanded, loud enough for me to hear through the door.

Menelaus.

My stomach twisted, bile rising, and I grabbed up the stained underdress of my Athenian gown, no longer caring how filthy it was, only that I could not be naked with his voice so near. I could not be here. I could not be seen.

I fumbled with the fabric, my fingers thick and clumsy with panic.

"I'm afraid my sister is in no condition to receive you," Pollux said. "It has been a long journey, and she has endured much."

"Helen is *mine*," Menelaus growled, and something thumped hard against the wooden door, making me jump.

The basin tipped, and I lurched to catch its fall. Too slow. My fingers too useless with fear. It fell with a crash, dirty water spraying everywhere.

"Helen?" Menelaus called. "Helen, open the door!"

The wood shuddered. As if Menelaus had pulled on the door and Pollux had stopped him with his greater strength.

"Would you truly invade her bath?" Pollux asked, a clear edge to his words. "There will be time enough for you to speak with her after she is recovered from her ordeal, Menelaus. But you will not see her this night."

"This is my home! You have no *right*—"

"I am her brother and her guardian," Pollux snapped. "I have *every* right. Whatever claim you think you have upon my sister, it is done, and I do not care what promises Leda made. A daughter of Zeus deserves better than a cursed son of Atreus. *Sparta* deserves better."

"You forget yourself and your place," Menelaus said with a snarl. "Were I not bound by law, I would spill your blood upon these stones and claim your sister upon your corpse."

"Were *I* not bound by law, you would not have lived long enough to bang upon her door," Pollux said coolly. "You forget you speak to a son of Zeus, and I am not the whelp you left behind in Sparta when you went to war. Not anymore."

"Menelaus!" Castor's voice rang clear and light, and I let out a breath of relief at his interruption.

Sacred law or not, the threats exchanged had not been idle. One more insult, given or perceived, and the gods would curse them both when it came to blood.

"We didn't expect you so soon," Castor said, nearer now. "Nestra let us believe we would be fortunate if you arrived before full dark."

There was silence for a long moment, and I crept toward the door, the better to listen.

"I was about to go in search of your kitchens, but perhaps you would show me the way?" Castor suggested. "I'm certain Helen will be better fed if the meal is sent by your authority, rather than my sister's."

Menelaus's snort of disgust was as familiar as his voice, and I held my breath, waiting. Castor had always had a talent for calming horses, though I'd never thought it might apply to men as well. I should have realized. I should have wondered when Theseus had professed his own abilities. So many nights, he'd soothed me back to sleep, and it had never occurred to me that my brothers might have some power of their own.

"Nestra was always a fool when it came to her sister," Menelaus admitted, the words grudging. "And she is likely to be even more foolish while Helen sleeps under her roof. She has not forgiven Agamemnon for his lust, though it is hardly his fault."

"Of course," Castor said, and I could hear the smile in his voice. "All the more reason for us not to linger, but I'm certain my brother told you we cannot stay more than the night."

Menelaus's reply was lost as they moved away, and I let my forehead drop against the warm wood of the door, relief making me weak.

"Are you well, Helen?" Pollux asked, his voice pitched low. "It's safe now, if you've finished washing."

I slid the wooden bar from the bracket that secured it and pushed the door open, letting my brother inside. He shut it firmly behind him, his gaze filled with concern.

"I'm sorry," I said, unable to meet his eyes. "When the door rattled, I jumped, and the basin tipped—"

He shook his head. "You've nothing to apologize for. Even if—if things had been different, and he had been your friend, still, I would not have let him barge in upon you while you bathed. He's lost all reason when it comes to you."

"I won't accept the blame for his madness, Pollux," I said. "What has become of Menelaus is not my doing."

"Do you truly believe I think so?" he asked. "Helen, it is not your fault you are beautiful, nor that the gods gave you such power over men. Of course I do not blame you for the results. I cannot imagine you would use such power maliciously to ruin even Menelaus if you could will it otherwise."

"You misunderstand me, Brother," I said, my hands closing into fists. I could not shoulder this burden. Theseus had been the proof of its falseness, along with the rest of Athens. The men had wanted me, certainly, but none of them had become so warped with lust and desire as Menelaus. "It is not my beauty that is to blame, either. Menelaus has gone mad because of his own weakness, the faults in his own mind, already present. Perhaps my beauty gave focus to his desires, but it might have been another woman just as easily."

Pollux laughed. "As much comfort as it might give you to think the power you possess over men is so trifling, I do not see how you can believe your beauty played no part in this. Do you think it was not jealousy that drove Menestheus to betray Theseus? The same light burned in his eyes in Athens as it did moments ago in Menelaus's. A flash of gold and fire, lust and desire, ignited by your very presence in their midst."

"And what of Theseus? Of the hundreds of other men who saw me in Athens?" I asked. "Why were they not so corrupted?"

My brother shrugged. "You ask me for answers only the gods possess. But I promise you, Sister, those other men did not survive unscathed. Theseus, perhaps, was an exception, though I cannot imagine he would have gone along with your scheme if not for some desire to possess you."

I stiffened. "Theseus stole me away at my urging and never demanded any favor from me in return. He would not have married me at all if it had not been *my* desire to become his bride and queen."

Pollux raised his hands, palm out. "I do not mean to say he did not act honorably, Helen. I am certain that he did, or he would never have earned your devotion, fierce as it is. Only to say that he wanted you, too. It was written plainly in every glance he gave you, every kindness he showed. And before he met you, the king of Athens had sworn never to marry again. What else could account for his change of heart but for the power of your beauty, granted to you by Zeus himself?"

"My beauty could not persuade him to remain in Athens," I snapped. "It was not power enough to keep him at my side, though you would have me believe it attracts Menelaus like a moth to the flame."

"Every man is different," Pollux said. "And Theseus was stronger and wiser than most. Of course he would not be ruled by lust the way another might be."

Was. The word struck me like a knife to the breast, and I turned away. "You truly believe he is dead."

He sighed. "Whether he is or not, I do not see how he will find his way back. And I would not have you suffer such a cruel disappointment. Not when it might be compounded by marriage to a man you may not ever love."

"Marriage to Menelaus, you mean."

"Marriage to any man who is not Theseus."

I closed my eyes, hating the truth of his words. No matter who Tyndareus chose, I would not be so fortunate as to find such joy, such love and affection and kindness again. Theseus had not only loved me, he had seen me as his equal in all things, respected me as his queen, and asked for my counsel. Likely, I would be treated as little more than a child when it came to the ruling of my people, but for the role Sparta's queen must play as priestess.

And that position, that of high priestess, would have challenges of its own. I had not thought of it before—I was more concerned with escaping my nightmares and averting the war that threatened than with what my duty might be if I became queen—but making sacrifices and offerings to the gods who had trapped me so utterly was likely to be torturous. I could not imagine Poseidon accepting any such offering from my hands on behalf of my people as queen. He had made it more than clear that he would grant me no more favors, for all the good it had done me to beg him for any aid at all.

I had still lost my daughter. Nearly lost my own life as well. And Theseus.

Oh, Theseus.

Had I known then what was coming, would I have traded my daughter willingly to stop it? To remain safe in Athens, with Theseus at my side? Part of me wished I had not fought so desperately. To have lost so much, to have seen even my daughter given up to the gods for supposed peace, and to find myself still in this place, facing this future . . .

"He will come, Pollux. I have to believe it."

Or else everything I had sacrificed, everything *we* had lost, would have been for nothing.

The nightmares returned again that night, old friends who would not be forgotten no matter how hard I fought against sleep.

I stand on the palace walls of the shining city, my arms wrapped around my own shoulders against the wind that whips around my body, tearing at my cloak and gown and pulling my golden hair free from its braids. Below me, four thousand men march out the city gate; the clink of metal and flap of leather bounces against the stone. Four thousand men going to their slaughter like so many lambs. The thought of the sacrifice makes my heart ache for Theseus, for all the days he spent upon his knees and so little now to show for it.

A dark-haired prince looks up at me, grim faced. His bronze armor no longer flashes in the sun, dulled by so many days of battle and thick with dust and blood. He raises his sword in salute when our eyes meet, and I wonder if he even knows why he fights this war.

"You've seen what we will do for you," my stranger whispers in my ear. The Trojan prince of my nightmares who has stolen me from my home, bringing me across the sea and imprisoning me behind these walls.

The warmth of his body against mine tempts me to lean back, but I keep myself stiff and turn my face away. "I've seen death brought to your people for my sake, though I have begged only for my release."

"You came to me willingly enough that night in Sparta." He brushes my hair over my shoulder, his fingers lingering at the column of my neck.

I shiver, jerking away. "To reason with you! But I should have known it was a fool's errand. Just as it is now. You've convinced them to fight for you, for me, but you can never have what you want. Even if I loved you, I am already married. Even if I loved you, you would be the last man I would ever give myself to. You ask me to trade the world for one night of your pleasure, and I cannot. I will not."

"But you tremble at my touch, all the same. And you've said your-self you have no love for Menelaus. Why cling to your marriage to that worthless man when he does not even treat you with the respect you deserve?"

"As you do?" I scoff, turning to glare at him. "Was it respect that drove you to abduct me from my own city? Respect that keeps me prisoner here now? Is it respect that makes you insist I will have you, though I have told you repeatedly all I wish is to be returned home?"

He smiles, catching my hand and tugging me back against his body. His hand on my skin burns hotter than the sun, his lust fogging my thoughts in the same way that his determination has infected his brother and father, convincing them to fight for us. I have seen him work his wiles over the two men, seen him turn the nobles into his slaves with a handclasp, and I know it is his gift, this charm, this persuasion that he will name only as Aphrodite's blessing. With it, he can make me love him, too, if he wishes. Make my body yearn for his. But he hasn't yet. I can only pray that he never will.

"Helen, my love." He holds me fast until my breathing quickens and my heart begins to race with fear. "If you did not have my respect, you would be beneath me in my bed, not standing atop this wall."

"If you had any respect for me at all, you would have given me up when I asked it of you the first time."

He laughs and I break free, tearing my hand from his and stumbling back. The moment he no longer touches me, my head begins to clear. I gulp cold air like a landed fish, leaning heavily against the wall while I struggle against the last of his lingering influence. This was the same power Theseus had used to soothe me in the night, but if I had ever doubted his claim that he had not used it for more, this was my proof. I had never felt this.

The prince fingers a strand of my hair, watching me, his lips curving in a knowing smile. "You'll change your mind when Menelaus is dead."

"Menelaus won't be killed." I knock his hand away. "Not by you."

His smile turns into a sneer. "Be careful, Helen."

"Or what?" I raise my chin, meeting his eyes. My heart is so filled with hate and pain, I do not care what risks I take. Theseus is gone, and no matter what happens now, the city will turn to ash and cinders. It will be a relief to go with it. "You'll take me by force? Rape me like Menelaus?"

"You can't fight the will of the gods forever," he growls.

"I don't need to wait forever. I need only last until the city falls and the blood of your people flows thick in the streets. But perhaps if I am lucky, the gods will see us both dead first."

Then I leave him, skipping down the stone steps to the temple of Athena. When my foot hits the paved street, everything turns to fire. I let it burn my skin, my hair, my clothing from my body, and keep walking. Women scream and children cry, but the flame wraps around me like a cloak, caressing my arms and legs, tickling my stomach. I fall to my knees and weep with the realization it will not take me.

I will never be free.

"Hush, Helen." Castor's voice slips through the fire, the brush of a hand upon my brow, smoothing my hair from my face and dousing the flames. "Hush, now, and sleep."

The darkness that swallows me has never been so sweet.

CHAPTER FIVE
MENELAUS

He could not sleep, knowing she was beneath his roof. Years spent in search of her, and she had been found by her brothers in Athens. Athens! And how convenient that it was only after King Theseus had been lost. He raked his fingers through his hair. If Agamemnon had only let him ride to Athens after that thrice-cursed Athenian, he might have had her in his bed these last two years. She might have been his, all this time!

But surely her brothers would not have given her up so easily, even to King Theseus. No, he decided, throwing his legs over the edge of the bed and rising to pace the room. No, if they had known that worthless Athenian had taken her, they would have raised an army to get her back. And if Theseus had taken her, they would have known. How could the king of Athens have hidden her, beautiful as she was? His men would have looked upon her and war would have broken out, even in peaceful Attica. They would have slain their own king to have her for themselves.

He would have murdered Theseus with his bare hands. The gods would have granted him the strength! Helen was his, after all, promised and claimed. He had claimed her, and she had been willing enough. Stripping herself of her gown with her own hands, offering her body. After torturing him for so long before, she could hardly have done otherwise. She had treated him cruelly for too long with all her teasing, and now she was returned, at last, at last.

Menelaus closed his hands into fists. She was returned and beneath his roof, his bedded bride, and her brothers had dared to turn him away? He threw open his door, making his way by moonlight through the cold stone halls of Mycenae. He knew his way, even in the darkest night. His childhood home, all its secrets revealed again since Agamemnon had reclaimed it. His sister-in-law had given Helen her own room, but when he had gone in search of her there, she had been hiding in her brothers' room instead. *Bathing.*

The thought of her naked and flushed, her soft skin bare and waiting, had almost undone him. How he had dreamed of having her again. Taken woman after woman to his bed, only to close his eyes and imagine Helen in their place, her softness, her curves, her shining golden hair, fisted in his hand. None of them satisfied him the way she could. He felt nothing when he spilled his seed into their begging wombs. And then they would come to him, months later, claiming he had planted them, that his seed had taken root. But he knew the truth. He knew their ways, the lies they told, thinking to win his favor. Thinking that with Helen lost, he would take them to wife in her place.

As if any woman could take her place.

The weeping drew him to her brothers' door. The cries so precious to him, so familiar. How often had he stood beneath her window in the night, listening to her sob in her sleep, imagining her tears were for him? Every desperate moan of his name made him harden all the more, until he ached with the pain of his need.

He listened now, again, hardly breathing, waiting for his name. If she still suffered from these nightmares, she had not forgotten him, no matter how long she had been away. She still belonged to him, by the will of the gods themselves. Fate had tied them together, and he would not let anything tear them apart. Not again. Never again.

"No!" she cried. "Please! Just let me burn, let me die!"

Menelaus growled, pressing his hand to the door. With her brothers inside, he did not dare enter. Not after the threats Pollux had made before. But to stand outside, to be barred from her—

"I never wanted this," she moaned. "I never wanted you."

His lip curled, the words lodging like spears in his chest. If it weren't for these dreams, she would have been his long ago. By now she would have had more than one babe at her breast, and he would never have had to suffer this humiliation. Over and over again, she pushed him away. She lied to herself about her desires, when he could see it so clearly in her eyes. She had followed him like a puppy before he'd left to go to war, eager for every scrap of attention he tossed her.

But everything had unraveled after he'd returned. She'd turned from him. Hidden the truth of what their future held and refused to give herself up to him as the gods demanded, as she ought. She had no right to deny him, not out of fear for this supposed war. Women had no place in the affairs of men, and she had never understood. How many times had she argued with him after he had told her he must fight for Agamemnon? She had sneered at his honor then, and why? Because he would be hardened by it? Because Agamemnon had never treated her with kindness?

Helen had never liked his brother. But when he had protected her from marriage to Agamemnon, ensured her place at his own side instead, she had thrown the gift in his face, not caring what it had cost him or how much he had sacrificed for her sake. Did she not realize he might have taken Mycenae for himself? He'd had the support of their men—their love, as he'd once had hers. He'd needed only the right moment, the right circumstances. But the thought of leaving her to a loveless marriage, to his brother or some other man, was too much. He could not let her marry a man who only lusted for her beauty and had no understanding of how great a prize she truly was. What was Mycenae, compared to a daughter of Zeus? Compared to Helen, of all his daughters!

There was no greater treasure in all the world, and whether she wanted him or not, it no longer mattered. She was his. Nothing she dreamed would ever change that.

He had only to wait for the right moment to reclaim her.

CHAPTER SIX
HELEN

The next morning, we were all three exhausted still. Pollux and Castor had woken me from my nightmares, the violent dreams repeating over and over and over again until Castor had climbed into my bed and whispered reassurances in my ears, calming me with words and touch and whatever gift the gods had given him. I wished Zeus had seen fit to offer me the same. Something I could use as I willed, instead of my beauty using me.

"We've a long journey yet," Pollux said, and I had never seen circles so dark beneath his eyes. "Go with Castor to the men, and I will offer Nestra and Agamemnon our farewells."

Castor grunted. "Better I speak to our sister and you see to the men. I can tell already you are short on patience, and Menelaus is bound to test you."

"No," I said, frowning. "Menelaus is more likely to be waiting for us with the men, unwilling to risk our slipping away in the dark."

Pollux drummed his fingers against the hilt of his sword, his gaze upon the door. "Helen is right."

"And you will keep your temper if she is wrong?" Castor asked, half smiling.

"So long as Helen is safe with you, I will find the strength to tolerate any insults he might offer."

I tipped my head, studying my brother. Small, tired lines fanned out from the corners of his eyes, and his movements were just a touch too forceful as he packed. As if he could not quite control his strength. His temper was already bubbling to the surface. "You must do better than that, Pollux. For all you know, he means to follow us to Sparta."

"Accidents can happen upon the road," Pollux said.

"Not to Menelaus, and not in our company," I said firmly. Though the gods knew I would not have grieved for his loss. We would have to fear Agamemnon then, and Sparta was not Athens, to endure such a siege. Perhaps I should have let Theseus have his way two years ago. Perhaps if war had come to the Rock while I stood at his side as queen, I would be in Athens still, and not in Mycenae, missing half my heart.

He sighed, looking up at last to meet my eyes. "How did you live like this for so long? Awake most of the night, crying and screaming in your sleep, tossing and turning as if possessed by some evil. I never realized how terrible it truly was. You never—you never told me it could be that way."

"It is worse now than it was then," I admitted. "And while I was in Athens, in Theseus's bed, I slept well. It was not until after he had gone that I suffered again."

Pollux's forehead creased, his gaze shifting briefly to Castor and then away. "I wonder."

"It would explain some of his accomplishments," Castor agreed. "The peace in Attica, even, could be attributed to his power, if he kept his nobles with him at the palace, or even spoke with them often enough."

"Theseus gave them all a say in their governance," I said, not liking what they implied. "He did not use his power to manipulate their minds."

Pollux's gaze snapped back to mine. "You knew of it?"

"He confessed himself before he left. But he never used it wrongly. Only to quiet me when I was disturbed by my dreams, to help me fall more easily back to sleep."

"Or to quiet your nightmares altogether," Castor said. "It would have been easily accomplished, and it is possible he did not know himself he had done it."

I shook my head. "I had other dreams. Dreams he did not know about."

"Then he could not know to soothe you," Pollux said.

"No." I turned from my brothers, busying myself by smoothing the bedding and furs. "I was safe with Theseus in Athens."

"You cannot know that for certain, Helen. Not if he had power like Castor's. He is subtle enough even I cannot tell when he employs it, but with Poseidon's blood in his veins, Theseus was surely even that much more masterful in its use. And if he wished you to feel safe, to be content in his bed, desired to help you sleep less fitfully . . ."

"He would never have betrayed me. He respected me. Treated me as his equal in all things. Even in his bed."

But my stomach had soured, my thoughts turning back to his hope that distraction might cause my dreams to fade. How determined he had been to keep me happy and content those last months before he had left with Pirithous for the house of Hades.

"He would not have needed to invoke his power purposefully, Helen," Castor said. "If he had been intent upon you and your happiness, it might not have taken more than that."

Theseus had always helped me to sleep. Helped me to forget my fears, my worries. I had slept so well at his side, and I had never stopped to question the comfort he had given me. Not from the moment he had pulled me from the basket where I had hidden in his hold.

But what if Castor was right? What if it had all been a lie, purposeful or not?

What if I had never been safe?

"Could your sister not have spared you a clean gown?" Menelaus asked, meeting us among the men, as I had feared. I couldn't bring myself to look at him, though the flame of his red hair had made him impossible to miss. "You look a fright."

Castor stepped between us before he could reach for me, and I forced myself to smile. "Nestra is still angry that I stained one of her gowns when we were children, I'm sure. But it hardly matters. I'll have clean clothes enough in Sparta."

"Leda will be furious to see your hair is ruined," Menelaus said.

"Will she?" I asked, ignoring the prickle of unease that traveled down my spine as he followed me to my horse. Castor, to his credit, remained at my side, and I spared him a glance, my eyes narrowing, for I felt none of the panic I had the previous night. His lips twitched, and one shoulder rose briefly, not quite an admission, and certainly not an apology. But it might as easily have been my own distraction, for my thoughts still dwelt on Theseus.

Had it been only his power that had persuaded me of our hard-won peace? Had I loved him of my own will, or had it been a wish of his, made truth by some trick? I could not imagine he would have done either purposefully. Pirithous, perhaps, sly as he was, but not Theseus. He was too honorable, too good. And Aethra would never have allowed her son to abuse me. Whatever other doubts Castor and Pollux had placed in my mind, I did not doubt that. Nor did I doubt that he had loved me truly. And even now, apart for as long as we had been, my heart ached for him. Neither my love nor his could have been false. It was only the rest I could not be sure of.

"Leda will be pleased you are returned," Castor said, his hand at my waist jogging me from my thoughts. He helped me up onto my horse, neatly blocking Menelaus from moving nearer. "You can hardly be blamed for what was done to you while you were held captive, and I am certain Tyndareus will remind her of it should she voice such a concern. The ruin of your hair will be nothing to him, I promise you."

My fingers found my hair of their own accord, and then I pulled the hood of my cloak up over my head, annoyed that Menelaus had made me think of it at all. I'd nearly forgotten it was dyed, traveling with my brothers. Every day felt as though another lifetime had passed since I had been in Athens. Since I had lived as Theseus's wife. It seemed strange that my hair should not have faded already or grown out completely in the time since. I would need to do something to wash it out before the suitors arrived and the games began. To look my best and entice as many men as possible in the hopes that any of them might be chosen over Menelaus.

Perhaps this once I might find a use of my own for the gift Zeus had given me. Let them see this curse of mine used to thwart the war they desired.

"And who, exactly, is to blame for her abduction?" Menelaus asked, far too casually for my peace of mind.

"I did not know the men who took me." I twisted my fingers in my horse's mane, grateful for the shadow of the cloak upon my face in the predawn light. "And I escaped them before I learned more. But I did not know where I was or how to find my way back. I had never been farther than Gytheio, nor permitted to ride beyond the landmarks I had known all my life. I do not know how long I traveled in circles before I found a road."

"You needn't speak of it, Helen," Castor said kindly. "The gods will see to their punishment, and we are only glad to have found you at last."

"And I will be all the more grateful to find my way home," I said.

"I would think you would wish to see her captors punished by your own hands," Menelaus said. "Were she my sister, I would not rest until the men who had assaulted her were dead."

Castor's fingers stilled upon the bridle, his whole body stiffening. He did not look at Menelaus, though I do not know how he resisted. "After I have seen my sister made safe, I will pray that the gods grant me the opportunity to pursue the men who abused her. Now if you will excuse me, Helen and I have much to do, and two long days still ahead of us."

My brother swung up on the horse behind me, settling lightly at my back, and with a cluck of his tongue we were riding away, down the clumsy column of yawning, sleep-tousled men. No doubt they had all hoped for another day of rest, encamped outside Mycenae's thick walls. I could not blame them, truly, but nor was I so sympathetic as to grant their wish with Menelaus's gaze still following me too closely.

"He will keep asking," I said, turning my head so only my brother might hear the words. "He will push and push and push until he has the answers he desires."

"Then we must guard our tongues," Castor said. "Pollux and I will do well enough, but I fear for you, Helen. You are so uneasy in his presence, and if he trips you in your story even once—"

"I will not give him the opportunity," I promised. "I will not give him anything at all."

Pollux and Castor drove the men hard, and we marched well beyond sunset that day, depending upon the moonlight to set up our spare camp. The men grumbled, and if they were as stiff and sore as I was, half falling from Castor's horse, I could understand why.

"No riders followed from Mycenae," Pollux said, after the last of his scouts rode into camp, long after most of us had found our furs and settled ourselves for sleep. My brothers had fed the man from their own supplies and sent him to his bed. "So long as the weather holds, we should be in Sparta before dark tomorrow."

"Assuming the men are not dead upon their feet come morning," Castor said. "Or refuse to rise altogether."

Pollux grinned. "I'm certain you could find some way to motivate them, Brother. For your sister's sake."

I wrapped myself more tightly in Theseus's cloak, trying to fight the chill that had not left me since Mycenae. But it was not the cold that made me uncomfortable. The idea that the safety I had been so sure of in Athens had been nothing but a trick of the mind still haunted me. I suspected it always would. "I will not have Castor abuse the men on my account."

"It is hardly abuse, Helen," Pollux said. "Just encouragement where it's needed, and the sharing of a better mood among the men. Is that truly so terrible?"

I pressed my lips together. "Perhaps if you were the one wondering how much of your happiness had been your own, you would feel differently."

Castor sighed, wrapping an arm around my shoulders to pull me near and press a kiss into my hair. "Had I known it would trouble you, I would not have spoken of it at all. But you should not think of it so. Your happiness, I am certain, was real. Theseus was too honorable a man to betray your trust so utterly. And he was too wise, besides. Using whatever power the gods gave him to comfort you in the night is no different than the use of his strength to defend you, or his influence as king to disguise you as an Egyptian."

"So you say."

"So I know," Castor said. "Or do you think it is a betrayal to calm a panicked horse before he does himself harm in his stall?"

"Am I nothing more than livestock now? My fears to be dismissed as nonsense?"

"Of course not, Helen," Pollux said. "That lesson we have learned well enough by now. I will never discount your fears again, nor mistrust your dreams. Castor only means that Theseus offered you the comfort he could as your husband. Just as he gave you everything else within his power. Truly, did you never fight at all, that you think he deceived you so completely?"

I swallowed, remembering the table he had thrown into the wall, furious that I had kept our daughter's fate a secret and risked my own life in the bargain. All those days and nights after, when I had refused him and we had lived for a time like strangers, though we shared a bed. Days that I had wasted, thinking I had seasons upon seasons to spend at his side. Thinking of them now, I would have given anything to have that time back. To have my husband back.

"Theseus never stayed angry for long, no matter what wrong I had done him," I said softly, unwelcome tears pressing at my eyes. I fought them back, refusing to give in to grief. Theseus would come for me. I had not lost him yet, not wholly. "I only wish I could say the same for myself."

Pollux smiled. "See? If he had used his power, it would have been the other way. Your anger would have been fleeting, soothed away at his whim. Though in truth, I cannot imagine any man holding sway over your temper for long, no matter what gifts the gods had granted him."

Castor laughed, but I went cold, thinking of my dream and all I knew of the strange prince and his influence over me. Perhaps Theseus had not sought to control me, but it was clear from my nightmares that the prince would. And if I did not guard myself, if I allowed him to have his way, we would all suffer for it.

"Is there some way I might learn to protect myself from this power of yours, Castor?"

My brother's laughter faded, a wrinkle between his eyebrows replacing his smile. "If there is, I do not know it, but in my experience, the stronger the will, the more difficult it is to turn it to my own desires."

I chewed on my lip, my stomach twisting. Because if Theseus did not return in time and I was forced to marry Menelaus, I could well believe my will to remain as his wife would be anything but strong.

Castor squeezed my shoulders again and let me go. "You should rest, Helen. I'll wake you at dawn."

He was right, of course, and I rose from my place beside the fire. But even when I found my furs and burrowed beneath them for warmth, I knew I was unlikely to sleep.

I had no desire to dream.

CHAPTER SEVEN
HELEN

Helen." Tyndareus took me into his arms, tears in his eyes, and held me tight.

I blinked back the dampness in my own eyes, hiding my face against his shoulder. So much frailer now than when I had seen him last. Somehow he seemed smaller, and the thought that he had aged before his time because of me broke my heart.

"I missed you, Father."

"I never thought to see you again," he confessed, his voice too low for any of the others to hear. "Thank the gods I was wrong. Thank Zeus you are returned to us, after all this time."

I bit my tongue on an ungrateful response and forced myself to smile. Just because I could not bring myself to thank the gods for delivering me back into the hands of the Fates, it did not mean I should insult them by saying so aloud. A lesson I should have learned long ago.

"For whatever shame I have brought to Sparta, I beg your forgiveness," I said. "And if you cannot grant it, I will dedicate myself to the gods instead."

"Don't be foolish, child," Tyndareus said, framing my face in his palms and holding me away to search my gaze. "I will not give you up so easily as that. Sparta has need of its heir, no matter what troubles have befallen her before now. You are forgiven a thousand times over, if you will only promise me the same for dismissing your fears too quickly. But you are safe, returned home, and now that this abduction is behind us and the threat of war is passed—"

I shook my head, pulling his hands from my face. I'd covered my dyed hair with a length of linen, scavenged from one of the men as we traveled, not wanting to incite more talk. Nor to risk anyone in my father's court mistaking me for the Athenian queen at a glance. It was too late to do anything about the men who had marched to retrieve me, but at least they knew nothing of my circumstances atop the Rock, only that my brothers had fetched me from it. "I fear this was not the abduction of my nightmares, Father. There is more yet to come. Pain and death and war, if we are not cautious."

He frowned, his gaze shifting to Pollux and Castor standing on either side of me, grim faced. "Is this true?"

"There was not a single night of our journey that Helen did not suffer nightmares," Pollux said. "If she says this is not the end of it, I can only believe her. Or else the gods torture her for their own amusement."

"Surely Zeus would never permit such cruelty without cause," Tyndareus murmured. "But I do not like this. And I like less that you spread word of her recovery far and wide without my leave. If she is yet to suffer the abduction of her nightmares, the more who know she is returned, the greater the risk."

"You swore to Zeus I would not be wed without all the proper rites," I said. "Would you break your vow to the gods?"

Tyndareus drew back, his attention falling on me with all the weight of his throne. As if he had seen me only now for the first time and was not certain he cared for what he had found. "You did this?"

"If I had not, I could not be certain it would be done at all. Pollux and Castor have agreed it is in all our interests that the assembly be held in accordance with your vow. And after speaking with my sister in Mycenae, I am all the more certain of the choice I have made."

"You forget yourself, Daughter," Tyndareus said, his jaw tight and his eyes flashing. "You forget who is king."

"A king who forswears himself to the gods does not serve Sparta," I said, keeping my voice low and calm. Tyndareus must listen, and I would not cower behind my brothers this time, hoping the choices they made were the right ones, until Menelaus climbed through my window. I would not sit here, passive, while Tyndareus decided my fate. "*I* do not forget what befell us the last time that *you* forgot *your* place. It is because of Zeus's anger, his punishment so long ago, that I live at all. The news must be spread and my suitors must assemble, that you might hear every offer of marriage and allow them to compete for my hand before the gods. We risk too much already without forgetting the promises made to Zeus."

Tyndareus's face had gone from white to red, but I stood my ground, unflinching before his anger. I was not the child he chastised for hiding her womanhood, or the girl he had punished for dyeing her hair. I was his heir and the future queen of Sparta, and I would have every man who arrived know that I meant to rule at his side. As I had in Athens, with Theseus.

"Let them come, then," he said, too coolly. "It seems I can do little to stop it. But do not think I will forget this, Helen. Whatever you suffered, wherever you were taken, it does not change what you are here, within these walls. Do not make the mistake of believing yourself queen before your time."

"Pollux, take her to her room. It is clear to me that your sister needs time to rest, undisturbed."

"Forgive me, Father," Pollux said, unmoving. "I must beg your permission to enter the women's quarters. I would see Helen kept guarded and safe, that she might not be stolen from beneath our noses again."

Tyndareus snorted, his eyes narrowing. "So you might plot that much more easily with your sister?"

"My loyalty is and always will be to you and to Sparta, above all," Pollux said. "But Helen is my sister, and as you say, she will one day be my queen. It is in all our interests to be certain she remains unmolested, to prevent further rumor in regard to her honor or virtue. Sparta has suffered shame enough without allowing more room for talk."

"You will take no further action without my explicit consent, Pollux. Guard her body, and keep her safe, but should I believe you or Castor follow her orders over mine, I will find other work for you and your brother to do, far from the palace."

Pollux bowed deeply. "It will be as you command, Father."

And with Tyndareus's warning ringing in my ears, my brothers guided me away.

"You should never have goaded him, Helen," Pollux said once we had left the megaron. He kept one hand at the small of my back, propelling me forward. Castor had moved ahead of us, hand resting carelessly upon the hilt of his sword. "He might have been your ally instead of your enemy, if you had only spoken less harshly."

I was not such a fool that I did not see it all for what it was—a new imprisonment, as punishment for speaking my mind. For daring to act in my own interests without my father's blessing. For acting as a son instead of a daughter.

"And what good did he do me as an ally before now?" I asked. "I love Tyndareus as a father, you know I do, but he was blinded by his affections for Menelaus from the start, and if Agamemnon is as powerful as Castor says, he is not any freer now. Better he realize how far I am willing to go to protect myself than believe he will be allowed to marry me off to Menelaus without a fight."

Pollux grunted, clenching his jaw to hold back his reply as we came upon our cousin Penelope and one of my father's guests. The man looked up as we passed, amusement clearly written in his features, and I recognized him as Odysseus, newly made king of Ithaca, no doubt come to exchange gifts and renew guest-friendship with Sparta. He touched his fist to his forehead in the Cretan gesture of respect, the same used by Theseus's men in Athens, and I looked quickly away before he saw the way the reminder cut through me.

Loss thickened my throat. Perhaps it had been foolish, but I had hoped we would hear some word of Theseus by the time we had arrived in Sparta. That he had returned to the land of the living, at the least, if nothing more, and proved all the whispers of his death false.

"I look forward to hearing of your adventures, Princess," he called after me, laughter in his voice.

My steps slowed, and I hesitated, forcing Pollux to stop beside me. Cunning Odysseus. He was not so much older than my brothers. Of age with Agamemnon and hardly a stranger to Sparta, for he had spent a year with us at his father's request, and another after that in Pylos, among King Nestor's sons. But he had never had much interest in me, nor the patience that Menelaus had shown for a small girl who wanted nothing more than to chase after her brothers.

"I fear we'll not have the opportunity to exchange such pleasantries, King Odysseus," I said, inclining my head politely, for he smiled like a man with a secret, and I wanted dearly to know if it was mine. If Odysseus had come to Athens while I was queen, I wanted to believe I would have recognized him, but he was not above disguising himself for his own entertainment, and I had more than once seen others fall for his tricks. "Unless you mean to stay as a suitor in hopes of winning my hand?"

His gaze shifted to Penelope, and he cleared his throat. "No insult intended, Princess, but even the goddess Aphrodite's beauty could not tempt me to give up my home. I have no desire at all to be Sparta's king."

"Then I fear we will have little time together. My brothers even now escort me to the women's quarters, where I believe my father intends to keep me for some time."

"For your safety, of course," Odysseus drawled, his lips twitching. "I am certain he has no wish to *lose* you twice."

My blood ran cold. "Indeed, a man would need your cunning to steal me away, now that I am guarded by my brothers."

"Fortunate, then, that I am ever in Sparta's service," Odysseus said. And then he bowed. "But forgive me, I would not delay you. I'm certain you long for the safety and comfort of your room, after so long spent . . . away."

I lifted my chin, ignoring his implications as thoroughly as he had ignored mine, and continued on. Pollux glanced back, however, his eyes narrowed, and a curse slipped from between his lips. Castor held open the curtain leading to the stairs and the women's quarters, and both my brothers seemed to falter at the bottom step. A heartbeat of hesitation before they retook their places as my guards.

Pollux waited until the curtain fell back into place, his shoulders hunched as he climbed the stairs beside me. "Odysseus knows something."

"He thinks he does, at any rate." I pulled the makeshift scarf from my hair now that I was out of sight of any of my father's guests. "I suppose he will let us know for certain one way or the other, before long."

"And use it as a weapon against us, no doubt. To negotiate for something he desires."

"Odysseus is too canny to think a war in anyone's interests, no matter what he knows. And what could he possibly desire from us? He has Ithaca, and you heard him—he doesn't want me."

Castor snorted. "He wants the peace and quiet away from the mainland more, but that doesn't mean he doesn't want you. Any man who says as much is a liar. Not that Odysseus wasn't always quick to fib when it suited him, and sly as a fox the rest of the time."

"Regardless," I said, not wishing to dwell on what Castor's words meant when it came to his own desires, or Pollux's. "Odysseus isn't going to start a war. Especially not if he prefers peace and quiet to a beautiful wife. He'll hold his tongue."

At least I hoped he would. A wrong word carried to Menelaus's ear was all it would take, but while Odysseus enjoyed his games, I didn't think he meant me any harm.

I am ever in Sparta's service, he'd said. And if Theseus did not arrive, and soon, I might yet have to take Odysseus at his word.

Let him put all that cunning and guile to good use for once in his life, and maybe we'd all secure ourselves a little more peace.

CHAPTER EIGHT
ODYSSEUS

*H*elen of Sparta.

The moment he'd heard Tyndareus dismiss her, Odysseus had taken Penelope by the hand and dragged her from the megaron, all amorous intentions. Not that he did not truly want to taste Penelope's clever lips, but he'd known she wouldn't yield to him so quickly. And he'd known, too, which way Helen and her brothers would come from the megaron to return her to her rooms, and he couldn't resist the lure. The famously beautiful Helen of Sparta, all grown up, and returned home, at last.

He watched her disappear with her brothers around the corner, not quite able to tear his gaze from the gentle sway of her hips—much too plumply shaped for a woman who professed to have been wandering the wilderness alone these last years, suffering only the gods knew what deprivations along the way. That she had lied was unquestionable, and he'd known it from the moment the messenger had arrived to announce her recovery, but what she had lied to hide, that was the mystery that taunted him.

"Do not tell me she's ensnared you as well, my lord," Penelope said, touching his arm.

He covered her hand with his own, granting her a warm smile to make up for his inattention. "It takes more than beauty to capture me, I promise you. And what use do I have for a princess and her kingdom when I have my own to attend to? I would be served much better by a woman who might love Ithaca as I do."

She peeked up at him from beneath lowered lashes, playing the shy maiden. She did it so well. All virtue, his Penelope. Or at least all the appearance of it. And he of all men could appreciate her harmless deceptions, though he hadn't quite determined if she'd realized how easily he saw through them yet. "Won't you tell me more of your home, King Odysseus? I'd dearly love to see Ithaca with my own eyes, but I cannot imagine my uncle would allow such a journey. Ever since Helen was stolen away, he's hardly let me leave the palace at all."

"He is a prudent man, your uncle. And cautious, as he should be when he is charged with the protection of such a flower as yourself," Odysseus said, leaning nearer. All the better to draw in the rose-petal scent of her hair. "And poor Helen's fate. I remember her most fondly as a child, all awkward limbs and sun-bright hair. An innocent girl, too trusting for her own good. But King Tyndareus must have been beside himself at the abduction of his heir."

"Helen was always his favorite," she agreed. "He's aged ten winters in her absence, though I could never understand why he spoiled her so. He treats her like a son more than a daughter, even listening to her counsel on matters she could hardly know anything about. And Menelaus was no better. I cannot say I envy the man who will be named her husband, willful as she's become."

"And only all the more so after her trials, I fear," Odysseus said, adding a pitying sigh for good measure. Poor, sweet Penelope. Beside

Helen, she was sure to be forgotten. By everyone but him, if the gods were good. "You are truly kind to warn me, Penelope. And I am grateful to have the truth of her character with which to blind me to the temptation of her beauty. So long as I remain in Sparta, I would have your support—I have no desire to forget myself."

Penelope's fingers tightened upon his arm, and she met his eyes, earnest and fierce. "If you ever fear you will be lost to her seductions, you need only come to me, and I will remind you of your true self, I promise you."

"I need only think of you, I am certain." He squeezed her hand, gazing longingly into her eyes. And perhaps the threat of Helen, come to steal his love, would be the encouragement she needed to give herself up. Not merely in body, for he rather preferred that she did not grant her favor to just any man, but in the form of sacred vows. Tyndareus had already told him he would not marry Penelope to anyone she did not desire. "But is there anything more I might use to armor myself? As her cousin, I cannot imagine there is anyone else who knows her faults so well."

"Besides her willfulness, you mean?" Penelope twitched one shoulder, warming to the subject. "Before she was stolen, she practically threw herself at King Theseus of Athens, thinking to bend him to her will. Can you imagine her audacity? And all beneath Menelaus's eye, driving him mad with jealousy. Everyone knew she was meant for him, and the way she had flirted and toyed with him until King Theseus arrived! Whoever she marries, the poor man will live in constant fear that she will abandon him for a more powerful husband. She uses her beauty as nothing more than a lure."

"Cruel and unfeeling," Odysseus said. "I am certain you could never treat a man so poorly, once you knew you had secured his affections."

"Never," she promised. "When I am married, my husband will know my loyalty is to him, and him alone."

Sweet, jealous Penelope, so happy to oblige him. So eager to prove herself the better prospect as a wife. Yes, perhaps Helen's return would suit him quite well, if it meant he need not wait so long to secure Penelope's affections. Another few days in the company of her cousin, and he imagined she would have no reservations at all.

And in the meantime, she would provide him with everything he needed to know to solve the greater mystery that called.

Helen of Sparta. If she wasn't lost in the woods, stumbling up and down mountains, just where, oh where, might she have gone?

CHAPTER NINE
HELEN

My room had not changed at all in the last two years, and I stood inside the door, staring at the small bed in the center, dread slithering down my spine. To be forced to sleep again in this room, in that bed. My gaze slid to the window, and I did not dare to so much as blink or be overwhelmed by memories of that night, already pressing themselves behind my eyes. Menelaus waiting for me in my bedroom, his hand closing around my throat . . .

"Helen?"

I shook my head, struggling to focus my gaze upon my brother instead. Castor stood before me, searching my face.

"Are you well?" he asked.

"Fine," I lied, turning away from his concern. My eyes caught on the second bed, nothing more than a sleeping pallet on the floor. "What's become of Clymene?"

"Father punished her for leaving you alone the night you disappeared, and she's served Leda in the washrooms since," Castor said. "But I'm certain she can be returned to you, if you wish."

"She shouldn't have been punished at all," I said. It hadn't been her fault, after all, that Menelaus and his brother had conspired to keep her from my room and from my side. Tyndareus was the one who had allowed the sons of Atreus authority over the servants in the palace, while they had lived in Sparta. And Clymene was a cousin to Agamemnon, besides. If she hadn't done as he'd bid, he might just as soon have had her beaten for disobedience. "But do not make it a command. Tell her only that if she would be happier to be my maid again, it would please me. At least then we need not worry about frightening another poor girl with my nightmares."

"I'll stay with you at night, if you would rather," Castor said. "Perhaps with my gift—"

"No," I said, before he could finish. I did not want to think of Theseus's power—nor feel the sinking sensation in my stomach that came with the knowledge that the happiness we had shared might have been a lie. Or at least the happiness that had come from believing we had changed my fate. Would I have loved him less if my nightmares had still haunted me? I wasn't certain it would have changed my feelings. Perhaps instead, I simply would have trusted that whatever came, we would conquer it together. Perhaps we still could, if he would only hurry. "If I am meant to dream, I will dream, and hope that I will have some small advantage because of it. A little lost sleep along the way will do me no harm."

And I did not want to wake in the night, thinking Theseus held me in his arms, only to find my brother in my bed, brushing my tears away. Nothing but a reminder of all I had lost. But even if all of that had been nothing, I could not ask it of Castor. I would not tempt him to forget himself. Not if there was the slightest chance that what had happened to

Menelaus was my fault. I did not want to see Castor's kindness replaced with desire, and then resentment and violence. I could not bear it.

"Just keep a guard beneath my window at night," I said. "One we can trust will not obey, should Agamemnon or Menelaus arrive and attempt to dismiss him."

"Castor and I will take that duty upon ourselves," Pollux promised, coming to stand before me, too. "You need never fear another invasion through your window while you sleep in the night."

"And the rest of the day?"

"You will not ever enter this room without one of us at your side," Castor said. "And if any man lurks within, he will not live long enough to trouble you further. Will that do?"

I threw my arms around them, hugging both my brothers at once, tight and hard. "Thank you."

"It is the least we can do, Helen," Pollux said. "And what we should have done before. You never should have had to look elsewhere for protection. Not even for a moment. I wished every day you were gone that I had listened to you more closely, guarded you more fiercely. You will not suffer any harm again while we live."

I shut my eyes tightly then, fighting against a sob. Because according to my nightmares, if I married Menelaus, my brave, foolish brothers would not live long.

Clymene arrived quickly after Castor left to fetch her, and she dropped to her knees and wept at my feet, whether with guilt or relief I could not tell. A glance at my brothers sent them from the room, and I crouched before her, murmuring assurances that I was safe and well.

"I am so sorry, my lady. Please, you must forgive me. If I had only been at your side, perhaps we might have raised an alarm, and you could have been spared so much."

"Hush, now," I said, smoothing her hair from her face. "I have never blamed you for what happened that night or any other."

"But you were stolen away," she wailed. "Stolen from your very bed in the night! And if I'd been with you—"

"If you'd been with me, you'd likely have suffered for it," I said. "And the guards never paid any attention to cries from this room. Tyndareus trained them too well to ignore my nightmares. Why should he have ever dreamed that a man would dare invade the women's quarters and steal away his daughter? You are blameless, guiltless in every way."

Her tears had quieted by then, and she gripped my hands. "Are you certain you wish me to serve you again, my lady?"

"I would rather you than anyone else. My nightmares grow worse, and I trust no one else to keep my secrets. If you are willing."

"Willing!" She sobbed a laugh. "You offer me escape from the lash of your mother's tongue, and think I will not accept? She has hated me since I told her you had been lost."

I bit my cheek to stop an apology, for though I surely owed her one, I dared not offer it. Poor Clymene. I had not thought at all about how she would be treated in my absence. How Leda would blame her. But I had not known then just how desperate Leda was to see me married to Menelaus, and even now, I did not understand why. What difference was it to Leda who I married, so long as Sparta had a strong king?

"I suspect she will hate me more now," I said instead. "For thwarting her with my abduction."

"She can hardly blame you for being stolen, my lady!"

But now that I had said the words, I knew them to be true. She would blame me for everything, even without knowing I had arranged it all. She would find ways of letting me know it, of ensuring that I suffered for my disobedience. And she was the only one, but for my brothers and Theseus, who knew what Menelaus had done.

Surely that night mattered less now. I had been abducted, and the men who came to win me would already doubt my virtue, no matter our protests—and though the truth of my marriage must remain a secret, I certainly had not been dishonored by Theseus. It would make little difference if she revealed Menelaus had assaulted me first. And if Tyndareus realized what she had done to me, arranging the rape of Sparta's heir beneath his roof, queen or not, he would have my mother punished for it.

I only feared that it would influence Tyndareus's decision, give him the excuse he surely wanted to wed me to Menelaus after all that I had done to escape it. And Leda must realize it, too. But would my father give me so easily to a man who had forced himself upon me in the night, even if that man was Menelaus?

I did not know.

I did not want to find out.

CHAPTER TEN
HELEN

I saw much of the inside of my room over the course of the next sevenday. My brothers visited often enough, guarding me carefully, and Clymene was my constant companion, refusing to leave my side unless the command came from my lips.

And for a sevenday, I tolerated it. I had spent longer days in Athens, with only Aethra's infrequent visits, and Theseus gone to see to the business of being king until after the sun had set. But in Athens, I had been hidden for good reason, and of my own choosing. It had not been punishment and spite. Always during those months, I had known it would be worth the sacrifice. That once all had been arranged, I would have Theseus as my husband, and we would put my fears and troubles behind us. Now I only stared ahead into darkness, worrying that Theseus would not come in time. Or worse, not at all.

Clymene had helped me wash my hair, over and over again with vinegar and honey, softening the black dye I had used for so long into a rich brown, and then an auburn. To lighten it further, I feared I had need of the sun, and so long as I was trapped within my room, I would never have enough light to turn my hair back to gold again before my suitors arrived. Not without turning it to straw first.

And it was not only for my hair that I wished my freedom. I longed to walk the walls, to search the horizon for some sign of Theseus. If I could only *look* for his coming, perhaps his absence would not weigh upon me so heavily. Closed in the women's quarters, in the bedroom I had thought left behind with my childhood, it seemed as though my life as Theseus's wife had been nothing more than a dream. I needed to stare at something else, beyond my four walls and the inner courtyard beneath my window. I needed to *act* somehow, as if I believed he was coming, even if it was only by pacing the walls, eager for any smudge of dust on the horizon. Otherwise, I was only preparing myself for the worst, resigning myself to a future without him that I did not want. It was giving him up, sitting there beside my window and letting Clymene lighten my hair, and Theseus would never give up hope for me.

"Please, Pollux," I said, when he came to see me on the eighth day. I had taken advantage of his arrival to send Clymene for more honey, and we were left alone, however briefly. "You must convince Tyndareus to let me out. I promise I will go nowhere alone. You can leash me, if you must, to keep me near, but I cannot stand another day spent inside the women's quarters. Inside the palace at all! I am suffocating."

He shook his head. "At best, he will allow you to eat dinner in the megaron. But you will find it no less stifling with Leda at the table."

"He cannot refuse me the right to make offerings to Zeus at the shrine. Can you not persuade him to allow us even that far? Surely some sacrifice is due to the god for my safe return."

Pollux laughed then, for I had not quite been able to keep the bitterness from my words. "You cannot possibly think the gods would not taste your scorn in the blood, should the sacrifice come from your hand."

"Then you can wield the knife, and I will lift my arms and pretend myself lost in prayers of thanksgiving and gratitude," I snapped. And then I sighed, struggling to control my temper. My brothers did not deserve to suffer from my own frustrations. "Pollux, I will lose my mind if I am not freed. I must *do* something. For Theseus, if not for myself."

He knelt before me where I sat on a stool in what sunlight the window allowed, and took my hand. "Helen, I will speak to him. Even beg if I must. But you must promise me you will do nothing foolish. The last thing we need now is a reminder of how you used to escape your room by climbing out the window. It is not so large a leap from escaping punishment to running away altogether, and Zeus protect us all if anyone learns the truth of your disappearance. Just pretend obedience for a few days more, until your suitors begin to arrive, and Tyndareus will have no choice but to let you out."

I hated that he was right. But I had so little to occupy myself, and I could not even trust my fingers to weave, afraid that what would be revealed in the loom would betray me. I squeezed Pollux's hand and nodded all the same. Clymene returned a moment later, and neither one of us could risk saying anything more.

When Pollux left me to speak to Tyndareus about a short trip to the shrine, I had little hope for his success. Even less hope that I might find any breath of freedom unless Theseus arrived.

Three more days I waited, confined to the women's quarters, with nothing but the washing of my hair for excitement. I leaned over the lip of the tub while Clymene poured more vinegar over my head to rinse the honey out. Her fingers worked carefully through the strands, and I shut my eyes, allowing small memories of Athens to rise in my thoughts. Aethra helping me to dye my hair, her fingers strong and gentle, never pulling too hard. Theseus coiling locks of my hair around his fingers as we lay in bed, studying me in the lamplight as if he needed nothing else in the world to live.

Theseus's lips pressed to the top of my head, my forehead, my eyelids . . .

"Helen!"

Pollux's voice jerked me from my thoughts, and I lurched, banging my chin upon the tub. My brother had burst through the door into the bathing room before I could respond, and I glared at him, snatching up a towel to stop the vinegar from dripping from my hair into my eyes.

"Could you not have waited in my room?" I asked, blotting the worst of the liquid from my hair.

"We haven't the time. You've got to dress quickly, before Tyndareus changes his mind."

"I'm allowed out?" I asked, scrambling to my feet. "Truly?"

"To the shrine and back," Pollux said, grinning. "Castor is finding us a suitable calf to offer in sacrifice. He'll be waiting at the palace gate."

"But your hair, my lady. You can hardly go out with it dripping around your ears," Clymene said.

"I'll wear a shawl over my head until we're out of sight, and no one will be the wiser," I said, waving away her worry. "Find me a clean shift and a fine skirt! I would not want Tyndareus to think I insult the gods."

I pressed a kiss to my brother's cheek as I slipped past him into the hall. "Thank you, Pollux!"

"I'll be waiting at the stairwell, but you'd better hurry, Helen. The day is already half gone!"

With Clymene's help, I was stripped out of my stained shift and dressed with only a minimum of fumbling, and then I was in the hall again, lifting my skirt to run for the stairs. Pollux laughed, racing me through the halls of the palace proper as if we were children again. He was so fast, so graceful, and how I managed to keep up with a gown fouling my legs, I wasn't certain, but then we were outside, and the sun kissed my face, warm fingers of light cupping my cheeks and heating me from the inside out. Like Theseus's touch, his teasing caresses.

"And I thought it impossible that the day could become more beautiful." I spun to see Odysseus leaning against the stone wall, arms crossed and lips curved. "You're radiant as the sun, Princess. Apollo himself must shade his eyes against the glare."

"I would have thought you'd have returned home to your beloved Ithaca by now," I said, moving nearer to Pollux, who had stopped with me in the courtyard.

"As you see, I am still here."

I couldn't quite keep myself from glancing up at the windows that surrounded us now. Too many. And all with ears. It was one thing to let the servants see me enjoy the sun, but another altogether to give them the fodder of a conversation with Odysseus. Gods only knew what Leda would make of his sly comments.

"You must not let me distract you from your purpose." I turned from him completely, slipping my arm through my brother's. Better to be rude than let him goad me here. "Come, Pollux, Castor will be impatient if we keep him waiting, and I am eager to offer thanks to my father."

Odysseus's footsteps echoed ours as we passed through the courtyard and across the outer porch. I refused to so much as glance back. Not that it stopped him from following.

"No gratitude at all for the man who persuaded Tyndareus to let you give thanks to Zeus?"

I sighed, knowing I had no choice but to answer. A debt was a debt, and if it were true . . . "Why should King Odysseus concern himself with my confinement?"

He laughed, jogging to catch up to us, but when he opened his mouth to reply, I shook my head, short and sharp, letting him see my gaze shift to the palace at our backs. He only grinned all the wider. "I hoped to speak with you about your cousin. That you might use what-ever influence you have to persuade her of my affections."

Pollux snorted. "I'd wondered what you were still doing here."

"In addition to offering my support to Sparta's king in his hour of need, of course," Odysseus said. "I wouldn't dream of abandoning Tyndareus with Helen's suitors on their way, descending upon Sparta like vultures starving for a fresh kill."

I grimaced, but by now we had passed through the palace gate and found Castor waiting for us on the well-beaten path up the hill-side, away from Leda's ears. "Vultures, indeed. Must you be so vulgar, Odysseus? I'd much prefer it if you could keep yourself from referring to me as a piece of meat, about to be picked apart by so many men. Bad enough I am already considered a prize."

"You're no prize, Princess, of that I am certain. Sparta, however—well, for a prince with no throne of his own, I can well imagine he would risk wedding you for a crown."

"You are truly too kind," I said, picking up my pace to take the calf's lead rope from Castor. All the better to put space between Odysseus and me. "I thank you for whatever role you played in freeing me, but I fear I owe the gods my gratitude now. If you wouldn't mind?"

"I'm afraid you won't dismiss me so easily as that," Odysseus said, smiling. "I've promised your father I'd act as his spy, to be sure you were not plotting against him with your brothers."

"Tyndareus will be grieved to know he chose such a poor infor-mant," Pollux said. "And I cannot believe you have any need of Helen's influence to win Penelope."

Castor barked a laugh. "Penelope is well won already, from what I saw of her yesterday, floating out of the stables starry-eyed. I hope you've already gotten Tyndareus's blessing, or she's going to be ripe and showing before you're wed."

"Gods above!" I stared at Castor. "Penelope, rolling in the hay? Of all people!"

"She could do worse than a king," Castor said. "And after watching Nestra throw herself at Agamemnon, what else would you expect?"

"Not that it's any business of yours," Odysseus said, his face flushed. "But Penelope is far too virtuous to be caught rolling in the hay with anyone before she is wed. You wouldn't believe what it took to wheedle a kiss from her fair lips."

"Ah, was that all it was?" Castor said.

"She might have been gracious enough to allow me some small amount of fondling as well," Odysseus admitted. "Or else she was too overtaken with desire to stop me immediately, at any rate."

Menelaus's sour breath tickled the back of my neck. An old memory I had hoped to keep buried, stirring with Odysseus's boasts. I could only imagine how Menelaus had convinced himself of my desire, my wanting, with similar words. Making what he had done merely an act of shared passion, rather than a rape.

"I may not be so innocent as I was, but I hardly need to hear stories of the women you've forced yourself upon," I said, before they could go on. My brothers both flushed, the smiles falling from their lips, but I could not meet their eyes, and had no interest in their pity. "What is it that you want from us, Odysseus?"

His eyes narrowed at the sudden shift in mood, his gaze flitting to each of us in turn. "You three share a secret."

"It is no secret that I was abducted, stolen from my very bed," I said, tugging on the lead to keep the calf at my side, grateful for the excuse to look away.

"My grandfather was Autolycus, son of Hermes. Do you think I do not know a trick when it is set before my eyes? That I do not have some sense for lies when they are spoken in my ear?"

"And what does your divine ancestry have to do with your business here?" I asked.

"You will be queen of Sparta one day, Helen. And sooner than you might like. Your husband will be king, and powerful. Is it so strange that I might wish to make myself your friend now, to avoid strife for myself and my people?"

I strangled a laugh. "Avoid strife? Do you truly believe there will be any peace at all once I am married? There are men who would kill to have me as their wife, and you are not so great a fool that you do not realize it. And even if, by some grace of the gods, all the men who come to win me agree that the worthiest among them has been chosen, there is still more than a good chance that war will follow."

"Helen," Pollux warned.

"No," I said. "This much is mine to share. The gods have granted me dreams of the future, and what purpose has it served to keep them secret? Tyndareus has only used them for his own ends, and if Odysseus truly desires peace, he has a right to know what comes for us all."

"So it is true," Odysseus said. "There were whispers, of course, and I heard you crying, but I could not be certain why. I would keep Ithaca safe, Princess, of that you must have no doubt, and if you know of our fate . . ."

"Death, Odysseus," I said. "War and death and blood. So many men killed, even the victors will never recover."

CHAPTER ELEVEN
HELEN

O dysseus stared at me in stunned silence, even his quick tongue at an utter loss for response, and I forged onward, tugging the calf along, up the path and through the arch that marked the entrance to Zeus's shrine.

The words had left a bitter taste in my mouth, my body flushed and my heart pounding. Perhaps I should never have spoken of it. Perhaps Odysseus would have been better off spending his days in ignorance. But I was tired of hiding the truth, and it made no difference now. I was too old to be dedicated to the gods and trained as an oracle, too sullied by the daughter I'd borne for the priests to have use of me, and too dangerous to steal from Mycenae's prince, besides.

When I stood before the face of Zeus in the rock, I finally stopped, glowering at the god who was my father. All of this was his doing, or else he had the power to stop it and chose otherwise. He could have spared me this future. He could have left me safely in Athens, awaiting

Theseus's return. He could have commanded Athena to protect me, to protect Theseus, and even our child, too.

He could have spared my daughter.

"You must tell him the rest," Pollux said quietly. I hadn't realized he'd followed so closely upon my heels. "It is cruel to leave him in such a state, when you know there is still some small hope."

I closed my eyes, forcing back the tears that had risen at the thought of our little girl. My stolen child, sacrificed for nothing at all but Zeus's pride.

"I do not know anything," I said. "I have never known."

"Your dreams change, still. And so long as that is true, there is a chance we might soften the blow. With Odysseus's help, we might yet outwit the gods."

I did not have the heart to argue, either way. To tell him that although my nightmares changed, it was the smallest details, not the largest bones. It did not matter if it was Ajax of Locris or Menelaus who found me in Troy. So long as my dreams still placed me in that burning city, I had changed nothing of any real meaning, and far too many would die.

"You'd better make the sacrifice with your hands, Pollux," I said instead. "I can't bring myself to do it."

His hand covered mine on the lead rope, the calf happily cropping the grass before the stone. And then I turned away from the rock, from the altar beneath. Zeus would have nothing more from me.

"What must we do?" Odysseus asked, after Pollux had made our offering. "There must be something."

"In the dream, I am married to Menelaus," I said. I had unwrapped my hair and now sat upon the stone bench, letting the sunshine do what it could to lighten it. Until the sun began to set, I had no intention of leaving, even if it felt as though Zeus glowered from the rock. "And I thought—I hoped—that if I could only avoid that binding, I might stop the war. But I am not so certain now that the gods will not take the blood they desire some other way. Ignite another war instead, just as devastating to our people."

"That's why you left," he murmured, realization shadowing his face. "You fled from Menelaus."

I said nothing, unwilling to confess myself so wholly. I owed Theseus and Athens my protection still, and I was not certain I trusted Odysseus. I was not certain Odysseus knew what trustworthiness was.

"Surely it is only a matter of ensuring Menelaus does not win the games, then," Odysseus said, unconcerned by my silence. "Or dispensing with the games altogether and bribing a priest to name another man as chosen by the gods to win you."

"Perhaps it would be," Castor said, "if Agamemnon were not so powerful, and Menelaus not so transfixed by my sister's beauty. He is determined to have her, no matter what blood will be spilled because of it. And Tyndareus—he wants Menelaus as a son-in-law. He thinks because Menelaus is so obsessed, he will guard her jealously enough that no man will possibly be able to steal her from him."

"But he won't," I said. "He'll try, I'm certain, and it will be a misery, but he will not succeed. The strange prince will come, and I will be stolen. Or somehow I go willingly. It has never been clear."

"There must be a way to stop it," Odysseus said, his gaze unfocused now. "Menelaus and Agamemnon are nothing more than brutes, wealthy or not. They can be outwitted. And Tyndareus, too, in his desperation to avoid a bloodbath beneath his roof. He is nervous as a rabbit in an open field about this assembly. Only give me time to think, and I will find us a way through."

"Time is one thing we are terribly short of, Odysseus," I said, hugging myself. "And if I only had more of it . . ."

But there was little I could do if Theseus was held by the gods. No matter how much time I stole awaiting his return.

The gods only knew what Odysseus told my father of our afternoon spent at the shrine, but Tyndareus granted me more freedom after that, provided his supposed spy remained in our company. And where Odysseus spent his days, soon after Penelope followed, though she did not seem pleased to find him spending his time with me.

"Won't you have suitors enough without seducing the king of Ithaca as well?" she demanded the following night, having pushed her way past Clymene into my room after the evening meal.

I did not so much as pause in combing my hair, though her words sent a flush of anger to my face, only half-hidden in the lamplight. "Despite what my sister might have told you, I would much prefer to see indifference in a man's eyes than lust. Even if it were otherwise, King Odysseus is far too distracted by thoughts of your favors and virtues to so much as look at me."

Penelope's eyes went wide, and she dropped suddenly to the low bench at the foot of my bed. "Truly?"

I sighed, setting aside my comb. We'd spent another day at the shrine, where it was safe for us to speak openly, even if all we did was repeat the same arguments. I still longed for the walls, but I feared what Tyndareus would think if I climbed them. "I don't suppose you're going to believe me if I say yes?"

She dropped her gaze, twisting her hands together in her lap. "Odysseus was meant to leave the day you arrived home. What else should I think than that he was taken by your beauty?"

"You should think that Odysseus is a king, and my return reshapes Sparta's future. Perhaps the future of all of Achaea. Certainly it will result in a shift in power, no matter who my father marries me to. Most likely, he wishes to learn what he can and ensure the winds change in his favor before he goes."

Her cheeks reddened. "Is that what you speak of all day long, then? As if you will have any power at all when you are queen."

I stiffened. "I will be high priestess of Sparta, if nothing else. And with Athena's blessing, perhaps I will have a husband who values my counsel. Who sees a daughter of Zeus as his equal, more than his prize."

"It's a pretty dream, Helen, but you'd be better served resigning yourself to the women's quarters. Whichever suitor wins your hand, he'll have to shut you up in these rooms under guard to keep you. After all, you've already been stolen once."

"Enough, Penelope." My fingers closed into fists in the fabric of my skirt. "I have no interest in stealing the man you desire, and King Odysseus has no interest in me. But if you mistrust him so completely, perhaps you should reconsider your choice. It takes far less than my beauty to tempt a man to stray, particularly if his wife has such a shrewish temperament as yours."

"At least I am not despoiled," Penelope snapped. "And I will never give him reason to believe me anything but virtuous. Unlike you, I know my duty and my place."

"You know nothing," I said. "And that is the entirety of your appeal. A woman who is willing to sit at the loom and wait for her husband's return, turning a blind eye to all his affairs and questioning nothing. But since it seems as though Odysseus desires nothing more than blind obedience from his wife, I'm sure you'll suit him perfectly."

"Just because you're beautiful, a daughter of Zeus, you think yourself so much better than the rest of us," Penelope said. "But you're wrong, Helen. A daughter of Zeus, no matter how pretty, is still just a woman. Meant to be bartered and bred, and nothing more."

"And perhaps that is true in Laconia, even in the whole of the Peloponnese," I agreed. "How fortunate for me that my suitors will come from farther afield."

She rose, her smile thin and brittle. "It does not matter how many come or from how far, Princess. Not when Mycenae's prince has already claimed you for his own. And I promise you, Menelaus will not tolerate a wife who reaches for his crown."

Then she left, floating from the room as if she owned it. And I watched her go, silenced by the blow of her words and the sudden certainty that she knew the truth. Perhaps not that I had fled, but that Menelaus had taken me, claimed me in body as his wife.

And I had just made her my enemy.

CHAPTER TWELVE
MENELAUS

Menelaus threw his cup against the wall, the gold ringing loud as it struck the stone. "You cannot mean this!"

But his brother sat unmoved, did not even look up from his plate, his fingers covered in grease from the carcass of the bird he ate. "You make me all the more sure of my decision with every word exchanged."

"Helen is mine!" he roared. "*Mine!* And you would keep her from me? Leave me here in Mycenae like a wayward child? And what will the others think, when Menelaus allows his brother to stand in his place? They will say I was afraid I would lose. That I had not the courage to face them myself and win Helen with my own hands!"

"And if I let you go to Sparta, you will lose her without question," Agamemnon said, infernally calm. As if he cared not at all. As if he had not just refused him the right to secure his own wife. "This madness in your eyes, the wild gleam—do you think Tyndareus would entrust Sparta to your hands now? No. You would have neither Helen nor a crown, and then you would return here in a foul temper, blaming me for your own foolishness."

"You seem to think she is not already claimed. Mine by right, promised by her mother. By Tyndareus himself."

Agamemnon snorted, still focused upon his plate. "Tyndareus made no promises."

"You lie!" He swept the meal from the table, knocking it all to the floor.

"You will remember who is king in this hall, Menelaus." His brother lifted his head, his eyes black with anger as he rose from his place behind the table, hands pressed flat against the finely carved wood. "Or you will find yourself without more than just your thrice-cursed bride. Do I make myself clear?"

Menelaus swallowed a growl, but did not back down. He was *owed* an explanation, at the least. "The words fell from your own lips, *my king*. And I spoke with Leda myself. Tyndareus—"

"Leda may have promised you the girl, but Tyndareus did not." Agamemnon bared his teeth. "And why would he, when you stalked his palace, pissing all over his daughter while his hall was filled to over-flowing with men all come to woo her? You knew your purpose, knew the plan we had all agreed upon, and even for the length of a feast you could not keep yourself in check. I only told you Tyndareus had agreed in secret to keep you from acting any more the fool. But even with that, you could not be satisfied."

"You saw her throwing herself at that Athenian," Menelaus snapped. "If it had been Clytemnestra—"

Agamemnon slammed his fist upon the table. "Do you know how much trouble you might have caused us, had you been seen climbing through her window? How much we might have lost? Did you think at all of anything but your own lust?"

He raised his chin. "I sought to save her from her own blindness. She does not know the power she has over men, does not realize how she tempts us. And what followed is the proof!"

"Proof," Agamemnon sneered, dropping back to his seat. "It was proof of something, that is true. Proof that I cannot trust you not to lose your head over a worthless woman. Which is why you will remain in Mycenae and I will compete for Helen's hand in your place. Once she is won, wedded, and bedded, perhaps you will have some sense restored, but until then? I will not risk the trouble you might brew among so many men, all mad with lust."

Menelaus swore, kicking a stool and sending it crashing into the dais. But it did not matter what he said now. Agamemnon had made up his mind, and so long as he was *prince* instead of *king*, he had no choice but to obey. Agamemnon would have him imprisoned if he believed for a moment he would not do as he was told. And there was more to this than his brother's belief that he would fail.

Agamemnon sought to undermine him. To keep him always in the debt of Mycenae, always subordinate. He meant to ensure that the other suitors would realize who was the greater man, the more powerful king.

He wanted Menelaus bound so tightly he would never break free, never have the smallest hope of rising up. Because Agamemnon was afraid, always haunted by their father's murder at his own brother's hand, by this supposed curse tainting their blood. Afraid that their father's fate would repeat itself again, and this time it would be Agamemnon who died.

And in moments such as these, Menelaus could not help but think he should be. For if it had not been for his desire for Helen, the woman Agamemnon thought so worthless, Menelaus would have stolen his brother's crown.

A throne for a throne, Agamemnon had promised him. And Helen, as his wife.

"Do not fail me," he said to his brother. "Not in this."

Or else the curse his brother feared would become all too real.

CHAPTER THIRTEEN
HELEN

Y ou take a great risk in coming here, Princess," Odysseus said, stopping to stand beside me upon the wall. Castor had been on guard beneath my window, and Clymene slept soundly. I'd been careful to avoid disturbing either one of them when I slipped out of the women's quarters, wrapped against the cold night air in Theseus's cloak.

Now I dropped my gaze from the dark horizon, the moon too shy a sliver to light Theseus's way this night, though it did not stop me from straining to see, from imagining he might stand just beyond my sight. I stared at the crown I held in my hands instead. The emerald glittered in its setting, catching the faint moonlight. "You bribed the guard, didn't you?"

"I didn't want Penelope's comings and goings made known to Leda or Tyndareus," he admitted. "I certainly didn't expect to learn that you had escaped your confinement and your guards."

I laughed, sliding the delicate gold over my wrist and up to my elbow, out of sight beneath the wool of my cloak. "Do you not see these men upon the walls? I have escaped nothing."

"If one guard can be bribed, there is no reason that others could not succumb to temptation. Of one form or another."

"I do not fear my father's men," I said, wrapping my cloak more tightly around me to ward against the wind. "Nor do I fear any thief in the night, come to steal me, though I would certainly be curious as to the outcome if he tried. Would he be smote by the gods for his impertinence? Or simply struck down by my father's guards? If only such a fate awaited Menelaus."

"The prince of Mycenae is never far from your mind," Odysseus said slowly. "But surely you do not truly wish him ill, when even I remember the kindness he showed you as a child. Would it not serve your cause if he were simply married elsewhere, far away from you?"

I let out a breath, struggling to steady myself. To consider carefully my words. "I fear the boy who treated me as a brother and a friend died in the war to reclaim Mycenae. Or else my cursed beauty ruined him soon after. And if he had ever truly loved me, truly cared for me or for Sparta, he would have given me up long ago."

Odysseus leaned against the stonework, his back to the horizon. "It is not so easy to thwart the gods, Helen. Surely you must realize that by now. Perhaps it is in their interests he pursues you, more than his own."

"And if I believed for a moment that was true, perhaps things would be different between us now," I agreed. "But he made it very clear to me that I was his prize. His brother promised him I would be his bride, once they had retaken Mycenae and Agamemnon was crowned, and Menelaus is determined to have what he believes he has earned with his loyalty. Escape from beneath Agamemnon's shadow. A kingdom. Me."

I snorted, staring up at the stars. How I wished I might disappear among them. How I longed for those days in Athens, when I had thought, however briefly, that I might never have to think of Menelaus again. That I might live my life loved by a greater man, a better man. I had been such a fool.

"Do you know what he said, when I asked him to give me up?" I heard myself say. Now that I had begun, it did not seem that I could stop. "He said it was all for my protection. That if he had not made me a condition of his service to his brother, Agamemnon would have taken me for his own. As if a marriage to Agamemnon was worse than the mountains of the dead, the seas of blood, the destruction of everything I loved. As if I should be *grateful* to him for sparing me the small irritation of suffering Agamemnon for a husband."

"Let it never be said that the sons of Atreus possess any great wisdom between them," Odysseus said. "But even if he is a fool, is he not at least a kindly one? Certainly he seems to care for you, to take an interest in your happiness."

"Only insofar as it ensures his own," I said, unable to keep the bitterness from my voice. "He cannot conceive of the idea that I might not want him as he wants me. I am simply a stupid girl who cannot recognize that he is the best choice, the best man to protect me. Everything he does is for my own good, in his mind, and my own concerns, my reservations, even my nightmares do not matter. And he blames it all upon me. His lust, his desire. But how can it be my fault, when I have done everything to discourage him? Just because I have shown my face within his sight, I am to be blamed for his urges?"

"I do not pretend that it is fair to you," Odysseus said. "But your beauty serves as encouragement enough for any man, caught unwitting. Gift or curse, the gods have made you so beautiful you draw men like so many bees to honey. Perhaps you do not control this power you have, but it does not mean your power does not work upon those who surround you."

"It does not mean I am at fault. If it is the gods who have empowered me, who use me for their own ends, the blame should fall upon them," I said. "Or are you to blame for the fact that you were born a prince? Or born a man at all, for that matter!"

"It is hardly the same," he said.

"I have done *nothing* but try to live my life. To serve my people and protect Achaea. Blame me for that if you wish, but do not blame me for the cruel use the gods have made of my form."

He grunted. "It might surprise you to know I did not come here to fight. Only to see that you were safe and protect you from your father's anger when he hears of your excursion. You should not wander alone, Helen."

"According to my brothers, I spent the better part of two years wandering alone. Living in caves like an animal. Why should I not be driven to continue?"

Odysseus half smiled. "It is a terrible story, truly. Unbelievable in every way, but for the fact that you are a daughter of Zeus. One can only presume he kept you alive with ambrosia, for I cannot imagine you have much talent for foraging."

"I am not completely helpless, Odysseus, despite appearances."

"I did not say that you were *completely* helpless," he teased, bumping his shoulder against mine. "Only that I find it difficult to believe you would survive alone in the wilds for so long, or that you might be found and returned home looking quite so well-fed. Did you not consider the delight of your many curves when you came up with such a story?"

I glared at him sidelong. "Careful. If Penelope heard you utter anything of the sort, she'd murder me in my sleep."

"Ah, Penelope," he said, staring up at the sky. "What a story she told me tonight."

"Oh?" I kept my tone carefully neutral, ignoring the roiling of my stomach. Odysseus was baiting me, and I had no interest in giving him the satisfaction of thinking himself successful.

"Nothing you'd be interested in, I'm sure. After all, it couldn't possibly be true, and repeating these kinds of horrid rumors only lends them legitimacy they don't deserve."

I rolled my eyes. "And yet you seem so desperate to discuss it. Or do you only want me to ask it of you so you can refuse?"

"It's only that it would explain so much," he said, still pretending interest in the stars. "Why your mother was said to have taken to her bed, pale and shaking, when she heard you had disappeared. This resentment you hold for the prince of Mycenae, to say nothing of his fury and obsession with getting you back. Even why you might have felt you had no choice but to flee. Why you felt you had nothing to lose by doing so. Such a strange, terrible knot, it is no wonder you need help to escape it now."

I shivered, in spite of myself, and looked away. All his questions. His subtle probing of my relationship with Menelaus. He had played me for a fool, and now what could I say? He would see through any argument I might make, any bluster.

"I suppose that is what rumors do best," I managed, before the silence betrayed me utterly. "But I find most often the explanations they provide are far too convenient for my liking. Men and women are rarely so simply motivated."

"If this one were true, however, it would make this knot we seek to unravel all the more tangled. One would think, if you truly desired to free yourself, you might have given your friends and allies all the threads, rather than let them worry upon only one or two and tighten the bond all the more, unwitting."

"I am happy for you that you have no trouble telling friend from foe, ally from enemy. It must be a great comfort to you, now that you are king. I fear, however, that I am not so fortunate. And if I do, in fact, keep secrets, perhaps it is because I know the knot you toy with is a noose, and it is already wrapped far too tightly around my throat."

I pulled up the hood of Theseus's cloak, covering my head and hiding my face in shadow. "I wish you dreams more pleasant than mine, King Odysseus, should you sleep at all this night."

I left him in the dark, and I did not bother to look back. But I feared it would not be long before Odysseus realized all the truths I had kept from him.

Theseus. Athens.

Queen Meryet.

CHAPTER FOURTEEN
HELEN

My suitors arrived first as a trickle, and then in a rush. Within seven days of that night upon the wall, the megaron had become a roaring banquet hall, filled with men of all ages, and even youths. So many, their faces blurred together, one after another, and I did not dare to leave the women's quarters without one of my brothers in addition to Clymene.

It was enough to make me miss even Pirithous. He had lied to me, betrayed Theseus with this mad journey to the Underworld, but when he had followed me through these halls, I had known myself to be well protected. Safe. Now, even with my brothers by my side, I cringed to enter the megaron and wade through so many men.

"Menestheus has come," Castor murmured in my ear. "If you can remember not to sneer in his general direction, it would be a help."

Sneer? No. I wanted to spit at him. The audacity of Menestheus coming here to win me for his own after betraying Theseus so utterly, after betraying *me*—the man deserved far worse than to be sneered at.

But I could hardly admit to dislike of the man who had returned me to my brothers. In fact, for appearances, I might have to pretend delight that he'd come. The thought made me sick.

"What of Menelaus?" I asked to distract myself.

Castor grunted. "He hasn't arrived yet, and when he does, we'll have our hands full keeping him from Menestheus. We put the fear of Zeus into him in Athens, but I don't trust it to last, and should Menelaus hear the wrong words exchanged . . ."

"If the gods are good, Menelaus will not show his face at all. We can only pray he's suffering from some mortal wound after being thrown from his horse."

"Not here, Helen," Castor said, glancing quickly around us to be sure no one had heard. Clymene walked at my heels, but we spoke softly enough that she would not hear over the noise in the megaron. "When he does arrive, if you cannot keep your temper, we'll all be sorry for it. I don't know what you said to Penelope to turn her so completely against us, but the last thing we needed was another enemy. And she has Odysseus's ear."

I grimaced. Odysseus hadn't mentioned that night on the wall or the concerns he'd expressed, but he hadn't been overly friendly since, either. "I'm less worried about what she's whispering in Odysseus's ear than I am what she might say to Nestra, if she comes."

"Just try to make yourself agreeable, would you? You need these men, and the longer they fight and argue over you, the better off we all are. Especially when there has been no word of Theseus at all."

I swallowed hard, hating how casually he spoke the words. Hating how hollowly they rang in my heart. Every day that passed without news—did he think I needed to be reminded? That I was not deafened by the silence? Even now, my ears were tuned to every whisper of his name, any mention at all. But when my father's guests spoke of Theseus, it was with regret and grief, and the soft, respectful tones reserved for the dead. And I hated that most of all.

"Princess!" Ajax the Great bowed low, stealing my hand before I'd even thought to keep it from him and pressing a kiss to my knuckles. "You are more beautiful than ever."

I forced a smile to my lips. "And I think you have grown taller still, Prince Ajax. Though I cannot imagine how it is possible. Have you come to win me?"

"I will certainly try," he said, returning my smile. "There is no greater prize to be found in all of Achaea."

"You refer to Sparta, of course," I said, all politeness even as I corrected him. "And I cannot blame you for desiring our beautiful lands for your own. We, too, would benefit from closer alliance with Salamis, should you become our king."

"The kingship of Sparta is nothing compared to the honor of wedding such a beautiful bride," Ajax said, his eyes warming. "Even if I must give up my father's throne, I would not be unhappy so long as you shared my bed."

I flinched, his words summoning memories I did not want, and Castor touched my arm, offering a balm of comfort with the contact.

"Do not frighten my sister with thoughts of facing your monstrous snake in the night," my brother said, and then he raised his voice to be heard by the rest of the assembly. "No one shall speak of the marriage bed within the hearing of the princess! What thoughts you might have of that nature, however complimentary, do her the favor of keeping them to yourself!"

There was a roar of laughter in response to my brother's command, and Ajax pressed another kiss to my hand. "I must beg your forgiveness, my lady, I was overcome."

"See that it does not happen again, and I will forget it at once," I promised. He had always been more boisterous than offensive, and if it had not been for Menelaus, I might have laughed. Ajax, at least, did not mind plain speaking, and he'd protected me from Leda's fury once before. "But if it counts for anything at all, you should know I would not be unhappy if the man who defended my honesty so long ago were chosen to become my husband and king."

He flushed, his smile broadening into a grin. "I will fight all the harder, Princess."

"I am glad of it," I said, meaning it. There were far more unsuitable men than Ajax the Great, and as the great-grandson of Zeus, no one could argue that he was not worthy. "If you will excuse me, Prince Ajax, I fear if I linger any longer with any one man, this banquet will turn into a brawl."

He chuckled, releasing my hand, and Castor led me on, pushing the men back when they tried to crowd me. How we reached the dais at all, I do not know, but I was grateful to find myself seated with only my family and Odysseus.

"With just a smile and a word, you win their hearts," Odysseus said as I sat down beside him. "Is it any wonder Menelaus is mad with jealousy?"

"Has he arrived, then, at last?" The thought sent a prickle of unease down my back.

"I have heard just this day that Agamemnon has come in his place, for he does not trust his brother not to lose all reason and sense at the sight of you so besieged by men. But I have not quite decided whether we should be grateful to the king of Mycenae or not. It is one thing to refuse a prince the bride he desires, quite another to insult the king himself by choosing another."

It was as though I could breathe again. As if until that moment, I had been drowning. I stared at my cup, clasping my fingers tightly in my lap to keep my hands from shaking with relief. If it were true—gods above, let it be true! Menelaus left in Mycenae, far away from me. Agamemnon was unpleasant company, to be sure, but to be free of his brother!

"The gods are good," I said, resolving to make an offering to Athena first thing the following day. "And with Athena's help, we will find our way free of Mycenae altogether. I must believe it."

"Let us wait and see what future your dreams predict at this turn of events, shall we?" Odysseus said, filling my cup with wine. "From that knowledge, and the prevailing mood of this assembly, we will form our plans."

But in spite of his caution, for the rest of the banquet, I could not keep a smile from curving my lips.

Pollux gripped my hand, laughing as I tripped over my own feet on my way back to the women's quarters. I grinned, pleased with the way the hall just barely spun. I'd had enough wine that I did not care how many men had come or what dreams I might suffer. When Theseus arrived, we would run away, and Menelaus would not be here to stop us. Menelaus would not be here at all!

"I haven't seen you in such good spirits since your birthday feast," Pollux said. "And what on earth did you say to Ajax the Great to make him so insufferably pleased with himself?"

"Nothing that wasn't true," I said, skipping from one blue-painted tile to the next. "Do you remember when we used to pretend the red tiles were the chasms of Hades, and if we stepped on them we'd be swallowed—whoops!"

My brother caught me by the waist before I fell, swinging me up into his arms. "I know Castor told you to make yourself agreeable, but perhaps a little less wine would be prudent?"

"I wanted to celebrate," I said. "And why shouldn't I? None of the men who have come to win me would dare do me any harm or risk losing everything they desire. And Menelaus is not coming at all!"

"For which I am certainly glad enough," Pollux agreed. "Though I think it far too early to believe we are saved. Agamemnon will do everything in his power still to win you for his brother, and while he stays away, Tyndareus cannot see how deranged he has become, which certainly works against us."

"Do not be so grim, Pollux." I kicked my feet, one arm wrapped around his neck to steady myself. "The brother I remember was all laughter and teasing."

"And then his sister was stolen from under his nose, and he realized how he had wronged her with his teasing and jokes when he ought to have been listening to her more seriously," Pollux said. "But once all of this is behind us, I promise we will laugh together again, you and I. And when you are queen, Castor and I will stand at your side, your loyal servants and guards."

"Will her husband not have that honor?" a man said, stepping out of the shadows as we reached the curtained entrance to the women's quarters, and Pollux stopped short, his body going stiff. "I cannot help but think the future king of Sparta might find such an arrangement . . . uncomfortable."

Pollux set me down carefully, his hand falling to the hilt of his sword. "And you are?"

"Polypoetes." The man bowed, a familiar smile tugging at the corners of his mouth, and even in the lamplight there was something strange about his eyes. Something in his expression that I thought I knew.

Ignoring Pollux's caution and emboldened by the wine, I stepped toward him and lifted his chin, that I might study his face more easily. "Who is your father, Polypoetes?"

He wrapped his hand around my wrist and pressed a kiss into my palm, all charm. "I am the son of Hippodamia, Tamer of Horses and Daughter of the Centaurs; and King Pirithous of the Lapiths, son of Zeus and loyal friend to King Theseus of Athens."

I grinned at him, closing my hand over his. Pirithous's son. And how I had never met him before now, I did not know, but no matter how infuriating I'd found his father, Pirithous had been trustworthy and good in his own way. "If you have even half of your father's virtue and courage, you are most welcome to Sparta, Polypoetes."

He laughed. "There are few women indeed who would use the word *virtue* to describe my father, but I thank you for your kindness."

"Didero," Pollux said, speaking to our faithful bribed guard. "Stretch your legs."

Didero bowed, though it was clear from the glance he threw over his shoulder he had wished to stay. No doubt to tell Odysseus what he'd heard, for some new reward or another.

"Has Pirithous come as well?" I asked the moment the guard had disappeared from sight, unable to keep from hoping. "All of Achaea has heard of his quest, but has he found his way home with his new goddess-bride? Or perhaps there is some word of Theseus?"

Polypoetes's eyes darkened. "My father has often found it to his advantage to play the fool, but in this, I fear he has gone too far. He is lost, my lady, and knowing the harm it has done you, I have come to do what I am able to make it right."

I tugged my hand from his, suddenly wishing I had not had so much wine, for my thoughts were sluggish and the things he'd said—

"What harm could Pirithous's quest have done my sister?" Pollux asked coolly, pulling me gently back to his side.

"If I did not know the truth, would I await you here, in the dark?" Polypoetes asked, laughter in his voice. "Why should I not have introduced myself in the megaron, where all the other men might hear and mark well your response to me? No. I would not have dared utter my father's name or Theseus's with so many watching, knowing the eager light it must bring to the princess's eyes."

Pollux had gone stiff again, his eyes narrowing. But I stopped his hand upon the hilt of his sword and put myself between them before my brother's temper offended the gods. Polypoetes was a guest. Protected by sacred law, no matter what news he brought.

"Who else believes as you do?" I asked, struggling to order my thoughts well enough that I might give nothing more away.

"No one, Princess," Polypoetes said. "Pirithous kept no secrets from me, as his heir, but he would never betray Theseus. My father's secrets die with me."

I nodded, looking back at Pollux. "Pirithous might have led Theseus into ruin, but he did not do it out of malice. He was infuriating, arrogant, foolish—but he was not an enemy. If Pirithous trusted his son, perhaps we should as well."

"You take his word so easily," Pollux said. "The son of a man who destroyed all your hopes with his hubris. You cannot even be sure he is who he says he is."

"There are others here who know me."

"Who?" Pollux said. "Menestheus? You might just as easily have bribed him to say as much."

His eyes narrowed. "What purpose does it serve me to lie? I would hardly dare steal Theseus's bride for my own with such a ruse. I have come to repay my father's debts and to protect my people. That is all."

"He has the look of his father," I said, stopping Pollux before he could snarl again. "And we have need of friends and allies, Brother. As many as we can find. The more who stand against Menelaus, the safer we all are. Provided that he does not fear Mycenae . . . ?"

"Among the Lapiths, we do not forget what is owed," he said. "And Thessaly is far enough north we are safe from even Agamemnon's grasping hands. Should he dare to strike at us, to raid our banks or march so far from home, he would find only defeat, his men trampled beneath our horses' hooves."

"Brave words," Pollux said. "Especially for a people who seem to have misplaced their king."

Polypoetes bared his teeth. "The Lapiths take pride in King Pirithous, son of Dia and Zeus, but do not make the mistake of believing he was our only strength. Or do you think while he was raiding with Theseus, we cowered behind our walls?"

"With a king like Pirithous, I cannot believe your people have ever cowered in their lives," I said, digging my nails into Pollux's arm now to silence him. I'd had too much wine, but I was not sure what Pollux would make his excuse. "I beg your forgiveness on my brother's behalf. It is the strain of uncertainty that causes him to speak so rudely. We are glad to have another friend, though I admit I am not certain how you might serve us by more than just your presence."

"He can fight for you," Pollux said to me. Then he stepped forward, urgent and entreating, his gaze fixed upon Polypoetes. "Fight as if you would murder any man who stands in your way, and let Agamemnon and Tyndareus know it. If you are truly Pirithous's son, I trust you can defend yourself?"

"Against any man assembled," Polypoetes agreed, and I did not think it was merely a boast. I had seen Pirithous fight, and I did not think he would send his son into the world without teaching him to survive.

"Stay on your guard," Pollux said. "I do not know how far Agamemnon will go to secure Helen's marriage to his brother, but I can promise you he will find a way to cheat. Be ready to protect yourself and the others should he resort to deadly means."

"And you, Princess? Is there nothing you will ask of me?"

I let out a breath. "Distract Menestheus, if you can, I suppose. Keep him from Agamemnon's ear. Should Mycenae learn I was Theseus's wife, it will go badly for Athens, but I do not trust Menestheus to realize it, or even to care overmuch, if there is something he might gain from it."

Polypoetes bowed. "You made a fine queen of Athens, my lady, and I do not doubt you will be a great queen of Sparta, as well. I will do all within my power to ensure that the man who is chosen as your husband is worthy of the honor."

It was a promise I was happy to accept, along with his friendship. But I would have been more reassured if he had brought instead some small word of hope, some whisper of news of Theseus.

There would never be any man more worthy than the one I had already married.

CHAPTER FIFTEEN
POLYPOETES

Polypoetes did not linger in the hall. The moment Helen disappeared behind her curtained passage, he turned back to the megaron. Bad enough he had been forced to reveal himself before the guard, the man's interest far too keen for his peace of mind. He did not need to be caught lurking by anyone else.

"Was the princess all that you hoped she would be?" Odysseus drawled, catching him as he entered the megaron again. "I shouldn't wonder that the son of Pirithous would be so bold, but I confess curiosity at the warmth of your reception. By all accounts, the princess cared little for your father's company when he came here last."

Ah, his father. Polypoetes had learned long ago that Pirithous was known far better for his piracy than he was for his heroics, and it surely did not help that he had provoked and fostered rumors that he had stolen Helen for himself. But whatever Pirithous's reputation, Polypoetes knew his father's heart. The Lapiths could not have had a better king, nor Pirithous a more devoted people, no matter how unsettled or even unsavory he might have appeared to others.

"I wanted only to match her against the stories my father told me some years ago," he said easily, for it was not untrue. "She truly is blinding in her beauty."

"Is that all your father told you?" Odysseus asked. "Knowing Pirithous's keen appreciation for women, I would have thought he'd have more to say on the subject than just that."

Polypoetes smiled. "My father most appreciated beauty, King Odysseus, in all its forms."

"What, then, did he make of the most beautiful woman in all of Achaea?"

In truth, Pirithous had not spoken at any length regarding Helen's physical splendor. He'd been far more interested in what lay beneath. She'd made Theseus a willful wife, Pirithous had said more than once. A stubborn woman, determined to have her way. He had been convinced she would bring Theseus trouble because of it, and from what Polypoetes had heard of their trials, his father had not been wholly wrong.

"He said she shone too brightly," Polypoetes said. "That any man who drew too near was likely to be burned by the flame long before he recognized the danger. Her beauty, he told me once, was like a Siren's song. Impossible to resist, but too dangerous to enjoy."

But it hadn't been Helen's beauty, her irresistible danger, that had ruined Theseus. That most shameful honor belonged to his father, in the end. For it had been Pirithous who had asked Theseus to accompany him to the Underworld, to the very house of Hades, in his quest to steal Persephone and claim her as his bride. Pirithous who had known his friend would not refuse him and had even counted on Theseus's honor to serve his own ends. Pirithous who had trapped them both beneath the earth.

Pirithous had cost Theseus not just his life, but the rule of Athens for his sons, and if everything his father had told him was to be believed, the peaceful future of all Achaea, which Helen and Theseus had woven so carefully, now lay in tattered shreds at Pirithous's feet. And at his own.

"I never realized King Pirithous spoke with such poetry," Odysseus said, his gaze shifting to the tables, still more full than empty of men. Many of them would carouse and drink until dawn, so long as Tyndareus allowed the wine to flow. "In spite of his reputation, I would not have minded if he had come back again to compete. And better he had sought Helen than the prize he pursues even now."

They spoke of Pirithous's loss so casually. As if all of Achaea had not lost a great man, a great hero. As if they had not lost even their own lives because of his father's foolish quest, if Helen's dreams were a true warning, sent by the gods. Polypoetes snorted, annoyed by all of it. These men who did not realize what they risked, or did not care, so long as they satisfied their lust.

"If he had come," he said fiercely, turning his irritation toward the part he must play, "he would have found himself shamed by defeat, for I would not have given up my own pursuit even for my father's sake. And I promise you, King Odysseus, I mean to win."

But perhaps Pirithous had not been wrong about Helen's Siren song, because in spite of all he knew, once the words had left his mouth, he did not mind the sound of them. The thought of keeping Helen as his own.

After all, he would hardly be the first king of the Lapiths to take a willful woman to wife.

CHAPTER SIXTEEN
HELEN

I had been able to avoid Leda since my return home, in part due to my brothers' presence in the women's quarters—an exception that had infuriated my mother—and in part by Clymene's faithful service. She would scout the hallway before I left, ensuring my mother was nowhere to be seen, and fetch what supplies I needed to be sure I would not meet her along the way. But I had known from the start that I could not keep on this way forever. It had only ever been a matter of time. And now that my suitors had arrived, I had no choice but to sit beneath her eye, morning, noon, and evening, at banquet in the megaron.

Whatever response I had expected, it was not the smug smile, the proud bearing. As if now that I had returned home, everything she had hoped for, everything she had dreamed of would be hers. As if she held my fate in her hands. Perhaps she was convinced she would see me married to Menelaus yet and she need no longer fear any reprisals for having lost his promised bride.

"Squirm as much as you like, Helen," she said to me one evening, a smirk upon her lips. She'd caught me outside the megaron with only Clymene to escort me back to my room. "It will change nothing now that Agamemnon has arrived to speak on his brother's behalf."

I had been forced to spend the meal beside Prince Ajax of Locris, a man who had not endeared himself to me in my nightmares. I could not look on him without hearing screams and smelling blood. In my earliest nightmares, Ajax had raped me. But so had many others since.

"Do you not wonder why Menelaus does not come to win me himself?" I asked. "Or does he mean to let his brother stand in his place as king of Sparta as well, should Agamemnon succeed?"

Leda's eyes hardened. "Agamemnon, at least, would have the good sense to silence you. Perhaps I should speak to him about his brother's leniency and ensure your future husband is prepared to discipline you properly."

"Tyndareus would never allow my husband to abuse me," I said.

"Tyndareus will not live forever," my mother said, far too pleasantly. "And any agreements you might have made with your father will die with him."

"And what do you think Zeus will say, should he see his daughter mistreated?"

Leda laughed. "All Zeus desires is his war, Helen. Haven't you realized that by now? You are nothing to him but a means to an end. Just as I was."

My hands closed into fists so tight my nails dug deep into my palms. "Jealousy doesn't become you, Mother."

"Jealousy?" She shook her head. "Pity, once, perhaps. When you were small and far less willful. Before you learned to bespell men with your beauty, turning them into fools. You are nothing but ruin. That is your gift, your curse and mine, for having borne you. Had I dashed your head upon the rocks so long ago, we would all be the better for it."

Ruin. And perhaps she was right. I hated her for saying it, all the same. Hated her for having brought me into the world, if this was to be my fate. "And if you had not been so ungrateful for Zeus's favors, I'd never have been born at all. Whatever punishment this is, let it rest upon your head. All the blood spilled on your hands, and yours alone."

"You're right," she said, smiling so serenely again, so smugly. "The gods have punished me justly, taught me my place. Which is why I will never be so foolish as to spite the gods again. Zeus desires his war, and he shall have it. And if I am very fortunate, perhaps he will grant me his favors once more."

And then she swept away, back into the megaron, as if I mattered not at all.

My mother's words haunted me, and I lay awake in my bed, afraid to sleep for what nightmares it might bring. It felt as though I was always afraid to sleep since I'd returned to Sparta. Not a single night had passed peacefully since my brothers had stolen me back from Athens. But tonight, somehow, I knew I would dream of Theseus. Of Theseus's ruin. My heart could not stand it. Knowing everything he had lost already was bad enough, but I had blamed Menestheus for it, Pirithous, even my brothers, until that moment.

Until Leda's accusation had run me through. Oh, my mother. Her tongue, as always, sharper than any sword. And she wielded it so well, so precisely. Perhaps, in that way, we were not so different after all, for I had surely learned the boldness of my own speech at Leda's knee.

I rubbed my eyes, rolling to my side to curl into a ball, hoping if I only made myself small enough, I could escape some of the guilt that threatened to crush me. I had ruined Theseus. I had tempted him, offered him my body and my love in exchange for his help, knowing he would not, could not refuse me. I had provoked him into stealing me away, and then basked in his love and attention in Athens, taking his mind and his focus from his duty to his people. I had helped him to betray them, without ever realizing fully what it all meant. I was the reason he had put distance between himself and Menestheus, between himself and all the rest of his nobles. And it was Menestheus's lust for me, I understood now, that had caused him to stew in his resentment and bitterness, to even go so far as to betray his king.

I had cost Theseus everything. The great hero brought low by my beauty, my foolishness, my gift for ruination. Perhaps Athens did not burn yet, but its men might still suffer and die. And that, too, would be my fault. For if Theseus had remained king, had I only given him a warning of what might come and left him to face it his own way, surely Athens would never go to war for me. If he had never loved me, Athens might still be his, kept safe by his wisdom, his leadership.

My eyes drifted shut, despite the twisted knot of my thoughts. Exhaustion overtook me all the same, not caring whether I dreaded the dreams that came with it.

Menelaus sits in Tyndareus's place in the megaron, red hair gleaming in the lamplight, and where my mother should have been, at his right hand, there is only me. A great feast has been prepared, the tables warping beneath the weight of all the food and wine, and I have never seen so many strangers at banquet. Castor and Pollux sit together at the head table, and between them is a man I do not know. He watches me, hungry, and I look away at once.

Menelaus calls for wine, and I pour him some. He takes my hand, but there is nothing gentle about his touch, and when he meets my eyes there is no friendship in his face, only desire and lust. He squeezes my hand so hard my bones press together, and then another man shouts to him from below. He turns away, releasing me and laughing at the joke.

I beg to be excused, and leave the hall. My feet do not take me to the room I share with Clymene, but to the room that had been my mother's. I back from it, knowing at once she is dead. A warm hand grips my shoulder, rough and hard, forcing me back inside.

The door closes and the room is dark, but when I turn it is not Menelaus who faces me. I try to pull free and open my mouth to call for help.

The man covers my mouth with his hand before I can shout, pressing me against the wall. "Shh, Helen. I won't harm you."

I stare at him, my eyes widening to make out his features in the moonlight. He is tall and lean, but I can see little of his face. He touches my hair, stroking it from my cheek, and where his fingers brush my skin I feel as though I have been kissed by fire.

"Your honor will not let you accept me, I know," he says. "But Aphrodite herself has promised you to me. You are mine, Helen. You have been meant for me since before your marriage to this man. Since that day, so long ago, when I found you bathing in the water. So beautiful, so young. We were both so young."

I shake my head, desperate to free myself now. I remember the boy. I remember Theseus, ready to plunge a sword through his chest. My pleading that he be spared. The kiss I gave him in payment for his silence, never dreaming I would ever see him again. The shepherd's son. *Paris.*

My heels scrape painfully against the wall as I struggle, and his hand falls to my waist, holding me in place.

"I have kept my promise," he says, his voice harder now. The sweet boy is gone, if he'd ever lived at all, and the man has come to claim me. "I let that Athenian take you, but he did not keep you safe. Did not keep you at all. But you needn't fear anything now that you're mine. Now that we have one another."

Then he covers my mouth with his, kissing me with a need that makes my stomach twist and my whole body tremble. My trembling seems to please him. Perhaps he mistakes it for desire instead of the agony that roots me to the floor. He releases me and I gasp, but before I can move or speak, he is gone.

I fall to my knees and the floor lurches. The moonlight melts into water, spraying against my face, and a ribbed wooden hull pitches beneath me. I fumble in the darkness, my hands searching until they find a ladder, and then I climb up into sun and wind. An empty deck. I fight to find my footing, grasping at the mast to steady myself.

And then I see him. Tall and broad and beautiful, his dark hair almost blue in the sunlight, like his father's. "Theseus!"

He turns, his gaze searching, but though he looks right at me, I am invisible to his eyes. I stumble forward, running down the center of the deck, between the empty benches and the abandoned oars. "Theseus, I am here!"

When I throw myself into his arms, everything dissolves into mist and darkness. Then smoke and flame. I cannot breathe. I cannot breathe, and Theseus is lost. And everything burns.

Everything but me.

"She is mad," Pollux said the next morning, after I had told him all that Leda had said. I did not speak of my nightmare. Of Theseus on the ship, or the young boy we had spared in Troy. The young boy who had grown into my strange prince, intent upon stealing me away. I could not face it yet. "Hera has driven her into madness in punishment for inciting Zeus's lust. It is the only explanation."

Castor pressed his lips together, stepping back from where he stood beside the door, listening for Clymene's return. Or Penelope's ear pressed to the panel as Leda's spy—or Odysseus's. "Is it madness, after all she's suffered? Zeus punished her once already for what he well might have considered disobedience. She is right to fear his anger a second time."

"But to sacrifice her own daughter to the gods' demands? To sacrifice all of us?" Pollux asked. "She betrays Sparta!"

I hoped he did not see my flinch, for this last month I had wondered if I had been a fool to fight for my daughter's life. Wondered if I might have kept Theseus, if only I had given her up more freely. Had I known, I was not certain I would have made the same choice.

"And what is Sparta to the gods?" Castor asked. "Where is her duty, if not to the gods, first? Sparta must always come second. The desires of men, her own will. None of that matters if she believes the gods have ordained this course."

Pollux snorted. "I know you and Nestra were always Mother's favorites, but I cannot believe you would defend her in this. You can't think it's true!"

Castor's gaze faltered, skating over my face and then falling away, his mouth too firm, too grim. I rose from my stool, taking his hands in mine. "But why have you helped me, if you think as Leda does? If you believe the gods desire the war?"

His lips twitched as he looked down at me, some small touch of humor in the lines fanning out from his eyes. He was so young to look so old. "I think between the gods and my family, it is my brother and sister who need me more. If this is the will of the gods, my actions are nothing to them. They will have their way in the end. But if it is not, if your dreams are meant as warning, or even opportunity, then I have done my duty still. The gods have not seen fit to command me otherwise, and until then, I will do what I can to protect my sister, my family, my people."

"Oh, Castor." I squeezed his hands. "You must know how much it means to me. How grateful I am for all that you have done."

Pollux made a soft noise of disgust behind us. "I still think she's mad."

"And if she is, we will learn the truth of it soon enough," Castor said, releasing me. "But whether she is right or wrong, mad or otherwise, she deserves our pity. She asked for none of this, and the gods have been as cruel to her as they have to Helen. Perhaps all the more so, for at least Helen has time still to fight. Mother was never given any warning of her fate, and she was powerless to stop it from coming. Perhaps this is her way of reclaiming some of what she lost, all those years ago."

I hugged myself, not wanting to admit that his words made sense. Not wanting to feel anything but anger toward my mother after she had betrayed me so utterly. That she had given Menelaus permission to rape me, for any reason, was a wrong I could not forgive. I had fought for my own daughter's sake, even in the face of death, of ruin. As a mother should. "It does not make what she has done right."

"No," Castor agreed. "And I do not defend her actions, nor the cruelty you suffered at her hand, Helen, but I cannot help but feel *for* her, all the same. She is only a mortal, caught up in the games of the gods. I know something of how that feels, after these last months."

"You are more than just a mortal, Castor," Pollux said fiercely. "Even if you do not have Zeus's ichor running through your veins, you are still blessed by the gods!"

But no matter how strongly Pollux protested, I understood. I may have been Zeus's daughter, but I had felt the same. I was not Theseus or Pirithous or Heracles, or even Pollux. I was only a girl, as Penelope had said, and but for the brief years I had spent as Theseus's wife, I had been treated as a prize my whole life—something to be given or taken away, but never to have any will of my own.

If that was the heart of Leda's pain, I knew it all too well.

But it did not mean I would do nothing. It did not mean I would not fight.

To save my brothers and Theseus, if no one else.

PART TWO: THE GAMES

CHAPTER SEVENTEEN
PARIS

Oenone delivered him a beautiful boy, with warm curly hair and dimpled cheeks, and a laugh that caused the flocks to huddle nearer, the ewes and nannies eager to claim him as their own. They were not rich, he and Oenone, but it seemed to Paris in those days that he had plenty—more than he could ever have dreamed of, with his lover and his son, and brave, steady Tauros, who still won every match he was set.

And perhaps Oenone had been right. He did not need to leave the mountain, where they were so content and his name was known, his fame undiminished in the years that had passed. What more could he truly desire than his son bouncing upon his knee and Oenone kneeling at his side, smiling and laughing along with their child?

The days were longer, in some ways. He shepherded their flocks alone more often than not, Oenone left behind to care for their boy, Corythus. But he didn't mind the solitude, not truly. Oenone had a way of watching him when he was at home, as if she searched for any small sign of unhappiness, ready to act, to save him from any small dissatisfaction. She was almost, at times, too eager to please him, too happy to distract him from his concerns, and too quick to forgive him, to give in to him, even when they teased and bickered over something so small as their evening's meal.

"She would make you a fine wife, Paris," his father said, during one of his visits to Agelaus's home, his own, too, until his nymph had found him. Oenone often came with him, but Corythus had been fussing, and she hadn't wanted to disturb him once he'd fallen asleep at last. "I cannot imagine what holds you back from claiming her as such before the gods. Surely you cannot think you will ever find a more fitting bride upon Mount Ida."

Paris laughed. "Not upon Mount Ida, no. Perhaps not even in all of Troy. But you know as well as I do that Oenone is too beautiful to remain a shepherd's wife."

His father grasped his shoulder, squeezing tight. "You are more than just a shepherd, boy. And more than worthy of a woman of her grace. Make her your wife and find happiness and peace."

"You assume she will have me," he teased, covering Agelaus's hand with his own.

The old man snorted, leaning back from the rough-hewn table. "She's put up with you this long, and I warn you, Paris, she will not wait forever. If your mother still lived—"

"If my mother still lived, she would have boxed my ears for raising my son in such a way, I know. She would say I am no king, no prince, to keep a woman as a consort instead of a wife. But we are happy as we are, Father. And you know I would not cast my son away. He will have everything you have given me."

Agelaus nodded, letting the matter drop, but there was something in his eyes, his face when they parted later—as if he wished he had said more. Some reassurance Agelaus hesitated to offer, perhaps.

"You needn't worry for me, Father," Paris promised him when he said his farewell. "Oenone will not leave her son without a father. Whether I call her wife or not, it does not matter to the love we share."

"I pray to the gods it is true," Agelaus said, embracing him tightly. "You have always been a good boy, Paris, a loyal son, foundling or not. Now that you are grown with a child of your own, I cannot imagine you will make a poor father. Give your Oenone my warmest wishes, and tell her I am eager to meet my grandson, when the time is right."

"She will be pleased to hear it," Paris said. "Perhaps we will bring him to you when I come again after the new moon."

And perhaps, too, he would consider his father's words in the meantime.

Perhaps it was time he gave up his dream for more and made peace with what he had been given.

CHAPTER EIGHTEEN
HELEN

I could not bring myself to confess everything to my brothers, to Tyndareus, or even to Odysseus. The last time I had tried, my family had been too content to let my fate come find me, thinking they could turn the tide at the last moment, sure of themselves and of me. I would not let Tyndareus marry me complacently to Menelaus simply because we knew the name of the boy, the prince, who would come. And I did not want Menelaus to know his name, either. Not because I wanted to protect the prince himself—I had tried that once, and it would haunt me for a lifetime—but if I were wed to Menelaus, I did not mean to give him the satisfaction of knowing his enemy. The knowledge of my fate would be the only weapon I would have left to protect myself, as his wife.

But should the boy arrive, the fool shepherd's son somehow made a prince, and should he succeed in stealing me away, I needed Theseus to know what had become of me. The brief glimpse the gods had given me of my husband alone upon the deck of his ship had given me hope that Theseus might yet follow me, even if he could not come in time to win me now.

"Tell Polypoetes that my mother is partial to silks," I told Clymene while she brushed and braided my hair, golden again at long last—a gift for which I had thanked Athena profusely. "I wish him seated beside me for the evening meal, and I do not see how we will accomplish it if he does not do something to ingratiate himself to Leda."

"The son of Pirithous, my lady?" Clymene asked.

"The same," I agreed, turning my head to catch a measure of her expression. "Or have you heard rumors of him among the servants and slaves? Tell me he does not spend his days in the kitchens among the maids as his father did."

She smiled, but it was strained. And not only from the concentration it took to arrange my hair. "Prince Polypoetes has declared he will have no woman but you. He threatens to murder any man who wins you in his place. I fear what he will say once you have given him encouragement. What he might do, even to you."

I pressed my lips together to stop my own smile, pretending concern instead. "King Pirithous treated me with great kindness. I would know what kind of man his son is for myself. And all the more reason to discern it now, that I might have time to dissuade him if he is as dangerous as you fear."

Clymene sighed. "It will be as you say, my lady. Though how he intends to rule both in Thessaly and here, I cannot imagine. By all accounts, King Pirithous is lost, and his son will have the Lapith throne before the end of summer."

I closed my eyes, tasting ash at her words. "We cannot know King Pirithous's fate, but if there is any man living who is capable of besting the gods at their games, it is him. I think Polypoetes must have some hope of his father's return, or else why would he have come at all?"

Clymene murmured some small agreement and finished my hair, but my own blithe assurances were sour in my mouth. Polypoetes had already told me what he believed—that his father would never return from this final quest. I could not believe the same of Theseus. I would not betray his faith by mistrusting his strength now, and I would not give up hope, for I was certain that so long as there was breath in his body, Theseus would fight to reach me. Besides, how could I have seen him sailing if he were to remain in the Underworld for all time?

I ignored my own doubts, pressing them down into the smallest, darkest places in my heart, and finished dressing. The tiered linen skirt, woven so fine you could see the shift I wore beneath its layers, fit more snugly than it used to. Nothing fit my waist as it had before, and no matter how determinedly I fought against the knowledge, it was not so easily ignored as the rest. But I did not have time for sorrow, nor to grieve the life I had lost, the daughter, the husband—

"Your suitors brought enough fabric in gifts that you'll have new gowns before your betrothal," Clymene said, frowning at the fit. "It must be all this feasting since you've been found, and I can hardly imagine Athens didn't feed you well while you recovered there. You're more beautiful now than you were before, my lady."

It didn't seem possible that it was true, and it brought me no comfort at all to hear it. "Perhaps it would have been better if I had come back scarred and ugly."

"I don't blame you for saying such a thing, having heard you cry and weep in your sleep, but please, my lady, do not tempt the gods any further. You suffer enough without letting them think you aren't grateful for the gifts you've been given."

"Yes, but perhaps if they smite me, all those men waiting in the megaron will think better of taking me to wife."

"Or else the gods will inflame them all the more, and your father will be cursed again, with blood drawn in his halls."

"You're right, of course," I said, for I had no real desire to argue, and the gods were fickle enough they might curse Tyndareus anyway.

Or leave me to Menelaus's mercy. "You can tell Pollux to come up to get me on your way out. But say nothing of your errand. I don't wish him to keep Polypoetes from a seat of honor at my side."

"Yes, my lady." Clymene slipped out, leaving me alone.

I tore a mint leaf from the plant I now kept upon my windowsill and tried not to think of how dark the circles beneath my eyes had become. More beautiful, indeed. I crushed the mint between my fingers, hoping the scent might soothe me. I did not feel more beautiful. I felt brittle and worn, like a thread pulled too tight. And every night was worse than the last. If I did not dream of the war, of the future itself, then I dreamed of my past and woke up weeping for my daughter or Theseus.

"Your suitors grow restless, little sister," Pollux said, not bothering to knock before entering my room. "If you are not there to pour the libations to begin the games, they're liable to start without you, and far more violently."

"At least they won't have swords," I said, taking the arm he offered me. The first day of the games, my suitors would be wrestling one another. And I had to admit that there were worse events to have to watch. "Should I offer them a small prize for the winner of each day's games?"

"I'd just as soon not have to choose a winner every day, if it's all the same to you. That way lies a brawl. Let them boast to one another and think themselves each in the lead until the end. Hopefully by then Odysseus will have thought of something to keep them from going to war immediately after your husband is named."

"We can only pray."

"Which reminds me." Pollux held the curtain for me at the bottom of the stairs. "Tyndareus intends to lead the whole mess of them up to the shrine before the wrestling begins. You're to make a sacrifice to Zeus."

"Does Tyndareus wish for these games to be cursed?" I demanded.

"Tyndareus does not realize fully your circumstances, Helen. Though I wonder if you ought to have told him the truth, if no one else."

I shook my head. "I cannot trust that he would not tell Menelaus or Agamemnon, or gods save us all, Leda, for that matter. And then where would we be?"

"Not at war, so long as Theseus remains missing. Even Menelaus could be persuaded to leave Athens be, with your kidnapper as good as dead. At least while there's a chance he might have you for his own. The risk will be after Theseus's return, if it should happen at all."

"Stop, Pollux," I begged, the dream too near, and Leda's words too haunting. "Do not speak of him as if he is gone forever. Please. Let me have this one small spot of hope, or the guilt of it all will suffocate me. I cannot have been his ruin, Pollux. I can't live with myself if it is true."

He stopped us, drawing me nearer and searching my face. "What happened to the woman who refused to accept any blame upon herself? You can't have taken Leda's words so much to heart."

I hid my face against his shoulder so he would not see how deeply I had been wounded. "Just please, pretend for my sake, whatever you believe. Pretend he will come, if not now, someday. Pretend he lives."

Pollux wrapped me in his arms, tucking my head beneath his chin. "Of course," he promised. "If that is what you need, it is the least I might do."

But it did not make me feel any better, and I still had a sacrifice to make at Tyndareus's command. Perhaps I would make it for Theseus, in my heart, instead. Tyndareus need never know how I had dedicated the victim. For Theseus's sake, for his safety, I would even bend my knee to Zeus again.

Though I did not have much hope my prayers would be answered.

"You make a most beautiful priestess, Princess," Patroclus said, escorting me back from the shrine.

I remembered him only vaguely from my birthday celebration, when Theseus and Pirithous had challenged the rest of the men by sword and Theseus had won. But not before Patroclus had defeated Pirithous, and Theseus had defeated him in turn.

"You're from Thessaly, aren't you?" I asked, for I could not bear the compliment while the blood of the bull still clung to my fingernails.

"Opus, in truth, though I live in the far south of Thessaly now, with my kinsman, in Phthia."

"Yes, I remember. Something about not trifling with Myrmidons?"

He smiled, boyish delight sparkling in his eyes. "Until my dying day, I shall have the joy of boasting that I defeated Pirithous, king of the Lapiths, by the sword."

I dropped my gaze, reminded too much of the boy. Patroclus may not want to be my hero, to set himself apart through me exactly, but it was clear he took pleasure in what small measure of reputation he had found. A measure the young shepherd boy—the prince Paris—had been denied. I hid a grimace at my own thoughts, not quite used to thinking of him by a name. I wasn't certain I wished to be. Nor could I afford to dwell upon him now.

"It is no small honor, I'm sure. King Pirithous, by all accounts, is a warrior born. But if you are Phthian now, surely you must know Pirithous's son, Polypoetes, who has come to win me."

"Mmm," Patroclus agreed. "We are, thankfully, some distance south of the river valley where the Lapiths are settled. Peleus holds some strange grudge against King Pirithous, though I have never quite learned what for. I am sorry to say, though we are neighbors of a sort, there is little love between our peoples, as a result."

I could well imagine any king might find Pirithous's manners to be offensive, but I had never truly considered how it might affect his kingdom or his people.

"Perhaps it is time those grudges were forgotten," I said. "Surely Polypoetes can have done nothing to insult you personally. Or are you one of the assembly who insists he will make war upon the man who wins me?"

Patroclus laughed. "Even if I wished to, I'm afraid I have not the men to accomplish more than my own doom. Myrmidon I may be, but I do not have command of an army, and as a guest of Peleus, no lands from which I might raise a force for the purpose. No, Princess, you have nothing to fear from me on that account."

I smiled. "Does that mean I can count you as a man in need of a kingdom of his own, rather than one who has lost himself to reason in pursuit of my beauty?"

He tilted his head, studying me sidelong. "Can it not be both?"

"It can," I agreed. "And I am certain there are a great many of you who I would count so. But surely Sparta deserves a king who can keep his wits about him?"

"In that case, let me assure you that while I am surely awed by your beauty and grace, it is not only lust which draws me. I am thankful for the kindness of my kinsmen and enjoy the pleasures fertile Phthia has to offer, but I would be happier still if I did not need to rely upon the hospitality of Peleus all my days."

"Should your kinsman ever turn from you, know that Tyndareus, too, is often sympathetic to those who find themselves bereft of their rightful homes, for one reason or another."

"You mean, of course, his support of the brothers Atrides, while they lived in exile, wronged by their uncle." He ducked his head, hiding his face. "My circumstances are, perhaps, not quite so sympathetic. I do not pretend to have been unjustly robbed of anything."

My gaze shifted past him. Polypoetes seemed to be stalking us, circling nearer and nearer. As a wolf follows its prey. I almost felt sorry for the other suitors, watching his show of a hunt. Even knowing he only played at the part, the intensity of his pursuit made me uneasy.

I touched Patroclus's arm, dutifully ignoring the way Polypoetes bared his teeth in response. He should have something to provoke his rage, or it would ring too hollow, and a perceived preference for Patroclus, who had already admitted to bad blood between his people and the Lapiths, was reason enough for his jealousy, and then some.

"You need not speak of it," I told him. "Not where others might hear, or even at all. Whatever your sin, I promise you, there are others with hands more unclean who seek to win me."

I had his attention now, fully, and he studied me with furrowed brow. "Why do your father and brothers permit it? Surely if they are unfit, they should be refused such an honor."

"I fear there are some men far too powerful to refuse," I said, dropping my hand. "But let us speak of happier things. Tell me instead what, beyond beauty, you seek in a bride, that I might know better how I am expected to behave."

He smiled then. "I am young, Princess, I admit, but not so young as that. You tease me unkindly."

"Perhaps I do," I said, some of my own good humor fading. It had not been so long ago that I had walked with Theseus on this very path. I could only pray that what I put in motion this day would not end so terribly for those involved. "But as I told King Theseus once before, I would know the men who seek to win me, to better prepare myself for my future. You are young enough, I hope, not to take offense, and I would much prefer to engage openly with my suitors than to begin falsely in a relationship with a man who might become my husband."

"And what, I wonder, did King Theseus think of your boldness?" Patroclus asked.

I pretended concern for my skirt, brushing away some false bit of dust, to keep him from seeing any hint of my affections. "King Theseus is wise and just. He understood my desires and obliged me. But of course I should have expected nothing less from a man who once took an Amazon to wife. Had he no appreciation for bold women, I cannot imagine he would have ever married Antiope."

"You spent a great deal of time in his company, as I recall," Patroclus said. "You must have been disappointed to learn he had married elsewhere. Did you meet his new queen while you were in Athens?"

"Of course." I swallowed, my mouth suddenly dry, and my gaze darted again to Polypoetes, desperation and panic twisting together like a noose around my throat.

"Is it true what they say, that Queen Meryet is nearly as beautiful as you are?"

Meryet of Egypt. The name I had taken while I hid in plain sight as Theseus's wife. The life I had left behind. I opened my mouth to answer, but no words came. Only the sound of my heartbeat, thrumming too fast in my ears.

If I spoke of Athens, I would break.

CHAPTER NINETEEN
PATROCLUS

Haven't you stolen enough of the princess's company?" a man snarled, grasping him by the elbow as if the barbarian would tear him from Helen's side. "You are not the only man here to court her."

Patroclus jerked his arm free, caught off balance by the intrusion. A glance told him it was Pirithous's son, Polypoetes, and he felt his lip curl in response. "I have accepted only what she has given freely."

"Then take your gift and go, insect," Polypoetes snapped. "You Myrmidons are all the same, lusting for what you have no right to want. You're nothing more than ants, thinking the meal set upon the table is for your enjoyment. Pests to be swatted away."

Patroclus stiffened at the insult, unprovoked as it was. "And you Lapiths are no better than barbarians." To think just a moment before the princess had suggested there could not be any cause for enmity between them. "But what should I expect from the son of centaur-kin?"

Polypoetes growled, but Helen caught his fisted hand before he lifted it to strike, stepping between them. "Stop this, please. There will be opportunity enough for you to prove your worth in the games. Save your anger for the fields, if you must carry it at all."

"Forgive me, my lady," Patroclus said, inclining his head. He would not have her caught in the middle, not for all the world, and he feared what would happen if he allowed the exchange to go any further, his anger stoked too hot. "I fear sometimes it is not so easy to set aside old grudges, as you suggested. But I hope you know I would have tried to oblige you, if not for this."

"Perhaps you may yet find common ground, my lord Patroclus. I have not lost hope, I promise you. But if one prince has taken exception to our conversation, I fear the others have as well, and I do not wish to cause any further strife this day. I'm certain we will speak again."

Patroclus had grace enough to accept his dismissal, offering her a small smile before stepping back. Polypoetes desired Helen's company, and for her sake, Patroclus would withdraw. This time. It was as she said, after all. They would certainly find time to speak again. He had the advantage of showing her his willingness even to sacrifice some measure of his pride to satisfy her wish for peace, while Polypoetes showed himself to be only the unreasonable, witless suitor, in comparison.

Or at least that was what he told himself, when Polypoetes took his place as smoothly as if they had planned the exchange, grinning wolfishly at his success. There was a light in Helen's eye, almost a relief, and her cheeks flushed a delicate pink at Polypoetes's attentions. As if he had pleased her with his insults—or simply with his intrusion.

Patroclus shook his head, forcing himself to look away. He was only imagining a partiality that could not possibly exist. Polypoetes could not have exchanged more than a half dozen words with the princess before this day. At the table, Helen was politely attentive to all her partners, granting no one else her favors, and the son of Pirithous had yet to sit beside her at the morning, midday, or evening meal. Surely if she showed him any affection at all, it was only for his father's sake, and he did not seem to remember that she had taken any great pleasure from Pirithous's company, either, at the time, for all he was her brother, through Zeus.

"A word and a touch, that's all it takes," Agamemnon said, joining him as he continued down the mountain. "She bewitches men so easily. If I had not seen her as a scrawny child, had not watched her work her wiles on my brother . . ."

Patroclus snorted. "If you think her so dangerous, why do you seek to win her for Menelaus at all?"

"Better to give the witch to my brother than go to war with every prince in Achaea who stands in his way," Agamemnon said. "Though if we are given no other choice, Mycenae has the men and the ships to win, and I cannot say the thought of all those kingdoms falling into my hand is not tempting."

Patroclus grunted, knowing a threat when he heard one and unwilling to give his own position away. Not after what Helen had told him just moments before. Her words rang like a warning in his ears now—the men who insist they will make war, and those too powerful to refuse, no matter how dirty their hands.

He risked a glance sidelong at Agamemnon and wondered. Helen was bold, of that there was no question, but he had not realized until that moment her cunning. Perhaps she had wanted to know him, yes, but as she had said, too, she had not wanted to begin falsely.

Mycenae would do everything in its power to obtain her, and with the barest of words, she had made it clear that she would do everything in *her* power to thwart them.

He had only to decide if, with no kingdom and no army and no power of his own, he dared support her.

CHAPTER TWENTY
HELEN

I must admit, Princess, I did not expect quite so many men to come for your hand," Menestheus said, much too close to my ear for my liking. His breath was foul and hot, and his voice made my skin crawl. "One look at you and they forget you were lost for more than two years, forget every thought they might have had as to your virtue after such an adventure. It is a true testament to the power of your beauty."

"If only you, too, could be made to forget so easily," I said mildly, keeping my eyes upon the field. Poor Patroclus had been set against Ajax the Great for the first match, and I was pleased to see he was faring better than I might have guessed possible. But the whole event made me think of Theseus, fighting with Pirithous at his back during the celebration of my birthday and besting every man upon the field simply to prevent Menelaus from winning my kiss. A prize he had won, but never claimed for himself until our wedding day.

"I wonder what they would say if they knew you had been hiding in plain sight all that time," Menestheus said, ignoring my words altogether.

"I suppose at least it would secure my honor," I said. "Stolen away and married is a much more virtuous fate than rape, after all. As for Athens herself, however, I am not certain she would fare quite so well."

"No?" he asked. "With Theseus and his sons removed from power, I fail to see how anyone could take exception to us. The moment we suspected the truth, we acted in all honor to return Sparta's princess to her people."

"Is it honorable to betray your king?" I asked, watching as Ajax finally pinned the much smaller Patroclus to the ground. "I hadn't realized."

His hand closed on my elbow, fingers bruising my flesh. "You think yourself so *above* me, Helen of Sparta. Your honor unstained. And what would your dear father think if he learned you had kept the truth from him? If he knew just where you had gone? Did you not betray your kin and king, just as thoroughly as I betrayed mine?"

I ground my teeth, tearing my arm from his grasp. "I did what I must to protect my people. To protect even yours, though I hardly expect you'll ever have the wit to recognize it. What was your reason, *King* Menestheus? Can you claim so noble a purpose, or was it simply desire and lust—for me, for power itself—that drove you?"

"You know nothing of what drove me," he sneered. "Nothing of Athens at all. Theseus never should have been made king! From the start, he had no right. And that fool Aegeus gave him everything, simply because he carried his sword. You were only the means I had hoped for to ruin him at last, nothing more. A convenient excuse to take back what should have been mine."

You are nothing but ruin.

I stumbled back, turning from the field, from Menestheus. But everywhere I looked, there were men. Suitors, eager for a moment of my attention, for the hope of my love and affection, my beauty and body. And their faces danced behind my eyes, blood-spattered, broken, bruised, and dead. I could smell the bronze of battle, the stench of burning flesh rising in thick, greasy clouds of smoke. I fell to my knees, gagging and retching, unable to breathe.

"Princess?" Odysseus called out, and then Pollux was at my side. "Helen, what's happened? What's wrong?"

The smoke stung my eyes, making them water, and my throat was too thick, my lungs heaving, gasping for air. I shook my head, clutching at my brother, blurred by tears but beside me. It could not be real if he was beside me.

"I'll be their ruin," I wheezed. "I'll ruin them all."

"The sooner you get her out of sight, the better," Odysseus hissed. "Already there will be those who take this as a sign, an ill omen, sent by the gods."

"You say it as if it isn't true," Pollux mumbled. But he caught me up, lifting me into his arms. "The princess is ill," he announced. "Too much excitement combined with rich foods, I'm sure."

"You cannot believe that," Odysseus said, continuing on with us as Pollux carried me toward the palace.

My brother shook his head. "This sounds as though it is her nightmares, haunting her. But if you would help Castor with the matches, I would be grateful. Any support he might need."

"Of course," Odysseus agreed.

And then we left him behind.

Pollux carried me straight to my room, sending Clymene away with a clipped command after I had been settled in my bed. He sat upon its edge, his hand wrapped tightly around mine, and I hid my face from his searching gaze, dragging the linens up over my head.

"Will you not tell me what happened?" he said, tugging them back down again. "What did Menestheus say?"

I closed my eyes, but it only brought the faces of the dead back into sight, and I rolled to my side, turning my back to my brother. "He said I was his excuse. A means to ruin Theseus. And then it was all I could see. So many of them. Lost because of me. Because of my curse."

"There is nothing shameful in beauty, Helen," Pollux said, reaching out to stroke my hair. "Nothing accursed. Your beauty is the surest sign of Zeus's favor."

"Not beauty," I said. "No, my curse is far more sinister. It is as Leda said. I am nothing but ruin. Everyone I touch. Even—" But I stopped myself, swallowing the words. I would not burden my brother with the knowledge of his own fate. He already knew too much of mine.

"Even what?" he asked.

I let out a breath, substituting a different truth. "I had a daughter, you know. With Theseus. I ruined her, too. Ruined everything. Better if Theseus had let me die then."

Pollux sighed, his hand stilling in my hair. "You cannot know that."

"I knew," I said. "I dreamed. And I hid it all from Theseus, for fear he would give her up. Theseus was nothing if not loyal to the gods, and I could not stand the thought, after they had already taken so much from me. You and Castor, Tyndareus, my people and my kingdom. Even the hope of peace. I went to Poseidon and made him promise me he would protect our child. Theseus, too. But he did not promise to save me. And he did not promise that Athens would survive. I almost died. If Theseus had not sacrificed the child . . . and I hated him for it. I would have rather seen the world burn than give her up."

"But it did not end so," Pollux said. "And you clearly forgave him, even loved him again. You did not bring ruin down on Athens, and Menestheus admits freely that he acted against Theseus, wanted Theseus undone and exiled. That is surely not your fault."

"If I had never gone with him—"

"If you had never gone with him," Pollux interrupted me, "he may well have lost his throne to Menestheus regardless. You do not know that Pirithous would not have persuaded him still to travel to the Underworld, to the house of Hades, to steal that god's wife. And Menestheus would have seen to it that he did not return a king, for some reason or another, with or without your presence upon the Rock."

"And yet, it was through me that this was done." I laughed bitterly. "Theseus never would have gone with Pirithous if it had not been for me, either. He would not have owed Pirithous the debt, would never have been trapped by his honor, and perhaps Pirithous might not have been so determined to take another wife. Least of all a goddess."

"You cannot do this, Helen. You cannot tie yourself in knots over the fates of others. It is as Castor said: if it is their will, the gods will find a way. Perhaps all of this was woven already, and you were only a single thread in the larger tapestry. But if you pull and tug, trying to unravel it, you will have no answers at all, no better understanding. And we must focus upon the present that has been wrought. The opportunity you have been given to *protect* all these men, to avert their deaths. You do not have to be their ruin."

"Unless it is the will of the gods," I said.

"In which case you will know it is not some fault of yours," Pollux said gently. "You will have done everything in your power to stop this future from coming to pass, and you may rest the blame and blood upon the shoulders of the gods and make your peace with what will come."

"There is no peace to be had in this, Pollux," I said, drawing the linens up again to cover my head. "Not for me."

But I could not hide in my room forever. The midday meal was one thing, but no matter how ill I felt, the evening banquet required my presence. There were too many men and too many cups of wine in their hands, and all of them were desperate for some small glimpse of me.

I did not know how I would manage, but I let Clymene dress me in a less wrinkled gown and smooth the mess I had made of my hair, chewing mint leaves outright to mask the bronze of blood and the grit of ash that still sat on the back of my tongue, imagined or otherwise.

"I heard that Queen Leda was quite pleased with the gift of silk from Polypoetes," she told me. "Though how you could be so certain he would have it to give, I still do not know."

"Pirithous and Theseus often raided together. It only stood to reason that if one of them had such fine fabrics, the other would as well."

Clymene sighed. "I do wish he had not married that Egyptian princess. Or lost himself in the Underworld. King Theseus was so kind when he was here last, and he worried for you so, after you were found missing. Every day that passed without you found, I would swear his face had grown more lined."

"Whether he had married or not," I said, pretending my flinch was only for the tug of my hair, "it does not mean he would have been free to come, or even that he would have wanted to. Sparta is a long way from Athens, and to rule a second kingdom from such a distance would have been far from easy. Likely we would have seen little of him here."

"You can't imagine he'd have left you in Sparta alone?" Clymene said, laughter threading through her words. "The way he looked at you, my lady, I do not think he'd have let you far from his sight unless he had no other choice at all. But I'm certain Sparta would have made do with some steward or other, if need be. We might yet, should your father choose a king for you."

"Or a prince like Polypoetes, I suppose." It was a mark against his suit, I knew. And precisely the reason Tyndareus had not been eager to promise me to Theseus, regardless of his vow to Zeus. "I would not mind it, I think, if my husband could be persuaded to return home and leave Sparta in my hands alone."

"I would not count upon such an outcome, my lady," Clymene said, finishing with my hair and patting my shoulder briefly to let me know she was done. "But if any woman might have the power to persuade her husband of anything, I believe it is you."

It was not much of a reassurance. Nor a comfortable one, for that matter, no matter how true it might have been—and I was not certain that it was. After all, if I were so persuasive as that, why did Menelaus still seek to win me as a bride?

A knock on the door interrupted my thoughts, signaling Castor's arrival as my escort. I had no doubts as to why he had come in Pollux's place this night—and I would certainly be grateful for whatever calm he could give me. Clymene let him in, and my brother gave me a long, searching look as he took my hand.

"You had us all worried, Little Sister," Castor said. "Is there anything I can do?"

"Don't short me on the wine at dinner," I said, forcing a smile. "Other than that, I can only pray that Leda has given me a less challenging partner for the meal. If it is Agamemnon or the like—"

"Polypoetes has won the honor," Castor said, and the relief that flooded me at his assurance could not all have been my own. I gave him a sharp look as he led me from the women's quarters, but he offered only the faintest smile in return. I did feel much better with my arm through his, and his hand resting upon mine. "I hope he proves to be as much a friend as his father, Helen, but I am not certain how far we should trust him. His threats ring . . . more than sincere."

I pressed my lips together, uncertain that I could frame a reply in such a way that Clymene would not wonder. Much as I appreciated my maid, I did not want her involved any further than she must already be. And I could not trust wholly that some small amount of my doings did not work their way back to Mycenae. Not when she shared blood with Agamemnon and Menelaus.

But even if Clymene had not followed so close, the halls beyond the women's quarters were full of guests and servants. Too full for any kind of privacy, with the evening banquet about to begin. If it had not been for Castor, his calm, steady presence, and whatever power he used to share it with me, I think I would have fled the stares and smiles, for I certainly would not have had the strength to return them otherwise.

"I will not be far," Castor promised me, just before we entered the megaron. "But it would be better if you did not show these men any further weakness."

And then Polypoetes descended upon us, drawing me away from my brother's side. I faced the banquet and the son of Pirithous with nothing but my own courage to see me through.

CHAPTER TWENTY-ONE
HELEN

I trust you're feeling more yourself again?" Polypoetes asked, guiding me almost at once toward the dais and the family table, where we would enjoy our meal.

My sister Clytemnestra had arrived with her husband sometime the previous evening, and a glance at the seating arrangement made my stomach sink. Castor had said nothing about having to endure my sister's company, seated as she was between me and Tyndareus. Thank the gods for Polypoetes on my other side, for if I had been forced to sit between Nestra and Agamemnon—

"My lady?" Polypoetes prompted, laughter in his voice. "You look as though you'll be ill again, and I hope very much it is not for dislike of my company after I all but bribed your mother to sit at your side."

I shook my head, swallowing my dismay. "I promise you, it is my pleasure to be seated beside you—in fact, I find myself more grateful than I had anticipated to have your support this night. I had only wished we might have a greater opportunity for conversation."

Polypoetes followed my gaze to my sister, who was already smiling far too smugly in my direction, and grunted. "The evening is cool and the courtyard quiet. Perhaps a walk together, after the meal. I imagine the stifling air will not serve your recovery, and we cannot have you collapsing again before your guests. In fact, I must insist upon it. With your maid to accompany us, of course. Or perhaps one of your brothers, if it cannot be avoided."

I cast him a glance sidelong and could not quite keep from smiling at his tone. "Do you truly begrudge me the protection of my brothers?"

He granted me one of his father's grins, overpowering in its charm, if a little less artful. "It is not that, exactly. Certainly I can understand their purpose, and I'm pleased they take such a determined interest in your safety—that you are not wholly without friends within your household. But I would not mind being a little less beneath their eye. You are not alone in wishing we might have the privacy for more open speech between us."

"Has there been some news of your father?"

His gray eyes warmed. "I wish I could say yes, Princess. And I wish more of the men in this hall shared your consideration. I realize they cannot fully understand how much has been lost—but my father was more than just an amusement, while he lived. He was a hero, though he would never admit to it, and it pains me to realize how poorly he will be remembered."

"You must tell me of his heroics, then," I said, as we climbed the dais. "That you might know one other person in this assembly appreciates him fully. But you should not feel that you grieve alone, Prince Polypoetes. Nor that you are without the support of family in this difficult time. Pirithous was my brother through Zeus, and Pollux's, too, after all."

A brother twice over, truly, when I took Theseus as my husband. But I could not say as much as I took my seat beside my sister. Polypoetes, however, kept my hand after I was settled, bowing over it to press a kiss to my knuckles before he took his own seat, and I knew he felt the words I dared not speak.

"You are as kindhearted as my father claimed," he said, filling my cup with wine. "Sparta is fortunate to have such a princess, such a woman as their future queen. Though I fear there are few men here who would feel the same way."

"You believe yourself to be so different from the rest of these men?"

"I am Lapith, Princess," he said, as if that were an answer in and of itself. The only explanation needed.

"And what does that mean, to be Lapith?" I prompted, for it was surely a topic even Nestra could not object to. "I have met only one before you, and I am not certain King Pirithous was wholly representative of his people, being a son of Zeus."

"He was," Polypoetes said slowly. "And he was not. The Lapiths, for example, are not all quite so lustful. But we are certainly loyal to one another, as Pirithous was to Theseus. We are hardy, difficult to discourage or defeat. Many believe it is arrogance to say as much, but we have survived great hardship, and through survival have grown strong."

"I'm afraid in Laconia we are not so familiar with the stories of Thessaly, and even less so those of your particular people," I said, cautious now. I had no wish to cause him pain, but he had certainly made me curious. "Is there one you might tell, as an example of your people and their resilience?"

"Many more than one," he said, taking up his cup. He lifted it, as if in salute, before taking his first sip. "Perhaps the story that might interest you most, my lady, is that of my father's wife."

I lifted my eyebrows. "Your mother?"

"The very same."

"Forgive me," I said, leaning forward now. "But was she a witch of some kind, to be thrown off? Is that why you would speak of her as hardship?"

"Not at all, I promise you. In truth, by all accounts, she was both beautiful and strong. A woman of great courage and will. Their marriage was arranged by Dia, my father's mother, who had ruled alone as queen of our people for many years before her death, in order to make peace between the Lapiths and the centaurs, our neighbors."

I stared at him, this strange son of Pirithous. As well formed as his father, and yet—"Your mother was a centaur?"

He laughed lowly, rich and warm. "She was a foundling, raised by them upon the mountain. An adopted daughter of Centaurus, their king. Do you truly know none of this? I thought all of Achaea knew at least of Ixion, the mad king, and the centaurs he begot when he thought to take Hera to his . . ."

All the humor drained from his face, and he looked away, throwing back what remained of his wine in one long draft. Every line of his body, a moment earlier at perfect ease, had gone tense and hard.

"My lord?" I touched his arm gently, unsure of what had upset him.

He shook his head. "I should have seen it before. All this time, and I did not realize. My father spent his whole life rebuilding what Ixion had ruined, only to suffer his same fate."

"King Ixion meant to steal Hera, to make her his wife?" I asked, struggling to connect the pieces of the story. "Just as Pirithous has gone now to steal Persephone."

"He was deceived, of course, and instead of Hera, he mated with a cloud," Polypoetes said. "From that cloud Centaurus was born, father and king to all the centaurs in the North. But my father . . . my father will not return. And if he does, if he is driven to madness just as Ixion was, in punishment, I am certain he would prefer death than the ruin he might cause his people as king. What my father did to deserve this fate, I do not know, but the gods are cruel to have treated him so. Crueler than I ever realized."

I let my hand fall away, feeling suddenly cold. Because there could have been only one sin great enough to result in this punishment. Pirithous might have failed to secure Persephone, but he had managed to steal something else. Someone else. Another daughter of Zeus, and the fate she had been meant for—the war the gods desired above all else—had nearly been averted.

And I knew suddenly, as if Iris herself had come from Olympus to whisper it in my ear, that Pirithous had been punished so cruelly for helping to steal me.

"Forgive me," I breathed. "I did not know what I was."

But I would remember now. I would never forget again.

The rest of the meal was spent in uneasy silence, Polypoetes withdrawn, his thoughts turned so far inward he took little notice of me at all. We drank, pouring one another more wine as it was required, and when our eyes met in passing, we both looked away, made all the more uncomfortable by those brief moments of shared pain. I had wanted so much to tell him of the Trojan prince, the stranger of my nightmares, that someone might know and pass that word along should the worst come to pass, but now . . .

What right did I have to involve him at all?

"You seem to have lost the interest of one of your most desperate suitors," Nestra said to me, a triumphant smile upon her lips. "Did he realize you would one day grow old, your beauty lost to age, and then he would be saddled with a shrewish wife who does not know when to keep silent?"

"It could be worse," I said, picking the chickpeas from the relish on my plate. I had never cared for their consistency, though eaten mashed they were not nearly so offensive. "I could have no beauty at all and still be shrewish. Or perhaps bitter and angry, always lashing out against my betters."

"You think yourself to be my better, then? When I am queen of Mycenae, and you are nothing?"

I looked up, my gaze floating over the megaron and all the men inside drinking and feasting and laughing at their tables. Men who would die for me. Whose lives I held in my hand. "I am worse than nothing, Nestra. And if you could see, even for a moment, through the blind jealousy you cling to so desperately, you might realize how great a fool you have been all this time, hating me for something I cannot control, something I never wanted."

"Yes, poor Helen," my sister mocked. "She is so *burdened* by her beauty."

"I suppose you would be terribly pleased to think your merest smile, your smallest encouragement, could drive a man to madness, to violence, to rape?"

Her eyes narrowed. "There was nothing small about your encouragements when it came to Menelaus, Sister. The way you followed him around like a lost puppy before he left for war. The way you flirted and laughed with him after he returned."

"I neither flirted nor laughed," I said coolly. "In fact, I wept. I begged him to leave me alone, from almost the moment he arrived in Sparta again. He would not listen. What has happened, he has done to himself."

"How convenient to always see yourself as blameless," Nestra said. "Whether you wanted it or not, you are beautiful. That you cannot be bothered to take any care in how you flaunt yourself, then blame these poor men for being seduced, proves just how blind *you* are."

I shook my head, taking up my wine. Neither Polypoetes nor I had been overcareful in our consumption, and at that moment, I wished only for a greater sense of oblivion. "I see all too clearly, Nestra, I promise you. And were it in my power, I would send every one of these men away. I might have even given up my place as queen for you, if I could have. Or let Pollux inherit Sparta, if that would not do. Anything, so long as it kept our people safe."

Nestra rolled her eyes. "This is about your nightmares again, I suppose. As if they have not already come to pass. You were abducted, and now you are returned, yet you still cling to these dreams in order to have your way. So you can abuse poor Menelaus's heart all over again."

"Can you not be happy with the husband you have?" I snapped. "Or do you forget how you lusted over Agamemnon? You did not care a bit about Menelaus until he returned from war—until you realized he wanted me over you. What did you honestly expect, Nestra? That all our years of friendship would be wiped away when you decided at last to grace him with your favors? You are queen now, as you said. You have everything you ever wanted, and the opportunity to lord it over me, besides. Why can you not let it rest!"

"Oh, I have everything, yes," Nestra said, her tone snide. "Everything but what you take for granted, believing it only your due, your right, because you are so beautiful. Everything but the love, the loyalty and devotion you seem so intent to throw away because it does not come precisely as you like it."

"Because it comes with *war*, Nestra!" And had she been anyone else, any less snide or offensive, I might have pitied her. But as it was, I could think only that she and Agamemnon deserved one another. "Should I not object to destruction and ruin, the death of everyone I love?"

"If that is what the gods desire, who are you to say otherwise? Take your short years of love, of happiness, and be content. But no, you are the beautiful Helen, and so you must remake the world to suit your desires, thinking it is your right."

"You are wrong, Nestra," I said, pouring myself more wine. "It is not that I think it is my right—it has been and always will be *duty* that drives me. Because I am princess and heir of Sparta, and I must serve!"

"You may tell yourself that, if you like. If it helps you to sleep at night. But the rest of us know better, Helen. I have watched you my whole life, and it has been clear to me for years on end that you have only ever served yourself."

CHAPTER TWENTY-TWO
POLYPOETES

He had only been half listening to Helen's low-voiced argument with her sister, barely aware that it was happening at all, so lost in his own thoughts, his own misery. But as their voices rose, he could not help but overhear—and it seemed to him it had gone on quite long enough. Other men in the hall were looking up now, their conversations trailing off as they strained to listen, to catch some gist of the exchange. Too many for anyone's good.

"Princess," he interrupted, touching Helen's elbow as she drew breath to respond again. "Would you be so kind as to join me for some air? A walk around the courtyard, perhaps, to help settle my stomach— if the queen of Mycenae might spare you, of course. I fear I am not used to such rich Laconian fare, nor the strength of your wine."

Clytemnestra's eyes flashed, but she only lifted her chin and turned her face away. A clear insult to a man who would be a king of Thessaly before long. And she had spoken of Helen's arrogance?

But Helen nodded, and in favor of removing her and preventing a greater scene, he ignored Clytemnestra's slight. Whatever his own private grief, or Helen's part in it, he had promised to help her, and he did not mean to be forsworn.

He rose and helped her from her stool as well, threading her arm through his as they left the table. Before they had sat down to eat, he had thought of getting her alone for other reasons—the delight of knowing the sweetness of her kiss, for instance, if he could manage somehow to convince her to offer him such a gift. But now, when they stepped from the megaron onto the porch, then into the courtyard itself, seduction was the furthest thing from his mind.

Her sister had suggested she saw herself as blameless, but it seemed to him that Helen had taken all upon herself. Her wretched, breathless apology when he had told her of his grandfather's fate, the echo of his father's own, was one small proof among many other moments.

"Forgive my interference," he said, the silence stretching too heavily between them. "But I did not think you wished to make your private argument an entertainment for the entire hall."

Helen's footsteps slowed, her eyes closing for a moment. The moonlight cast bleak shadows over her fair skin. "I always promise myself I will not let my sister provoke me, but somehow she always manages it, and I find myself helpless to resist."

"The joys of family," he said, matching his pace to hers. "I suppose I am fortunate that I have no acknowledged siblings, and my half brothers and sisters are scattered across the lands, rather than living so near to taunt me."

"I had not considered—but surely Pirithous has claimed some number of his children? Those he fathered off his slaves, at the least?"

Polypoetes shook his head. "He sees them cared for, to be sure, and the women married to deserving men, but he would not risk the kingship falling into any hands other than mine. To honor my mother, you see, and protect me. It is in part, I think, why he did not consider taking another wife for so long."

"Until Persephone," she murmured, dropping her gaze. "I am truly sorry, Polypoetes. More sorry than you may ever realize. Had I known then what I do now, I would never have asked for Theseus's help, nor accepted Pirithous's aid."

"You need not apologize to me, Princess," he said, offering a rueful smile. "My father was not a man who did anything he did not wish to do. Certainly he did not help Theseus only because of the bonds of their friendship. And if Theseus had not stolen you for himself, I would hazard that my father might have done so in his place."

She made a low noise of irritation, deep in her throat. "Theseus said something similar once. And that Pirithous would never have admitted it. But if he had tried to steal me, I would have fought him every step of the way."

He grinned. "That is only because he did not turn his charms upon you, Princess. You have your beauty, and it is powerful, but there are very few women who could resist my father when he set his mind upon them. Even my mother was persuaded, and by all accounts, she had declared him the last man she could ever love."

"And you?" She met his eyes, searching them for something, though he knew not what.

"Did I fall prey to my father's charms?"

She smiled. "I would not need to ask that question—it is clear enough that you love him."

"Then what?"

She pressed her lips together, studying him again. "Have you Pirithous's same charms?"

"Ah." Of course. And he should not have been surprised she knew of his father's particular skills. "I fear, Princess, that I must rely upon my own more natural attributes. Persuasion of a more conventional kind, composed merely of soft words and fine gifts. But even so, I think, were we married, you would have few complaints."

Her good humor faded, her expression shuttering, and she turned her face away. "Then Castor is not wrong. The threats you make—the favors you do me—you mean it all, sincerely."

"Is that so wrong?" he asked, tightening his hold upon her hand when she stiffened as though she might pull away. "You would be better off with me than any of these others. I know the threat you face, and I know, too, that you have suffered a great loss. Even better, you would never have to fear me—we Lapiths like our women strong and our queens bold. Sparta would be yours to rule as you pleased."

"And if Theseus returns?" she asked softly. "Would you give me up to my true husband?"

He released her hand upon his arm, his heart aching—for her, for himself. He had known she loved Theseus, of course, but he had not realized how closely she still held the hope of his return. "Princess, if you desired it, I would give him time yet to reclaim you. Even another full year before I asked anything of you as my wife. But you must know it is more than hopeless. And even if by some grace of the gods he is set free, you will be married to someone else by then. You could do far worse than to let that someone be me."

Her jaw tightened and she shook her head. "I would not have Theseus forced against the son of Pirithous; surely you must understand that. And I cannot imagine you wish for it, either."

"Oh, Helen." He sighed, drawing her to a stop at his side and turning her gently to face him. That she might see, once and for all. That she might know the truth, as he did. "If there was even the smallest hope that my father was not lost, do you think I would ignore it? If there was the slightest chance that Theseus did not share his fate—"

"You cannot know it, Polypoetes. None but the gods can. Theseus swore to me upon the Styx that he would find me if I were stolen from him. That he would find me, wherever I was in the world. You must understand that I cannot abandon faith in him so easily. What kind of wife would I make any man if I were so disloyal? So faithless?"

He took her face in his hands, stroked her cheek, her hair. "He would not begrudge you happiness, if you found it elsewhere. If you found protection elsewhere, in his absence, he would not begrudge you that, either."

"You say what you think I wish to hear," she said, drawing his hand away and stepping back. "But what I wish above all is for his return. His safety. His life, still bound to mine, that we might find wholeness together again. You would be kind to me, I am sure of it. And I do not doubt any of the rest. But my heart is his. And to pretend otherwise, to let you believe it might be yours one day—I am not so cruel as that, Prince Polypoetes. I beg you not to make me so."

He let her fingers fall from his and forced a smile to his lips, as if her words did not twist like snakes around his heart. As if the things she said did not make him want her all the more, no matter how hopeless his cause. Or hers.

"Promise me you will consider it, at the least," he said. "And I will swear to you by any power you name that even after we live as husband and wife, should Theseus ever return, I will give you up, if you still desire him. There is no other man here who will make you such a promise."

She smiled sadly. "I have already ruined your father, my friend. And the great Hero of Attica. Are you so eager to be next?"

"It is as I said, my lady, that first night. We Lapiths do not fear Mycenae."

"And the gods?" she asked. "Do you not fear them, either?"

But of course she couldn't have known just what she asked. She didn't know his mother's story. His mother's life, or her sacrifice. She did not know the lesson he had learned far too young.

"The gods will take what they are owed," he told her. "And they are welcome to it. But until that day comes, I will live for love. Our days are too short for anything less."

CHAPTER TWENTY-THREE
HELEN

Polypoetes's words, his conviction, kept me awake well into the night. So much of what he had said was true—of all the men who had come, he was the only one with whom I might live my life honestly. The only one who had any hope of understanding my heart. But knowing what I was, the ruin that I would bring him, how could I accept his offer? Or any offer belonging to a man I cared for, a people I wanted to protect?

I was not certain I should even allow myself to become queen of Sparta, though short of fleeing a second time, and all the risk that came with it, I did not see how I could stop any of it. And what purpose did it serve if I only exchanged one war for another?

No. I could not flee Sparta a second time. Would not. And not only because here, at least, Theseus might know to find me, but also because I could not be certain that my first escape had changed anything of the fate I was given. To put my father and my brothers through so much pain, to shame Sparta itself a second time—I would face my future here, boldly, not slink away in the night, hoping to outrun it.

And if Polypoetes stood beside me?

I could not trust he would do as he said, not wholly. I knew well enough the temptation of my body, and while Theseus might have had the fortitude to resist me, to wait until the time was right to claim me as his wife, I was not certain I trusted any other man to do the same. And as for giving me up—he would have to swear it upon the Styx. I would trust no other bond, no lesser vow. And even that, I was not certain was enough.

None of it would matter if Tyndareus chose another, and Odysseus had not yet devised a plan to protect us all from the results of such a choice. Which meant Polypoetes, no matter how bravely he spoke, would be endangered, along with his people, should I make any prefer-ence known. Nor was there any guarantee that Tyndareus would take my feelings into account, and so long as Agamemnon remained to compete in his brother's name, fortune surely would not favor me.

But I knew I would consider his offer. It was the only hope I had been given yet, and no matter how dangerous it might be for him, how little I wanted him to fall at my hand, I could not turn from it, not completely.

I could not turn from him.

Clymene painted my face to hide the dark circles beneath my eyes the following morning, as I struggled to fight off the lingering dread of nightmares and, far worse, memory. Now my dreams were not con-tent with presenting me only with the burning city of my future, but retraced, too, the failings of my past. Between glimpses of my Trojan prince, I found myself chasing Theseus and Pirithous as they rode out from the walls of Athens, begging them to turn back. Or pleading with Theseus alone, on his empty ship, knowing he could not hear me, could not see me, but desperate for any sign that he might recognize me, all the same.

"You call King Theseus's name in your sleep, my lady," Clymene said, fastening the tiered skirt around my waist.

I smoothed the fabric and shook my head. "He was kind to me, and the thought that he is lost forever—it seems so impossible that it could be true."

"Are you certain that is all that it is?" Clymene asked gently. "You spent so much time with him while he was here. It seemed to me that you hoped he might win you. And now you've come home to find he married another in your place."

"It does not matter now," I said, for I could not speak of it further without losing what little composure I had managed to find. "He is both married and lost, and I must find another protector."

"There was talk among the servants, my lady. Whispers about your nightmares. I've not said a word to anyone of anything I've heard, but it will reach the ears of the men before long. Especially after yesterday."

I sighed, but it had always only ever been a matter of time. Even with my brother beneath my window at night, it was impossible that we could keep the secret from so many for very long. "And what will they hear?"

"That you dream of war. That the gods have declared you will be stolen from your husband. Some argue that your nightmares have already come to pass, but it is bound to make the men suspicious all the same. And the way King Agamemnon and Prince Polypoetes talk, I cannot say they don't have reason to worry."

"They should," I said. "They should know what they risk, marrying me. That I am more than just a beautiful woman brought to bed for their pleasure. They should know they risk ruin. Even death."

"I am not sure it will stop them," Clymene said. "Not now that they've spoken with you, some of them. There's not a slave in the palace who hasn't heard your name while they've been used."

"Like Menelaus," I murmured, my stomach twisting with disgust. "So weak that they cannot spend a day in my company without abusing one of our women."

"They aren't unkind, my lady. Not that I've heard. Except, perhaps, for the new king of Athens. And Ajax of Locris, but you've never cared for him overmuch, I think."

"Even so," I said, hating how easily they were excused for their rutting. It was not uncommon for the men of Achaea, particularly those of high rank, to keep women enough to satisfy them when they grew bored of their wives, and I knew I should not take offense or exception that they took advantage of Tyndareus's hospitality in such a way. But after Theseus . . . After Theseus, I could not help but think them pathetic. And if they could not control themselves for a day, I did not like to think how they would treat me, should opportunity arise.

With any luck, I would not have to marry so unworthy a man. Though perhaps if I did, and led him into ruin, I would not be entirely unhappy to see him fall.

"Are you certain it is wise for you to ride out for the hunt?" Odysseus asked, his horse steady beside mine while we waited outside the city gates for the rest of the men to mount.

Castor had provided horses from Tyndareus's stables for the suitors who had not brought their own, and I watched him while he whispered in a mare's ear before giving her up to the Cretan commander, Idomeneus. Crete belonged, nominally, to Athens. Or it had, beneath Theseus's rule, and from the way Idomeneus and Menestheus had been circling one another, I was not certain how much longer that claim would hold. Likely when King Catreus, grandfather to both Idomeneus and the sons of Atreus, passed away, Crete would be its own kingdom once again, if not before. Another small piece of Theseus's legacy destroyed.

"I'm certain I intend to do it," I told Odysseus, turning my gaze from the Cretan. He'd come to Athens once, but it had been before I was made queen, and thankfully, he could not have known me. "Besides, with my brothers riding, and you, who will guard me if I remain behind?"

He chuckled lightly. "A very practical position, Princess. But I would wager it will be a challenge for your brothers to guard you on the hunt as well, and just as many dangers in the wood, if not more."

"Then I suppose you should remain at my side," I said, allowing him his game. I could not avoid Odysseus forever, and I was curious what he thought of the other men so far. "Since you have no need to prove yourself as my suitor, of course."

"Of course," he agreed, smiling. "In fact, this very day, Tyndareus has promised me Penelope's hand, for one small service in exchange."

"And what service might that be?"

"The same service I've promised to provide you, in fact," Odysseus said. "A means by which to avert a slaughter, should some few of your suitors feel slighted by the choice of your husband. It seems the thought has weighed as heavily upon your father's mind as it has yours."

"And you waited until now to make your offer in order to ensure he responded with proper gratitude, I've no doubt." Once, Tyndareus would have trusted me with those fears. We would have discussed the challenges together. Now, even all these weeks later, he would barely look at me. I turned my horse, guiding her away from the larger press of men, toward the wood and the poor boar who would meet his end in my honor. "I cannot say I'm surprised, but it wasn't terribly compassionate of you to let him suffer so."

Odysseus followed, keeping his horse beside mine. "I could not very well offer until I had a solution in mind."

I nearly lurched off my horse, I turned so quickly, and only his hand at my elbow kept me from falling. "You've devised some scheme?"

He grinned. "Two, in fact. And put together, Tyndareus will be blameless, your new husband will be kept safe from harm, and Sparta will be protected from war."

"Truly?" I was half-strangled by relief, my fingers curled so tightly around my horse's reins that she came to a halt beneath me. "Odysseus, do not tease me. After yesterday, I could not stand to be the victim of such a cruel jest."

He laughed again, tipping his head toward the trees. "I do not tease you, I swear. But come, let us ride out a little farther. We have a few moments, I think, before the others will be ready to follow."

He put his heels to his horse's ribs, kicking the gelding into a canter, and I followed, leaning low over my mare's neck and urging her to a gallop, overtaking him easily as I raced for the trees. He had a plan. A plan that could protect us all, at last! I laughed into the wind. If just one threat of war could be set aside, there was hope that the other might be stopped as well. That I might be *free*, at last, of this small portion of my heartache.

I stopped at the trees, reining my mare so quickly she reared up and whinnied in protest. I laughed again and settled her to four feet, stroking her neck. Odysseus was grinning still when he reached me just a moment later, and we both circled our horses to watch the men we had left behind, their own mounts dancing and pawing with the excitement of their riders.

"Tell me everything," I said. "I would know how we will thwart the gods."

CHAPTER TWENTY-FOUR

HELEN

First, we will invoke a drawing—blessed by sacrifice and overseen by the priests, of course. We will say, when the games are through, that the men who have come to win you are all equally worthy and the choice must be left wholly in the hands of the gods. This will please them all, I think, and give no man the excuse of slight or insult."

I strangled a laugh. This was what the great cunning of Odysseus had come up with? He was truly fiendish in his simplicity. "You do not think it is too obvious?"

Odysseus smirked. "Have you not learned by now, Helen, that men are blinded by their pride? They will all preen, knowing themselves to be the better. But most importantly, Tyndareus, your brothers, even you will be made blameless. It will not matter what favors you bestowed, or what encouragements, nor who has which natural strengths, be they gifts or titles or power, and how they might have been weighted against the others. They will *all* be made equal."

"Even Agamemnon," I said, understanding him more completely. In fact, Agamemnon would be brought low. His power, his gifts, his skills—they would mean nothing.

"Even Agamemnon," he agreed. "But a drawing of names, in and of itself, will not be enough. There is nothing, then, to prevent a man not chosen from inventing some plot of his own to steal you from the man who has won, or simply to kill him, if they are not bound by some other means. Polypoetes and Patroclus, for example, whose people have for so long been at enmity, might find the awarding of your fair self the perfect excuse to make war."

"Mmm," I said, remembering how near they had come to blows the day before. "Polypoetes and Patroclus both know my feelings on the matter, but I cannot say it will stop them beyond this assembly."

"Nor will it stop Agamemnon, who has men and ships and arms aplenty to rain destruction down on the head of any other man here."

"And what solution do you propose?"

Now he grinned again, far too pleased with himself for someone who had just admitted that pride was a man's greatest weakness. "This is the true genius, addressing not just this threat, but that which you may face in the future as well. We will make them all swear an oath to uphold the right of whoever is chosen to keep you as his wife. Should the day come when you are stolen away, all your suitors will rise in your defense and his, to retrieve you."

I stared at him, his words sinking like so many rocks in my stomach. All my suitors. If I were ever stolen, all my suitors would fight, would be sworn to retrieve me. *Oh, Theseus.* Every prayer for his return would be turned into a curse upon myself, upon Achaea.

"Tell me you have not already suggested this to my father."

Odysseus laughed. "What do you think convinced him to promise me Penelope?"

"No. No, no, no." My horse shivered beneath me, pawing the ground, and I softened my hold upon the reins only with an effort of will. Then I slid from her back altogether, feeling too faint to remain so far from the ground. I pressed my face against her neck, fighting to breathe, to keep from losing my morning meal. "Theseus, forgive me."

"Helen, I don't understand," Odysseus said, a rustle of fabric and the huff of his horse signaling his own dismount. "This was what you wanted. Safety for your people, as small a threat of conflict as could ever be possible—and protection, too, should your dreams threaten your future. I thought you'd be pleased with my ingenuity, all things considered."

Pleased. I wanted to weep. "You don't have any idea what you've done. If you'd only come to me first—" I swallowed the rest. It hardly mattered now. He'd told Tyndareus, and Tyndareus would never give up such a scheme, seeing it precisely as Odysseus did. A promise of protection for my future, against any threat. He could not have dreamed of such an advantage.

But Theseus aside—and I could not think any more upon that, or I would never recover—it was another piece of my nightmares falling into place. Another tangle to the knot that I would never get undone. It was the means by which Menelaus might make such devastating war upon Troy. The reason so many of Achaea's kings and princes, so many of her men, would lay siege upon that great city, and ultimately die.

Odysseus had not thwarted the gods; he had given them everything I had fought so hard to stop. And he did not even realize it. Could not see beyond his own foolish pride.

"Tell me at least," I managed to say, my voice hoarse and my throat so thick the words choked me. I lifted my head, letting him see what he had wrought. "Please tell me that you have divined some way in which we might prevent Menelaus from winning me. Promise me that much has been accomplished. That I need not fear his name called out as my husband, now that you have stolen away my every smallest dream for happiness."

He drew back, startled, his face paling at what he saw in mine. "He has the smallest of chances, only—"

"How could you?" I flew at him then, my hands fists, my tears breaking, coursing down my cheeks. He had made it all possible. He had tied me to my fate as surely as the sailcloth to the mast. He had thrown me to the mercy of the gods, and I knew, I *knew* how they would choose. "How could you!"

"Helen!" He grasped me by the wrists, forcing me back, throwing me away before I could beat upon his chest, his face. I would tear the hair from his head, rend the tunic from his body, and scrape the skin from his flesh with nothing but my nails. "Helen, stop this!"

"I have nothing left!" I sobbed, falling to my knees in the dirt. "You've taken everything. Ruined everything. But you demand I stop? You dare! Even if Theseus should come now, it will not matter! These men will hunt us down—because of you!"

He shook his head, his eyes narrowing. "What has Theseus to do with any of this? He is lost, Helen. And even if he survives this foolishness of Pirithous's, he is married!"

"To me!" I cried. I buried my face in my hands, unable to keep from weeping aloud. Because he was truly lost to me now, my hero, my husband, my king. He was lost to me, even if he lived, and the knowledge tore me apart.

"Helen . . ." He crouched before me, touched my shoulder, then drew his hand back again, as if unsure of what I might do. "Gods above, Helen. If I had known . . ."

"It was all I could do," I gasped. "I was queen, and Athens—it was all I could do to protect her. To protect his people. No one can ever know, Odysseus."

He let out a long breath, then clasped my shoulder again, more firmly this time. "I'll find a way to keep Menelaus's name from the drawing. I'll . . . I'll find a way. Somehow. And your secret will be safe, I swear. But as for the oath—I fear it is beyond my power now."

I was not so certain it had ever been in his power at all.

"Helen!" Polypoetes charged toward us, sliding off his horse before the animal had even stopped in order to reach me. Odysseus withdrew, stepping back, and I struggled to control myself. "What's happened? What did he do to you?"

I shook my head, letting him draw me into his arms, though he could never shield me from this pain. I was heartsick and even more sore-hearted. Bruised and broken, the once solid urn of my hopes turned to so many scattered shards of pottery, ground beneath Odysseus's sandaled feet.

"I . . ." But Odysseus's cunning failed him, and no excuse fell from his lips. No explanation at all. He only grasped the base of his horse's neck and vaulted up onto his back. "I'll think of something, Helen, I promise you. I'll make this right."

But he wouldn't. How could he? The gods had used him for their own ends, and they would hardly give him the means to work against them now. I knew it even before he had turned his horse away, turned back to the palace itself, and left me.

"Helen?" Polypoetes prompted, ducking his head to look at me. "You need only say the word and I will run him down. Punish him with my own hands for whatever wrong he has done you."

A laugh caught in my throat, emerging as a sob instead. "You should be grateful to him, Polypoetes. Whether Theseus lives or not, it no longer matters, for he has found a way to keep my suitors from warring. To keep me for all time in the power of the man who wins me."

His forehead furrowed, his gaze chasing after Odysseus, watching as he disappeared inside the city's walls. Poor Polypoetes was not quite so fine as his father, for when he looked back at me again, behind the pity, the compassion for my plight, there was a spark of something else, something far more selfish in its desires.

He stroked my hair from my face and offered me a small, sad smile. A lie of a smile, projecting a sympathy that did not reach his eyes. "Then I will do everything in my power to ensure that you are made mine."

And then my brothers arrived, just ahead of the rest of the men, and I was glad to be saved from answering.

Polypoetes still thought he could persuade my heart. He believed I might love him as he did me. But a life as his wife would be only a reminder of all my sorrows, a pale shadow of everything I had lost.

And I knew in that moment, he could never understand.

He desired me too much.

I did not speak to my brothers of what had happened, ignoring their questions when they asked and only riding on, silently, with the rest of the men. I placed myself near Ajax the Great, hardly able to bring myself to offer him even the smallest of encouragements. But at least as his companion, I need not fear another man's interruptions. Not even Polypoetes would dare, though he rode close on my heels, always watching.

It wasn't that I did not like him, even appreciate him. It wasn't even that I did not think myself capable of caring for him, were he to become my husband. But I feared what would happen if I encouraged him at all, even now, with Odysseus's accursed plan ready to be set in place.

I feared he would become as twisted as Menelaus, and all the more powerful for the secrets he kept safe. Athens and Theseus were too dear to my heart to put at further risk, and all the more so now that it seemed that part of my life was torn from me forever.

The small hope I might have carried that Polypoetes might let me go, might return me to Theseus should he arrive, was buried now. Once he swore Odysseus's vow, it would change everything. His promises would become empty, hollow things, and even if he had the strength to keep them, the other suitors would keep us trapped, imprisoned by their own desires. If just one man forswore himself, it would shatter the too fragile peace between them—and then it would become a matter of honor and pride. And if there was one thing I knew, it was that the god of war stepped close upon the heels of both.

In the end, Polypoetes would be just like the rest. Another man I would never be able to escape. Not without destroying everything I held dear.

CHAPTER TWENTY-FIVE
ODYSSEUS

He could have cursed her for keeping so impossible a secret. And cursed himself for not realizing just what it was she had kept from him so carefully. How could he have believed for a moment it was only Menelaus's rape she'd hidden, when he had known how thin her story was from the start? She could never have escaped for so long without help, of that he'd had no doubt, but it had never occurred to him that she might have secured it from King Theseus! That she might have *loved* the hero who had helped her steal away.

It had never occurred to him that she had hoped, still, to be stolen again.

"My lord?" Penelope came out to meet him on the wide porch, frowning. "I thought you meant to join the others in the hunt?"

He forced himself to smile, sliding from his horse's back and turning him over to the stableboy. "I thought better of it, remembering you here. And why should we not take advantage of our time alone to celebrate privately our betrothal?"

"Hush!" she said, laughing. "You know Tyndareus does not want it known until after this business with Helen is settled! He cannot be seen to favor you so kindly, or the other men will suspect something amiss."

"The other men know already I do not compete for Helen's hand, and if you think for a moment they do not already watch me with suspicion, you are as daft as you are beautiful," he said, taking her in his arms. "And who is here to see us now, besides? It is the perfect moment, and even if we ran through the palace shouting our joy, it would not matter."

"The servants would hear," she chided. "And the news would spread like wildfire. You know that."

He sighed, releasing her at last. "I suppose, then, that I should go speak with Tyndareus and pretend I did not return to see you at all."

"Perhaps that would be best," she said, always so proper, so attentive to her duty. And it would take a man of Theseus's strength to keep a woman like Helen in her place, as a wife. But not Penelope. Penelope could be relied upon always. Nor would she blink an eye if he left her in Ithaca for any length of time. He would never need to fear returning home to an army come to steal her from him. And that was all he could ever ask for in a wife—peace and loyalty.

Helen would provide neither. Not to any man but Theseus.

"Find me after," Odysseus murmured against Penelope's ear. "I would have you know my pleasure, all the same."

And then he left her to find Tyndareus. Because he had made Helen a promise, and if he was fortunate somehow, perhaps he might persuade her father that he had been wrong. That his plan would fail or cause some other trouble, unrealized until then.

He had to try, at the least. And if he did not succeed there, then he would turn his mind to the means by which he might exclude Mycenae.

He must think of something. And he was running out of time.

"King Odysseus," Leda said, offering him her hand in warm greeting. "You have brought us such joy. We will miss Penelope, of course, but surely she could not have made a better match. And to offer Tyndareus, too, a means by which to safeguard his daughter—we are both more than grateful, my lord. Truly, Sparta can have no greater friend!"

"Not even Mycenae?" he asked, bending to kiss her hand. "I would think Agamemnon might still exceed my place, as the husband of your daughter. And the man who wins Helen, too, must certainly become another son to Tyndareus."

"With any luck, the man who wins Helen will already be as a son to Tyndareus," she said, smiling. "And I am pleased to think Menelaus will have your protection, when all of this is done."

"You seem very certain of his success, my lady."

"Who among the suitors could ever hope to compete against Mycenae and win?" she asked, laughing. "Perhaps there are some who are more skilled in one way or another, but none will ever be richer. And we must not forget that Menelaus and Helen have long years of friendship with which to forge their future."

"I have heard, however, that the princess would have it otherwise. That she is not amenable to a marriage to Menelaus at all, in fact. Surely to wed her against her will would only weaken Sparta."

Leda flicked her fingers in dismissal. "Helen will do as she is told, you needn't worry about that."

"It is little difference to me, my lady, one way or the other. In Ithaca we are far enough away that we need not concern ourselves with the troubles of the mainland. It is only as a friend to Sparta that we dare speak at all."

"Of course," she agreed, her smile cooling. "But even Ithaca, I am certain, cannot desire to make Mycenae its enemy."

"Ithaca has only ever desired peace, Queen Leda, as I'm certain you must know." He touched his fist to his forehead, all politeness. "And it is in search of such that I would speak with your husband and king, if he is free."

Leda dropped her gaze. "You know he is not well, my lord. Even with the relief you have granted him, this business with Helen has worn him thin. I would not have you disturb his rest. Can it not wait until the midday meal?"

He hesitated. He more than anyone knew how desperately Tyndareus needed his rest, particularly now. To show his weakness with so many wolves in his house would only invite more trouble for Sparta—for Helen, too.

"I would speak to him alone before the others return from the hunt. If it must wait until midday, it can, but not later. There is too much at stake."

"Oh, Odysseus," she sighed. "Tell me you have not been taken in by my daughter? You, of all men."

He forced himself to smile, even to laugh as he lied. "I promise you, it is not for her sake I have returned, but for my own. For Ithaca's."

"Let it always be so," she said. "And you will have a friend in me for all time."

"Then let us be friends," he said, keeping his face a mask of lighthearted amusement, though her words surprised him. By all rights she should wish him an ally of her daughter, no matter what trap she feared Helen might set for him. Because to protect Helen was to protect Sparta, and what higher calling could there be for the queen? "I will return midday to speak with Tyndareus about my concerns."

"As you wish," Leda said, touching his arm in farewell. "But I warn you, King Odysseus. She has a way about her, my daughter.

And I would not like to see you brought to ruin by her beauty. For Ithaca's sake."

"Of course," he said, and bowed.

Of course.

But he was beginning to wonder if Leda did not play her own game, and if she did, just what she meant to achieve.

He had Ithaca to look out for, after all.

CHAPTER TWENTY-SIX
HELEN

"We meet again, Princess," Menestheus said, his smile thin as he sat beside me. I stiffened, swallowing my disgust at the way his eyes raked over me. "Should you not be more pleased? We are certainly old friends by now."

"Perhaps I have never been certain of you," I said mildly, offering a false smile in return. "I was King Theseus's friend first, after all. And it is only natural I might be concerned that his cousin would so easily forget his loyalties and make himself king in his absence."

"Ah," he said, pouring us both wine. "I cannot imagine it would be wise of you to support him still. You must realize I'd much prefer to be the hero in your little story, rather than the villain. For the good of Athens."

I let my gaze fall to my plate, forcing myself to remain pleasant, though his veiled threat made me want to spit in his face. "I wonder, if you care for me so little, why you've come so far, *King* Menestheus. Why should you want me as your queen at all?"

"I have seen with my own eyes the power of your beauty, Princess. Why should I not desire to keep you at my side, knowing what I do?"

"You truly think Athens would be fooled so easily?" I asked.

He shrugged. "I will have won you fairly. The rest will hardly matter by then."

"The rest will bring Mycenae to your door, and you cannot be certain I would not let them in."

"Can I not?" Menestheus smirked. "Would you truly condemn so many innocents just to hurt me? Condemn yourself as well? No, Princess. When I have won you, I will have no fear of your betrayal."

My lip curled. "Theseus will return, Menestheus, and should he find me held against my will as your bride—"

He laughed then, loud and rough. "Oh, Princess, you cannot imagine how it would delight me to see his face when he realizes that you are mine. That I defeated him in every way that could ever matter. The great Hero of Attica, cast out of his city, made to beg at my door, and you—perhaps I would let him in, bound and gagged, just to make him watch."

My face flushed, the blood roaring in my ears with his words, his threats. The picture of pain and anguish he painted with such glee.

"You worthless dog," I breathed. "You are not fit to lick his sandals, never mind rule his city. So long as Athens is yours, it is doomed."

"Have you dreamed of our future, then, my dear?" he drawled. "How encouraging to know you think of me even in sleep. I will be sure to tell the others you've said as much."

"If you knew half of what I dreamed, you would not be so eager to claim me," I snapped. "But if I must bring ruin, let it be upon your head, before any other man in this hall."

"Little Sister," Castor interrupted, his hand falling heavily upon my shoulder, "is that any way to speak to our friend? After Menestheus was so kind to deliver you home?"

I bit back a curse, turning my face away, for Menestheus had only laughed again. At my words, at Castor's reminder that I must pretend friendship, though I could not stand even the *thought* of him. And he would see Theseus dead. My dreams had told me that. I wished I could see Menestheus die by my own hand first. That I might rend him limb from limb, scratch out his eyes, and leave his body to be ravaged by the wolves. He deserved nothing better.

"The princess does like to tease, doesn't she?" Menestheus said. "And I must admit that I admire her fire, if not her willfulness. When she is my wife, it will be my pleasure to see her broken."

Castor stiffened behind me, and though I had calmed considerably with his touch, he did not have the benefit of his own power. But he smiled and leaned down, the better to be heard.

"Have a care, Menestheus. Now that we know the way into Athens, it would be a simple thing to take back what we have given."

"Is that a threat, Prince Castor?" Menestheus asked. "And after you just reminded your sister of the kindness I had done you. Perhaps you should remind yourself of the same. Nor should you forget that once your princess is wed, what becomes of her is no longer your concern."

"That is where you are wrong, *friend*," Castor said, baring his teeth. "We will serve our queen until the day we die, defending her from all threats. Her husband included, should it come to that."

"You will not live long, if that is your intent," Menestheus said, far too casually, and a chill went down my spine. "Those from whom she might require protection will hardly have qualms about putting you down like the dogs you are."

"He can certainly try," Castor said. "And when he has shown his true nature, and Sparta sends him into exile for his crimes, my sister will still remain, still rule as our beloved queen. So I say again, Menestheus, have a care. Our sister is not without protection, and our patience is far from endless."

Menestheus snorted. "Did she spread her legs to earn your devotion, as she did for Theseus?"

Castor snarled, but I shoved back my stool, hitting my brother hard in the shins with the wood as I rose. "Perhaps I will retire early, if you would be so kind as to escort me to my room, Brother."

He glared still at Menestheus, who smiled to himself as he filled his plate, secure in the hospitality that bound us. But I had no intention of allowing Castor to be goaded into his own exile by striking at a guest.

"Please, Castor. Do not give him what he wants. Keep your honor and the favor of the gods, that you might serve me as you have promised when I am queen."

"By all means," Menestheus said. "Go and take your pleasure between her thighs while you are free still to do so."

Castor lurched toward him, but I pushed my brother back, both hands against his chest. "He is not worth your disgrace," I hissed.

"What's this?" Pollux said, joining us at last and disguising a firm grip upon Castor's arm with a clap upon his shoulder. "It seems not a moment passes without some new disagreement within this hall. I blame you, Sister. Your suitors are so desperate to win your heart, they forget all sense."

"Yes," I agreed. "It must certainly be that. But Castor was just escorting me to my room—I fear I did not sleep well, and as King Menestheus has had the benefit of my company in Athens, I knew he would forgive me for retiring."

"Of course," he said, all graciousness. "I am already at so great an advantage over the others, I can hardly begrudge you your rest."

"Indeed," Pollux murmured, his eyes narrowing. "Off you go, then, Little Sister. And Castor, too. I'll see that our friend is entertained in your absence, shall I? We wouldn't want King Menestheus to feel slighted. Perhaps a slave to warm your bed?"

"Better a slave to slit his throat," Castor grumbled as we turned away.

I laced my arm through his and said nothing. Who was I to begrudge him such a pleasant dream? A slave to slit the throat of every man who would abuse me, and surely the horrors of the war in my nightmares would be halved. But we would be cursed. Not just my brothers or me, but Sparta itself and all her people.

Hospitality and guest-friendship were sacred bonds, and I had done enough twice over to offend the gods without doing harm to one of our guests.

I dared not risk it.

No matter how much he might deserve it.

"What on earth was that about?" Pollux demanded of us some time later. Castor and I had remained in my room after we'd abandoned him to Menestheus's company. I'd sent Clymene to the feast to observe the men in my place, allowing my brother a bit more privacy in which to vent his anger. As it was, he had spent half the evening pacing my room, cursing Menestheus for the insults he'd given us.

I had watched him carefully from my stool beside the window, afraid of what it meant. To have taken such grave offense from Menestheus's accusations—Castor was too honorable and too good a brother to impose himself upon me, but it seemed by his response that the temptation troubled him, all the same.

"We should send him from Sparta, reject him utterly as a suitor for Helen," Castor said. "I will not see her married to that dog."

"His exclusion will be easily accomplished, from what Odysseus has told me," Pollux said, pouring us all wine from a pitcher he'd stolen from the banquet table. "It seems we're to have a drawing at the end of the games. The choice of Helen's husband is to be left to the gods."

"Then Odysseus could not persuade Tyndareus otherwise," I murmured, accepting the wine he offered and turning my gaze to the courtyard beneath my window. From where I sat, I could see the lesser porch leading into the megaron. "And we have lost all."

"Not all," Pollux said. "Odysseus means to substitute another token, for a man we prefer, in place of Agamemnon's."

"How does he think he'll accomplish that?" I demanded, staring at my brother. "Does he think these men will be so careless? That Agamemnon will be?"

Pollux sighed. "We must trust him, Helen. He will find a way, and he will do as we wish. You have only to name the suitor you prefer. We'll have Menestheus's token replaced as well, and he will have that much better a chance to win you."

I shook my head, watching the megaron again. Light still flickered, streaming out into the courtyard, and I could hear the men boasting and laughing together. No doubt retelling their glorious victories or exaggerating their hunting prowess. "You know the only name I desire. There is little difference between the rest of these men."

"You cannot tell me you'd be pleased to see Ajax of Locris made your husband," Pollux said. "You flinch from his every movement."

"What of Polypoetes?" Castor asked gently.

"Neither one of you care for him overmuch," I said. "Would you have him be raised up as your king?"

"If he were kind to you. If you thought you might be happy as his wife."

I swirled the wine in my cup. "He promised to let me rule Sparta as I desired. But I do not think he would let me remain here. I would rule from Thessaly, abusing some poor young man as a messenger between us."

"Then you see, it would not matter if we cared for him or not. We would hardly see him," Castor said.

"Or me."

"You speak of it as if you did not run away with Theseus and tell us nothing of your whereabouts," Pollux said. "At least this time we would know for certain where you had gone, even have the freedom to visit. You would be safe from Mycenae so far north, and safer still from the strange prince of your dreams."

"I suppose so," I said, studying the dark liquid in my cup. "But would I bring him ruin, still? As I did his father?"

Castor laughed. "You can't blame yourself for Pirithous's foolishness. That was no one's doing but the gods."

"Yes," I agreed. "The gods, who sought to punish him for his sins. And what was his greatest sin, Castor? His most obvious transgression?"

"Hubris," Castor said at once. "Anyone could see that. He thought himself equal to the gods, and it was his pride that led him into the house of Hades."

I set the wine aside, my stomach too sour to drink it. "Pirithous knew what he was. Whatever games he played, whatever acts he put on for others, he knew himself nothing more than a servant, at best. A plaything, more like. No. His sin was stealing me from Tyndareus after accepting his hospitality and friendship. I am the reason the gods ruined him. And I do not mean to bring the same dark fate down upon his son. On any of these men. Those who might be worthy of me can hardly deserve the destruction I would sow."

"Helen—"

But I lifted my hand, silencing Castor before he could speak further. "If you wish to give one man greater opportunity in this lottery, in place of Mycenae and Athens, then choose from among them yourselves. I want no part in it."

"You're certain, Helen?" Pollux asked.

"Let me be blameless in this one small way, Pollux, or I feel I will be crushed beneath all this weight."

My brothers exchanged a glance between them, but I ignored their obvious concern. I could not think of it any longer. Not when I faced four more days of games and suitors with the knowledge that every happiness I had yet hoped for was gone.

And of course that night I dreamed of Theseus.

The gods must have enjoyed watching me weep.

CHAPTER TWENTY-SEVEN
HELEN

I kept my distance from the suitors after that, barring the midday meal and the evening banquet, where I could hardly avoid the partners Tyndareus and Leda chose for me. Idomeneus of Crete was harmless enough, and my instincts regarding his desire to break from Athens were confirmed the moment he began to speak of Theseus.

"You cannot have known him well," Idomeneus said, "but he was a good king. A fair man. He made no decisions without first conferring with his councilors, and every land he held was given the right to put a man forward, that their interests might always be weighed. In Crete, we had expected the worst after Minos's death, but he treated us as friends. Even took our princess to wife as proof of his respect for our people."

"Yes," I agreed. "I have heard something of his way of ruling—but do not all kings keep a council?"

"Not all kings, and of those that do, even fewer listen to their people so closely. Menestheus, I fear, means to keep Theseus's councilors merely as ornament, rather than true and trusted advisers. And it will not be long before he begins losing support upon the mainland because of it. It was one thing to be ruled by a man who respected them, who understood that each land had its own traditions, and recognized their ways. It is another to give allegiance to a man who looks down upon us all from the height of the Rock."

"And what of King Theseus's sons?" I asked, pretending ignorance. "Menestheus cannot have the right to steal Athens from them, even if he claims some share of their blood."

"I have heard they live in exile," Idomeneus said, his gaze slithering away, searching for those who might overhear even as he lowered his voice. "But if they desire to continue living, they are better off forgotten, wherever they have gone. If Demophon has even the smallest measure of his father's wisdom, he will bide his time. Should Menestheus believe he is a threat, those boys will not survive long."

I hated to agree, but I feared he was right. Just as Theseus would not survive if he returned from the Underworld and Menestheus feared his hold over Athens would slip. "It is a great shame, all of it."

"It is certainly that," Idomeneus said. "But I worry most for the queen he left behind. She has not been seen or heard from since Menestheus took the throne. He cannot have dared to kill her outright, of course, for Egypt is far too powerful to anger so, but I cannot imagine she will be given a pleasant end. Why he did not simply take her to wife himself, I do not begin to understand."

I mumbled something sympathetic and turned the conversation elsewhere. But at least if my suitors believed Theseus's queen still lived, locked away by Menestheus, they did not suspect me. And it was not wholly untrue. That life I had led, the person I had been—she might as well have been imprisoned now, and some days I wondered if I would be better off dead.

But there was still time. Despite Odysseus's scheming, there was still time for Theseus to arrive, to claim me for his own again before any oaths were sworn. It was a sliver of hope, but I clung to it, just as I clung to the memory of his love.

Please, Athena. Please, let him come!

The games went on. Boxing, archery, spear throwing. Races by foot and upon chariots. I watched them all. Fleet-footed Patroclus won the foot-race easily, and the Great Ajax was unbeatable in any test of strength. Agamemnon's horses were undone only by the midnight-black Lapith stallions Polypoetes had brought from Thessaly, and once they were unharnessed from their chariot, he presented them to me as gifts.

"Bred from the mares of Magnesia and foals of my mother's most prized stallion, Podarkes. They are brave and true, if wild. Your brother will know how best to treat them, and I will train them both to your hand, Princess, before I go, that they might be safe for you to ride."

The other men mumbled among themselves at his words, eyes widening at the richness of such a gift. There were no finer horses in all of Achaea than those belonging to the Lapiths, and to receive *two* such stallions for Sparta's stables—our animals would certainly be worth far more in trade, once they were bred.

"You are too generous, Prince Polypoetes," I said, though I could hardly refuse the gift without giving insult. "And I cannot see how I am deserving of such a prize."

"You are deserving of every good thing, Princess," he said. "And as I have told you already, this is only the beginning of what I would offer you, should you become my wife."

I dropped my gaze, avoiding his eyes. What he had promised me was never far from my mind, and perhaps I had been a fool to refuse to make any preference known to my brothers, who watched now, but I could not bear the thought of disappointing him so completely. Nor to look upon Theseus when he returned to find me in the bed of Pirithous's son.

And he would return. My dreams made it clearer every night that wherever he was, he searched for me, as desperate to find me as I was to be in his arms, as if now that our cause was nearly hopeless, the gods delighted in reminding me of everything I had lost. But Theseus still lived. And so long as he lived, I would not plan a future that did not account for his arrival. When he came to reclaim me, he would see my faithfulness, my loyalty, still. He would have no doubt of my love for him.

"Princess?" Polypoetes stepped forward, lowering his voice. "I can't have offended you?"

"No, of course not." I forced a smile to my lips and pressed a kiss to his cheek in thanks, for I could offer him nothing else. "I am certain you will make some woman a very generous and loving husband, my lord. But I cannot hope I will be so fortunate. For your sake."

"Helen," he murmured, reaching out to catch me by the hand as I pulled away. "You cannot mean that."

The echo of Menelaus's own words drawn from Polypoetes's lips struck me like a sword through the stomach. It was the same, all of it, and I would not see him warped into madness with my kindnesses, my friendship. "Do not make this harder for me, I beg of you. If you truly care for me, you must let me go."

"And what?" he demanded, his jaw tight. There was no one to hear but my brothers, for we stood apart, but there was no hiding his anger from the others, even if they did not know his words. "Give you up to Mycenae, when I know you would rather die than become Menelaus's wife?"

"I don't know," I said, more to myself than to him. "I wish I did, Polypoetes. I wish I knew. I wish I could save you from what I am, but you must understand, if I am the reason Menelaus is what he is, I cannot risk doing the same again to you. The Lapiths remember what is owed, you've said, but in Sparta, we remember, too. I will not repay your father's kindness by cursing his son."

He closed his eyes, his lips pressed thin with grief. "Gods above."

"Tell me you understand. That you are not so lost in thrall to my beauty that you cannot see reason."

His jaw worked for a moment longer, but when he looked at me again, it was with clear eyes. "I would have welcomed madness if you had asked it of me. I still will, if you should change your mind. But I am not lost to it, Helen. Not yet."

And then he let me go, with a stiff bow of farewell, following the others back to the palace and the baths to wash and dress for the evening banquet.

I could only pray that he was not wrong.

"I am at last favored with your company," Antilochus said at the feasting that night. A son of King Nestor and prince of Pylos, he was far from a stranger to our halls, and even less of a stranger to me.

Wily Nestor had sent his sons as guests, one by one, to every city of worth in the mainland, the better, as he claimed loudly and often, to foster the bonds of friendship. Antilochus was neither the oldest nor the youngest of them, and I was certain Nestor had chosen him as my suitor in great part because of the time he had spent among us in his youth.

"I wonder if I should be insulted or gratified that I was not permitted such an honor sooner."

"You hardly had need," I said. "We all know you're a troublesome fool, after all. Never missing an opportunity to push a poor girl into the mud when she only wanted to fish with her brothers."

He laughed, and I was glad to have one meal during which I could pretend I was not on display. "You cannot still hold that offense against me, all these years later."

"It does not seem reasonable that I should," I admitted, smiling in spite of myself. "And yet I cannot seem to look at you without tasting the grit of the riverbank on my tongue."

"If I could do it all again, my lady, I would lend you my own pole instead of treating you so unkindly."

"You mean now that you know how beautiful I was to become?" I asked.

"Of course," he agreed, letting me have my fun. "What other reason could there be?"

"Certainly not the growth of your character in the years since, my lord."

He grinned. "Careful, Princess, I begin to think I was not wrong, after all. Still the same wildling you always were. Does Tyndareus still indulge your every whim?"

"If only he did." I passed him a relish to pair with his bread, ignoring the sinking feeling in my stomach at the mention of Tyndareus, grown all the more distant since Odysseus had found the solution he required. I feared the rift between us would not heal. "But clearly it is not so, or you would have hardly found yourself seated at my elbow."

Antilochus chuckled low. "I shall choose to be gratified, then, that I was permitted the honor at all."

"A wise choice, my lord. Truly discerning."

"I strive to be so—can you imagine the disappointment of my father, were I otherwise?"

"Surely your father has sons enough that he can afford one or two who have not inherited his wit."

"Oh yes," Antilochus said. "But just as surely he would not send such a poor example to Sparta to win *you*. Even if he was sent with the knowledge that he had little hope of success."

"And why should the son of Nestor consider himself so poorly?"

"I'm certain you noticed the son of Nestor did not win a single event in your games."

"I'm certain the son of Nestor has more tact than to outshine his rivals so boldly. You might have beaten Patroclus, if you'd desired it. And the chariot race was simply a matter of who had the finest horses."

"Ah, the horses," Antilochus sighed. "I don't suppose you might allow us to borrow your fine Lapith stallions to seed our own stables in Pylos?"

"And offend Prince Polypoetes after he showed me such generosity?" I almost believed Antilochus desired the horses over me. Perhaps he did, for he'd always preferred the stableboys to the kitchen maids. Nestor might have just as easily sent him as my suitor to see if he could be tempted to take a wife at all. And judging by Antilochus's performance, I was beginning to think his father would be left disappointed.

"I feared as much," he said. "Which means I have no choice but to be reduced to raiding. Do you suppose Castor might be persuaded to help?"

"You wish to enlist my brother in the raid of his own horses?" I asked. "Perhaps I was mistaken in my earlier compliments—clearly you are not so wise as you first appeared."

"There, you see?" he said, smiling again. "Another reason I should not expect to win you, Princess. If I needed one beyond the clear intentions of Mycenae."

"And now we reach the heart of the matter," I said, grimacing. "Did your father command you to yield to Mycenae, then? I wonder that he bothered to send you at all, if he is so sure of Menelaus's cause."

"My father always hopes for the best, my lady. To have a son made king of Sparta would please him, no question. But he is practical enough to prepare himself and his son for disappointment. And King Agamemnon has made his feelings on this matter more than clear. Those of us who stand in his way cannot expect to stand long."

"And if I told you that King Agamemnon's hands would be tied on this matter? That he will not, in the end, be free to make good on such a threat?"

Antilochus lifted his eyebrows. "If that is so, my lady . . . I would wish I had given my honest all to the footrace."

I snorted. "You still would have let Patroclus win."

"That may be true," he agreed, pouring us both more wine. "But I would have made sure I had come in second."

"Your attention, please," Tyndareus called out, rising from his seat at the center of the table. I frowned at the thinness of his voice. "Your attention!"

Below, Odysseus banged his fist upon the table, and my brothers did the same. Antilochus joined them, and then Polypoetes and Ajax the Great, all signaling for silence in the megaron, that my father might be heard. When the rest of the men had quieted, my father nodded his thanks to the assembly.

"You have all competed well," he began, drawing himself upright. "And Sparta has been honored by your coming and your friendship. But we have no desire to be the cause of strife among you, nor do we wish for Helen's marriage to begin with bloodshed."

A grumble rippled through the room, and Antilochus gave me a questioning look, but I only shrugged and sipped my wine.

Tyndareus held up his hand, waiting for silence to fall again. "To this end, and because you are all so well matched as suitors for the princess, at the urging and advice of our peace-loving King Odysseus, we will ask each of you to swear a solemn vow to protect not only our daughter, but the rights of the man who has won her as his wife."

"Just how long did you know of this?" Antilochus murmured against my ear, hardly alone among the burst of talk brought forth by my father's announcement. "And why did you not tell me sooner?"

"That would hardly have been fair, my lord," I said, hiding my words behind my cup. "But hush now, or you'll miss the rest."

"You have all heard the rumors," Tyndareus went on, speaking over them, though his voice warbled as he raised it. "And should the day come that my daughter is stolen by any man, be he foreign or otherwise, I would give her chosen husband every help in bringing her home again, to his side!"

"Then it's true you suffer nightmares," Antilochus said, still speaking in an undertone. "No wonder you've looked so ill."

I thrust an elbow into his ribs at his teasing, but he caught it and masked his laugh with a cough against his hand.

"But there is more," Tyndareus said. "From the beginning, we have promised Zeus would have a hand in the choosing of our daughter's husband. After watching you compete and seeing no one man set apart in such an even match, we have chosen to leave the decision wholly in the god's hands. We will have a sacred lottery, consecrated by Zeus at the shrine. Each man will be allowed one token, and Helen herself, blindfolded, will draw the winner. Whoever's name is upon the token, he will become Helen's husband and my heir."

There was a roar of sound then, some of the men rising to their feet, banging upon the table with either glee or fury—Polypoetes only shifted his gaze to me, worry furrowing lines across his brow. He did not need to ask how long I had known. He had comforted me when I had learned of it. And of all the men, he understood what it meant, what this plan of Odysseus's had taken from me.

I looked away, draining the rest of the wine from my cup. Now was not the time to dwell upon what I would lose the moment those oaths were made.

"Clever," Antilochus said. "And this was Odysseus's idea as well, I suppose?"

"Yes, he's quite cunning," I mumbled, not quite able to keep the bitterness from my voice. "Of course it does not take into account any desires *I* might have, should my husband prove himself unsuitable."

Antilochus threw back his head and laughed.

All the better, I supposed, that he thought it a joke.

But for me, knowing what I did, it never could be.

CHAPTER
TWENTY-EIGHT
POLYPOETES

Polypoetes watched as Agamemnon rose, fury in every line of his body at Tyndareus's announcement. For a moment, he feared the king of Mycenae would strike at his quailing wife when she caught at him, but the moment passed with only a terse reply. Agamemnon left the dais, shoving his way through the other men, who raised their cups in honor of their host and the princess they'd come to win. Agamemnon sneered at them all, not bothering to hide his disgust.

It was clear that of all the men in the megaron, Agamemnon felt himself the most wounded. Polypoetes eased his way nearer to the king of Mycenae, unsure of what he intended, but Pollux's warning rose in his thoughts. If trouble came, it would come from Agamemnon. But more than that, if any man were to find a way to cheat Odysseus's careful plot, it would be Mycenae's king, and Polypoetes had no desire to give him the opportunity to scheme.

"Careful, my prince," Leonteus said, jostling his elbow as he placed a wine cup in his hand. "Wounded lions are unpredictable creatures."

A son of one of his father's most trusted advisers, Leonteus had always been his dearest friend among the Lapiths. His closest companion in all Achaea after the death of Theseus's son, Hippolytus, whom he had been raised to love and admire as a brother. Sometimes when he faced some new challenge, he still asked himself what Hippolytus might have done—but if Hippolytus had lived, Polypoetes was certain that Menestheus would never have taken Athens so easily. For all he knew, Helen might have still been safe upon the Rock.

"Are you lost, King Agamemnon?" Polypoetes called out, raising his new drink as if it were an excuse for his boldness. Leonteus moved nearer to his side, laughing along with the other men who heard his shout, but ready to act in his defense.

"Do I look it?" Agamemnon demanded.

"There is no other explanation, surely, for your appearance among the rabble," Polypoetes said, clapping the nearest man upon the back and grinning. "You've never strayed from your position upon the dais before now."

"Before now, we were not all made equal," Agamemnon said.

"Some of us are still more equal than others," Leonteus drawled.

Polypoetes smirked, lifting his cup again in salute, like a man who had enjoyed the wine too much. "And the gods would know it best!"

Agamemnon's smile was thin and forced. "Yes, the gods can certainly tell a prince from a peasant, and a king from a prince as well. But while this oath protects Helen's husband, it does not offer any comfort to those who will lose her. There are many here who might be wise to consider that."

"The Lapiths do not fear Mycenae," Polypoetes said, goading him. After all, an angry man has not the wit to plot. If he could only enrage Agamemnon, provoke him to violence—Helen would have much less to fear, if the king of Mycenae no longer competed in his brother's place.

"Whether we win or lose, it will make no difference. Thessaly will not bend its knee to any Peloponnesian king."

"Brave talk for a prince who has lived beneath the protection of Athens his whole life," Agamemnon sneered. "You Lapiths have lost your ally along with your king, though you're not clever enough to realize the significance. Pirithous had few friends, Polypoetes. And fewer still after he took your mother to wife, tainting his line with centaur savagery."

Polypoetes's eyes narrowed at the insult, his hands balling into fists. That Agamemnon spoke of his mother so coarsely, dared to speak of her at all, made him want to spit in his face. But more than that, it told him all that he needed to know about how Mycenae's king would treat Helen. These Peloponnesian fools could not stand to think any woman might be their equal, her companionship the greatest source of their strength.

"You would only give him what he wants," Leonteus said in a low voice, grasping Polypoetes's arm to hold him back. "He cannot defeat us with his wealth, but if you violate the sacred laws, attack one of Tyndareus's guests . . ."

Polypoetes growled, jerking free of his companion, all the more irritated that Agamemnon had managed to provoke him, instead. "When Helen is mine and you are sworn to protect us both, I will make you eat your words, Agamemnon."

"You had better hope that is how this ends," Agamemnon agreed. "Because winning Helen will be the only thing that will save your people from my sword when all this is behind us. They say the Lapiths are rich with more than horses and King Pirithous kept a hoard of gold and bronze beneath his palace, ripe for the plucking now that he's gone."

"Come and try," Polypoetes said, baring his teeth. "And we Lapiths will ride your army down, trampling your men into the dust. We will feed your flesh to our horses and grow all the stronger for it."

"I would expect nothing less from centaur filth," he said mildly, turning away.

"Even centaurs would not eat their own kin," Polypoetes spat to his back. "Say what you will about my mother, but there is no curse upon my head because of her blood."

Agamemnon stiffened, his hand falling to the hilt of the knife on his hip. Polypoetes held his breath, and it seemed as if the whole room had gone silent but for the crackling of the hearth fire. He kept his hand from his blade, for if blood were to be spilled in this hall, it would not be done by his hand. Let Agamemnon cut him, let Agamemnon alone suffer the consequence of his rage.

Agamemnon's hand flexed around the hilt, and then slowly, deliberately, he released the knife.

"Patroclus!" the king of Mycenae called, careless now, as if Polypoetes were no threat to him at all. "A word with you, if you've a moment to spare."

The moment passed; Polypoetes had failed.

"That was a fool's game, my prince," Leonteus murmured. "I would not risk it again, were I you."

He let out a breath. "I had to try."

"Is she truly worth so much? Even as beautiful as she is—it might have been your life you traded in that moment."

"It isn't only for her that I would have traded it, my friend. But if it had been . . ." He glanced up at the dais, where Helen sat in deep conversation with the suitor at her side, seemingly oblivious to what had passed among the men below. "I do not think my mother would disapprove."

Leonteus snorted. "I think she would like it better if she did not greet your shade in the Underworld so soon. Have a care, Polypoetes. Remember that the Lapiths have need of you still."

It was a kind rebuke, but a rebuke all the same. And he nodded, accepting it.

"We'll find another way," Leonteus said, clapping him upon the shoulder. "Only try not to get yourself killed before we do."

CHAPTER TWENTY-NINE
HELEN

Antilochus was pleasant company even after my father's announcement, no doubt believing himself made all the safer by a drawing than he would have been otherwise. Certainly his prospects had not improved, for his familiarity with our people and our customs had set him apart from the start. Pollux and Castor would not have overlooked the time he had spent in Sparta in his youth, and even Tyndareus could not have argued against his suit—not without arguing against Menelaus, too.

All the same, I had hoped for a better outcome. For days I had prayed that Odysseus would manage some twist to his game that would allow Theseus to reclaim me. But I ought to have realized Tyndareus would not be persuaded, not once he had made up his mind. It had been the same before, with the celebration of my birth, when he had thought inviting all those men from the far corners of the earth would lure out my stranger before his fated time.

Of course it hadn't worked, and now I knew better why. Paris, the boy whose life I had spared, would never have had the means to come. In truth, I did not truly understand how he would have the means to find me now. How did the son of a shepherd become a prince?

"I would not have expected Agamemnon to be in such good spirits," Antilochus said, startling me from my thoughts. "Not once in all the time I've been here have I seen him make such an effort with the other men. But look at him with Patroclus now."

Seeing Agamemnon in happy conference with any of the men below the dais made me uneasy, but the way Patroclus's gaze slid to me, almost longingly, was all the more discomfiting. "He's plotting something. It's the only explanation. And poor Patroclus looks as though he's been caught in a spider's web."

"Shall we save him?" Antilochus asked.

I pressed my lips together, considering, but shook my head. "Even for poor Patroclus, I would not set myself in Agamemnon's path."

Antilochus laughed. "Then I suppose it is fortunate that you have a champion. Unless he's offended you in some way, and you'd prefer to watch him squirm?"

Champion. I'd had one once, that was true. But Antilochus made a poor substitute for Theseus. There was not a man among my suitors who could have matched the man I had lost.

"Save him if you dare," I said. "But do not blame me for any ill will you earn from Agamemnon. Patroclus may be young and cornered, but I do not think he is incapable of extracting himself, should he desire to do so."

"It's true," he said. "And I haven't any real need to impress you, now that I depend upon the blessing of the gods alone with this drawing. But one might suppose that if you chose to pray to Zeus with a certain man in mind, your divine father might listen . . ."

I snorted, not caring how undignified it sounded. "You would be mistaken, I promise you. If Zeus had any regard for my preferences, I would not today be in want of a husband."

"That settles it, then," Antilochus said, helping himself to several honeyed figs. "Patroclus hasn't done anything to offend me personally, but it's entertaining to watch, all the same. And I'm in need of some amusement now that you've decided to spend the meal in such a dour temper."

"I'm hardly dour," I said, flicking a crumb at him. But it was not without effort. I could not believe wholly that Agamemnon would not find a way around whatever trick Odysseus meant to use to keep Menelaus's name from the drawing. Not when he smiled and drank as he left Patroclus to join his cousin Idomeneus instead.

"Perhaps you'd like more wine?" Antilochus offered. "To drown your sorrows before you frighten off your suitors with your scowling."

I sighed and accepted, raising my cup in his honor once it was filled again. "May the gods smile upon you tomorrow, Antilochus. Or if not you, another just as worthy."

"How kind," he said wryly, but he smiled again. "And may the gods grant you the freedom you so crave, whoever you must marry."

It was a pleasant thought.

And a great shame it was altogether impossible.

"Come along, Helen," Pollux said, scooping me into his arms. I was half-asleep from the wine Antilochus had kept pouring into my cup. Enough that I had passed giddy and slipped into exhaustion before I'd realized what had happened. One thing was certain: if I found myself married to Antilochus, my days would not be dull.

"No, they would not be that," my brother agreed, carrying me from the megaron. I hadn't meant to speak aloud. "But I am not certain he would please you, in the end. Even if he didn't neglect your bed entirely, he hasn't the temperament required for a king, too inclined to laugh away his councilors' concerns."

Castor walked ahead, clearing the way. He clapped Polypoetes upon the back and nodded to Ajax the Great, who roared for the rest of the men to stand back.

"One of them will be my husband," I said, resting my head upon Pollux's shoulder.

"Yes," he said.

"I only ever wanted to save my people, Pollux, to spare them. But tomorrow, one of them will be named my husband, and I fear I will drive him mad."

My brother grunted. "Hush now, Helen. We'll have you in your bed before long, safe and sound."

"Sleep is never safe," I murmured. "Not so long as there are dreams."

"All the same," he said. "Just rest now. You'll have need of it come morning."

I would have argued, but my tongue felt too thick, my words too slow. After Pollux laid me down in my bed, Castor smoothed my hair back from my face with a troubled frown. I caught his hand in mine and held tight.

"Keep the dreams away?"

Castor hesitated, his gaze shifting to Pollux, and then to the pallet where Clymene stood dithering, waiting for my brothers to leave before she saw to my needs. I had only one. A night of sleep, undisturbed. A night of sleep without seeing Theseus, whom I would lose forever the following day. All the careful hopes for his return that I had nurtured these last weeks had sharpened into blades, and I was not certain how much longer I could dance upon their edges without cutting myself into pieces.

"Please, Castor."

"It would not hurt to give her a guard. Not with the way Agamemnon was carrying on, and we all know there are others, just as unscrupulous, who might see tonight as their final opportunity to steal her away," Pollux said. "But if you mistrust yourself, I would stay in your place."

Castor shook his head. "It is the rumors that concern me, nothing more."

"Let them believe what they will," Pollux said. "So long as Clymene remains as her companion, what's left of Helen's honor is preserved. And by tomorrow evening it will not matter, either way."

Because tomorrow, my new husband would be named. If the priests thought the day auspicious, I might even be wed before night fell again.

And Theseus had not found me. Theseus had not come. Once the name was drawn, it would not matter anymore. The web had been woven, and I was cocooned at its heart.

"Please," I said again, tears pressing behind my eyes. "Just for one night, give me peace."

Castor sighed. "Make room, then, Little Sister, and I will do what I can."

It was the first full night of sleep I'd had in weeks.

And likely the last I'd have for years.

CHAPTER THIRTY
HELEN

"You look beautiful, my lady," Clymene said after I was bathed and dressed and she had finished with my hair.

Two oiled locks framed my face, a portion of the rest was gathered tightly atop my head, and what was left hung loose down my back. Nestra's hair was almost twice the length of mine, falling all the way to her hips, but Leda had been forced to cut mine before I had fled with Theseus, after I had ruined it with walnut dye, and I had never bothered to let it grow back. How foolish I had been then, to believe even for a moment that my beauty resided only in my hair. Or perhaps I had only been desperate to think I might have some power over that part of me, blessing or curse, which would bring ruin down upon our heads.

Zeus had since made it more than clear to me that I had none. My determination to prevent what was coming had only woven my fate more securely into the loom. But how could I stop fighting? How could I give in to all the destruction that awaited my people?

I wouldn't. I couldn't. Not so long as there was the smallest thread of hope to be teased and tugged upon, that it all might unravel yet.

I stared at the circlet in my hands, brushed my fingers over the polished emerald that I had worn upon my head as queen of Athens. It was only that I had wanted so much for Theseus to be part of that thread. Now he had been ripped from the loom altogether, taking a small piece of my spirit with him, and the knots tightened all the more as I scrambled to find another way to untangle the mess.

And so long as the name I chose today was not Menelaus's, there was hope. Whichever man I married, I would have time before he was made king. Perhaps my beauty might be of some small use then, in persuading him of my value as more than just a prize. If even just one of Sparta's friends and allies were willing to treat with me, to ask for my counsel and my presence when decisions were made, it would give me the foothold I needed to ensure my people were protected. That was all that mattered, all that I could ever have truly hoped for in a marriage.

"Beautiful, but unhappy," Clymene amended, her forehead creased with concern. "Is there anything I might do to help?"

I shook my head, forcing a smile to my lips for her sake. "Once, long ago, I believed I might be so fortunate as to love the man the gods would name my husband. I suppose I'm simply realizing, after all this time, that it was a child's dream, and one I ought to have given up years and years ago as foolishness."

"You might yet love him, my lady," Clymene said. "And he will certainly love you."

It was kind of her to say, and perhaps, to her, it seemed as though it might be true. But I knew what these men loved, what they desired. It was not my companionship so much as my body, though I could not deny I might yet be surprised. But I knew with certainty I could not love them. Not now. Not so long as Theseus might live.

Perhaps not even after he was gone.

The morning meal was quiet, the megaron half-empty. Most of the men, it seemed, had decided to offer sacrifice to Zeus. In a way, it was a relief, for it meant I need not worry they would do something foolish in the hopes of impressing me. Let them brawl before the gods, if they desired it, and leave me in peace.

"What's the matter, Helen?" Penelope asked, sitting beside me at the table. "I thought you didn't care in the least which of the men won you, so long as it wasn't Menelaus."

"It makes no difference now, either way," I said, picking apart a pomegranate.

"So you did have a favorite, after all." She stole one of the ruby seeds from my plate, no doubt hoping to irritate me.

"Of course she had a favorite," Nestra said, settling on my other side. "Helen always has favorites. But only so long as they snub her. Once she's won their hearts, she wants nothing more to do with the poor men."

I said nothing, popping six of the seeds between my lips and sucking the tart flesh from the pits. No good could come of any comment I might make in response.

"Then it must have been Menestheus," Penelope said. "Didn't you hear the way they fought? I thought Castor was going to break him in two for the insults he gave."

"Poor Castor." Nestra sighed. "Agamemnon's offered him a place in Mycenae, but he's refused to leave your side. He says he's promised to guard you, not that you'll have any need of him once you're married."

"Guard." Penelope scoffed at the word. "Is that what he calls it? Spending the night in your room that way?"

The pomegranate rind exploded between my fingers, and the jeweled seeds sprayed out in every direction, rolling off the table and onto the floor. I wanted to curse, but if I opened my mouth, I would regret it. Of that, I was certain.

Nestra's eyes widened. "What?"

"I saw him slip out this morning, rumpled still. It was obvious he'd slept there. What else they did together, I can only guess."

"Not another word, Penelope," Nestra snapped, grabbing me by the arm. Her nails dug into my skin so sharply I feared she'd draw blood. "What did you do?"

I tore my arm free of Nestra's grasp and glared. "The last night before the men were all sworn to protect the man who was named my husband, did you really think Castor and Pollux would leave me unguarded? They feared I'd be stolen from my bed! Honestly, Nestra, how could you think so poorly of Castor, even for a moment?"

Her hands balled into fists. "Why shouldn't I believe you capable of bewitching him along with all the others? The gods know you spend enough time with both our brothers, locked away in the women's quarters where they have no business being at all. Who knows what you've done to them."

"I've done nothing," I said, struggling to keep the anger from my voice. "I would never hurt Castor and Pollux, or any other man, though I hardly expect you to believe it. We don't all take pleasure from the pain of others, no matter what Leda might have raised us to think."

"Always the innocent," my sister said. "I suppose it's the only way you can sleep at night, hmm?"

"If telling myself lies helped me to sleep at night, I would be far better rested," I said. "But if you think I have even a moment's peace, day or night, you are wrong. I want none of this, Nestra. As I've told you again and again."

"If you hate your beauty so much, why not be rid of it altogether?" Penelope said. "Scar your face, mark your body, and ruin yourself."

My fingers stilled, the pomegranate in my hands forgotten. How had I never considered it before now? Tattoos and scars would not be undone the way dye could be. Perhaps I had some power still, however small the opportunity. But did I dare to frighten off my suitors now? Risk losing all but Menelaus?

"Forgive me," I murmured, rising from my seat. Theseus would never have been offended by scars or tattoos—he'd married an Amazon, after all—and I wondered now who else might overlook them. Menestheus might have been the most obvious answer, for he must have known Antiope when she lived as Theseus's queen, but Polypoetes had mentioned his mother was related somehow to the centaurs, and if that was so, she might have had strange ideas of beauty as well. Menestheus's name would be withdrawn regardless, if I trusted Odysseus and my brothers, and Menelaus's, too, somehow, if Agamemnon did not withdraw his brother willingly, out of disgust. I had only to ensure that Polypoetes would not abandon me.

"You're not truly considering it?" Penelope said, catching me by the arm before I left the dais. My expression must have given her all the answer she needed, for she sucked in a breath, her face white. "Helen, it is madness!"

"Is it madness to wish to stop a war? To free the men and women around me from death and sorrow?" I shook my head. "Scorn me if you like, but if I did nothing, I could not live with myself."

Penelope pressed her lips together, searching my face. "You would truly give up your beauty, scar your face, your body, to end these dreams? To protect your people?"

"I would give up my life if I believed it would not bring about a war still, among men who felt themselves cheated."

"Do you not believe they will think themselves cheated if you pursue this scheme?" she asked. "If you mistrust my counsel, I cannot blame you. But speak to King Odysseus, to your brothers, they will say the same!"

I stared at her, confused by her pleas. "I would have thought you'd be pleased to see me scarred, my beauty forsaken."

She flushed. "We are all blind fools when we believe ourselves threatened. But I know what Odysseus bargained for, what he was promised for his aid."

"And yet."

Penelope dropped her gaze. Even knowing, she had been happy enough to spite me. But perhaps she had not fully realized how far I was willing to go—how desperate I was. Nestra would have made it difficult, I supposed, for her to see the truth, and Penelope had certainly never given me much in the way of opportunity to explain myself. Not before she had made up her mind already.

"I have no desire to lose my husband to a war fought over something so foolish as a pretty girl," she said at last. "And my lord Odysseus is as knotted up in this as all the rest of the men. If you mean to protect him, I will not stand in your way."

It was as near to an apology as I imagined I would ever receive. "If there is any way I might spare him, I will see it is done, I promise you."

She nodded and let me go.

And I? I went in search of a blade.

Even if I was not yet certain how, or if, I meant to use it.

CHAPTER
THIRTY-ONE
PATROCLUS

P atroclus leaned against the crenellation of the palace wall, looking out over the city of Sparta. Beautiful and serene, nestled
safely between the mountains, Sparta was wealthy enough
in land and livestock that he need never rely upon the hospitality of
another man again. Better, he could repay Peleus's kindnesses with
friendship, one king to another, should he be so lucky as to win Helen
as his wife.

He ran his thumb over the shard of pottery in his hand, blank still,
for he had not yet made up his mind which name he would scratch
upon its dull red surface, Menelaus's or his own.

"Think, boy," Agamemnon had said, his voice low. "Tyndareus
allows each man to put forth one name, but he did not say it must be
his own. If you do as I ask, nothing will be left to chance. You'll have
secured the solemn and binding friendship of Mycenae for your king

and kinsman, and wealth enough that you need not live by his favor alone. But stand against me, and whether you win Helen or not, Peleus will suffer for it, I promise you."

The king of Mycenae was powerful, to be sure, and Patroclus had no interest in making him an enemy, but Agamemnon was more than insufferable. He was vicious in the games, never satisfied by merely beating a man. More than one of Helen's suitors had left the wrestling match with shoulders twisted out of joint, and Agamemnon had broken at least three noses and four sets of ribs during the boxing, then gloated over the men he had laid low. When Polypoetes had defeated Agamemnon by half a length in the chariot racing, Patroclus had wanted to cheer.

But he had known all along that he must be careful. He did not dare to show his disgust, or even a hint of his dislike. Peleus would not be pleased if he brought home a war with Mycenae instead of a bride, and he owed his kinsman far too much to betray his generosity with carelessness. Up until Tyndareus's announcement, he'd even been tempted to withdraw altogether from his pursuit of Helen, rather than borrow the greater trouble of winning her. Between Polypoetes and Agamemnon, he wouldn't have survived a fortnight as her husband, besides.

Now everything was changed. No man in the megaron was given more consideration than any other with this drawing. And better, if his name was drawn, not one of the suitors assembled could strike at him. Even he, with so little to offer, might yet have opportunity to call Helen his wife. He'd had hope for a bright, shining moment, before Agamemnon had turned it all to ash again with his scheming. For perhaps he might be safe with his bride in Sparta, but if it meant Mycenae turned upon Phthia like a fell wolf, if it meant he had betrayed his kinsman and his king . . .

He closed the shard in his fist, letting the sharp edges cut into his palm. He wanted the princess, wanted Sparta, too, but the price was high. And had she not said herself she desired a man not lost to reason in pursuit of her? He'd had time enough to reflect upon her words since, heard the wry humor as they wound their way through his thoughts: *Surely Sparta deserves a king who can keep his wits about him.*

He might win her, but to do so in this manner would ensure he lost her favor. And then what would he have? A cold bed and a cloak of guilt, if not the curse of the gods for his betrayal, after all Peleus had done for him.

And yet. She had said more, too, during their brief encounter. Spoken of powerful men with stained hands, whom she would not have at all as her husband if she could prevent it. She had not named names, of course, for she was too cunning for that. But he knew, all the same. They all knew, by now, who the princess did *not* favor.

Prince Ajax of Locris, from the way she stiffened when he neared, wary as a rabbit in the field. The newly made King Menestheus of Athens, by the daggers in her gaze when she looked upon him and the curl of her lip when he spoke whispered words against her ear. And Prince Menelaus of Mycenae, whose brother she avoided at all costs, even the barest mention of his name draining the warmth from her cheeks.

So he stood upon the wall, staring out over the land he had dreamed of claiming as his own, his fist clenched tight around a blank shard of pottery, while he wondered whom he would betray: the woman he had come to win, or the kinsman who had sent him to her side.

No matter what choice he made, he suspected it would not end well.

CHAPTER THIRTY-TWO
HELEN

I ought to have realized it would not work. I should have known, when I saw the marks of my pregnancy fade into smooth, untouched skin, that it would not be so simple, so easy. I should have realized, but it was not until I held my hand over the hearth flames in my room and felt only the tickle of the fire, the gentle play of its heat against my skin like a lover's caress, that I knew. The gods had given me some small gift of my own, beyond this beauty, another that I could not control, for it was meant to preserve me as their tool, their toy.

"Gods above, Helen!" Pollux said, snatching me back from the hearth. "What in the name of Zeus do you think you're doing?"

He pried the knife in my other hand from my fingers and threw it across the room before I realized his intent, then held me by the shoulders, searching my face, my body, his eyes wild with fear and worry.

I dropped my gaze, my face flushed with sudden shame for my own foolishness, and Pollux shook me.

"Tell me you did not mean to take your life, at least!"

I shook my head, a noise escaping my lips that was almost a laugh. Almost, but for the hard, bitter edge of the sound, like shards of pottery in my throat. "It would only mean another war, but it does not matter. There's nothing to be done."

His hand found mine, his fingers gentle as he examined the flesh I had failed to burn. Been prevented from burning, because the gods required me whole and beautiful still, to drive all these men into ruin.

"You're fortunate you weren't hurt," he said.

"Fortunate, yes. Of course." And I felt that noise again, rough and harsh and scraping its way out, then the press of tears behind my eyes. I blinked them back. "Today I must stand beside Tyndareus and choose a husband, and they will all be watching me, devouring me with their eyes. Because I am too *pretty* and there is not a one among them who is worthy enough to turn away. But I am fortunate I cannot do myself any lasting damage. That all of Troy will burn, but not me. I'll emerge from the flames as beautiful as ever."

Pollux's gaze softened, his fingers lacing through mine. "Troy?"

I closed my eyes, turned my face away. I had never meant for him to know. All the better to keep the truth from Menelaus, that I might have some power over my life if all this ended poorly.

"Helen, look at me." He caught my chin between his finger and his thumb, turning my face back to his. "Menelaus will not win you. The strange prince of your dreams will not steal you. The war will not come, and Troy will not burn. Odysseus will see to it. And should he fail by some cruel trick of the gods, or should you marry elsewhere and this prince still come, Castor and I will remain at your side."

"I do not know how you can be certain," I said. "Not after making it so clear to me that what little certainty I had was a lie." That small peace I had found with Theseus in Athens—I would never know if it were true, if for those brief years I had changed my fate, or if he had only soothed away my nightmares with some power of his own. I would never know, because Theseus had not come, and now I must marry another.

"Your certainty depended upon fickle dreams; mine is drawn from Odysseus's particular skills."

I pulled away, turning my back to him and hugging myself. "His particular skills include deceit, Pollux. He could have played us false from the start."

"And if you believed he was capable of it, truly, you would have told him nothing. Odysseus may not be entirely honorable, but he is honest in his goals. Betraying us to Agamemnon would not give him the peace he so desires for his people. And he is not so different from you, Helen, in that respect. Perhaps that's why you've trusted him, until now."

"I trusted him because he did not want me for his wife," I said. "I begin to wonder if I ought to have seduced him, instead."

"Penelope would have murdered you in your bed."

I flexed my hand, but the skin was not even the slightest bit tight. If she had tried, would she have succeeded? I could not help but wonder how far this seeming protection extended. Not so far that I could not be violated, bruised, beaten, if it served their purposes, but far enough to keep me alive and relatively unscathed, come what may? Until the gods were through with me.

And perhaps that was why I mistrusted Odysseus's plans, why I could not place my faith in my brothers to protect me. As much as I wanted to believe I could thwart the gods, reweave my fate, it felt more and more like a child's foolish, powerless protest when she cannot have her way.

Maybe that was all I was, too. A child, dreaming still that I had some control over my fate.

After the midday meal, dressed in my richest gown, I stood before the hearth in the megaron, beneath the streaming sunlight from the light well above. Tyndareus had sacrificed his finest horse—barring the matched pair Polypoetes had gifted me—to sanctify the oaths my suitors made now.

The golden bowl in my hands was heavy, and my arms began to tremble as each of my suitors dropped his token inside, repeating Odysseus's oath and sealing it further with a drop of his own blood, collected in a shallow phiale on the table at my side. I was glad I had not given in to the temptation to don the garb of a priestess in the Cretan style, with my breasts bare. As it was, the eyes of my suitors lingered, and I did not want to consider their thoughts.

Ajax the Great stepped aside, and Polypoetes stood before me, his gaze searching mine. "I do not forget the promises I made to you, Princess. Should you draw my name, I will keep my word, regardless of Odysseus's oath."

His promises. I swallowed hard against the longing for such a simple end. Polypoetes, taking me as his wife in name only, keeping me safe until Theseus could claim me. But it would never be so simple as that now. I could not hope for Theseus any longer.

Polypoetes dropped his token into the bowl, then dragged his dagger across the calloused flesh of his palm, bleeding for the phiale as he swore his vow. His eyes held mine, still promising more.

If I had not married Theseus, had not come to realize what the gods truly used me for, I might have hoped for Polypoetes to be named my husband. Perhaps some small, selfish part of me still did, even knowing what ruin I might bring him.

He stepped back then, and I watched him go, aching. Before Theseus, I might have loved him. Even now, I might have lived happily as his wife.

I forced my gaze to the next man, pushing the thought from my mind. It did me no good to dwell upon what might have been, what could be. Polypoetes was one of two dozen names, and I knew better than most how easily even the smallest hope could be stolen.

The next man was his friend Leonteus, another Lapith warrior. He winked at me, setting his token into the bowl with exaggerated care. I glanced at it, unsure of what he meant by his display, and my breath hitched at the name scratched on the shard. *Polypoetes.*

I did not hear his vow through the roaring in my ears, but I saw his grin, all mischief and self-satisfaction for his trick.

And Polypoetes was two of two dozen names, just like that.

That small, desperate flame of hope, so carefully banked, licked one breath higher in my heart, and I said a silent prayer, begging Athena not to let it burn me from the inside out.

Even if you have no love for me, I said to the goddess, *guard me from this fate, from the path that leads to war and death and ruin, for Theseus's sake.*

But Theseus had been right, so long ago, when we had walked in the courtyard and he had warned me of the troubles we might face after he stole me away. Knowing the gods heard me did not change things for the better.

Likely, it would not change things at all.

Castor and Pollux escorted me to the shrine after all the names had been collected and all the oaths had been made. We followed Tyndareus and the white bull he had chosen up the sloping hill, Odysseus beside him. I watched Tyndareus, frowning at his stiff steps and his hunched back. My father had been tall and strong once, if never particularly broad. Straight and lean, all wiry muscle, and too proud to stoop. Now, walking with Odysseus, he was nearly wheezing.

"He is not well," I murmured to Castor. "How is it possible that I did not realize how ill he had become?"

"He was not so ill before. Just a winter cough, nothing more," my brother said, and I was grateful my suitors did not follow upon our heels, but waited with Leda in the megaron, plied with wine and prayers. She must have known, kept his secret all this time. "I expect it is the weight of all this, pretending his strength in front of so many men. If they knew . . ."

He did not need to say more. If my suitors had realized how ill Tyndareus truly was, we'd have had a war, not these games, and I would have been the spoils. He needed me married, and a strong heir in place, for Sparta's sake. The sooner the better. But it also meant I would have less time to win my husband's respect before he was made king, whoever he might be. My thoughts shied from Polypoetes and his promises—I could not hope for it. Would not.

"At least the gods have spared us that," I said, and Castor grunted his agreement. "But I still wish he had named Pollux his heir and given me up altogether."

Pollux barked a laugh. "And I thank the gods daily that I need not live my life with a circlet weighing upon my brow. I love Sparta, and I am happy to serve our people as their prince, but just the thought of spending my days listening to petitions and complaints . . ." He shuddered. "I haven't the patience to sit for it."

"Or the wisdom," Castor said, then ducked Pollux's swing.

I caught his arm before it turned into a good-natured brawl. They were in such good spirits, even with the evidence of Tyndareus's illness, the sacrifice looming, and my husband about to be named.

My stomach roiled and my heart drummed too loudly in my ears, their confidence making me all the more uneasy. I had been confident once, too, so sure I had escaped my fate, only to find myself here, facing the same threats still. If I had not seen the fury in Poseidon's eyes when I had crossed him, I would have thought the gods laughed at my misfortunes.

To think I had believed once that the gods took no interest in me at all.

"All will be well, Helen," Castor said, as if he read my mind. "You do not face your future without friends."

Tyndareus and Odysseus had entered the shrine, disappearing behind the trees and shrubs planted on either side of the stone entrance. Behind us, the sound of men's voices rose on the wind, and I glanced back, my steps slowing as I watched my suitors begin their climb. Menestheus and Agamemnon walked together, and I shivered at the sight. Agamemnon had been far too pleased with himself when he dropped Menelaus's name into the bowl, and Menestheus's smile had been too full of malice for my comfort.

"I do not face my future without enemies, either."

"And that is why the gods gave you brothers," Pollux said with a smile.

I could not bring myself to return it. For the gods had given me my brothers, that was true, but the gods might yet take them from me, too.

CHAPTER
THIRTY-THREE
HELEN

The priest scattered barley, and once more, Tyndareus's hand covered mine upon the knife as we sliced the bull's throat. Hot blood washed over my fingers, my toes, and then the priest pressed a silver bowl to the bull's neck, catching the spray. I stepped back, watching the bull sink slowly to his knees and then fall sideways without so much as a moan. Consenting to his sacrifice.

Odysseus stood beside the altar, and when I lifted my eyes from the victim, he gave me the barest of nods, a flash of his hand showing the shards of pottery with the names of Menelaus and Menestheus. The priest cut the tail from the bull and dunked the tip into the blood, sprinkling it over the golden bowl filled with the names of my suitors, while he murmured prayers to Zeus. And then again, this time mixing the bull's blood with the drops of the men's collected in the phiale.

Pollux picked up the golden bowl, raising it high before the face of Zeus in the rock, and Castor tied a swath of rolled linen over my eyes. A shudder rippled down my spine as the world went black, and I struggled to breathe, still haunted by the memories of so many days spent in the dark before we fled for Athens, folded into a too-small basket in the hold of Theseus's ship, waiting for him to arrive.

Castor's hand brushed my cheek, then pressed warm against my shoulder, and a flood of calm washed through me. The pressure around my heart eased, and I gulped a breath of clean air, untainted by the sea and my sweat. It tasted of bronze, instead, the scent of blood thick in my nose. I stretched out my hand, conscious now of the soft mumbling of my suitors saying their last prayers, the shuffling of their feet and the rustle of their clothes. My fingers touched the rim of the bowl, cool and smooth, and then I reached inside, letting the sharp edges of the shards scrape against my skin as I dug through, feeling their shapes, hoping for some small mark to help me choose.

But there was nothing but the smooth baked clay, the scraped symbols of their names impossible to discern. I picked one and withdrew my hand, a fist of fear and longing. *Let it be Polypoetes. Let it be Pirithous's son.*

I forced my fingers to uncurl, and the priest plucked the shard from my open palm.

"Zeus, our lord and father, has chosen a husband for his daughter," he announced. "I remind you now of your vows, the oaths you have all sworn to guard Helen, to protect the rights of the man who calls her his wife."

Polypoetes, Polypoetes, Polypoetes. Please, gods, please.

My brother untied the blindfold, and I let my fingers twist into knots, my palms sweating and my heart racing hard. My gaze found the shard in the priest's hand, and I wanted to steal it from him, to swipe it from his fingers and read the name myself. He nodded to me, a tight smile upon his lips, as if he read my impatience, my dread.

"Who will have this honor?" Tyndareus asked, his voice ringing firm and clear.

The priest raised the shard high for all to see. "Zeus has chosen Menelaus Atrides, prince of Mycenae."

I fell to my knees and retched.

PART THREE:
QUEEN OF SPARTA

CHAPTER THIRTY-FOUR
PARIS

D o not go today," Oenone said one morning, nearly a full year since Corythus's birth. She nestled closer to Paris beneath the furs, caressing with sure hands where she knew it would do the most good. "Stay home with me, with your son, and let another guard your father's flocks."

He laughed, drawing her closer still and nuzzling her throat. His Oenone, always eager for his love, and so determined to keep him sated and satisfied in their bed. "You know I can't. There is no one else but us, and we haven't any feed to tide them over until tomorrow. They must be grazed."

He had been so content this last year, so happy, and he had been thinking more and more of what his father had said, so many months past. Why should he not make Oenone his wife? Settle with her upon the mountain and enjoy this quiet life with a good woman and whatever children the gods might grant them.

"Please, Paris," she said, clinging to him when he pulled away. "It will not hurt them to go hungry for just one day."

He frowned, studying her face, the fever-brightness of her eyes and the lines of pain, poorly hidden. There was desperation behind her words, though he could not begin to imagine why. "Every day I graze the animals, Oenone, and never before have you begged me to stay. What frightens you so?"

But she hid her face against his neck, tightening her hold. "Is it not enough that I have never asked it of you before? You must realize I would not do so without reason."

"Then tell me your reason, that I might decide for myself what is best."

She moaned. "Would you abandon me now? Abandon your son?"

"Oenone." He lifted her face that she might see his. "You have given me such a gift of joy. Why would you believe for a moment I could leave you?"

"You won't return," she said, just as she'd said it once before, after Tauros had won another fight and he'd spoken of taking him to the festival at Troy. "You'll leave us, and you'll never return. Not truly. Not as you are now."

"That's hardly an explanation, my love. What will you have me tell my father when he finds his flock half-starved?"

She shook her head, tears in her eyes. "Please, Paris. Your father would understand, I'm certain of it. He would not want you to leave if he only knew. In Lord Apollo's name, I beg of you, stay."

He searched her face, brushing the tears away. Oenone did not invoke the gods lightly, that much he knew, but the last time she had spoken this way, she had brought Ares down from Olympus, and he had no interest in facing a god again so soon.

"I can stay through the morning," he said. "Will that do?"

Her gaze lost focus and she stared at him, unseeing. "Through the midday meal?"

"If it will please you, yes, but I cannot remain any longer, Oenone, truly."

She sighed, coming back to him at last, still far too grim. "Then we must make the most of what we have."

She nearly convinced him to stay the afternoon as well, after she'd seen him fed and dragged him back to their bed for another round of shared pleasures. But Corythus began to cry, no doubt feeling neglected, and while Oenone soothed him, Paris dressed.

"I'll return before dark," he promised her, and dropped kisses atop both their heads. Oenone did not argue, at least, though she watched him go with such sorrow he nearly turned back again.

His strange nymph—if she could only explain. But when she suffered these moods, she rarely knew what it meant. Perhaps she glimpsed a bird flying west instead of east, or the clouds passed over the sun, just so, and dread would grasp tight hold of her heart, impossible to ignore. He humored her when he was able, of course, or she grew all the more stricken, and before long Corythus would be in tears as well, catching his mother's ill feelings. But Paris could not ignore the needs of his father's flocks for much beyond a morning, even for Oenone's sake.

He clucked at the goats, nudged the sheep along with his crook, and followed the eager flock up the stony track to the field where they grazed, his thoughts still with Oenone and Corythus. Perhaps he should have insisted they join him. Surely an afternoon of herding would not harm his son, and Oenone would find no peace at all while he was gone from her sight. He hesitated at the top of the rise, looking back, but the thought of a day spent listening to such gloom chased the intention away, and if he did not follow close upon their heels, he would lose his father's goats, besides.

So instead, Paris climbed. A call here, a prod there, keeping the animals together and a wary eye for wolves and lions. Raiders came now and again, though this part of the coast was sheltered behind the isle of Lesbos, and more often the Achaeans aimed their ships north to Troy's richer lands and wealth. But that did not mean the flocks were not threatened by common thieves, and upon the rocky mountain, an unwary goat might be taken by a tumble into a crevasse or lost if it went running too deep into a cave.

Before Corythus, Paris had lost more than his fair share one way or another, but without the distraction of Oenone at his side, it was easier to give the animals the attention they deserved—at least it would have been, had Oenone not done her best to exhaust him all morning, no doubt hoping he would fall asleep and forget his duties a little longer.

Paris found a likely rock on a rise and settled upon it, his staff across his knees. The day was quiet, the sun warm on his skin, begging him to close his eyes and bask in its comfort. So long as he remained upright, he told himself, he would not sleep, and surely not even the goats could find trouble while he shut his eyes against the glare. He'd taken his gaze off them for far longer with Oenone, making love to her in the grass. Corythus had likely been born from one such moment, and no real harm had ever come of it. He'd simply tune his ears to any sound of danger, and rest.

The bleat of a goat woke him from a deep sleep, and thank the gods the sun had not fallen far. Paris rose at once, searching for the source of the sound. The billy bleated again, then charged off behind a tumble of protruding rock, disappearing from sight. Paris cursed, chasing after him, glancing once over his shoulder to be certain the rest of the animals were safe enough. Likely it was a snake or vermin of some kind, startling the fool goat, but his father would never forgive him if he lost the pride of the herd, and it would be too easy for the animal to break a leg or take a tumble, racing off that way.

Paris rounded the rocks and skidded to an abrupt stop, nearly overbalancing in his haste, and half stumbling over the billy, who was preening before a trio of women, all crouched and fussing over the goat. Women so beautiful he had to look away, feeling as though he had been blinded by a flash of the too-bright sun in his eyes.

"Paris Alexandros."

Paris spun, finding a man sitting lazily atop the rock outcropping. He wore winged sandals made of shining gold upon his dangling feet and held a short staff with two serpents twisting and writhing around its upper half.

Paris dropped to his knees, bowing his head before his patron— Hermes, god of shepherds and messenger of the gods. "My lord Hermes, I beg your forgiveness."

The god laughed, vaulting down from his perch to land lightly on the rocky ground with a flutter of his sandals. "Have you given some offense I am not aware of, Paris?"

"I did not see you at once, to grant you all proper honor," he said, his gaze lowered.

"And why should you see a god of thieves if he does not wish to be seen?" Hermes asked, clapping him upon the shoulder with a warm hand. "Rise, Paris Alexandros. For it is we who come to beg your favor today, not the other way around, and you cannot judge the beauty of our fair goddesses with your face in the dirt."

Hermes hauled him up, not giving him the chance to protest, and Paris found himself facing the trio of women—goddesses!—again, all three smiling now and studying him as they had his goat just a moment before.

"He is handsome, isn't he?" The auburn-haired beauty placed a hand upon his chest, turning the innocent contact into a lingering caress as she circled him. Myrtle flowers floated in her hair, and the scent of the sea filled his head. "But he is so young to have such judgment, no matter what Ares has said."

Paris swallowed hard, Oenone's warnings echoing in his ears. *You won't return.* It was not difficult to believe, while he stood before them. He had been fortunate enough with Ares, so long ago, but he could not count upon a blessing now, not with so many to please.

"Forgive me, ladies, my lord Hermes, but I do not understand what business brings you here to me."

"That is the message I bring, of course," Hermes said, "though I am forbidden to influence your choice. An unfortunate apple made its way to Olympus, inscribed 'for the fairest,' and Athena, Hera, and Aphrodite, all three, seek to claim it."

"My lord and husband Zeus, in his wisdom, has made you our judge," the second goddess said, her sun-blond hair falling in rich curls down her back. He could not tear his gaze from her large, dark eyes, rich with promise. Hera, queen of all the gods.

"You must examine us closely, young Paris," the third goddess said, her arm threading through his. Her silver eyes flashed with some hidden emotion as she cast a glance at the other two women. Athena, he knew, from the helm upon her head. "And determine which of us is the most beautiful, for we cannot settle the dispute for ourselves, it seems, and Zeus, wisely, will not choose. You, however, must."

He turned to Hermes, speechless and unsure. To name one goddess fairest would certainly make enemies of the other two. "And you are certain this task should fall to me? I am only a shepherd boy, unworthy even to look upon your feet."

Hermes lifted one brow. "A mere shepherd boy, you say, with a nymph for a bride. Surely you must have wondered how you had earned such a prize?"

"For my courage," he said, though it sounded feeble now. "Just as I earned my name."

"Alexandros," a goddess purred in his ear. And the way her body pressed against his, the delicate flick of her tongue along the shell of his ear, he was certain now that the auburn-haired beauty must be Aphrodite. And then she laughed, her breath tickling his skin. "Defender of men."

"Perhaps you would rather be a *ruler* of men," Hera said, her eyes narrowing. "I could make it so, Paris, should you name me fairest. You could be the greatest king who ever lived."

"Or a *conqueror* of men, if you'd prefer," Athena said, releasing his arm to circle him again, presumably that he might see her more easily. "And a blessing of wisdom beyond anything you could ever dream. You would never lose a war, never be betrayed, and men the world over would come to beg your counsel."

"Or," Aphrodite said, a sly smile curving her lips, "perhaps you'd rather have something . . . warmer."

"Warmer, my lady?" he heard himself ask, lured by the huskiness of her voice. Even Oenone was not so tempting as the goddess before him, and he struggled to keep his desire in check.

She stepped back, a ripple of liquid light shimmering over her skin, turning her hair to so much gold and her eyes to deep green pools. The full curves of her body slimmed by just a breath, her gown falling from her shoulders until she stood naked and transformed.

Paris stared, his heart racing, his whole body flushed. The girl of his youth. The woman he had longed for all these years, dreamed of from afar, made flesh again before his eyes.

"Choose me, and I will give you Helen of Sparta. The most beautiful woman in all the world made yours."

CHAPTER
THIRTY-FIVE
PARIS

He stumbled back, shaking his head. Hermes chuckled, the god's firm hand falling hard upon his shoulder to hold him when he might have preferred to flee. "Steady, young Paris. Do not let your courage fail you now."

These goddesses sought to bribe him, and Paris found himself sorely tested by their gifts, but they had chosen him for his judgment, and if he made his decision this way, based only upon what they offered, he would know he had failed.

Helen of Sparta.

To know her name after so many years dreaming only of her face— did Aphrodite realize how she tempted him? Did she know how many nights he had lain awake, thinking of her soft, chaste kiss?

"What of her hero?" he asked, in spite of himself. "What of the man who guarded her, who sought to keep her hidden? The Athenian."

Aphrodite gave a little flick of her shoulder, her hair darkening once more to auburn and her still-naked body returning to its natural form. Gods above, she was beautiful. Her breasts two ripe apples, a perfect handful each, and the quirk of her lips, full and red, begging to be kissed. But not as beautiful as Helen. And now that he had seen her face again, her body bared, he could not forget, could not force her from his thoughts.

"Theseus," Athena said, her eyes suddenly hard, cutting to Aphrodite as sharply as any blade. "Helen was taken from his care. My sister betrayed him, and though he may yet return from the house of Hades, it will be some time before he recovers his strength, if at all. Beware, young Paris, or you will find your own future turned to ruin at my sister's hand."

He closed his eyes, struggling to keep his thoughts in order. Helen was no longer safe, no longer protected. The man she had loved could no longer care for her, and she was no longer Helen of Athens, as she ought to have been known; she was Helen of Sparta now.

Helen of Sparta, and his if he desired her. Promised by the goddess of love herself. And with such a promise, he need not fear that she would not want him. Surely the goddess would not be so cruel as that—to give him her body, but not her heart?

No.

He lifted his gaze to the goddesses, all three watching him too closely. Did they read his thoughts? He did not know, could not think of that now. He could not think of the prizes they had offered him at all, though it was impossible to give up the vision of Helen completely, and perhaps it was not so wrong to hold her in his thoughts, for with her beauty bright and blinding in his mind, surely he would be more able to judge.

"Choose, Paris," Hermes said. "Zeus, king of gods, lord of Olympus, demands it."

Paris straightened, focusing on Athena, with her words of warning, and Hera beside her, all pride and splendor, queen of all women.

"My ladies, I beg you to forgive my boldness, but having seen the beauty of Aphrodite in all her wondrous glory, if I am to make a choice, I would not leave you at a disadvantage. I must see your beauty, too, in full."

Hera pressed her lips into a thin line and raised her chin. "You would dare look upon the queen of Olympus unclothed?"

"For the sake of fair judgment only, Queen Hera," he said, bowing low.

"Then look, Paris Alexandros, and look long." A rustle of fabric, and her gown landed at his feet, still warm from her skin as it brushed his toes. "But do not think for a moment my nakedness suggests invitation beyond that."

He lifted his gaze, careful to keep his expression controlled. Perhaps they knew his thoughts, and perhaps they didn't; either way he would not forget himself or his place. But Hera—she was indeed glorious to behold, even stiff and disdainful as she was. He clasped his hands tightly behind his back to keep from reaching for her, though he longed to touch the softness of her smooth, unblemished skin. What he would not have given to taste the hard pink buds of her breasts, to feel his hands filled with her warmth.

He dug his nails into his palms instead, his knuckles creaking with the strain of maintaining his composure, and he circled Hera, studying her form. When he had seen all he could see without temptation breaking his self-control, he nodded to Athena.

"You as well, Lady, if you do not wish to withdraw."

Athena's eyes were hard as stone, but she removed her gown all the same, letting the shimmering fabric pool around her feet. Paris kept a respectful distance, unwilling to press the patience of the goddess of war. Since she had spoken of Theseus, he could feel the simmer of her rage, hot waves lapping at his ankles, and he wading through its shallows. Athena was deep night and starlight, her hair raven black in its rope-thick plait and her skin pale and rich as cream. But beneath her beauty lay a terrible strength, softening the roundness of her figure into leaner lines and muscle where Hera and Aphrodite were lush.

"Have you seen enough?" she asked coolly.

"Thank you, Lady, yes."

His gaze shifted to Aphrodite again, and she smiled, stepping toward him as he approached. "You needn't hold yourself back from me, Paris," she said, tossing her rich chestnut hair and letting it flash with Helen's gold—a reminder of the gift she had offered. He felt his body stir at the thought. "I promise you, I will not bite."

Athena gave a soft snort of derision, even as Aphrodite drew his arms free, guiding his hands to her breasts, her hips, her woman's cleft. Paris could not stifle his groan, and his eyes drifted shut of their own accord, the silky heat of her center filling his palm even as she urged his fingers deeper.

"This is the true beauty of a woman," she murmured against his ear. "But only imagine Helen's body here beneath your hands. Imagine her whimpers of pleasure muffled against your throat. I will give you all the power you need to bring her home. My blessing, and she will be yours."

He tore himself free from her grasp, closing his damp fingers into a fist behind his back. Part of him could not help but wonder if she tasted as honeyed as her words, but he forced the thought away. And Aphrodite, delighted with her own game, laughed.

"Come now, Paris, will you not make your choice?" she asked, sweet as a songbird singing in the tree. Athena had been right to warn him, for Aphrodite was songbird and viper, both. And yet . . . Of the three, it was Aphrodite who drew his eye again and again.

"You are all more beautiful than words can describe," he said. "But if I must choose only one, it must be the goddess of love, the fairest lady, Aphrodite."

He told himself it had nothing to do with Helen. That he had not been swayed by the goddess's words or her gifts, but rather the plump curve of her bottom and the ripeness of her breasts, combined with a boldness in her manner that could not fail to bring delight to any man.

But when he met her gaze and saw the golden-haired girl reflected in those deep blue pools, he knew.

Helen of Sparta.

At long last, she was his.

Hermes had helped Paris to gather his flock, but the sun had long set by the time he made his way home. He still did not know what he meant to say to Oenone when she met him at the pens, Corythus on her hip. But she gave him one long look and turned away.

"If you had only stayed, you would not be so silent now."

Paris sighed, urging the last of the sheep inside before he secured the gate. "Do you think it would have stopped them had I been in your bed? That Zeus would have chosen another in my place?"

"If you had stayed—"

"No, Oenone," he said, stopping her complaint. "It would have changed nothing had I remained, except that you might have been caused more pain. Better if you had made your peace with what was coming than try to change my fate."

She drew herself up, looking more goddess than woman in the fading light, her features all liquid and fire. "If you think it was my choice to become the bride of a poor shepherd boy, you are a fool, Paris Alexandros, but if I had known your fate before all this—I wish I'd had warning enough to guard my heart, to stop my love. I wish you'd only been a slave and not the man you are, that I might have hated you instead!"

He dropped his gaze, grinding his teeth on all words he should not say. He couldn't be surprised she hadn't wanted him at first, and she'd readily admitted that she was his prize, his gift from the gods. "I never meant to hurt you, Oenone. I never wanted to hurt you. Just as I never asked for this—any of it. I would have been content upon this mountain with you and our son."

"Would have been," she repeated bitterly. "But no longer."

Paris could not deny it, and at the least, he owed Oenone the truth. "Before you came to me, I loved another. She needs me now, and I cannot turn from that call."

"Is that what the goddess has told you?" she sneered. "And you truly believe it?"

"Aphrodite did not have to say it. When we met before, Helen made her situation clear. And I must go to her, Oenone. I will have no peace until this is done."

"Then you will abandon your son," she said. "You will leave us behind and never think on us again. You will give up everything that you loved and ruin more!"

"If that is what must be done, then for her sake, I will do it. Just as I would have done the same for yours."

She shook her head, a harsh laugh escaping her throat. "No, Paris. It was for me to do what must be done. Me to keep you upon the mountain all this time, to stop you from venturing to Troy. Now that I have failed at the task Lord Apollo set me, I will suffer alone, cursed by this love. And when the day comes that you have need of *me*, I must serve you—the favored son."

"Agelaus can hardly compel you. If you are pained by me, you need not see me again, need not ever serve me."

"It is not Agelaus whose commands I must suffer," Oenone snapped. "And like you, I will have little choice in the matter. Only a fool would defy Lord Apollo, and he will be unhappy enough with me already, when this all ends in fire because of you. Because I could not keep you content!"

Lord Apollo. How often she had spoken of him, of his blessing and desires. How often she had used his name—and now, only now, he understood. "Lord Apollo sent you to me to stop this? To keep me here?"

"And I have failed. Just as your parents failed before me. Fate will have her way, after all, even against the will of the gods."

CHAPTER
THIRTY-SIX
PARIS

Paris took Tauros and what few possessions he had, leaving with the dawn's light. What purpose was there in remaining with Oenone when he knew now what he was meant for? The gods had given him a gift—a greater gift than his nymph—and he could not, would not turn from Helen. Not now that she was his.

He spent the first night with his father in the small hut where he'd lived as a child. Agelaus had always been old, his skin leathery and brown from the sun, lined with his years of labor. Now Paris could see nothing else beyond his age, his infirmity, knowing that in repayment for all his father had done, he meant to leave him behind.

"No, Paris," Agelaus said, his hands still strong as they grasped his across the table, where they had shared a meal while Paris had confessed his tale. "You must not defy the gods for me. And you have left me a grandson, a boy to shepherd for me in your place. I will go to Oenone and offer to raise your son, to care for both of them while you are away. But you must go, and in truth, I expected it long before now. A foundling child rarely escapes his fate. The gods will always find a way to set them back upon the path they were born for."

"Can you not give me some greater direction? Was there not even the smallest clue of where I came from when you found me?"

Agelaus shook his head. "You were just a babe, swaddled tight, with no mark or sign as to your birth beyond that small wooden rattle, clutched tightly in your hand. But if your Oenone did not want you to attend the festival with Tauros, going so far as to bring Ares down from Olympus to persuade you otherwise, perhaps you should begin at Troy. At the very least, you might find your way to Sparta from there, by ship. There is sure to be some trader willing to take you on as an oarsman."

It was sound reasoning, and with his father's encouragement, his assurances of Oenone and Corythus's care, and the rattle in his pack, he continued on, descending the mountain with Tauros at his back and traveling north toward the golden city and Aphrodite's promised reward.

The sooner he reached Helen, the happier they both would be.

It was three days' travel by foot, for he could not walk as the crow flew, and with the bull, it was necessary to take the better-worn route. He would not risk losing Tauros along the way, not when he needed to barter the beast for food and lodging when he arrived. If he was fortunate, perhaps he could arrange a fight and trade his winnings, but either way, he needed Tauros sound.

It was simple enough to find a bed the first night after leaving his father's home, for he knew most of those who lived near Mount Ida, and was known by reputation to more. Even on the second night, a kind stranger seemed to recognize him and offered him a place to sleep upon his porch. Paris could only assume it was the work of Hermes, flitting ahead by Aphrodite's command, for she had promised to give him everything he needed to reach Helen and bring her home again. It wasn't until the third day, when he reached the walls of Troy among a large group of fellow travelers, that he realized just how blessed he was.

"Come to test your bull at the games tomorrow?" a guard asked, stopping him at the gate. "Circle round to the Scaean Gate, nearer the citadel. Lord Aeneas's men will direct you on from there."

Aphrodite, Hermes, I give you my thanks! He gave Tauros's rope a tug and followed the guard's finger, a smile upon his lips. Whatever the occasion, this festival served his purposes, and no matter what happened to Tauros in the ring, there was sure to be compensation from the king. Priam was well-known for his generosity in such matters. The king might take his share of the flock, and the best animals when they were required, but he did not cheat the men who cared for them, and Paris did not think he would do so now, when so many had come.

The Scaean Gate was thick with herdsmen, their bulls snorting and pawing the ground, heads low and bodies threatening. Some were larger than Tauros—larger even than the beast Ares had been, when they'd fought so long ago.

A scribe took his name, carving it into a soft clay tablet, and with a sharp-eyed glance at Tauros, nodded acceptance of his entry. "Lord Aeneas hosts the bull fights, in honor of his lost cousin, given up by King Priam to the gods for the glory and honor of Troy, that there might be everlasting peace," he droned, obviously bored by his own words, having repeated them so often. "You'll have a place to sleep until your bull is defeated, as well as food and wine, but I'd send your man to keep an eye upon your animal in the stables, if it were me. Lord Aeneas is only offering prizes to the winners, and there's many a country cattleman who would hurt another man's beast to ensure his own victory. Unscrupulous lot."

Paris lifted a brow. "Do you say as much to all of them?"

The scribe lifted his gaze, squinting at Paris. "Cloaks like that aren't usually found on common herdsmen. The wool's too fine, and the dye too rich. Purple belongs to princes and kings, so far as I've ever seen."

"My lady will be pleased to know her work is so admired," Paris said. Oenone had spun, dyed, and woven all his clothes for years, but he'd never realized their worth. Then again, upon the mountain, it was warmth that mattered most, not color or weave, and the women wove what was needed for their men.

"Get on with you, then," the scribe said, his face flushed with his error. He jerked his chin toward the gate. "I haven't the time to gab about all day with country fools. A stableboy will see you settled."

Paris laughed, leading Tauros through. By the time he reached the stables and saw his bull to his small pen, he was half convinced the scribe's mistake had been some trickery of Hermes, for he was nothing but dust and sweat when he took the time to look at himself.

"My lord, your pardon, but the banquet's set to begin at sundown, and you'll want time to wash and change," the stableboy said, watching as Paris stripped off his filth-covered cloak and picked up a brush to see to Tauros's hide.

"Is it a princely banquet?" Paris asked, for though King Priam was generous, he could not be so generous as that. The boy nodded, confusion written in the wrinkle between his brows, and Paris laughed. "I can't have fooled you, too."

"My lord?"

"Do I look so much like a prince to your city eyes?" he asked gently. "I'm only a poor shepherd from the mountain, nothing more. Certainly no one worthy of such a banquet."

The boy looked doubtful, but the stable master called for him, and he set off at a run, calling another apology over his shoulder as he went.

Tauros snorted, his hide shivering beneath Paris's hand, and he smiled, patting the bull's shoulder before beginning to brush him down. "Peace, my friend. At least we know the gods are with us."

It was the only explanation, and before he slept that night, in the corner of Tauros's stall with little more than a horse blanket to keep him warm, he made sure to offer them his thanks.

Tauros fought and won his first match early in the day, and with the winnings Paris was able to find a boy to sit by his pen while he watched the afternoon games. They were funeral games, it turned out, for the prince who had died, held annually in his honor by King Priam and Queen Hecuba, though it sounded as though the games weren't always quite so celebratory as these. This year, King Priam's sons and nephews each hosted an event, the older ones paired with the younger in teams, offering prizes of their own to honor their kin.

"Didn't I see you enter your name for the boxing?" a familiar voice asked as he stood in the line of men waiting to join the footrace. Paris turned, finding his father standing at his shoulder. But the walking stick he leaned upon was strangely wrought, with snakes carved coiling in the wood. "It's about to begin now, unless I miscounted the chariots taking their laps. You'd better hurry if you mean to compete."

"Father, what are you doing here? The journey is far too long!"

Agelaus rolled his eyes and straightened, every stooped line melting from his aged body. "The boxing, young Paris, and be quick about it. You'll find the others waiting before the dais."

Hermes, he realized suddenly, as the walking stick—his caduceus—hissed. "My lord, forgive me. I thought I'd run rather than box—"

"Both, then, assuming you aren't knocked senseless. I'll see your name is added to the lists. But hurry now, or you'll have another year to wait before you find your way home, and your poor Helen will have suffered that much longer."

Still, Paris hesitated, questions begging to be asked on the tip of his tongue. But Hermes, in the guise of his father, gave him a shove, and he knew the god's patience would not last. A backward glance at Agelaus, looking far too young and strong, and Paris left, shouldering his way through the throng toward the dais and setting his mind to the fight ahead. He'd defeated Athenian raiders as a boy, so why should he not win today, older, stronger, and wiser now?

He must trust in the gods, that was all. Hermes would not have come himself if it were not necessary that he listen. So he joined the others before the dais, at the back of the assembly, and thanked Hermes and Aphrodite both for their aid.

Home. That was what Hermes had said. He must take part in the boxing to find his way home. And from there to Helen, by the way he had phrased it. His heartbeat sped at the thought, but he couldn't afford the distraction. Not if he wished to win.

"Paris, son of Agelaus, against Adamaos, son of Nikostratos," one of the princes called, among a list of other matches, all to be fought at once. Hector, probably, by his age and his size. Who else would host the boxing but the prince best known for his skill as a warrior?

Paris stepped forward, wrapping his hands and wrists in the leather straps offered to each participant, and swallowed back a lump of fear when he faced Adamaos. The man was immense, larger even than Hector, and when he grinned, he had only half his teeth. Likely he was an experienced brawler. The sort of man hired to travel with traders to guard against raiders and thieves. This man would crush him like a bug.

"The winners will move on to the next round, but you will fight only until the first fall," Hector called out. Then, after a pause to be sure they had all found their partners, he shouted, "Begin!"

Adamaos had the greater reach, but after a few exchanges, Paris found he was far more nimble. He wove and dodged and ducked and spun, and Adamaos was breathing hard, growling with frustration as his blows glanced instead of striking solidly, when he landed any at all. It was the only hope Paris had of winning—exhausting Adamaos until he lost focus on the match.

Paris took a solid hit to the jaw, his head snapping back and his vision swimming, but Adamaos's feet had begun to drag and shuffle through the dust instead of lifting. Paris waited only for his sight to clear before he made his move, coming in close and fast and knocking Adamaos off balance with the attack, then using one foot to trip the larger man as he took a startled step back.

The huge man fell, letting out a roar of outrage as he did, and Paris danced out of reach before he could retaliate. "Paris, son of Agelaus, wins against Adamaos, son of Nikostratos," one of the judges announced, and two of the palace guards appeared to escort his foe from the field. "Adamaos is dismissed."

"Watch your back, son of Agelaus," Adamaos snarled as he was led away. "You'll regret your victory before this day is through."

The rest of his matches were more of the same. Paris was paired against the largest men still standing, and he took hits enough to make his ears ring and the earth spin, blood filling his mouth with bronze, but somehow he stayed upon his feet. Each man he defeated seemed angrier than the last, and after the third tackled him, bringing him down hard to the ground, he made sure to keep a careful distance from the brutes he'd defeated.

"Lord Apollo will not let you live," the last growled, spitting blood into the dirt between them. "He's marked you, son of Agelaus, and as the sun sets, so will you fall."

Paris grimaced, his body protesting the abuse he'd taken already, but his mind still sharp and focused upon his goal. Helen, golden and beautiful and his. Just the thought of her licked like flames through his limbs. Oenone had spoken of fire, and he knew it well by now, the fire of his passion for Helen, his love. And Lord Apollo might threaten him, might stand between him and his prize, but surely Aphrodite would not be so easily thwarted.

"I have come too far to fail now," Paris said.

And then the final match began.

He did not remember much of it, for he caught a fist to the side of his head early on, and had it not been for the goddess, the warmth and strength of her body behind his, holding him up, he would have certainly fallen. But Aphrodite kept her word, and he kept his feet, and before he had regained his senses, he stood over his opponent, fists aching and body bruised, and Prince Hector himself set a crown of gold upon his head, proclaiming him the victor.

"Where do you hail from, Paris, son of Agelaus?" the Trojan prince asked. "I would not wish to face an army of your people in battle, as determined as you have shown yourself to be."

"I am only a shepherd, come down from Mount Ida," he said, dropping to one knee before the prince. "But I cannot accept all credit for my victory. Aphrodite, goddess of all that is beautiful, is the reason I have won."

Hector frowned and flicked his fingers, drawing Paris back to his unsteady feet. "Are you some son of hers, to be so blessed?"

"A son of her heart, perhaps, but not of her body," Paris said. "As my father, Agelaus, found and adopted me, so too has the goddess."

"A foundling boy from Mount Ida," one of the princesses murmured from her place beside the king, all color draining from her face. "Send him off, Brother! Give him his prize and let him return home this very night. Before we are all cursed!"

"You must forgive my sister's ravings." Hector smiled, but his shoulders stiffened, and the warmth of his congratulations faded with her words. "I bid you join us for the banquet at the palace tonight. As the winner of this contest, it is your right, and we would all know better the shepherd from Mount Ida who is so blessed by the gods."

Paris bowed again, though he could not quite take his gaze off the princess, her fingers clawing at the arm of her father's chair, her expression wild with fear. He'd seen such desperation before, in Oenone's eyes, when she begged him to remain upon the mountain at her side.

"I would not grieve the princess with my presence if it is not wanted," he said. "And I've a bull in the stable I must see to, besides. But I thank you for your generosity, Prince Hector, King Priam."

He felt their eyes upon him as he walked away, and suddenly the threats of the men he had defeated weighed more heavily upon his shoulders.

If the princes of Troy desired to be rid of him, they need not look far to find men willing to see the grim deed done. But if he remained among the crowds, hidden in their midst, it would be that much more difficult for them to act. And he had the footrace still to run.

Though as unsteady as he was, at least he need not fear that he would win.

CHAPTER THIRTY-SEVEN
PARIS

I t took all his strength to keep upright as he made his way to the racing post, but Hermes, still in his father's guise, awaited him there. "You'll make few friends this day, Paris Alexandros," the god said, grinning. "But the trick of it! I have not had so much fun among mortals since Autolycus's day."

Paris shivered, the god's glee making him suddenly afraid. Athena had warned him, had she not? That he must be cautious of Aphrodite, or see himself brought low. But Hermes and Aphrodite had both helped him, both smoothed his way forward and given him the strength he needed to continue on.

"Quickly now," Hermes said again, his smile strange on Agelaus's lips. He pressed a pair of sandals into his hands, and Paris stared, aghast at the fluttering wings. "Put these on if you wish to race."

"My lord, I cannot . . . I am not fit—"

"Do you refuse a gift from your god?" Hermes said, gripping his hands too tight. "Do you refuse the aid we might offer?"

"No, of course not," Paris said, sure it was the only answer he could give, judging by the gleam in the god's eye. "Forgive me, please."

Hermes gave a nod to the sandals. "Put them on, and do not doubt me again, young Paris. I do not care to have my amusements spoiled by disobedient boys."

Until that moment, he had trusted blindly. But of course he had been a fool. His fingers fumbled with the laces as his thoughts flew. Hermes and Aphrodite served themselves; that much the god had made clear. How had he not realized it before now? Not seen the signs? And worse, it seemed with every step he took along this path, he defied the Lord Apollo, too.

Lord Apollo, who had sent him Oenone, to keep him upon the mountain. Who had employed Ares in his scheming, to satisfy Paris's desire for greater renown. Apollo had given him everything, had brought him happiness and joy in his simple shepherd's life, and if he had only stayed, as Oenone had wanted, perhaps he would be happy still.

But no. The moment he had seen Helen's face again, learned her name, he never could have returned. It was enough to make him wonder if the goddess had not stricken him from the start, brought him Helen so long ago, knowing already his fate and seeing how she might have her way.

Lord Apollo, forgive me, he prayed. Then Hermes shoved him out into the race.

The sandals knew their task too well, and no matter how Paris tried to slow his feet, it did not matter. Dust flew in his wake as he ran, unbalanced and flailing, but far ahead. Too far, and Paris groaned, then leaned into the speed Hermes had gifted him, for if he had no choice about it, he did not wish to look the fool quite so utterly as he felt one.

The sandals slowed to a more human pace, and he found himself steadied by the wind as he ran. It was one thing to win a race by leaps, and another to do so by a nose. Now that he had control, he allowed the other men to catch up, and he did not need to pretend his exhaustion as they gained ground.

But he could not lose, for the moment he thought to let another pass, the sandals sped him on. He could not lose, and it was as Hermes had said—today he would make few friends.

He only prayed the gods meant to save him from the enemies he had made instead.

After the footrace, he made his way back to the stables, too tired and sore to hold his own in the festival crowds. The footrace had won him a gold spiraled armband, and he tucked the crown from the boxing inside his tunic and out of sight. The boy he had engaged to watch Tauros was nodding off before his pen, and Paris gave him a shake.

"You're free to go, lad," he said, when the boy half leapt to his feet, blurting desperate apologies for having been found asleep. "Enjoy the evening's festivities, but if Tauros wins tomorrow, I'll need you again."

"Thank you, my lord, thank you!" And he was gone. As it should be, Paris thought. The quicker a boy was, the more likely he'd keep himself from trouble.

He let himself into Tauros's stall, checking the bull over again, just to be sure he'd missed nothing. Part of him was more than tempted to take his prizes and go, though he knew not where. His future seemed to be here in Troy, if Hermes's words were any indication, but the longer he remained, the less certain he was that he wished to claim such a fate, whatever it might be.

"You ought to have left, as my sister suggested," a voice said, and Paris spun, finding a stocky man leaning against one of the central beams. A prince, judging by the band of gold upon his brow. "And perhaps we might have overlooked her concerns had you disappeared into the crowds. But then you took the footrace, too, making quite the spectacle of yourself, and I imagine, if we let you continue on, your bull would win all his fights as well."

"Deiphobus, do not be so rude to our guest," Hector said, stepping out of the shadows. "After all, he claims it is the gods who have supported him, and no true skill of his own."

"If only he *were* our guest," Prince Deiphobus said, sauntering forward. "But he refused our invitation, as I recall. Scorned our table and our generosity, and in public no less."

"I meant no insult, my lords," Paris said, watching them both draw nearer. "I swear, I only wished to spare your sister any distress. I am only a shepherd, and I promise you, I do not forget my place."

"A shepherd boy who wins every match against men twice his size," Deiphobus said. "A shepherd boy who the lads in the stables call a lord, a prince. No. Whoever you might be, it is not so simple as that. You have come here to undermine us, to trick us somehow, and I will not suffer it. No man comes to Troy and makes fools of Priam's sons!"

Paris held up his hands to show he carried no weapons, placing himself between the princes and Tauros. Whatever happened to him now, there was no reason the bull should be harmed. "I will go," he said. "At once, if you desire it. I will leave this city and never return."

Deiphobus sneered. "Gutless dog."

"He's only a shepherd, Brother. He cannot help his cowardice," Hector said.

"A coward would not have earned the name Alexandros," Paris said, stiffening at the insult. "Perhaps I am only a shepherd, but we are hardly a craven lot. It takes bravery to guard our flocks, our herds!"

"Then prove it," Hector said. "You may have defeated those untrained fools, but I promise you, you will not win against me."

Paris hesitated, but the gloating smile on Deiphobus's face, Hector's smug expression beside his, as if they knew he would refuse . . . "To the first fall?"

"To the finish," Hector said. "This is a matter of honor, after all."

He nodded, unsurprised, and though the whole of it made him uneasy, he would not show his fears now. "If you wish to reclaim your honor, surely the challenge must be met before an assembly. Tomorrow, perhaps, before the dais and under your father's gaze."

Hector tapped his fingers against the fine linen of his kilt, his eyes narrowing. "Our guard will remain here, to be sure you are not disturbed until then."

To ensure he did not flee in the night, more like. But Paris bowed his head, accepting the terms. "Until tomorrow, Prince Hector."

And may Aphrodite protect me.

No one else would.

Paris let the guards lead him from the stable to the wide dais before which the games had been played, and faced Prince Hector, the greatest of King Priam's sons. This was a fight he would not win, not even fresh from his bed, but he would not give up easily, either. Hector would have to knock him senseless to keep him on the ground, and even then, Paris decided, he would still struggle to rise. For his own honor, to prove himself still worthy of his name.

There were no leather straps to wrap their hands, their wrists, and Paris was not fool enough to think any Trojan would act as a fair judge, but he couldn't refuse the challenge. This was where the gods had brought him—to this place, and this moment—and he had no doubt that Hermes had intended precisely this outcome. He must simply trust that Aphrodite would not betray him quite yet.

"Paris Alexandros, son of Agelaus, challenges Prince Hector, son of King Priam," the judge called out, and a murmur rippled through the gathered crowd, thick with laughter. Only a fool would challenge Hector, after all, and Paris certainly had not done so. But why would the prince and heir of Troy challenge a shepherd boy? No one would believe him if he argued as much. Not against the word of Troy's princes.

"The fight will continue until either Paris or Prince Hector lies senseless or dead."

Paris closed his eyes, drawing a steadying breath even as the laughter turned to startled silence. To the finish, Hector had said, but he had not imagined he meant to take it so far as this. A concession by one opponent always ended a match, but it seemed Hector was determined to be rid of him. And no doubt if anyone asked, he would be happy to say Paris had set the terms as well.

All the more reason to give his all to the fight. And once he survived, he would know without question that he had earned Helen as his prize.

"Begin!"

Hector circled slowly, and Paris countered, his hands tightly fisted in anticipation. But even watching him so closely, Paris did not see the moment when Hector moved. Fast as a snake, Hector's right fist struck his face, his left driving hard into his ribs, and Paris gasped, stumbling back a step with the shock. Hector fought with the speed and grace of a god.

"You see now what the difference is, *Alexandros,*" Hector taunted. "The difference between fighting a man and a prince."

"I never doubted, my lord," Paris said, allowing his body to slump, his shoulders curving inward to protect himself. "I have known you from the start to be my better in all things."

Another punch caught him square in the stomach, and Paris fought the rise of his gorge. At least he did not stumble, did not retreat, no matter how near to retching he was.

"Then why fight at all?" Hector asked.

Paris shook his head, unable to answer without losing his morning bread and wine. He tucked himself even smaller, his elbows guarding his gut.

"A shepherd would not boast of his name," Hector said, hitting him in the side of the head. Hector was relaxed now, a cat toying with a mouse in the grain. "A proper shepherd would not dare argue with his prince at all."

"And a noble prince would not disparage his shepherd," Paris spat, feinting high before striking hard and fast at Hector's unprotected ribs. The prince grunted, surprised. "You insulted me, and you wonder why I would reply?"

Hector swung, but Paris blocked and returned with a swing of his own, aiming for his nose. An audible crunch and the strange shift in his hand told him he'd hit his mark too well, even before Hector staggered back, cursing aloud.

Blood streamed down the prince's face, and Paris flexed his fingers, biting his tongue against the sharp stab of pain. A knuckle out of joint or a bone broken, likely, and one glance at Hector told him the prince was done with this game.

Hector threw himself forward, all taunting set aside, and Paris ducked too slow. His jaw, his ears, his stomach and ribs. It was all he could do to protect his head after the first furious rain of blows, and by the second, his very breath stolen from his lungs, Paris found himself upon his knees on the ground.

"Get up!" Hector snarled, circling him now. "Or are you truly so weak as this? Have you only one good hit in you, shepherd boy? And you claim to guard my flocks so bravely!"

The earth rocked beneath his feet, but Paris could not wait for it to steady before he rose. His ribs protested any movement at all, every breath, but he climbed up, stood tall.

Hector struck again, and his vision went black. Paris swung blindly, his blood roaring in his ears, but Hector batted his fist away and hit him in the face. He choked on the gush of his blood, gagging on it, but at least he could see again.

"Where are the gods now?" Hector growled. "You said they favored you before, and I begin to believe they must have, for you surely have no skill. So where is Aphrodite to save you from this humiliation? Even from your death?"

Paris blinked slowly, lurching out of his reach as he searched the crowd. So many had gathered to watch. But the gods had turned their eyes away, it seemed, and he did not know how much more of this he could take. Even as he thought it, he tripped again, falling for the second time and landing much too heavily on his knees.

"One more blow, Paris Alexandros," Hector said. "And all of this will end. You will never threaten my family again."

"King Priam!" The thin familiar voice of his father rose up over the cheers and laughter of the crowd. They were all too pleased to see their prince victorious, but Paris's gaze found Agelaus, pushing his way through. Too strong for such an old man, even desperate as he appeared. "King Priam, you must stop this at once! He is your son, Paris is your son!"

Hermes, Paris thought. Hermes had come to reveal his trick.

And then he fell face-first into the dirt.

His mouth was full of grit when he woke again, staring into the dark eyes of Queen Hecuba, her soot-black hair streaked with just the faintest traces of white. He hadn't noticed it before, seeing her only from a distance.

"Dear boy," she said softly, holding his injured hand far too tightly, until he moaned in pain. "My dear, dear boy."

He coughed then and groaned at the ache in his ribs, and Queen Hecuba, blessedly, let him go, reaching for a cup.

"A potion for the pain," she said, lifting his head and pressing the golden rim against his lips, forcing him to swallow. "Drink it slowly now. And not too much, or you'll only make yourself sick. Hector's already had the sharp edge of my tongue for this foolishness of his, but you'll mend. The physician has promised me you'll be on your feet before the moon begins to wane."

His thoughts spun almost as violently as the room when he turned his head to look at her, the queen, tending him as a mother would her child. What was it that Hermes had said? He could hardly remember now. Just the disturbance and the shouting and the jostling that followed, with so much pain. Hermes had clutched something in his hand, waved it broadly as he sought the king's attention, but Paris hadn't been able to make it out.

"Agelaus?"

"I'm afraid he did not linger. He said he didn't wish to make things any more difficult for you, now that you'd found your way home." And then she smiled, her dark eyes going liquid. "It broke my heart to give you up the first time. I could not bring myself to abandon you again. Tell me you will stay. Tell me you will take your place as a prince of Troy, as my son!"

Paris is your son!

The rattle. Hermes had held the rattle in his hand, no doubt stolen from his pack. Paris closed his eyes, his chest aching—and not from the bruises upon his ribs this time. That was Hermes's grand trick. The reason the gods had brought him here, and why they had set him against Hector, knowing he could not win, even intending that he should fail. So the king and queen would recognize their son at the last moment. So he could be made prince.

And how better to reach Helen? How better to protect her than with the whole of Troy behind him, its armies, its walls? Aphrodite had given him everything, just as she had promised. She had not betrayed him at all.

"Yes," he said, looking into his mother's eyes. "Yes, of course I will stay."

She smiled, tears spilling down her cheeks. "My beautiful boy. Returned to me at last, and all this time we mourned! How much I have missed. You must tell me everything, of course. And we will celebrate! A festival to mark your return and put these years of grief behind us."

He laughed softly and closed his eyes, exhausted by even the thought of more celebration. But if he was to persuade his new family to give him men and ships to sail to Sparta, he must be accepted by them, welcomed into their embrace. They must love him, or why should they stand beside him or support him in his hopes, his dreams?

"As you say, my queen," he agreed.

She made a soft sound, half pleasure, half distress, and grasped his hand again, hard and determined. "Mother," she said. "Or Hecuba, if you do not wish to offend the memory of the one who raised you. But please, I would not have you address me as a servant or a stranger. You are my son. A prince of Troy now."

"Forgive me," he said, squeezing her hand, though it felt as though a knife had lodged itself in his knuckles. "I was but a poor shepherd before I fell, and I fear my head still spins with all that has been revealed."

"Of course," she said, leaning forward to press a kiss to his brow before she rose. "And I must let you rest, to recover your strength. We've all the time in the world now."

But he did not.

He must rest and recover—and quickly, for Helen's sake, if not his own. And he could only hope that Aphrodite had not forsaken him quite yet, for he feared he would need her support still, when the day came that he must beg the king and queen to let him sail.

Soon, he promised himself.

And Helen of Sparta would become *his* Helen, safe and loved and guarded for all time.

His Helen, of *Troy*.

CHAPTER
THIRTY-EIGHT
MENELAUS

Helen of Sparta. Menelaus stared down at her, tossing and turning in his bed, small whimpers and sobs breaking from her lips as she slept. She did not speak of her nightmares, not since they had married nearly a year ago, and he could not help but wonder how they might have changed. Every night, it was the same. Moans and whimpers and small, choked sobs. She did not scream the way she used to, nor cry out in pain, but it was impossible for him to sleep through the noise.

"Theseus," she murmured. "Theseus, please. Hear me!"

His lip curled, and he turned away, pouring himself a cup of wine. Married and bedded, and she still was not his. Not even while she slept. *Theseus.* That Athenian dog. He did not forget how she had looked at the king of Athens when he had come so long ago. The adoration in her eyes, the laughter falling from her lips. He did not forget that Theseus had stolen her affections before his very eyes, and to hear her call for him in her dreams, in her nightmares—it made him want to retch.

"Wake up." He kicked the bed, then grabbed her by the arm and pulled her bodily from it, letting her fall, startled and confused, to the floor. "Wake up!"

She shook her head, settling back upon her knees and blinking at him owlishly. It wasn't the first time he'd torn her from the bed, nor the first time he had heard Theseus's name upon her lips while she slept, and always her response was the same as she struggled to wake.

"You were dreaming again," he said.

She swallowed, rubbing her face. "Was I?"

"Are you going to lie?" he asked, unable to keep the disgust from his tone. "Do you think I don't remember this game from when you played it before? When you told Tyndareus you remembered nothing of your dreams, that they fled the moment you opened your eyes? When you said the same, even to me, before I went to war?"

She lifted her head, looking up at him from the floor, and said nothing at all.

He grabbed her by her hair and dragged her up from her knees. "I listened to you then, too, Helen. To your cries, your weeping. The small begging sounds you would make as you slept. I listened to you sob around my name, night after night after night. A pleasant reminder that even in sleep, you were mine."

Her eyes sharpened, going hard as she grabbed his wrist, but he pulled her closer, until she stood so near he could feel her heat. He wanted to beat that look off her face, to throw her down and claim her. To spear her so deeply it pierced her faithless heart.

"It isn't my name you whisper anymore in the night," he said. "Do you know what you say? Who you call for?"

Silence, still, though her face had paled. Whether it was from the pain of his hand tearing at her hair or fear that he had learned her secrets, he did not know. Did not care.

"Perhaps I shouldn't tell you," he said. "Perhaps I should let you stew, instead, wondering who of your loved ones you might have betrayed in your sleep. And in the meantime, I will wait. I will wait and I will plan, and should they ever come for you, I will make you watch while I tear them limb from limb."

Her eyes fluttered shut, her chest rising fast, and he threw her away, disgusted with himself. With the man she had turned him into, the madness she had leached into his blood with every touch, every kiss, every smile, only to steal it all away and spurn him.

"Dream of that," he snarled.

And then he left. Before he did something he would truly regret.

She had made a fool of him. That was the heart of it, more than anything else. She had made a fool of him before half the princes and kings of Achaea, and his brother had done nothing to stop it, by refusing to let him compete in his own name. And then the way she had treated him, after, when he had taken her to their marriage bed. The things she had said. She had made him believe they could leave it all behind.

And he had been willing to forget it all. The nights she had spent on Theseus's arm, fawning over the great hero-king. The years she had been gone, and all her protests before she had been taken. He had been willing, even, to forget the way she had treated him in Mycenae upon her return, and the insults of her brothers.

But that was before he had learned the truth, seen it in the eyes of the men who had stayed for their wedding feast and the celebrations that followed. Before he had realized how they pitied her, how obvious she had made her disgust. Every guest in the palace knew what he had not. That Helen had not wanted him at all.

Oh, she had blamed it upon her dreams. From the start, he supposed, she had used them as an excuse, and now he looked back upon it and wondered how much of what she had told him had been lies. She had kept her dreams so secret for so long, pretending she remembered nothing, and only when he had made his feelings known did she speak. How much of what she had confessed was the truth of what she saw, and how much was just to keep him from claiming her as his wife, to delay what she feared he desired?

It was all so much clearer now, her distaste, her dislike. The coolness in her eyes when he came to her and the way she would lie beneath him, her head turned to the side, that she might not have to look at him at all. He held her in his arms, joined his body to hers, and still she did not give herself up. Not truly. Not in the way his body yearned for, not in any way that satisfied his needs.

And worse, it had been a full year now, and she had not quickened. Another way in which she had found the means to humiliate him before all. No man could look at her and think she was barren, but they would see him and laugh. Her curving waist, still delicate as any maiden's, was the proof that he had been unmanned.

He had hoped to take a goddess to his bed, and perhaps he truly had. A fickle goddess, with ruin in her heart, hoping to drive him mad.

CHAPTER
THIRTY-NINE
HELEN

Menelaus shook me awake before dawn, his face drawn with deep grooves in the lamplight, and Clymene stood over his shoulder, a cloak draped over her arm.

"Tyndareus," he said, his voice low and tight, and I sat up at once, reaching for the cloak. We'd been at odds with one another since he'd come to claim me as his wife and heard the whispers of the other men, the suitors who had stayed for my wedding banquet—Menestheus being the most troublesome of all. But for this small moment, he seemed more like the boy I had known. "Leda says he wishes to say his good-byes, but there is not much time."

I covered myself quickly and followed my husband into the hall. Tyndareus. My father in every way that mattered. And the only protection I had left, the only hope I had for any freedom while I lived as Menelaus's wife.

My gaze rose to his back, his shoulders stooped with grief and his hands balled into tight fists at his side. *He could have left me sleeping.* The realization twisted through my thoughts. Menelaus could have denied me this. He could have locked me in my room and kept me from my father's bedside. And after everything else that had passed between us, I wouldn't have been shocked if he'd tried. I might have even expected it.

He turned back to me when we reached the door, his hand outstretched, his face shadowed. I stared at his open palm, unsure what it meant. So often he had raised it against me in violence, in punishment for some imagined offense. It had been years since he had offered me his hand in friendship, and I could not help but fear a trick of some kind.

"For his sake," he said, not meeting my eyes. "If not for yours."

I pressed my lips together and fit my hand in his. For my father's sake, and perhaps, in some small part, for mine. Because seeing Tyndareus, pale and still in the flickering lamplight, I felt myself a child.

"Helen," my father breathed, not even strong enough to reach for me. One finger rose, then fell again, and I knelt beside the bed. "Beautiful Helen. You must . . . you must forgive me."

"No." I pressed his hand to my cheek. "Oh, Papa. There's nothing to forgive."

"I only wanted . . . you safe. Happy." He closed his eyes, swallowed thickly. "Forgive me."

"It was never your fault," I said, wishing I could promise him more. Assure him that I was happy, that I was safe. But I couldn't bring myself to lie. Not then. I lifted pleading eyes to Menelaus, looking for something more to say. He dropped his gaze, avoiding mine, and I had never felt so alone.

If only I had been able to keep my brothers near. To have their support in this moment would have been a comfort, but after Menestheus told my husband I had taken Castor and Pollux to my bed, I'd had no choice but to send them away. The gods had made it clear I could not escape *my* fate, but I still hoped I might guard my brothers from death at my husband's hands, no matter what my dreams had said.

Tyndareus let out a rattling breath. "Menelaus."

My husband sank to one knee at my side, his hand wrapping around my father's arm, just beneath the elbow. As if he might anchor him to this world. "I am here."

"Promise me," Tyndareus wheezed. "Promise me . . . you will remember. The boy I loved. The boy who loved . . . my Helen."

All this time, I had thought him blind to what I suffered, unwilling to see my unhappiness or Menelaus's cruelty. I pressed a kiss to my father's hand, unsure of my feelings. To know he had seen yet done so little—but there had been so little to do, once the gods had made their choice known. And he'd had Sparta to consider, too.

"Treat her kindly," Tyndareus said, the words barely more than a whisper. "Keep her safe. Happy."

His jaw tightened, but Menelaus nodded.

"Swear it," my father said, struggling up.

A strangled sound escaped my throat, and I pressed him gently back down. "Father, please, save your strength."

But Tyndareus pushed me away, grasping for Menelaus and catching him by the hand, the arm, the shoulder. "Swear upon the Styx."

"Upon the Styx," Menelaus said, his voice rough. "I swear to keep your daughter safe, to treat her kindly. This is my oath."

Tyndareus let him go, falling back, even paler than he'd been before. His lips moved, but no sound followed. Until: "Leda."

A servant rose from her silent place at the other side of his bed and slipped out of the room. Tyndareus's gaze stayed on me, a strange calm falling over his face. The tight lines of pain smoothed away, and his hand found mine again. I gripped it tight.

My mother came just moments later. Tyndareus looked at her, smiled, and was gone.

"We must have games," Leda said, joining us for the morning meal in the privacy of our room. Menelaus and I had hardly spoken since Tyndareus's spirit had fled, and until he was entombed with all proper rites, everything we did, every word we exchanged, would surely be heard by him. Just as he had heard my mother wailing all night. "A chariot race, at the least. And a banquet befitting our king."

I supposed I ought to have done the same, mourning my father loudly as was right and proper, but I was too numb, too terrified to carry on. And if I had dared tear at my garments, scratch my face, pull out my hair, what difference would it have made? Menelaus did not let me leave my room without covering my hair, and he would surely find my torn clothing too immodest.

"There will be a footrace as well, both for the men and women," Menelaus said. "Helen will compete, to honor her father, and so will I."

It was the first I had heard of it, and I could not help my stare, but Menelaus did not lift his eyes from the wine cup he held in his hands, though I was certain he must feel my shock. "You wish me to race?"

"And your brothers. Send them word they are to return with all haste. I would have them compete in the chariot race, with those Lapith stallions of yours. I will not have the people of Sparta say I refused Tyndareus's sons the right to honor their father."

"Of course," I heard myself say, though in truth, I could scarcely believe my ears. To have my brothers here, invited by Menelaus, even if they could not stay beyond the funeral rites—I wanted to weep with relief. "I'll send word to them at once."

"I'll send a messenger to Agamemnon as well, to summon your sister. My brother owes Tyndareus at least that much. I trust, Leda, that you will see to the rest, no expense spared. Tyndareus was my father in all but blood, and I will heap upon him every honor, and beg the gods for more."

"A bull to Zeus, of course," Leda said. "The sacrifice offered by Helen's hand."

Menelaus looked to me then, to be sure I consented.

"As you wish, of course," I said quickly, my thoughts spinning. "I would not dishonor my father's spirit by refusing."

"You've never cared overmuch for offering sacrifice," Menelaus said. "If you wished me to stand in your place, I would be willing. A sacrifice given by the new king can hardly offend Tyndareus's shade."

"It is not for me to refuse the command of my king," I said carefully, combing through his words to find the trap. Surely he could not mean to offer me a true choice simply because he knew I did not care to take the victims' lives. "Nor the desires of my husband."

"Perhaps, then, we should do it together," he said. "My hand atop yours, as Tyndareus often did before."

"It would be fitting," I agreed. "If that is your desire."

"Have you truly no opinion on the matter?" His hands tightened around the cup, a flash of anger passing over his face. "Must I command you to speak your mind, when until this day you have refused to be silent?"

Would that it were true, but even when I sat at my father's side in the megaron, I had not been so foolish as that, no matter what he believed. And I was careful now, still, as I chose my words.

"My desire is only for peace, my lord. Peace between us until Tyndareus's body is safely sealed within the tomb. His journey is long, and I would not give his shade reason to linger here."

"Nor would I," Menelaus said. "And to that end, I must have your honesty. I will not be forsworn and cursed because you expect me to know your mind."

And then I understood. This was my father's last gift, his final command and wish, brought into the light. I'd heard Menelaus swear upon the Styx, knew his oath, but somehow I had not believed it would last through the dawn.

"You mean to keep your vow."

"Vow?" Leda asked. "What vow?"

Menelaus ignored my mother, setting aside his cup and reaching for more bread. "I seem to have little choice in the matter."

But I shook my head, watching him. The shift of his deeply shadowed eyes away from mine, the inward curve of his shoulders, and the lines of grief marking his face. "You could have refused to swear it at all."

"Whatever feelings I might have toward you, whatever pain you have caused me, I am not so lost that I do not know what I owe your father. Nor do I mean to forget it now. If you desire peace, as I do, you will let the matter rest."

"What is this about, Menelaus?" Leda asked. "If Tyndareus bound you in some way—"

"You will *both* let the matter rest," he snapped. "And you, Leda, will arrange the appropriate rites and see that Tyndareus's body lies undisturbed. You will trouble me with nothing else until it is done. Am I understood?"

My mother rose from the table, stiff and strong, and bestowed upon us both a withering glare before she swept from the room.

Neither Menelaus nor I gave her the satisfaction of watching her go. But my husband had not finished yet, stranger that he had become. Once Leda had left the room, he poured us both more wine. "If you wish to be named high priestess, I would know it now. Before your mother is given opportunity to cause us both further grief."

"If you allow her to remain high priestess, grief is all she will bring us," I said. I had known for some time that she meant to keep her position after Tyndareus's death, and I had thought the matter settled, and Menelaus agreed. Anything to keep me within his power.

"And what would you bring us, instead?"

I stared into the wine, exhaustion falling over me like a cloak of gold, heavy and awkward and dragging at my shoulders. "Only the gods can know."

CHAPTER FORTY

HELEN

My brothers arrived soon after, but I stopped short of the courtyard at the sight of Polypoetes in their midst. Fool man, to have come so far, to have risked so much. I pressed myself back into the shadows, hoping to calm the race of my heart. Polypoetes of all my suitors would have made me the finest husband, even if I had not loved him, but I had not realized how much I had come to rely upon his silent support until he was gone. If Menelaus believed for a moment I favored him, it would be his death now.

"Athens will be returned to its rightful heirs, young though they might be to rule," Heracles was saying, for he'd arrived just the night before, and of course he would be among the first to greet my brothers, to do honor to Tyndareus's shade. "Demophon does not lack wisdom, thank Athena, but if Hippolytus had lived, Menestheus would never have succeeded in his coup. You must have known him, surely, Polypoetes."

"I did," Polypoetes said, old grief hanging upon his words. "We spent a great deal of time together as children, he and I, for our fathers wished us to be friends, that we might have some small measure of what they shared with one another. Hippolytus was by far my better."

"A good lad," Heracles agreed, and I could hear the sorrow thick in his voice. "So many good men and women lost before their time, and yet we must have faith. The gods do not act without purpose. It is my only comfort—but for food and wine and lovers, I suppose."

Polypoetes laughed. "Food and wine and women are a great deal more comforting, I should think."

"Women, yes, and strong young men who you need not fear breaking," Heracles said, grinning. And like that, all his sorrow seemed forgotten, and I heard him give one of the others a hearty slap upon the back. "Pleasure in all its forms, and such a glorious gift from the gods!"

I took a deep breath, steadier now, and forced myself to leave the shadows, a smile of greeting upon my lips. "King Polypoetes. We did not expect the son of Pirithous to travel so far."

"I fear I suffer from my father's wanderlust," he said, bowing over my hand. Or lust of a different sort, in any event, I thought, for his eyes were more than warm, concern written clearly upon his face. "I must confess, I came for you, more than your father. I know you loved Tyndareus well."

"As you see, I suffer no dearth of support," I said, a subtle warning in my words as I withdrew my hand. "My husband, too, grieves deeply, but as king and queen of Sparta now, we have not the luxury of wallowing in our pain."

And then I froze, my gaze falling on a group of women standing apart. Two were young, beautiful—gifts for Menelaus, I was sure, and wise of my brothers to offer them. But the third was an older woman, gray-haired and sharp-eyed. *Aethra?*

Polypoetes smiled, his short nod answering the question written far too clearly in the surge of hope I could not quite keep from my face. "Your brothers brought gifts for King Menelaus, but I thought you might have use for a wise woman, now that you are queen. Call her Physadeia."

"Physadeia," I breathed, then swallowed my emotions, struggling to gather my wits. Theseus's mother. And here, acting as my servant. I was too grateful for words. Clymene was good to me, and loyal, but with Aethra's wisdom, surely I would find a way through this madness, a means to tame Menelaus's cruelty. "Are you . . . are you quite certain you wish to give her up?"

"If she does not suit you, send her back to me in Thessaly," Polypoetes said, shrugging as if it made no difference at all. As if he and Aethra had not given me a gift beyond measure, and even better, a means to reach him should I require his support.

"Polypoetes is our friend and guest," Pollux said, before I could respond. "It is at our invitation that he has come, in gratitude for the hospitality and kindness he has shown us in the North these past months."

"Then we are happy to repay him with the same," I said, turning a smile upon Castor and Pollux, whom I was truly glad to see, despite my fears. And all the gladder now that they had brought Aethra with them. "Any friend to my brothers is a friend of mine."

"And any friend of your father's as well, I hope," Heracles said, catching my hand in his and bringing it to his lips. "Though I hope, too, you will allow me to call you my sister."

But I did not miss the way Polypoetes's hands balled into fists, or the way he fought to keep still as I freed myself from Heracles with a smile and some rote politeness.

Fool, fool man. Much as I appreciated his kindness, I almost wished he had not come.

I was careful not to speak to Polypoetes overmuch. Menelaus might have sworn to keep me safe and treat me kindly, but I was not sure I trusted his pledge to extend so far as ignoring my friendship with Pirithous's son. Heracles, our most honored guest, sat with us at the head table, and Leda kept him entertained. From what I could tell from my place by Menelaus's side, Heracles had already drunk an entire amphora of wine.

"When will the games begin?" Heracles demanded. Even in regular speech he was loud, but now that he was half-drunk, he seemed to roar. "I challenge any man here to test his strength against mine. Pollux, you will wrestle with me, will you not? A son of Zeus against a son of Zeus, surely there is no fairer match to be had!"

"It would be my pleasure," Pollux agreed, and I spared my brother a glance. He could hardly have refused, not without offending our guest, though son of Zeus or not, I did not think there was any chance he could win.

"He'll crush your brother like a bug," Menelaus said, as if he knew my thoughts. He did a poor job of hiding his delight at the prospect. "Pray Heracles hasn't been drinking, or he's likely to forget his own strength and do Pollux real harm."

"If you are sworn to my safety, surely you cannot wish ill upon my brothers," I said. "They are my fiercest protectors."

Menelaus's eyes narrowed. "That is my duty now, and you would do well not to forget it."

"From here I travel to the house of Hades," Heracles boomed, speaking to my mother. "I mean to see Theseus and Pirithous set free on my journey there, and after I will help Theseus reclaim his city from that usurper Menestheus."

I nearly dropped my cup, the wine sloshing over the rim to spill upon the table before I managed to right it. Heracles meant to go to Hades. After all this time, he meant to free Theseus! I swallowed my emotions, all the relief that flooded through my limbs, all the joy.

Menelaus's fingers closed around my wrist, and he took the cup from my hands, all solicitude. "Is something the matter, Helen?"

His words came back to me, from that night weeks ago, when he had woken me from my dreams and thrown me upon the floor.

Should they ever come for you, I will make you watch while I tear them limb from limb.

I met his eyes, dark with the threat of his promise, and I could not breathe. *Theseus.* It had been Theseus's name I had called in my sleep. It must have been. And likely not for the first time. Now Heracles promised to free him, and Menelaus—Menelaus would never let him anywhere near me.

"Perhaps you'd like to retire to your room," he said. "Rest yourself until the rites tomorrow. We would not want you to dishonor Tyndareus's shade in the footrace because you have not *slept*."

"I—"

"Old woman," Menelaus called, jerking his chin at Aethra behind me. He had not batted an eye when my brothers and Polypoetes had presented her to me as their gift, but I had not yet found opportunity to speak with her alone. "See to your lady. She is unwell and needs her rest."

"Menelaus—"

"Would you prefer to remain ill for the duration of your brothers' stay?" he asked, his voice too low to be heard by the others. "I am sworn to keep you safe, and perhaps I fear they have brought some threat. Your suitor Polypoetes certainly looks on you as if he has forgotten that you are married."

My blood ran cold, and I rose. "Too much wine, that is all," I said to the table. "I am certain I will feel much better after I've rested."

"Let me escort you," Pollux said, pushing back from the table.

But I shook my head, pinning him to his seat with a glance. "Do not disrupt your meal on my account. My maid will see me to my room."

Pollux's gaze slid from me to Menelaus, his mouth a thin line, but he did not argue. "As you wish, my queen."

Heracles's chuckle followed me from the megaron. "Are you certain she's Zeus's get? Too much wine, indeed!"

I slumped against the wall once I was in the hallway and out of sight, and Aethra pressed a cool hand to my forehead. "You do look flushed, my dear."

"You do not know what it has been like, living as his wife. Knowing what I've lost. But if Heracles finds Theseus, and he comes to reclaim me—"

She pressed her lips together, sliding an arm around my waist to urge me along. "Menelaus is no match for Theseus, with or without Athens. He will strike Menelaus down and you will be freed. Surely you cannot doubt it."

Suddenly, I did feel ill. "In my nightmares, Menelaus whispers that he has had Theseus killed. He says that is why he did not come to find me in Troy. That he was pushed off a cliff and drowned in the sea. Theseus and Pirithous thought it only proof they would return, but what if Heracles sets him free only for Menelaus to defeat him? To bring about his doom?"

"Hush," Aethra said, squeezing me harder against her side. "If that is the future you saw, we will change it. You will not go to Troy, for one. You will remain here in Sparta and rule for long years as queen."

I shook my head. "I have tried, Aethra. I have fought so hard to change my fate. But I am married to Menelaus now. The one thing I wished to avoid at any cost. I am not so certain there is any stopping the rest, not anymore. And if it all comes to pass as my dreams have foretold . . ."

"Then we will destroy your enemies in the fires of your burning city," Aethra said, her voice low and determined. "And they will wish they had never looked upon your beauty at all."

But as much as I wished to believe it was possible—that I might at least have some power over Menelaus's fate, if not my own—I was not sure it would be so simple as that. For in my dreams, one thing was always the same.

Menelaus always survived.

And somehow, he always stole me back.

I rose before the sun the next morning, slipping from the bed while Menelaus still snored, and met Aethra outside my door. Early mornings were the safest for us, and Clymene thought nothing strange of my desire to be bathed by my new slave, allowing her to sleep a little longer. In fact, she had seemed rather pleased by the change in circumstance, though she insisted on helping me to dress after, and I could not refuse her without drawing more attention to Aethra than was wise.

The women's bathing room was deserted, as it always was, and I stripped quickly, sinking into the large spring-fed pool up to my neck. I had missed Sparta's bath while I'd lived in Athens. While I had been grateful for the bathing room we'd shared in Theseus's palace, ours required much less work.

"Did you sleep at all?" Aethra asked, joining me in the water.

I pressed my lips together. I'd dreamed. Not of Theseus, for which I could only thank the gods, but of my shepherd boy who would become a prince—perhaps he even was already. I had stood upon the wall of Troy and watched the men of Achaea die, searching for familiar faces, men I might have known. And Paris had laughed, drawing me away, murmuring encouragements and suggestions that made my face flush and my blood heat.

In my dreams, Prince Paris loved to toy with me, to see how far he could press me, and I knew I could not last. That one day, he would forget that he had sworn to wait until I came to him of my own free will, and my resistance would crumble under his power. Aphrodite's blessing was too strong, too insidious, and after so many long months, despair had sunk sharp claws into my heart, leaving me weak.

"You'll never find happiness with Menelaus, but Aphrodite herself will grant us pleasures beyond imagining if you will only accept me as your husband, your lover," he'd breathed against my ear.

And part of me knew he did not lie. He would give me pleasure, of that I had no doubt, but pleasure alone did not grant happiness. And I knew, too, that whatever we shared, it would not be love. It would be a hollow thing, paid for in too much blood to ever bring me anything beyond guilt and heartache. I could not betray my people for so little in return. Would not, no matter what lies Paris had told. The army of Achaea might believe me to be faithless, but I would not be so in truth.

"Helen." Aethra's hand upon my shoulder drew me back to the bathing room, concern shadowing her eyes. "Truly, you must find some way to rest. A potion, perhaps—do you have a physician you might trust to mix one?"

"I do not dare ask for anything from anyone," I said, leaning forward to let her scrub my back. Clymene had helped me gather the herbs required to keep my stomach flat and my womb barren, but even she did not realize what I used them for. "If Menelaus or Leda suspect me even for a moment, I do not think it will matter what oaths have been sworn. And I fear for my brothers, Aethra. There are so many ways he might ensure their deaths without bloodying his own hands."

"Hush," she said, pushing my hair over my shoulder, that it would not tangle while she did her work. "You twist yourself into knots over futures you have not even seen with your own eyes. Whatever Menelaus might whisper in your dreams, it does not mean he speaks truth. You say he has claimed to arrange the deaths of your brothers, but perhaps he only says as much to hurt you. To convince you that you have no allies left, no protectors, no friends. You have said yourself he is

Agamemnon's brother, that he would not hesitate to lie if it secures his desires. Until you see it yourself, do not trust the words."

Aethra was always so confident, so sure that Theseus would free me from my fears. I wanted to believe her, to let myself be reassured. But how could I? Once, I had let Tyndareus and my brothers convince me I had nothing to fear, and then again, I had placed my faith in Theseus, only to find myself here, facing everything I had fought so hard against.

"I do not know what I am meant to do," I confessed. "But every day, I wonder if I should not follow as my mother leads. The gods have granted me these dreams, and I am trapped within them. But why would they force me to see such a terrible fate if I was not meant to act in some way? To fight this future?"

"The gods are not always united in their cause, Helen. Did you never consider that one among them might have placed their faith in you, hoping that you might change what they could not? And once Theseus is returned, you will have the strength to see it done, I am sure of it."

"If they meant for Theseus to free me, why did they not curse him with these dreams?" I asked. "You tell me I have only to await his return, but I do not think that is enough. I love your son, Aethra, more than my own life, but surely this battle is mine, not his, to fight."

"Then you must find your own strength, my dear girl, and make use of it. Perhaps you cannot be a hero, woman that you are, but you cannot be a daughter of Zeus for nothing, and beauty is no small power to hold."

"Beauty has done me little good," I said, taking up another sponge to scrub my shoulders and arms, watching the dead skin slough from my body. "I have driven Menelaus into madness, and Theseus and Pirithous to ruin. If I turn my beauty upon any other man, he is likely to suffer the same again. What strength is that, when I only bring myself greater danger than that which I have sought to avoid?"

"You do not know that is true, Helen. You blame yourself for his ruin, but his journey with Pirithous—you did not know them in their youth, but I promise you, Pirithous would have found a way to persuade Theseus to join him, whether he had helped in stealing you or not. He always drew Theseus into trouble, relying on Athena's favor and Poseidon's love of his son to bring them home safely again. It was bound to end badly sooner or later, and you can be certain that Theseus's regret is only that his misfortune has harmed you."

"If they had only listened to me, we would all still be safe in Athens," I murmured, thinking of my brothers and Tyndareus, too. "Always they think they know better, and instead it is all made worse."

"And whose fault is that, truly?" Aethra asked, laughing. "Not yours, my dear. It is their own hubris that undoes them, not you. And if a man can resist *your* persuasions, the gods have already decided his punishment. Do not take so much upon yourself, Helen, for to believe it is your power which has caused so much harm, not the will of the gods, is just more hubris, too. Better to think yourself blameless than to rob the gods of their glory, do you not think?"

I could not help but smile at that, for Aethra was not wrong, and some of the weight that settled upon my shoulders lifted with her words. "You do not blame me in the slightest?"

"I know my son too well to fault you. For all his wisdom as a king, he has always behaved like a fool boy in the company of Pirithous. If I blame anyone at all, it is that Lapith son of Zeus, and even then . . . Pirithous did Theseus as much good as he did harm, just as you have. I am not so blind that I do not see that, too." She pressed a kiss to the side of my head and rose from the bath. "Now come and let's ready you for your race. If Menelaus means to allow you to compete, you must look every bit the queen."

CHAPTER
FORTY-ONE
HELEN

I t had been a long time since I had felt so free.

Aethra and Clymene had woven a crown of flowers into my hair, plaiting it all tightly against my scalp, and I had abandoned my heavy flounced skirts for a shorter tunic embroidered richly along the bottom edge, sleeves, and wide neck. It reached no farther than midthigh, that I might run without restriction, and Aethra had even helped me bind my breasts. Menelaus had given me a grudging nod when he saw my legs exposed, acknowledging the need, but his gaze felt hot and possessive on my back as I stood with the other women at the starting line.

"Ah, to have those thighs wrapped around my waist," Heracles remarked far too loud, elbowing Polypoetes, who murmured a response I didn't hear. I flushed all the same and turned my attention from the dais to the post that marked the turn, carefully avoiding the sight of the humped tholos tomb where Tyndareus's body had been laid to rest that morning.

It still did not feel possible that my father was gone. In truth, the year since my wedding had all felt like one long nightmare, familiar and strange, utterly unreal. Now I was queen, and it was nothing like I had imagined it would be. Leda had always been so strong, so powerful in her own way, a force within the palace and a helpmate to my father. I had never been more helpless, more trapped than I was now. Not even during those months I had been hidden away in Athens had I felt this suffocated.

I had not run, truly run, in years, nor had I so much as ridden a horse in months, since Menelaus had forbidden me to leave the palace, and I knew this race would leave me sore, but I did not care. For Tyndareus's honor, for my own, I meant to win. And I would not give up what Menelaus had granted me for this one day.

For Tyndareus's honor, and mine, I would win more than this race. I meant to win my freedom, too. I meant to be a queen in truth. And this was where I must begin. Here in this place before my father's tomb, surrounded by my people, by the women I might rule. The women I had overlooked for so long, had been reminded of only now, with Aethra's coming.

Because just as the king kept his court, his assembly, so did the queen, and how many wives counseled their husbands, mothers their sons, as Aethra had counseled Theseus? All this time, I had looked to the men—my father, my brothers, my husbands, and their friends—thinking it was their power I needed to make Sparta safe, to save myself. And it was only now that I understood what I ought to have learned years ago at my mother's knee: we women had power of our own.

I need not exert my influence over my husband the king directly, if I began with the wives of the men whose support he needed. Their whispered words in their husbands' ears would be my weapons, my secret strength, and there would be little Menelaus might do to stop it.

In Athens, I had resisted such a role, worried my lies would be discovered, but in Sparta, what did I have to fear? If I told the women of my dreams and they understood my concerns, my fears for their men, for mine, surely they would wish to help, to stop this war before it came, before it devoured their husbands, their brothers, their sons.

Leda lifted her hands, a brilliant red scarf fluttering in her grasp, and silence fell upon the field. "In honor of my husband, of your beloved king, let these games begin!"

Wind and laughter and joy, and I flew, leaving the other women and girls behind. I was lightning and the storm, impossible to slow, to stop. My lungs burned and my side spasmed, but I ran, fast and fleet as a deer in the wood, with the speed of an eagle as it dove. I ran and ran and ran, and when I came to the post, I did not want to turn. But I spun around the post, passing the other women as they fought to reach me, and I pushed my body harder, begging my legs for more, though they protested my pace.

I could hear my brothers cheering, hooting, howling with glee, urging me on, and I answered with another burst of speed. The flowers in my hair tore free, my bound breasts bounced with every stride, and when I looked back, I had left the others far behind.

The finish came too fast, too soon, and as I crossed the line, a new ache blossomed in my heart.

Before now, I had not truly known, had not realized what it meant. But now I understood.

To be a daughter of Zeus was to be always alone.

"You were glorious!" Pollux said, sweeping me up into his arms and spinning us both, before Castor did the same. "Tyndareus could not have been prouder."

Castor released me as Menelaus approached, a golden circlet in his hands.

"A queenly prize for the queen of Sparta," he said. "Though it seems you already wear a crown."

I touched the flowers in my hair, or what remained of them, and bowed my head. "The flowers belong to the princess Tyndareus raised. Now that I am your queen, I must leave that part of me behind."

He set the circlet upon my brow, his face a mask of pride, but his eyes glittering with something else, something harder beneath. "It was the princess I loved, when she was but a girl."

"And the woman?" I asked, for my brothers had stepped away, laughing with Heracles.

"It is the woman I have come to loathe," he said, and dropped his hands as though I had burned him. "But perhaps there is some small hope for the queen, beautiful and strong as she is."

My fingers went to the golden band, the place in the center where an emerald had rested in another crown, long ago, when I had been queen of another city and wife to another man. The life I had lived to stop this one from coming. The life I had lost, and still longed to have again. For whether Menelaus might love me or not, as I was or as I would be, I could never want him. Not after all that he had done to hurt me.

"May Aphrodite bless us both," I murmured in reply.

Because whatever he might desire between us, it would take nothing less than the force of that goddess's power to change my heart and mind.

Castor and Pollux won the chariot race, even after Agamemnon clipped their wheels, hoping to push them off the track with his dirty driving, and while the men readied themselves for the footrace and my brothers stabled my horses with Polypoetes, Heracles joined me upon the dais.

"Will you not race, my lord?" I asked, careful not to appear too warm in my address. I had not yet had opportunity to change from my tunic, and I dared not give Menelaus cause to chastise me for my behavior, or accuse me of tempting our guests.

"Not today," he said, smiling. "I will win the wrestling, after all, and I would not leave you alone upon the dais. The way your husband guards you, we will likely have no other chance to speak but this."

I kept my gaze upon the field, watching Menelaus. Clytemnestra had begged off after the chariot race, excusing herself from the dais to see to her husband, his expression murderous after his loss, but there was still Leda to consider upon the dais with her scarf, and my husband's glances, even from below. "It is truly kind of you to come, but I am not certain what you could want with me."

Heracles grunted. "I am loud, I know, and brash, but I am not dim-witted, for all of that. Even a blind man must see the way your husband looks upon you, as if he tastes something foul on the back of his tongue. It cannot be that he does not desire you, nor can I imagine that he finds no pleasure in your bed, but still he is dissatisfied. And your brothers tell me that is not all. That you live within your palace like a caged bird. But perhaps you are right, Little Sister, that it is not what I could want with you, but rather what you would have of me, that matters more."

I let out a breath, glancing up at him then, but his face was all but indecipherable behind that beard, and I was not so sure yet whether I trusted his plain speech. Heracles was known for his love of women, even of men, and though he called me sister, I did not think it would stop him from desire, even outright lust. Worse, he was a blustering drunk, loud and brash, as he had admitted himself. If he spoke so openly as this to me now, how much more might he say after he'd had too much wine?

"You are very kind," I said again, praying I did not offend him. "But I am not certain what, if anything, you might do. You are our guest, Heracles, bound by sacred laws of hospitality and friendship."

"And it is in friendship I offer my services to you," he agreed. "As Tyndareus's daughter, and as Sparta's queen."

I closed my eyes. That even Heracles might do my bidding—but surely he would refuse the only help he could give me. I did not think even loyalty to my father would be enough to convince him that Sparta would be best served by Menelaus's death, nor could I ask it of him. Sparta owed Heracles too much to betray his kindness with such a cruel request.

But there was another task I might ask of him, one for which he had already expressed intent. "Do you truly mean to travel to the house of Hades next?" I asked.

"I do."

"Then if you truly wish to help me, do as you have said," I told him. "Bring Theseus home, and the rest will not matter for long beyond that."

His eyes narrowed, his face flushing lightly above his beard. "What aid do you believe Theseus might offer you that *I* cannot?"

I met his gaze, refusing to be cowed by his bluster. "Perhaps it is not Theseus himself, but rather the threat of Menestheus removed, which I desire."

"You speak in riddles," Heracles accused, as if the thought of such a thing was a personal affront. "If it is Menestheus you wish to see brought low, you could have said as much outright, and risked nothing."

"We are not all so powerful in our own right that we need not fear what trouble our speech might bring, my lord. You have asked me what aid you can provide me, and I have answered as plainly as I dare. If you would demand more of me in payment for your kindness, I cannot grant it, though I dearly wish I could."

He studied me for a long moment, a low growl in his throat while he seemed to digest my words. "Theseus's freedom, then, is all that you desire of me?"

"If it can be granted without causing some greater harm to you," I agreed.

Heracles snorted. "I have nothing to fear on such a quest, my lady. Cerberus and I have already come to terms, and not even Hades would dare hold the favored son of Zeus in his house."

"A great shame the same cannot be said for Pirithous," I said, seizing on the smallest shift of conversation, before anyone else might hear our discussion.

"Even the gods cannot always favor fools," Heracles said, though it was clear he took no joy in Pirithous's misfortune. "His offense is by far the greater, but I will do for him what I can, all the same. Polypoetes, I think, will not be unhappy to give his father back his kingship, but in Athens, there will be trouble. That rat Menestheus will see it is so."

"Menestheus does not deserve to be king," I said. "Even if Theseus is lost, it should be Demophon who wears the crown. He is good and noble, and far more worthy of his people's trust."

"Indeed he is," Heracles said, studying me again. "Though I might wonder how you know his character so well."

I flushed and turned my gaze back to the starting post of the footrace, training my eyes upon Menelaus where he waited with the others. "I do not need to know Demophon to know that any son of Theseus must be more worthy than Menestheus."

"Two years you were gone, is that not so?" Heracles asked. "And after all that time you were found in Athens, by Menestheus, as I heard it."

I clenched my jaw. "It was not Menestheus's city then, but Theseus's, and Demophon ruled in his father's absence. Demophon took me in, though Menestheus would have the credit for it."

"Ah," he said, laughter in his voice. "Now I see."

And whatever explanation he had created for my request, for my desire to see Menestheus ruined and Theseus freed, he let the matter drop, and so did I.

Let him believe whatever he wished. So long as Theseus was safe and well, I did not care what Heracles thought of me.

Menelaus finished first in the footrace, though whether it was by his own skill or the consideration of those who ran at his side, I would not guess. Either way, he was in good humor that night, smiling and singing and raising his cup to our many guests. I sat at his side, a dutiful wife, dressed for the banquet in full skirts and a shawl to cover my hair, to prove my obedience, and in return he was attentive, even kind, passing me the most tender pieces of meat, giving me first choice of every dish, and keeping my cup filled with wine.

Always, he kept a hand upon my thigh. I drank far more than I should have, relieved by his manner and hoping to leave all the rest of my sorrow behind. And that night, Aphrodite must have pitied us both, for when he came to claim his husbandly rights, for the first time since Theseus had left me, I found pleasure of my own.

If this was the husband I would have now that my father had died, the king Sparta had been given, perhaps it was as Menelaus had said upon the field when he had awarded me my prize.

Perhaps there was some small hope.

CHAPTER FORTY-TWO

HELEN

I pressed my hands to my stomach, smoothing my skirts again. But no matter how many times I ran my hands over the fabric, it would not smooth away the thickening of my waist or the slight rounding of my womb beneath. "How can this be possible?"

Aethra caught my hands, holding them tight in her own. "No potion will stand long against the will of the gods, my dear. No matter how desperately we desire it."

"But it worked—before, in Athens. Theseus and I were saved the heartbreak of another child."

"I do not think you were meant to have even the child you did with my son," Aethra said. "Or perhaps the gods only granted you the girl as a test, to be sure Theseus remained loyal, as he had sworn. But either way, it was in their interest to keep you barren. Now a child only ties you all the more firmly to Sparta and Menelaus."

"No," I said, tugging free of her grasp. That night. It must have been. The night of my father's funeral games, when Menelaus had, for once in his life, seen to my pleasure as well as his own. It had all been a trick, and how Aphrodite must have laughed on Olympus every night since. "This has nothing to do with me. Better if I had remained childless if it is war they want. I am meant to run away, after all, to allow my abduction by this strange man. This is for Menelaus. To bind him to me. To ensure that when I am stolen, he will be all the more determined to win me back."

A child. Menelaus's child, planted and growing in my womb. And if Theseus came now, if Menelaus was killed by his hand, a child, a son, changed everything. He would be a risk, a threat to Theseus, even to me, should he believe I had plotted against his father. A son would have no choice but to avenge his father's death, or be driven into madness by the gods.

"There are ways to rid yourself of the babe," Aethra said, always so infernally calm, so steady, when I felt so storm tossed, so lost. "But if the gods will it . . ."

If the gods willed it, whatever potion Aethra spoke of would be just as useless as the one I had hoped would keep me barren.

"Pray for a girl," I said, the words bitter on my tongue. Sparta's heir, if it was, and everything I had tried to prevent. But I could not wish for a boy, in the hope of denying Menelaus his heir. Not knowing what a son would mean, should Theseus be set free as Heracles had intended. Spite was not reason enough to doom the man I loved, should he find a way to keep his vow and claim me as his own again.

"Are you certain?" Aethra asked.

I closed my eyes and steadied myself. "Better Sparta's heir be born of my body, with no question of her rights. You've seen his slaves, how many of them have ripened so quickly. He will take Sparta from my family altogether if I cannot provide his heir."

"If he lives."

She said it so simply, but Heracles had left more than two months ago. No word had come since, of Pirithous or Theseus or Heracles himself. "Aethra, I cannot live this life hoping for another. The gods have given me to Menelaus, and now they have given Menelaus the child he desires. I must make my peace with this, as I have the rest."

"Have you truly?" she asked. "Do you resign yourself to the future as you dream of it as well?"

I flushed. "That is hardly the same. Why should I resign myself to what has not yet come to pass? No. It is not the same at all as making peace with what is now."

"You speak as if it is nothing," Aethra said. "As if you can wave it all away, all your pain, all the suffering. As if you would let your daughter's death, your love for Theseus, mean nothing at all."

I dropped to the bed, hiding my face in my hands. "You know that isn't what I want. It isn't the choice I would make, were I free. But is it wrong to concern myself with Sparta? To make the best of what I have now, when I cannot be certain what will come?"

"No, of course not." She sighed, kneeling before me. "But do not lose faith, Helen. Do not lose hope. Theseus will come, I promise you."

"And he will find me swollen with another man's child," I said, misery squeezing a hand around my heart. "Why should he fight for me then?"

"Because he loves you," she said. "Because you love him."

"It isn't enough, Aethra. With so many lives in the balance, so much at stake, it is selfish of me even to consider it, any of it. I cannot let the world burn only for love. Not even for Theseus's sake."

"And if you turn from him, Helen, what good will it do?" Aethra asked. "As long as you are Menelaus's wife, as long as Menelaus lives, fate tightens a noose around your neck, threatening all your people, all of Achaea's sons."

"No one wants to thwart the gods in this as much as I do," I said. "But I fear they will have war either way. I fear all roads lead to death and ruin, and all because of me. Would you want to live with such a burden? With so much blood upon your hands?"

"Then you must ask yourself which is worse," she said. "A war that destroys us all, or a smaller conflict between Mycenae, Sparta, and Athens."

"It will not be only Mycenae, Sparta, and Athens who war." Of that I was certain now, though if it had not been for Odysseus, it might have been otherwise. "Where Theseus fights, the Lapiths will not be far behind. And Mycenae has her own allies. Any of my suitors might rise to Agamemnon's call, drawn by the oath they swore. We will fight among ourselves until there is no one left standing."

"You give our men less credit than they deserve. There will be many of your suitors who will not feel there is any purpose in defending the rights of a man who lies dead."

"But just as many who will fight for the hope of winning *me*."

"Against the claim of Theseus?" Aethra shook her head. "Just as the Lapiths would stand beside you both, so will Heracles and your brothers. Few men would dare wage a war against the children of Zeus and the son of Poseidon. All you need do is confess yourself and your love, and it will weaken their resolve all the further. No man wants a woman who is devoted to another, nor will they desire to find themselves compared to a demigod and found wanting by their lover."

"And Menelaus's child?" I asked.

Aethra shrugged. "With any luck, Theseus will arrive before the babe is born, and she will know no other father. He would not begrudge the child his love."

"Then his heart is bigger than mine."

Aethra's eyes filled with compassion. "You say that now, but when the baby comes, you will love her, too."

"No," I said, sure of myself. "I am Leda's daughter in this way if no other. Son or daughter, it will not be mine. This child and any other will only ever be another way in which I have been punished by the gods."

Menelaus felt differently, of course, and his honest joy, his solicitous fawning only sharpened my resentment. "You will have anything you desire," he said. "Anything at all." And then he laughed, the first time I had heard the sound since before Theseus had stolen me away. "Thank all the gods! I feared I would need to set you out upon the riverbank, your body an offering to Zeus, and pray for the swan to come."

I bit my tongue to hold back a surge of fury at his words, so carelessly spoken. As if the swan's coming had not been an act of humiliation, of violence and cruelty toward my mother. As if it had not been the seed that had planted all this pain.

He took my face in his hands, smiling. "You need not worry, Helen. Now you are with child, it will not come to that. And if the gods will grant us one, we will have another after. You will give me a handful, at least, before I am through. A little army of Spartan sons, enormous as Ajax with Zeus's ichor in their veins. And let Agamemnon try to lord over us then, eh? Clytemnestra may have bred first, but she has not your blood."

Always it came back to this, to Agamemnon and his power, his strength, his shadow stretching even so far as Sparta. No doubt Agamemnon had mocked his brother for his lack of children, when Nestra had given him a daughter almost at once, and was heavy with a second child, likely conceived while Tyndareus had languished in his deathbed. But I did not care what the king of Mycenae said of me, or even how he pricked his brother's pride. Agamemnon could rot in his cold, wet palace, and his children with him. My sister, too, for that matter. As far as I could tell, Nestra had no kindness left at all, any last thread of it snapped by Agamemnon's own cruelty.

"I thought I might walk the palace walls," I said, struggling to keep my temper in check. My brothers and Polypoetes had left Leonteus behind, pretending him one of Tyndareus's guards, and I knew more often than not I could find him there. Aethra had delivered more than one message to my brothers through his hands, but I longed to hear the news from Thessaly with my own ears, eager for any whisper of Theseus now that Heracles had gone. "A little sun and fresh air will do your child good."

"Of course," Menelaus agreed. "But not alone. Take that old crone with you, and Clymene as well, and you will rest in your room after the midday meal. I will not have you exhausting yourself, am I understood?"

"A walk upon the palace wall will hardly be so tiring I require the whole afternoon to recover," I said.

"You will rest, all the same. Every afternoon. There is little else that requires your attention."

"The queen's megaron—"

"You will rest, Helen," Menelaus said, his voice going hard. "If you wish to gossip with the other women, you will do so in the morning, rather than walking upon the walls. But I will not risk this child because you do not know enough to preserve your strength."

I snapped my mouth shut, though I wanted to protest. He did not know I'd carried a child before this one. He could not ever know of the daughter I had lost, and if I let my anger get the best of me, that secret would not be kept for long.

"Anything I desire, you said."

"Anything the child needs," he agreed, as if it were obvious from the start what he had meant. And perhaps it should have been. I ought to have known. "And above all, the child will need you fed and rested. I mean to see to both. Certainly I cannot trust you to ensure either. You've hardly eaten these last days, and you cannot tell me you sleep any better. Every night you toss and turn, moaning and weeping."

Of course he would hold my nightmares over me now. Menelaus had done nothing but use my dreams for his own ends since I had confessed them as a child. Now they were simply another means by which he thought to control me, and why should he hesitate?

"I will walk the walls and return to the queen's megaron," I said. "There, I promise you, I will rest. No doubt Leda will tell you if I exert myself in any way I should not, but no woman in the palace will ask anything of me that would risk your child. I am safer among our women than I will be in this room alone, and I will surely benefit from their wisdom, besides. Confine me, and you will only cause concern. Unless you want rumors to spread of my ill health? Or do you wish for us both to appear weak?"

He bared his teeth. "If anything should happen to my child, I promise you, Helen, you will regret it."

I lifted my chin, refusing to be cowed. "Lay a hand upon me, Menelaus, and we will see who regrets it more. The gods do not forgive broken oaths."

"I need not beat you to punish you, *wife*. Or do you truly believe your brothers are safe in their travels? That Clymene is safe here, simply because she shares my blood?"

"Then you will be cursed by the gods again," I said. "And if anything happens to my brothers, to Clymene, to anyone I love, I will make sure Sparta knows how their king betrays them. How you betray us all. Whatever love these people might have had for you, I will turn it into hate. Until you are king of nothing, and a usurper stands in your place."

He grabbed me then, his hand hard around my throat. I did not breathe. Could not draw a single breath. "You excel at that, don't you? Twisting love into hate, bringing men to ruin. But you will not take Sparta from me, Helen. You are both mine, and I will kill any man, any *hero*, who so much as suggests otherwise."

He threw me away, and I stumbled, falling to my knees and gasping for air.

"Go walk the wall, if you wish, and then gossip with your women, but remember what I have said. Bring this child to term, or you will wish you had died instead."

CHAPTER
FORTY-THREE
THESEUS

Theseus!"

The voice sounded far away, muffled by the roar of the sea and waves breaking against the wood hull. He scanned the horizon for another ship. Nothing stood on the water but gulls, as nothing had stood on the water for longer than he could remember. No land in sight, no others sailing these seas. But it was not the first time he had imagined someone calling his name. So long alone, he expected nothing less.

Theseus broke off another large flake of the dried fish and chewed carefully to avoid the smaller bones that he could not seem to remove no matter how much time he spent at the task. Inevitably one found a way to lodge in his throat or gouge the roof of his mouth. Just like the wood of the deck seemed always to drive splinters into his bare feet, no matter how cautiously he stepped. Just like, even in the burning sun, he could never quite find warmth. He rubbed at the chilled skin of his wrists and forearms, grimacing.

"Theseus!" Louder this time. And familiar?

A shadow passed across the deck, and Theseus's vision blurred. He shook his head. What had he been about to do before the voice had interrupted him? He couldn't remember now. Nor could he quite place where he had heard the voice before, but he knew it.

The deck heaved, sending him face-first into the worn wood. Theseus barely had time to catch himself on his palms, hissing at the sharp pinpricks in the heels of his hands. It would be a good day's work plucking the splinters out, and the sun had already begun to fall toward the east. He had given up puzzling out the backward sunsets long ago. It didn't matter. He sailed on. Searching for . . .

He frowned, hauling himself back to his feet. The ship pitched, but he clung to the rail. What was he searching for?

"For the love of Zeus, Theseus! Open your eyes!"

A wave crashed against the side of the ship, threatening to tip it, and Theseus whirled, looking for the source of the voice. Cold water and sea spray lapped over the rail, though he had grown used to the fact that his feet were always cold. This time, when the water washed back into the ocean, it seemed as though some warmth had returned to his toes. He stared at them, wondering. Had Poseidon taken pity upon him, after all these endless days?

The ship rolled, and Theseus looked up to see the wave cresting high above the deck. He cursed, lunging for the mast. If he could just reach the ropes—his left leg gave, and he cried out at the tearing pain in his thigh. As if the muscle had been ripped free of the bone.

"Theseus!"

Water filled his mouth, salty and foul, as the wave fell, knocking him to the deck. Tendrils of ice and shadow wrapped themselves around his limbs, and his fingers fell short of the rope that dangled from the mast. The deck slipped out from beneath his feet, and he flailed for something, anything to grab onto.

A hand grasped his and Theseus clung to it, ignoring the bite of the splinters forced deeper into his palm. He squinted through the rushing water, struggling to make out the face that stared down from above.

Did Zeus himself grip his hand? Theseus nearly let go with the shock of such a thought.

"Ha!" Another hand caught him under the shoulder and pulled him up. "If you think after all the trouble I took to release you from that chair that I will let you drown in waking, you are sorely mistaken, my friend."

Theseus gasped, his head breaking the surface. A hulk of a man bent over him, straw-colored hair falling into his sharp blue-gray eyes above a full beard. Heracles grinned, hauling Theseus onto the bank to drop him in the grass and mud. A riverbank, Theseus saw now, though he had been certain he sailed upon the sea. His fingers dug into the dark, wet earth and he pressed his face against it, breathing it in. Good, clean, solid earth. He had not seen so much as a smudge of it on the horizon in so long. It almost made him forget the throbbing in his thigh.

"You may not thank me for it, I'm afraid. Hades's chair mangled your leg when I pulled you free of its embrace, and it will be a long time healing, if it ever does." The grin on the hero's face faltered, and Theseus saw the lines of strain around his eyes. "Nor would Hades allow Pirithous to be set free."

Theseus closed his eyes. Pirithous. The name brought to mind the face as he spoke of Persephone and how they might steal her from Hades, grinning with the same smile Heracles had shown. Aphrodite had led them both to ruin in the Underworld. It came to him clear as sunlight now. They had been searching for the goddess that Pirithous insisted he would have as his wife. And they had found her husband waiting, ready to devour their souls.

The last thing Theseus remembered before the vast sea and the unending ocean was the thought of Helen, her hair golden again, her eyes shining like emeralds. His Helen. His wife.

"There is more, Theseus. And you must hear it."

Theseus rolled to his back, feeling the sun on his face and arms, pressing down upon him with welcome warmth. He had not felt warm, fully through to his bones, for what felt like years.

"Menestheus has taken Athens, expelling your sons and your mother. No one knows what has happened to your wife, but Castor and Pollux rode off from Athens and announced the return of their sister Helen."

Theseus's eyes flashed open, and he would have sat up but for Heracles pushing him back to the ground. "When?"

"Well over a year past now, at least. Menestheus claimed the city not long after you left, and we're on our way to autumn next now. Persephone has already rejoined Hades for the season, or I might not have found even this much success in my quest."

Helen. She had warned him, and he had not listened, and now her brothers had returned her home. Did they realize what they held? She had told Pollux about her dreams, he was certain of that much, and Tyndareus as well, for all the good it had done her. And Menelaus. More than a year he'd been gone, and if she was not in Menelaus's hands already, she could not be far from his grasp.

And Menestheus had betrayed him, just as she'd said.

"Demophon and Acamas? My mother?"

"Safe and well. Aethra bids you to seek out your wife, and in doing so you will find her near."

"My wife." Theseus stared at the sky, blue and cloudless. "What has become of Helen?"

"I had wondered what made you take a wife when you had sworn a hundred times you would never marry again, but if it was Helen, I see how you might have been tempted. It wasn't until she bid me to set you free that I realized the truth. At first, I thought Aethra only hid among her serving women to protect herself from Menestheus."

"You've seen her, then. Helen. Tell me she is well, Heracles, I beg of you."

Heracles crouched beside him in the mud, swinging a skin from his shoulder before taking a long swig of wine. He wiped his mouth on the back of his hand and passed the drink to Theseus, who took it. If Heracles hesitated to speak, the news could not be welcome. Theseus drank. At least the pain in his leg would dull with the wine, if nothing else.

"I went to Sparta for Tyndareus's funeral games, and there I met Polypoetes again. Grown into a man, a king now, with Pirithous lost. He reminded me of his father's plight, and yours. As it happened, I had other reasons for traveling to the Underworld, and upon hearing you were both still held by Hades, I hastened my journey. I thought I might free you and help you win Athens back after."

Theseus glared at him, struggling to sit up and managing only to lift himself up on his elbows. "This is not the time for your boasting, Heracles. I need not hear the entire story, only the end. Helen! If she bid you set me free, you spoke with her, saw her, and if Tyndareus is gone . . ."

He swallowed the rest, fearing the words. Tyndareus would not have left his city without an heir, without a king.

Heracles turned his face away, staring at the rushing water of the river. "She is married to Menelaus now, and he is king of Sparta as well. Menelaus won her by lot, and the pact made by her suitors will bring war on the man who might steal her."

"Fools!"

"With Agamemnon threatening to kill any man who married her, other than his brother?" Heracles shook his head. "No. I would not say they were fools. If some vow had not been made, her suitors would have slaughtered one another."

"They will see one another slaughtered yet," Theseus murmured.

He sat up carefully and pulled his good leg beneath him. The other burned where the flesh was missing, and he supposed he ought to fear festering, but surely if Hades had let him go, he was not to die yet. Heracles clasped Theseus's hand, helping him to his feet, but a shock like lightning ran through his leg when he put his weight upon it, and he nearly fell back to the mud.

"It will be some time before you can walk again, longer still before you have strength enough to take back Athens," Heracles said, support-ing him. "But Hades threatened to change his mind, and I had not the time for caution."

"It will heal," Theseus said, gritting his teeth in pain. "It must heal."

"I suppose that is in Lord Apollo's hands."

Theseus said nothing. Having lost Helen once, he could not fail her again. But to protect her, he needed to be whole. How else was he to fight off the Trojan prince when the man came? Or, more immediately, Menelaus? Lame as he was, he would only succeed in getting himself killed. And he would not give either son of Atreus the satisfaction of skewering him on the end of a spear. Not while Helen had need of a champion.

"Will you help me to the nearest shrine of the archer, my friend?"

"The walk will do you good, but might I suggest some wine to wash the ash from your mouth, after all that time below?" Heracles ducked his head, pulling Theseus's arm across his shoulders to lend himself as a crutch.

Theseus grunted, but took the wineskin from Heracles's belt and drank deep. Perhaps if he were fortunate, he would be drunk enough when they arrived not to feel the poking and prodding of the priests.

Gods above, Theseus thought, *have mercy upon me now, if ever. Help me to reach Helen. Help me to save us all.*

CHAPTER
FORTY-FOUR
HELEN

Months passed. My stomach swelled, and though we had heard that Heracles traveled the Peloponnese, there was no whisper of Theseus, not even among the women in my megaron while we sat with our spinning, weaving, and sewing.

Most of the work of clothing our households fell upon slaves and servants, hired or owned by the palace and working together elsewhere in the city. Only peasants *needed* to spin and weave, but there were some small duties that fell upon a wife—burial shrouds and wedding clothes, or a blanket woven for a longed-for child's bed. Those with the skill wove fine hangings, family stories remembered in the threads.

Leda had not approved of my weaving when I was a child, thinking it beneath a princess, though as queen she had done her share of spinning, offering the illusion of industry to guests. But Leda had not often needed to pretend. She had ruled by Tyndareus's side more fully, and run the palace besides, with four children to keep out of trouble and any number of other sons sent from our friends and allies to strengthen the bonds of peace and uninterrupted trade.

"I've heard Clytemnestra has given birth to a son," Leda announced that morning, while we worked and gossiped together.

Menelaus had allowed her to remain high priestess, but only after she had sworn to serve his needs first, and the running of the palace had fallen to me—though there was little the steward could not address, and now that I was heavy with child, Menelaus had taken even his daily reports from my hands. It was nothing more than an excuse, I was certain, to keep control of Sparta firmly in his grasp. And he was not wholly wrong to do so. While the careful inventories had been reported to me, I had been freer to offer gifts to those whose support I desired. Now Menelaus watched every bit of fleece, every ingot of copper, silver, and gold; even the immense amphorae of wine and olive oil did not escape his careful inspection.

But he had not stopped me from walking the palace walls, nor forbidden me from spending my days with the wives of his men. So long as I did not exclude my mother, it seemed he thought himself secure. And perhaps he was, while Theseus remained lost, for I would not see my people cursed by spilling his blood. Zeus would never forgive a queen who murdered her king, and I did not think Hera would protect me, either.

"Agamemnon has named him Orestes," she said. "A fine, strong boy. He latched upon his mother's breast the moment he was placed in her arms."

"Agamemnon must be relieved to have an heir at last," I said.

"Just as Menelaus will be, should you give him a daughter," Leda said. "It will be a fine match when the time comes, the heir of Sparta married to the heir of Mycenae."

"I had heard that my cousin Agamemnon was so besotted with his Iphigenia he meant to make her queen if Clytemnestra could not give him a son," Clymene said.

I doubted it, knowing Agamemnon. I did not think him capable of seeing even his own daughter as more than another tool to secure his power. He'd marry her to a man he trusted, or one too weak to challenge him, and then wait for a grandson worthy of his crown. The poor husband of Iphigenia would be disposed of then, to make way for the child Agamemnon wanted upon the throne.

"Then King Menelaus will surely promise Helen's son to Iphigenia, and unite our lands twice over," Leda said.

It was exhausting, listening to my mother plot, and I set aside my spinning, my fingers fumbling and weakening the thread.

"Old Nestor might have something to say about that," Aethra said, careful to keep her gaze upon the sewing in her lap. "All those sons and grandsons of his need wives, and he did not raise them to be useless. I'd be surprised if he hadn't already sent to Mycenae, hoping to arrange a match."

"And Agamemnon will let King Nestor shower him with gifts," I agreed, "promising nothing either way. Why commit himself to any alliance at all so early, when it will be ten more years before Iphigenia can be wed, and some more valuable suitor might come to call between now and then?"

"A prince of Troy, perhaps," Aethra suggested, innocently enough. "Granting Mycenae trade rights in the bargain for her hand, giving him power over all Achaea's kings."

"Troy will never give up so much," Leda said. "Not unless it was the king himself taken with one of our women, and even then, they're just as likely to steal her in a raid as have her honorably."

"You speak so ill of the Trojans, Mother," I said, aware of the other women listening, and choosing my words with care. "But did not King Telamon steal his bride from Troy? Queen Hesione, the mother of Teucer, was a Trojan princess, as I recall, and the sister of King Priam, himself."

"And not even Salamis has been granted the right to trade beyond Troy, though they have made their Trojan princess into a queen," she said, as if that proved her point.

"And Sparta would never give hospitality to any man who allied himself with my uncle Hippocoon after he stole the crown from my father, Tyndareus. Why should Troy offer favors to those who have wronged her? Salamis should be grateful Troy did not launch ships and lay siege."

"Over a woman?" Aethra asked, laughing as if there were nothing more ridiculous in the world. And nor was this the first time we had worked together this way, to undermine any justification Menelaus might use to raise a host for war. "No king is so great a fool as to go to war over a stolen bride. Can you imagine such a thing? Why, think of all the women Heracles alone has stolen, or Theseus, for that matter. We would have no men left in Achaea if we made so much of so little."

"Theseus did not steal anyone who did not want to be stolen," I said. "But the same cannot be said for most. Hesione, queen of Salamis or not, was wronged, and Troy as well. We should be glad they allow us any trade at all, as shabbily as they have been treated, and as often as Achaean men raid their coasts."

"We would not have to raid if they were not so greedy," Leda said with a sniff of disgust.

"And no doubt they would treat us more generously if we were not stealing from them with one hand while we begged for their trade with the other."

"This is how it has always been, Helen, and how it will always be," Leda said. "Do not think to meddle in things you do not understand."

I smiled, forcing a lightness to my voice that I did not feel. "Forgive me, Mother. I certainly would not dare to speak so boldly to my husband. But we are among our friends, are we not?" I let my gaze travel over the others in the room, from the woman nearest me, Alcyone, the wife of the steward, to shy Pandora, daughter of a man Menelaus had appointed as one of his collectors. "And as queen, I would have this megaron be a place where we might all speak our minds freely, safe from the censure of men. Certainly we ought to be able to speak within these walls of the fates of our sisters, if nothing else."

Leda's lips pressed thin, and I knew she did not trust my words. But she could not argue. Not when she had used her megaron as a sanctuary in the same way.

"We should all be so fortunate as Hesione," she said then. "And Troy should be honored that good King Telamon made her his queen."

My lips twitched, my eyes meeting Aethra's, though I kept my words mild. "Then I suppose we should not fear any Trojan prince coming to steal away his own bride, for surely she will be treated with the same honors when he brings her home."

It did not matter if I believed the words, I told myself—I did not like to think of any woman treated so. What mattered was that the women heard them, and should the day come that I was stolen from this very palace, they would remember what had been said, thinking of the husbands they would lose, the sons, and use their influence to make them hesitate.

These moments were small victories, I knew, not enough to change the nightmares I still suffered, for to do so I must be heard by more than just Sparta's women, but perhaps it would mean these mothers would keep their sons at home, instead of letting them sail after their queen, eager to spill Trojan blood.

It wasn't much, but perhaps if I kept fighting, it might build upon itself into something more. Perhaps they would see that whatever encouragements Leda might offer, they need not follow where she led. With a little persuasion from their queen, they might even protect their men.

And though I did not say it to Aethra again, I knew I could not depend upon Theseus. Or anyone else at all. Whatever could be done to stop this war, it must be done by me.

Me alone.

CHAPTER
FORTY-FIVE
HELEN

Thank the gods it was a daughter. Let Menelaus have as many sons by the slaves as he wished, but his heir, at least, would have some of Sparta's proper blood in her veins. Leda's blood and Zeus's ichor, and what part of her belonged to my husband, I prayed would never surface. But a daughter was safest—for me, for Theseus, for everyone involved.

Once I had assured myself of her sex, I passed her off to Aethra and the milk mother she'd found. Leda could have the raising of her if she liked, but I would not give the gods another rope with which to bind me.

"You're certain this is what you wish?" Aethra asked, watching me too closely.

"She is Sparta's heir and Menelaus's daughter, not mine."

"Helen—"

"The gods cannot replace the child they stole from me so easily as this," I said, staring Aethra down. I did not forget the part she had played in encouraging Theseus to give up our daughter, even if I had forgiven it. "Send her to the woman to nurse, and keep her from my sight."

Aethra's lips thinned, but she turned away, the baby bundled in her arms. "You must name her at least. By custom it is the queen's right to name Sparta's daughters."

I closed my eyes, leaning back. The delivery had been quick, of course, almost easy, and though I was tired now, it was not the exhaustion that I remembered. I almost wished the gods had not spared me from it, for at least then I might rest. The dreamless sleep of the ill and the dying, with no nightmares to wake me.

"Call her Hermione, then," I said. She would need whatever strength her name and the gods might lend her, for she would not have me. Even if Theseus came to claim me, and Menelaus died tomorrow by his sword, I did not see how I could love her.

"You know what it is to live with your mother's disdain, Helen," Aethra said lowly. "To be scorned by her for nothing more than your birth. Will you truly do the same to your daughter now?"

"She will not have my scorn or my cruelty," I said. "But nor can I give her my love. Should I pretend otherwise?"

"You might try now, while she is still too small to know if the arms that hold her do so with love or disinterest. You might try at all."

But I did not want to. I did not want to love her of my own will or to be made to love her even by her own charms. I did not want *her* at all. A reminder of nothing but my sorrow, my heartbreak, my pain, and the husband I despised.

"No," I said. "And it is better this way. If I am stolen, she will not feel it as a loss. Leda will love her, if only to spite me, and when she is older, it is not as though I will be unkind."

Aethra sighed and left me alone. It would not be the end of it, I knew, for Aethra was nothing if not stubborn.

Just like her son.

My throat thickened with longing for Theseus, for the daughter he'd given me, the child the gods had stolen from us both. I knew I would never look on this daughter, this Hermione, without grief for my lost child clawing its way up out of the dark pocket in my heart where I had buried all my hopes, my memories of that other life.

And Menelaus would see it all, written in my face so clearly. He would see, and he would know the truth, and that was a risk I would not take.

Certainly not for a child I'd never wanted by a man I loathed.

"Awake at last?"

I kept my eyes closed for another breath, wishing I had not stirred at all, but I would have to rise before long, if only to relieve myself, and Menelaus, clearly in a temper, would merely grow more enraged by the wait.

"Your mother tells me you refuse to feed the child from your breast," he said, unconcerned that I had not responded. I hated that he knew me so well.

I sighed, opening my eyes a slit. "A child's rearing is her mother's affair, not yours."

"Hermione is my heir," he said, his jaw tight and his whole body coiled with anger—he must have already waited far too long. "That makes her a concern of mine as well."

"Then take her," I said. "Take her and make her yours. Raise her as you wish, and I will not interfere, but you cannot make me love her."

He rose, large and looming, his teeth bared in a snarl. "You will keep our daughter by your side, Helen, and at your breast, or I will tie you to the bed and force you. I will not see my child weakened because of your spite."

"And when my milk runs dry, what then?" I asked, sitting upright despite my discomfort. I'd fought against terrible cramping all night, aches and strains I did not remember from my last birth, buried as they'd been beneath so much other pain and suffering. "Do you think for a moment that more milk will come simply because it is your command?"

"I warn you, do not test me," he growled. "My patience for your foolishness is already stretched far too thin. You've taken advantage of me, Helen, of my kindness, and I swear by the gods, you will not be given the opportunity to do so again."

"Your *kindness*?" I snorted. "You do not know what kindness is, Menelaus. Not anymore. How could I take advantage of what I was never given?"

He slammed a wooden tablet down upon the table beside my head. The same on which I had written a message in soft wax to be sent to my brothers in Thessaly, through Leonteus, still upon Sparta's walls. Wax could be easily smudged or melted, obscuring the words and the message itself from prying eyes, but clearly Menelaus had found this one intact.

Aethra had passed along my letters a dozen times, and each had been a risk. This small note, informing my brothers of my daughter's birth, was the least objectionable, and I thanked the gods for that. But if he had seen any of the messages Polypoetes had sent to Leonteus, to me, he might have brought me Leonteus's head, rather than this.

"How long have you and your brothers had your spy upon the walls, Helen? How long have you been sending them messages behind my back?"

"How else could I be certain my brothers were safe and well, without putting them in greater danger?" I met his eyes, refusing to show my fear or even to acknowledge any guilt. He had done this, not me.

"If you had not threatened them, I would not have felt the need to hide our exchanges. You have only yourself to blame for that."

"It stops now," he snapped. "Your spy has fled, and should he ever return, I will have his throat cut. If your brothers desire to write to you, they will do so through me, as will you."

"Are you so afraid of what we might say to one another?" I asked, mocking now. "Do you think they do not realize how unhappy I have been? How miserable you have made me? If they sought to do you harm, they would have done it long before now."

"Perhaps if you did not undermine my rule at every turn, I would believe such a lie. But after this? After seeing all the gifts you have given to the men who oppose me, who argue against the ships I would build and the arms and armor I would see forged? No, Helen. You will not convince me this is all coincidence. That you and your brothers have not taken action from the start to weaken me and my position. As if my brother does not already seek to control me, now you do as well?"

"If I could control you, Menelaus, I would have sent you far from here long ago. I would have never married you at all!"

"Of course," he sneered. "If you'd had your way, you would have taken Theseus of Athens as your husband, I know. The way you call to him in the night, I can have no doubt where your affections lie. But he took another wife, Helen! Married and left you behind. And do you know what has become of your great hero now? Shall I tell you what word has reached us, after all this time?"

My throat closed, all my courage shriveling to dust on the back of my tongue. "Theseus is lost, trapped in the house of Hades."

"No longer," Menelaus said, gloating now. "No, he is freed, thanks to Heracles, and do you know what's become of him? All his strength, all his famed wisdom means nothing now that he's been crippled, the flesh of his thigh left behind in Hades's chair when Heracles tore him from its embrace."

"He is fortunate to have escaped at all," I said, struggling to hide the rising tide of my grief, to mask it with disdain I could not feel. For Theseus of all men to be crippled—this news changed everything. Aethra had counted upon his strength, his skill with a sword and his fists, but he would not survive if he challenged Menelaus with only one good leg. "He deserved far worse punishment than that for trying to steal Persephone from her husband."

"He'll suffer more, still," Menelaus promised. "Truly, the gods could not have treated him more cruelly than this. To give him back his life, and take from him all his triumphs, all his glory, all his strength and skill. He will be Oedipus, wandering and homeless and cursed by the gods, watching everything he built be torn apart."

"You should not take such pleasure in the misfortune of others, Menelaus," I said, wishing him away, that I might weep. "You will tempt the gods to see your own fortunes turned."

He painted so pitiful an end, and he did not know how much I had lost with his words, how much he pained me. My Theseus, brought so low. Lower still, if he came for me. I could not let him. Somehow, I must tell him so. Keep him from returning to my side. I could not live knowing that he had died for me, and I did not see how it would end any other way now.

"If I take pleasure in his fall, it is only in the knowledge that he will never take what is mine," Menelaus said. "No matter how you long for your hero, he will never come. And no amount of scheming with your brothers will change that."

I could not send for Aethra at once, for now that Menelaus had discovered Polypoetes's spy and the letter to my brothers, I had no doubt he would watch me all the more closely. Nor did I dare let myself sob aloud, but only turned my face into the bedding to muffle what cries I could not stop. Theseus. Poor Theseus. And now I understood how he could be killed with a push. A crippled man might be shoved from a cliff far more easily than one still whole.

Clymene came soon after, Hermione in her arms, and stopped short by the bed. "My lady, forgive me. My lord King Menelaus said you had called for your baby, that you'd decided to nurse her at your own breast."

"Leave her," I said, too exhausted to argue. "And find Physadeia."

Clymene placed the child in my arms, and I set her upon the bed beside me, unable to look into her face. If Menelaus believed telling me of Theseus's fate would bend me to his will in this, of all things, he would realize soon his mistake. I would not take his child to my breast or my heart. I would not be made to forget all that Theseus and I had suffered.

My maid left the room, and I waited. For when Aethra arrived, I must find a way to tell her of her son, and then, I feared, I must send her away.

If Theseus were truly so lamed, his need of his mother would be far greater than mine. And it was long past time I gave up the small flames of hope Aethra had fanned in my heart. She would go to her son and bring him a message.

Do not come for me, I would tell him. *Only find what peace you may.*

CHAPTER
FORTY-SIX
HELEN

Aethra did not like to leave me, but she went all the same, sorrow in her wise old eyes. Like me, she grieved for her son, and I think she knew as I did how much Theseus would need his mother, for she did not so much as argue, beyond one hard look at the message I begged her to give.

"He has sworn a vow, Helen. These words cannot change that."

"If he comes, he will die. Better that he should live a half-life than not at all."

She stroked my hair, studying my face. "Do you love him any less, knowing he is crippled?"

"Of course not," I said. "If he had lost the leg entirely, I would still long for him, still love him more than my own life. Do you not see it is for his sake that I ask this, not mine?"

She nodded, satisfied. "I will tell him, then, as you wish."

But I was still desperately afraid it would not be enough to keep him safe.

My days stretched long and slow and aching, but within a week, I rejoined the women in my megaron. Another excuse to keep small Hermione from my side, and I had need of every one I could find, for Menelaus had not forgotten his threats and, mistrusting me, had begun to accompany his daughter when she was sent to me to be fed, watching until he had seen her latch onto my breast.

I hated him then more than I had ever believed I could.

And then my brothers arrived, with Polypoetes in their midst, all three scuffed and bruised and bloodied in their armor as they burst into my hall, shoving through the guards who tried to stop them.

"Let them pass," I called, tripping over my skirts to meet them. Pollux looked the worst, and I found myself tracing the marks upon his skin, searching for broken bones, for wounds still bleeding. "What's happened? What's wrong?"

"We went with Theseus to Athens," he said, too loud. I hushed him, my gaze finding Leda among the other women, surrounding us now. But Pollux shook his head, continuing on. "Menestheus told them everything, and Menelaus will know, too, before long, if he does not already."

I drew back, my heart thundering, but when I looked to Castor, to Polypoetes for some reassurance, their faces were just as grim.

"Leave us," I said, to the room at large. "All of you. I must speak with my brothers alone."

"King Menelaus—" Leda began.

"King Menelaus will have the truth of this from my own lips, once I know all that has happened," I said, drowning her objection beneath my own firm command. "Now go!"

I watched them leave, waited until the guards had closed the door. My hands were trembling, the shock of Pollux's words turning to fear. "Tell me Theseus is safe, I beg of you."

"He lives, though it was a near thing," Polypoetes said. "I dare not say more within these walls."

"Then tell me everything," I said to Pollux. "Tell me what Menelaus will know, if he does not already."

But Pollux looked to Castor, and my eyes followed his. My quiet brother, so blessed by the gods—even he looked shaken.

"I did everything I could," Castor said. "We all did. But the Athenians—Helen, they turned him out. For betraying them, for stealing you and hiding it all. Menestheus told them you were Meryet, stolen in violation of the sacred laws. He said the gods had marked Theseus, crippled him, that he might be made unfit to rule for his sins, and they believed his words, turning on their rightful king like winter-starved wolves."

"I fear Menestheus will never be ousted," Pollux said. "Certainly not by Theseus, or even his sons, tainted now by their father's supposed wrongs. I do not know what Menelaus will do when he hears of it, but we could not leave you to face him alone. I won't abandon you, Helen. Not now."

Menelaus would hear all this, and it would be betrayal heaped upon betrayal, humiliation and insult he could not overlook. Even his vow to Tyndareus might be forgotten in his rage, unless I found some way to soften it, to bend this truth into something else, something new. Lies upon lies, until it sounded more like truth, combined with a gift the likes of which he had only ever dreamed . . .

It would cost me everything. Everything of myself that I had kept, fought and bled for from the start. I sank to the long stone bench that lined the walls, digging the heels of my hands into my eyes before they filled with tears I could not shed. "But you must leave me, all the same."

"You cannot be safe here," Pollux argued. "You did not see how twisted he had become, after you were stolen. When he learns it was Theseus—gods above, Helen. Just the knowledge that you had given Theseus a child—"

I lifted my head, ignoring Pollux, heartsick with the knowledge that my brothers were right to fear for me, and I looked to Polypoetes instead. "He will kill them if they do not go. For helping Theseus now, for keeping the secret of it for so long. He cannot hurt me, not without suffering my father's curse, but he will kill my brothers, and you, to punish me. He's threatened as much already, more than once."

"I would trade my life away for your sake, Helen," he said, his voice rough with emotion. Words I knew he'd say. Polypoetes would never betray me, bound by honor and friendship more than lust, now. "Just as I would have lived with madness to be your husband. To know you were my wife."

"For my sake, then, protect them. If you ever loved me at all, drag them from these halls and take them north. Keep them safe in Thessaly. Keep yourself safe, that you might yet come when I have true need of you."

"And how will we know?" Pollux asked. "Without Leonteus, without even Aethra to send word?"

"When the stranger comes, the prince, you are seated at my husband's table," I promised him, taking his hands in mine. Then Castor's, too, in turn. "You are both with me when it matters most. But if I do not send you away now, you will not survive to see that night—I know it. Go with Polypoetes, help Theseus if you can, and leave me to handle Menelaus."

"Are you certain of this, Helen?" Castor asked.

"I have known for some time that these are battles I must fight alone," I told him. "Theseus's failure in Athens, his wound . . . it is only the proof. I must give him up. Give up all hope of love, of joy, and live the life the gods have given me by the terms they have set."

Polypoetes shook his head. "No matter what you say, what you intend, Theseus will not give up on you. No man who has known your love could."

"He will see soon enough he has no choice," I said, though the words hurt me. "Just as I have. Just as you will, too."

And then I made them go.

I would face Menelaus alone.

"You filthy whore!" he spat, throwing down the golden circlet at my feet. It bounced and spun, skittering away, and I paid it no mind. I'd returned to my room to find him there already, my belongings strewn everywhere as he ransacked my possessions, searching for what, I did not know. That very circlet, perhaps, or some other proof of the news that had already spread. He'd been railing at me since. "You *lied* all this time. To your mother and father, to me!"

"I thought if I gave myself to Theseus then, before we were wed, it would stop all this from coming. To spare us both this pain! And if I returned—when I returned—it would be behind us. We could live our lives in peace, in love, happy together, as we had both always dreamed."

"Then it is true," he said. "All of it is true. Your dreams—you have been lying about those, too."

I pressed my lips together, for I had promised myself long ago he would learn nothing more of my nightmares, and this seemed the simplest way. He had always wanted to believe my dreams were false somehow. I would give him the excuse to dismiss them now, and perhaps, just perhaps I could turn all this to my advantage.

I could not control my fate, but that did not mean I could not hold Menelaus to my will, for Sparta's sake if not my own. He had lusted for me until today, believing he could have nothing more. That was the madness in his soul, the knowledge that no matter how he tried, he could not have my heart.

"Theseus was the man who stole you, all along," Menelaus accused. "And you hid it all that time, thinking to stop the war I would fight to take you back. All the rest of this, all your whimpering and tears in the night. Just more lies, to keep me from marching on your precious Athens and burning it to the ground."

His reasoning was convoluted at best, but with any luck, he would never realize how wrong he was. Why should he? It was not as though he would speak of this to his men. Theseus and I had humiliated him. Menelaus would want nothing more than to see it buried, to stop it from haunting his every step. And I knew what he wanted to hear; I'd always known, though before now, I had not been nearly so convincing, holding a part of myself back from the lies I told. This time, I could not keep myself apart. I must mean every word I said, and not only in the privacy of our room, but outside it. This time I must weave my tapestry of lies so tightly that not even Agamemnon would find any threads to unravel.

"I gave myself to you first," I said, pleading now. "You must understand, Menelaus, I only wanted us to be free. But it only made everything so much worse. And I did not know how to make it right, how to make us right. The stories my brothers told when they found me—I was so frightened it was too late, that I had ruined everything."

"And so you lied."

"I did not know what else to do." I dropped to my knees, grasping the hem of his tunic and pressing my face to his thigh in supplication. "I feared he would return for me, still. That I had not escaped my fate, after all. That was why I walked the walls. That I might have some warning, to stop him from stealing me a second time."

Menelaus stared at me, his face still red from shouting. He wanted to believe it. I could see it in his eyes. He wanted to believe that I had done it all for him, for us, and in truth, there was a part of me that wished for it, too. If only I had loved him, if only I could love him now.

Hermes, help me. Let us both be tricked by my words.

"I have always been your Helen," I said, the words bitter upon my tongue. "I have always been yours. Only let me prove it now. Let me give you everything you have long deserved."

"All this time you have denied me," he said. "All this time."

"Out of fear only," I said, letting my hand creep up his thigh. "I thought you would reject me, even send me from your side, and that fear kept me still, stiff and wooden in your bed. But let me show you my love, Menelaus, my devotion, I beg of you. Let me be your wife and queen in body and spirit as well as name. Let us be true partners, now that there are no secrets between us."

He wanted me, he had always wanted me, and I had let him abuse me, but he had never had me. Not until now. The only use for this beauty Zeus had given me, though I had shrunk from employing it before this moment, that when Theseus returned, I might know I had remained true to his love, true to myself. But I could not be his any longer. I could not be mine. I was the queen of Sparta, and I must serve my people first.

I would serve no one locked away, mistrusted and reviled by my husband, and though it made my skin crawl to welcome him, and I could never love the man he had become, it was long past time I did what I must.

"Menelaus, please," I murmured against his thigh, caressing him in the manner Theseus had once loved. "Please, let us have peace."

He groaned, desperate and low. "Promise me. Promise me you will be mine. That you are mine, even now!"

"As a child, I wanted no one else but you. And I promise you, I am yours. I have been yours from the start."

"Show me," he said. "Show me you are mine."

I showed him every pleasure I knew, and after he had fallen deeply asleep, I crept from the room, through the halls, until I climbed the palace wall, wearing a long underdress and Theseus's old woolen cloak.

One last stolen moment, and I lifted the thick wool, pressing it to my nose. It smelled of nothing now, though for weeks after I had left Athens, I had taken deep breaths, catching faint traces of his scent from the cloth.

"Forgive me," I breathed into its warmth.

Then I took it off and threw it over the wall.

I was Menelaus's now, and would not let myself think of Theseus again.

PART FOUR: FATED ENDS

CHAPTER
FORTY-SEVEN
PARIS

It had taken him years. Months upon months of ingratiating himself, of small longing suggestions of how sheltered his life had been, and how desperately he desired to see more of the world than the slopes of Mount Ida and the high walls of Troy. Years of subtlety and charm, of moments when he felt the goddess near and his words snaked into the hearts of his brothers, his sisters, his father and mother, convincing them of his need when they might otherwise have laughed his wishes away.

But Aphrodite had been true to her word, and the ship he required awaited him upon the shore. She had even given him a pretense for sailing so far as Achaea, for Priam wished for news of his sister Hesione, wife of King Telamon, and he was sending Paris with men enough to reclaim her should she desire it, and from Salamis it would be a simple matter to travel on to Laconia before making his way back home.

A month, perhaps two, and he would hold Helen in his arms, know the softness of her lips and the sweetness of her kiss. A month, perhaps two, and she would be safe again, protected from all who might abuse her. Paris would honor her as no husband had honored his wife before. He would shower her with gold and silver, with silks and linens so fine they were nothing more than a gentle breath against the skin. She would want for nothing, and he, too, would at last be satisfied.

"Do not go."

He whirled, startled by the voice when he had thought himself alone upon the balcony—his own balcony, in his own luxuriously furnished rooms, within the royal palace itself. "Who's there?"

Oenone stepped out of the shadows, her cheeks stained with tears, her clothing filthy and torn. A woman in mourning, her beauty obscured by her grief. "Do not go, Paris. Do not follow where Aphrodite leads, I beg of you."

He let out a breath, crossing the balcony to her side and guiding her to a bench. "You are too far from the mountain, Oenone. Truly, you look ill. Water!" he called inside to the servants, always waiting for his command. "Bread and wine as well for my guest, quickly!"

She clutched his hand. "Please, Paris. Please. If you leave upon that ship, you will never have peace. *We* will never have peace."

"How did you come so far?" he asked, ignoring her words. "To arrive here, inside the palace, in this state."

"I helped her to find her way." Another woman stepped into the light, and he frowned at his sister, Princess Cassandra.

She had never warmed to him, never treated him with anything but scorn and agitation. From the moment he had won the boxing match, it seemed she had set herself against him, and even with Aphrodite's blessing, he could not turn her heart to fondness for the brother she made no secret of wishing dead.

"Mother and Father are blind and deaf to my warnings, as you have been, but Lord Apollo does not give up so easily." Cassandra's gaze shifted focus, rising to the sun. "We are his beloved Troy, and he will not rest. He will never rest so long as you draw breath, so long as the fire in your heart threatens to burn us all within its flames."

"A flame of love," he said. "Nothing more."

Oenone moaned softly, falling to her knees. "Do you not see what you have done already? Look at me, Paris Alexandros, and tell me these flames have harmed no one!"

He shook his head, urging her up, prying her fingers from his knee and setting her again upon the bench before him. "From the start you knew my heart lay elsewhere, Oenone. You knew, and yet you stayed at my side. That you have suffered for it—I wish it might have been otherwise, but I will not take the blame for the gods' choice."

"*Your* choice," Cassandra hissed. "Your choosing, now and then. *You* have chosen to pursue the Spartan whore, to follow the goddess and turn your back upon the gifts Lord Apollo gave you. You might have chosen otherwise, even from the moment the goddesses revealed themselves to you."

"You would have had me lie?" he demanded.

"Did you not?" his sister sneered. "When you promised yourself you would not be bribed, only to succumb to Aphrodite's lure? The gods are fickle, Brother, and cruel to those they bless. Better if you had refused the task and died at the whim of Zeus than follow this path."

He ground his teeth, turning away from them both. They didn't understand. And how could they? They had not seen Helen bathing in the river. They had not heard the fear in her voice, the regret when she had realized what her Athenian protector meant to do.

"She saved my life," he heard himself say. "She spared me."

"If only she had let you die, instead," Cassandra said. "Then she might have spared us all."

Oenone remained in the palace at Cassandra's invitation, and when he took the short ride by chariot to his ship, she followed, weeping and begging him to turn back.

"We will all burn," she cried out, when the driver pulled the horses to a halt and he leapt from the chariot car. "And you will not survive the flames. You will be ash and bone upon the pyre before it is finished, unless you heed my words."

All night, she had wailed beneath his balcony, a cruel torment arranged by his dear sister, and in the morning when he had taken his last meal with his family, he'd endured the mocking of his brothers as well.

"Our Alexandros thinks so highly of himself he believes he'll do better than a nymph for a wife!" Deiphobus said, elbowing Polydorus beside him. "Shall we see if we can find a better use for that mouth of hers while he's away?"

"So long as it will silence her incessant moaning," Helenus grumbled, filling his cup with strong wine. Cassandra's twin, he was as dour as his sister, if not quite so outspoken. "I cannot abide the thought of listening to her weep for another night."

"Then perhaps you should take her to your bed, Helenus," Deiphobus said. "A few good pokes will quiet her, and by your foul temper, you're desperately in need of a woman's touch."

"Bedding the nymph would solve only half my troubles," Helenus replied. "Not that I would expect so simple a man as yourself to understand, but not every inconvenience can be solved by the pleasures found between a woman's thighs."

Deiphobus shoved him from the bench for the insult, always quick to take offense and quicker to use his fists to settle the matter. Paris slipped away in the confusion that followed, having learned within months of his arrival that it served no purpose to respond to his brother's baiting. Had he demanded Deiphobus leave Oenone alone, his brother would have made a point of taking her to his bed, just to spite him. As it was, Paris could only hope she would be well away before his brute of a brother thought to try, and if she wasn't, he had great faith in the ability of Cassandra's sharp tongue to turn Deiphobus aside.

Now he took Oenone by the arm, drawing her away from the ears of the driver and the men who waited to board his ship. "Return to Ida, Oenone. Go home to our son, to Agelaus, and find what happiness you may. For your own sake as much as mine."

"Do you truly believe there is anything but grief for me in this life?" she asked, fresh tears welling in her eyes. "If you leave, I have failed, and Lord Apollo's curse will rest upon my head. Mine and my son's!"

"He cannot curse you, surely, when the fault is hardly yours, and he is not so unjust that he would punish our son when he has done nothing to offend the gods." He brushed the tears from her cheeks and sighed. "You must realize I cannot turn from this. No matter how you beg, I *must* go. I will have no satisfaction without her, no joy. I will be nothing."

She shook her head, tearing free from his grasp to turn away and hug herself tight. "One day, Paris, you will need me more than you need her. Do not forget me then. Return to me, or it will be your death. Return to me, remember me, and I will see you healed."

"I could never forget you, Oenone," he promised, catching her hand to squeeze it. "I swear it."

And then he turned from her, bounding up the steep plank onto his ship. Because bringing Helen home, at last, was worth any risk. And besides, the gods themselves had granted him this. How could it be wrong to claim the prize he had been given? Oenone and Cassandra were only jealous, afraid of the light of Helen's beauty and how it would cast them into shadow.

But some small part of him wondered. He'd heard Cassandra's story after he had been welcomed home, told by Helenus late one night when he was deep in his cups. Cassandra had been beloved by Apollo once. Chosen by the sun god and blessed with the gift of his prophecy. But

Cassandra refused him when he came to her bed, and Apollo had cursed her, stripped her of every favor and left her without even the reason of her own mind. That was why she raved and wept, when once she had been beautiful and wise.

It seemed Lord Apollo had done the same to Oenone, though Paris could not imagine what offense she had given the god. But the nymph he had loved, who had herded and hunted at his side, was lost to her strange grief, buried beneath this terror and jealousy. His Oenone was gone, and it was not only because he had left her behind. She had been far too sensible to fall to pieces this way, far too wise.

Paris shook his head and put it all from his mind. Oenone would sort herself out, and his father would care for their son if she didn't. Either way, the gods had given him a greater task, and he must look to the future, to *his* future.

"Push off!" he called out. "We sail for Salamis with all speed!"

And then Sparta, with the blessing and aid of Aphrodite.

Before this journey was over, Helen would be his.

CHAPTER
FORTY-EIGHT
PARIS

S o this is the nephew I have heard so much about," Queen Hesione said, after they had been given food and wine, as hospitality demanded, and Telamon had welcomed Paris and his men into the palace for the duration of their stay.

Paris would not say King Telamon was precisely pleased with his arrival, but he could hardly turn him away when his wife made her pleasure known, and Telamon's son by Hesione, Teucer, had been happy enough to greet him as a cousin.

"Saved by the gods and returned to Hecuba after all this time, to bring joy to her and her people and dispel the dark clouds of grief and sorrow that had settled over Troy after your death," Hesione said. She was older than Priam, her dark hair streaked with white. "That is a great deal of weight to rest upon one man's shoulders, particularly if he is not used to the demands of the people upon their prince."

Paris inclined his head, smiling. "I am happy for the burden if it brings joy to my people."

"And when joy is no longer foremost in their thoughts when they look upon you, what then?" Hesione asked, her gaze shrewd.

"Then I am still their prince, one of Priam's sons, but we are so numerous, whatever offense I have given, it is sure to be forgotten before long."

Teucer laughed, nudging his half brother. "In that you have the advantage of us, and be glad. I fear we are neither one of us ever forgotten, or not for long."

"Speak for yourself, brother," the Great Ajax said, smiling. "I have no reason to desire myself forgotten for any length of time. But then, I did not put an arrow through the heart of the most beloved hunting dog of our father's friend, either."

Teucer grimaced. "An unfortunate accident, and one I will never outlive, so long as I remain in Salamis."

"I'm certain Prince Paris did not come all this way to hear stories of your youthful indiscretions," King Telamon said.

"On the contrary, King Telamon," Paris said, raising his cup to his cousin. "My father, King Priam, has no wish to continue this estrangement from his sister, and how better to strengthen the bonds between our peoples than through friendship and storytelling? We are family, after all."

"Is that why he sends us a son he barely knows? A boy raised as nothing more than a shepherd? If he truly desired peace and friendship between our peoples, then it would be Hector seated here in my hall, Priam's firstborn son and heir."

"And Hector would have been sent, had I not asked to come," Paris said, ignoring the insults both implied and explicit. Telamon was not wholly wrong, after all, and it had not escaped Paris's notice that Priam expressed little in the way of concern for his well-being as the time of his departure had grown near. If Priam were to sacrifice a son to such

322

a venture as this, Paris would surely be the most disposable. "After living a life of such simple means, I longed to see the greater world my brothers have boasted of, and my father was kind enough to oblige me. No doubt that I might serve my brother Hector all the better when he is made king."

Telamon grunted, his gaze sliding to his immense son Ajax. Paris pretended not to notice the exchange, turning again to the queen. "I do hope we might have the opportunity during my stay to know one another better, Aunt. And I trust that you will tutor me in the ways of the Achaean nobility, that I might not give offense where none is meant. After so long on the mountain, I fear I do not always know the manner in which I should address those who are now my equals. In fact, I thought I might look among our friends in these lands for a suitable bride, if there are any likely women you might suggest, with fathers who might be eager for alliance with a prince of Troy."

"You come too late to Achaea in pursuit of a worthy bride," Ajax said, stealing a handful of grapes from the platter before leaning back in his seat. "The most beautiful prize is long since married, though I doubt the gods would have smiled on your attempt to claim her. Helen of Sparta was fated for one man, and one man alone, though we all prayed otherwise."

Paris limited himself to a slight lift of his brows, careful to conceal the surge of anticipation coursing through his limbs like lightning. "Helen of Sparta? Surely there are other beautiful women in Achaea."

"None as beautiful as Helen," Ajax said. "And once a man looks upon her, he is spoiled by the sight."

He smiled, pretending a lightness he didn't feel. "I have looked upon the goddess Aphrodite and not been blinded, but you suggest a mere woman is so beautiful she would put even a goddess to shame?"

"A daughter of Zeus," Ajax said. "Not any mere woman, but a demigod, more powerful than Heracles in her own way. Some say even King Theseus fell under her power, that she cost him his throne. King

Theseus! One of the wisest of men, favored by Athena and a son of Poseidon himself. But if you travel that far looking for a wife, you'll surely see with your own eyes and live to regret it, I promise you."

"Or perhaps I'll steal her away for my own," Paris said, forcing laughter into his words as if it were a joke. "Is that not the time-honored tradition among your people here in Achaea?"

Telamon slammed his fist on the table, making the platter jump, loose grapes spilling onto the floor. "You dare come into my hall, claiming friendship, and speak in such a fashion? I have given you food and wine! Treated you as my guest! And this is how I am repaid?"

"Husband," Hesione said, covering his fist with her hand. "He has said already he does not know our ways. I am certain he meant no insult by his words, and he is, as you have said, our guest."

"And were it not for the gods, I would throw him from my hall and back into the sea. Were it not for you, my *wife*, I would spite the gods, too, and send him away." Telamon rose, his eyes narrowed and flashing. "Envoy after envoy I have sent to Priam's gates, and he has spurned me time and again, refusing me despite our bond, despite Hesione's own pleading. Now he sends you, and I am meant to suffer further insult? Inside my own walls? No." He jerked his chin toward his sons and let his gaze fall heavily upon Hesione, too. "Let him eat and drink, and entertain him if you will, but he is no friend, and he will carry no gifts back to Troy from my stores, nor will any man or woman in this house accept his. Am I understood?"

Hesione bowed her head. "It will be as you say, my king."

Telamon pinned his sons with the same glare until they both murmured their assent, and then he turned his back upon Paris and swept from the megaron, leaving them behind. Paris said nothing, forcing his fingers to remain loose, rather than balled into fists as they wished to be. Priam had told him nothing of Telamon's envoys, though he was not sure that if he had known he would have spoken differently. Peace with Salamis mattered little to Troy, and Paris had come for Helen, above all, besides.

"You must forgive us," Hesione said lowly. "My husband's anger is for Priam more than you."

"Father would not wish to hear you make these excuses, Mother," Teucer murmured, glancing at his brother, whose face had turned to stone. "He has no reason to ask forgiveness, and every reason to expect King Priam to beg for his."

She sighed, flicking her fingers in dismissal of the whole of it. "If you feel as your father does, Ajax, I will not take exception to your withdrawal. But surely you cannot refuse your brother the right to know his cousin, nor me the pleasure of my nephew's company."

Ajax rose, offering the queen a respectful bow. "Perhaps we will meet another time, Prince Paris, under less unhappy circumstances."

"I would be pleased if it were so," Paris assured him, the words almost meaningless. So long as Telamon lived to bear his grudge against Priam, there was little hope of such an encounter, and they both knew it. He did not wait for Ajax to leave before he turned his attention to Hesione again. "Perhaps it would be better if we left with the dawn?"

"No." Hesione pursed her lips, her face flushed with her own well-kept emotions. Irritation, he thought, and frustration, too, with how this reunion had ended. "My lord husband has made his feelings known, but the storm of his anger with you will pass quickly enough."

"There will be other guests to distract him soon," Teucer agreed. "The Dioscuri will arrive any day now from the north, unless I have mistaken the season, and there will be a banquet, surely, when they do. If you truly desire an Achaean bride, you might speak to our nobles then, and it would serve you well to meet with Castor and Pollux, even to travel on with them from here. There is no king in all of Achaea who would refuse you in their company."

"Save perhaps the sons of Atreus," Hesione amended. "But while Agamemnon might desire the benefits of a marriage bond with Troy, he cannot be trusted not to take more once he has been given the smallest taste. And there is little for you in Sparta, unless you wish to gawk at Menelaus's queen."

"Helen of Sparta," Paris said, savoring her name now that he was so much nearer to his goal.

"Sister to Castor and Pollux," Hesione warned, her eyes narrowing at his tone. "And her brothers will hardly take kindly to a man they think lusts for her sight unseen."

"I would see her, only because Ajax has spoken so persuasively of her beauty, but I have no desire to provoke a war. Whether I lust for her or not, she is another man's wife. A king's wife, and surely he would not allow such a prize to slip from his grasp without a fight."

Hesione snorted. "You see me here now, do you not? Make no mistake, Paris, no man would wage a war over the loss of a woman, no matter how beautiful she might be, or I would not be the wife of the thief who helped steal me from my home and family."

"Surely it is not so terrible as that," Teucer said, leaning forward to lay his hand over hers. "I have never seen my father treat you with anything but respect, and if he did otherwise, I would rise to your defense."

She caught up Teucer's hand and pressed a kiss to its back. "And for you, I will always be grateful. But you must realize by now this is not the life I would have chosen. Telamon might treat me with respect, but it was hard won, and there is little love between us, and less affection."

"You cannot know that you would have been granted anything more if you had remained in Troy," Teucer said. "Priam would have used your marriage to his own ends, to secure the loyalty of some nearby king, like as not."

"But I would have been given the choice of which king," she said. "And I wouldn't have suffered the humiliation of being taken as some man's prize."

"If you had loved King Telamon, would it have mattered how you were brought together?" Paris asked. "If he was fated for you, and the gods had declared it was so, would you resent him still?"

"It is one thing to know the gods' will, to know even your own fate, and another thing to choose it," Hesione said. "If I had loved Telamon, if he had persuaded me to leave Troy for his sake, of my own free will, it would have made all the difference in the world."

Paris stayed that night and the next, keeping himself in Teucer's company and from beneath Telamon's eye. Hesione's words haunted his thoughts. Helen was fated to be his, he knew, but what she knew of him, he had never considered. All these years, he had thought of her, dreamed of her, longed for her—but did she remember him at all? Would she wish to leave her husband, or, if he stole her, would she resent him, as Hesione did Telamon?

He had thought it would be a simple thing. That she would see him and love him at once. He had not paused for a moment to consider what he would do if fate and the goddess's word were not enough. And yet it had been clear that Hesione would not abandon Salamis even before he had offered to bring her home to Troy.

"Better if Priam had offered Telamon free trade beyond the Hellespont, as he has long desired, than offer me this. It is far too late to think of fleeing, and my future can only be here, through Teucer, my son."

He had not argued, for there was little purpose in it, and had she chosen otherwise, it would have forced him to reconsider his own plans. But it gave him further thought, more to fear, for when the Dioscuri arrived, so came news of Helen and the young daughter she had borne, now a child of four.

"Has there been news of Theseus?" Pollux asked late into the banquet that followed on the heels of their arrival. It seemed these brothers of Helen traveled widely through Achaea, roaming from kingdom to kingdom, performing small services as they could, friends to all.

"Little since he retired to Skyros," Telamon said, "though I have heard Demophon and Acamas have grown strong, and what part in that Theseus has had, I can only guess. Lycomedes believes Theseus has given up hope of reclaiming Athens for himself, but I cannot imagine there is any truth to it. Even all these years later, it seems strange to think there is any other king upon the Rock while Theseus still lives."

"Then perhaps he claims disinterest to preserve his life," Castor said, nodding thanks to Hesione when she filled his cup with more wine. "We dare not travel to Skyros ourselves for similar reasons."

"Menelaus still fears Theseus means to steal his wife?" Telamon asked.

Paris had been careful to hold his tongue, and had spent the meal pretending great interest in his plate and the food that had been offered, but he had listened closely, and he did not mean to leave the megaron before Castor and Pollux retired. Not so long as they spoke of their sister, or the hero who had left her behind.

"Menelaus fears everything," Pollux said, the words sharp with clear disgust. "Helen has him enough in hand to protect herself, even to ensure Sparta's prosperity, but it has cost her, and I cannot see how it will last."

"It will last as long as it must," Castor said. "As long as she believes it will keep peace in Achaea, and those she loves safe from harm. She has become all the more determined since Heracles's death, the great hero brought so low that he threw himself upon a pyre."

"Which is why we dare not travel to Skyros," Pollux said. "I will not test my sister's strength any further than I must, and if Menelaus believes we are aiding Theseus—"

"How she persuaded him to spare us before now, I do not wish to know," Castor murmured.

"—he will not hesitate to arrange some accident to befall us."

"Surely no Spartan would dare act against their prince!" Ajax said.

"Menelaus need not ask it of a Spartan when his brother will happily supply men of his own," Pollux replied. "And you know the men Agamemnon has drawn to him in Mycenae. Men without families, without honor or worth beyond the strength of their sword arm."

Telamon grunted. "Mercenaries, bought with land and gold."

"You need not fear the threat of Mycenae or Menelaus here," Ajax said. "And know, too, that should Menelaus act against you, Helen will not be without protectors."

No, Paris agreed. She would not be without protectors. He would keep her safe within Troy's high walls, and guard her to his last breath. And surely if this was her life, married to such a fool as Menelaus, she would not want to stay in Achaea, given the choice.

CHAPTER FORTY-NINE
HELEN

My lady," Clymene panted, lanky Hermione on her hip. They'd been walking the walls, I guessed, and had come running to the megaron with news of what they'd seen.

Menelaus would never deny Hermione anything, but I dared not ask for even the smallest portion of his daughter's freedom, so I sat in my small megaron, surrounding by Sparta's women, and fought the resentment that threatened to boil into a fury I could ill afford. Not if I wished to keep this hard-won peace with Menelaus, or my brothers' heads upon their shoulders.

"My lady, it's your brothers at the gate. They've come with another man. A prince of Troy, they said."

The words froze my fingers on the yarn I spun, and after a breath to steady myself, I set the spindle and distaff aside. *Paris.* I'd dreamed of him so often, and these last years, I'd almost come to welcome the thought. While I made love to Menelaus, a willing partner in his bed, I consoled myself with the knowledge this day would come. My strange prince, come to steal me, to begin the end of us all.

I forced my mouth to form a smile. "What a pleasant surprise."

My voice sounded flat even to my own ears, empty of any true emotion. I could not seem to summon any joy, though I was always glad for the time I shared with Castor and Pollux, brief as it must be. Every visit to Sparta was a risk, and Menelaus had been more agitated than usual these last weeks. Perhaps in response to my nightmares, which still woke us both in the dark, driving Menelaus from my bed to find more restful sleep with one of his slaves. He'd rarely spent a full night with me in the last month.

Adjusting the shawl Menelaus still insisted I wear to hide my hair, I rose. My husband would want me at his side to greet our guests, to give the appearance of a unity I would never feel, and I wanted to see my brothers, to know them safe and whole for myself.

But more than that, I could not deny a twisted curiosity.

If Clymene was right, today I would face my fate.

"We travel with Prince Paris of Troy, son of King Priam by his queen, Hecuba, and nephew of Queen Hesione of Salamis," Pollux said, introducing their new companion after food and wine had been served to all. From the moment he had set foot inside the king's megaron, Paris's eyes had followed me, but I pretended not to notice, ignoring him utterly to fuss over my brothers. Menelaus never allowed me to speak with them alone, but under his eye, I could at least clasp hands with Pollux, then Castor, and press chaste kisses to their cheeks in greeting.

Now Pollux's gaze flicked to me, a question he did not dare ask passing between us in a glance. *Is this your strange prince?* I inclined my head just slightly—*Yes*—and turned my attention to our guest.

"Have you traveled so far alone, Prince Paris? Surely the son of King Priam must have a guard of some kind."

"My men, but for the two you have seen, remain with my ship in Gytheio. Castor and Pollux assured me I would have no need for a greater party while we journeyed together in Laconia, and I would not insult the princes of Sparta by arguing the safety of their lands."

"My lands," Menelaus said, too sharply and too quickly to suggest anything but insecurity. I laid my hand upon his wrist, hoping it would calm him before he took insult instead. "Though I must grant that Castor and Pollux know them well enough to avoid what little danger our roads might offer. And you are welcome here, Prince Paris. Indeed, we are honored to shelter a son of Priam beneath our roof, and pleased to strengthen the ties between our peoples with guest-friendship."

I had always wondered why Menelaus would welcome such a stranger inside our walls, when he looked on me with obvious desire, if not lust outright. But in those words of welcome, Menelaus made everything suddenly clear. He wanted alliance with Troy, and no doubt the same trade rights King Priam had denied every other king in Achaea. He wanted to steal this prize from Agamemnon, and prove once and for all that he was a king in his own right, a king to be reckoned with, with power and influence of his own.

And he believed himself safe from the future of my nightmares, from the abductor who would steal me from his grasp—I had seen to that when I had allowed him to think that Theseus was the man who had come for me in my dreams.

I swallowed the surge of grief that always followed even the barest mention of Theseus, the slightest recollection, and dropped my gaze to Menelaus's hand, his fingers curled tightly upon the arm of his throne, the muscles of his arm taut with anticipation for the opportunity he believed, by sheer happenstance, he had been granted. The poor, desperate fool of a man.

It gave me no pleasure to know that in that moment, with my continued silence, I might cause his ruin. Strange. I had always thought it would be more satisfying to hold his fate in my hand, his fortunes, after all I had suffered for his desires.

Instead, my heart beat hollowly. Destroying Menelaus meant causing the deaths of so many others. And it would not give me what I truly wanted, what I longed for so fiercely I had forbidden myself from naming it even in the silence of my thoughts, buried deeply and locked away when I had thrown the cloak over the wall in the dark of night.

Menelaus's other hand fell heavily over mine, squeezing my fingers almost painfully, and I looked up, startled. "My king?"

"You are to show Prince Paris to his rooms and see to his needs. A bath, at the least, I should think, to wash the dust of the road from his skin before this evening's meal."

I stared at my husband. Surely he had not just demanded I bathe this man? A queen oversaw the hospitality provided to guests, certainly, but Menelaus had always, until this moment, demanded Leda see to their baths in my stead, and always servants and slaves were called to the task of washing.

"Prince Paris is our *most* honored guest," Menelaus said, his dark eyes holding mine, hard and determined, with a promise of fury if I did not act upon his words, and with haste. "It is only right that he be served by no less than the queen's own hands."

"Of course, my lord," I said, dropping my gaze again, that he might not think I challenged him. But I did not dare to respond too quickly, either, or I would risk offending him in an altogether different manner. "I will draw his bath myself, and see that our finest women attend him."

He squeezed my hand again, harder this time, and I bit my lip to stop a hiss of discomfort. "You will remain to oversee them as well."

I closed my eyes, nodding once, briefly, as his hand slipped from mine. "As you wish, of course."

It seemed Menelaus could not quite bring himself to whore his prized wife in exchange for trade beyond Troy, but I had never imagined for a moment it would be so near a thing.

"This way, please, Prince Paris," I said, rising. I did not so much as glance at my brothers, but I caught the elbow of a maid on my way out of the room. "I will need Clymene, at once, and water for our guest's bath drawn. Pass along my command and then remain at my side from the next moment on."

"Yes, my queen," she said, and darted off.

I paused at the doorway, turning to Paris, who followed me like a lion stalking his prey, the barest touch of a smile upon his lips, and his gaze branding my skin. "After you, my lord."

But I hesitated even then to follow. For beyond the prince, Menelaus watched me, too, his expression the careful neutral of a king's mask, and I knew we had never played a more dangerous game, he and I. One false step, one imagined breath of immodesty, of delight in my assigned tasks, and it would be my ruin, too.

Paris was beautiful, of that there could be no doubt. His body was lean with muscle, as honed as any warrior's, though I knew he could hardly have been raised as one. I lowered my lashes, careful not to let the maids see me look, but I could not help but notice the sun-gilded skin of his back when they pulled his tunic over his head, or the dimples of his bare bottom, just as golden as the rest of him.

He grinned at me, whether because he knew I watched or because he wished me to, and sank slowly into the tub. True to my promise to Menelaus, I stepped forward, lifting the pot of steaming water from the hearth and adding it to his bath.

"Shall I call for more water to be heated?" I asked, keeping my eyes trained to his now that I was so near. He would not have the satisfaction of seeing me admire his body, and I would not give the maids any fodder that might reach Menelaus's ear.

"This will do," he assured me, his grin relaxing into that same predatory smile—the smile of a man who knows he will have what he desires. I moved away, memories of Theseus rising too easily to the surface of my thoughts. Paris had Theseus's confidence, and I could not let him see how it affected me, certain he would take it as encouragement, when it ought to have been anything but.

When I was queen of Athens, Theseus had never made me watch while his guests bathed. Nor even to wait upon them outside the door, to personally oversee the maids. But I knew as well as any woman what was expected of the slaves sent to scrub their backs, and I could not help but wonder if I was meant to stand here so that Paris might better imagine himself pleasured by my hand.

And what did Menelaus truly hope to gain by this strange seduction? Did he hope if Paris desired me desperately enough, he would persuade King Priam to grant us some promise of trade?

Paris moaned softly as the women went about their work. I folded the towels, keeping my back to the tub, and struggled to control the flush burning my cheeks at the sound. He watched me, I knew. And I could almost feel his pleasure as my own, the whisper of his panting against my skin, the coil of need wound too tight in my belly, causing a familiar dampness between my thighs.

It had been so long since I'd felt true desire, and I hated that it was his. That he imposed it upon me, from across the room as he satisfied himself with another.

A desperate groan broke from his throat, and I left the room, shutting the door behind me and leaning back against the thin pine, wishing it were oak and bronze and stone, wishing I could not still hear his moans through the wood.

"Has he finished?" Clymene asked, for she'd been waiting just outside in the hall.

Paris cried out his pleasure, and I swallowed hard. "Near enough."

"The king should not have asked this of you," Clymene said, her voice low. "Does he not realize the risk? He will not let you walk the walls, but he will set you before this strange prince—"

Clymene clamped a hand over her own mouth, her eyes going wide.

I pressed my lips together, begging her with my silence. She stared at me, stared and trembled, and slowly her hand fell from her mouth, pressing hard over her heart instead.

"Menelaus wants freedom," I said gently, ignoring what had gone unsaid. "Power and influence that Mycenae will find impossible to match. And it seems that he is willing to sacrifice even me if it means he will have it."

"Oh, my lady," she breathed. "He's done it to himself, hasn't he? Everything you feared would come to pass."

"From the moment he refused to give me up, when I was still a child," I said. "And again on the day he reclaimed me as his wife. Menelaus has made his choices, and now I must make mine."

"My lady, my lady!" I straightened, frowning at the call. One of the serving maids dashed toward us, collapsing at my feet.

"What's happened?" I bent to help her, but she shook her head, pushing my hand away.

"My lady, it's your servant, the old woman Physadeia. She's come back, but the king—he means to whip her for running off, and she's thrown herself into your brother's arms, begging protection, shouting for you."

Aethra. Aethra had come back, after four long years. She was never meant to return to me. Not unless . . .

I grabbed up my skirts and ran for the megaron.

Because Aethra had come with news. And if she had come so far, it was surely Theseus who had sent her.

CHAPTER FIFTY
HELEN

top!" One glance at the room and I could see the sword's edge, my brothers protecting Aethra, and Menelaus with his hand upon his knife, face red and blustering, demanding his right. I fell to my knees at his feet, imploring. "Menelaus, my lord, I beg of you— Physadeia is mine. She is mine to punish if she is deserving, and it is my right to judge!"

He growled, lifting his hand as if he would strike me, and I held my breath, my heart racing and Zeus's own thunder in my ears. If he hit me now, before my brothers . . .

Menelaus closed his hand into a fist, sneering as he lifted his gaze. To Aethra, sheltered behind Pollux, to my brothers, ready to act in her defense. In mine. He grabbed me by the arm, lifting me up and dragging me two steps away, three, five.

"Should your brothers dare challenge me again within these walls, they will suffer for it, Helen. Do you understand me?" he snarled. "If they cannot remember their place, they will have no place at all."

I nodded and he released me.

"Do what you will with your slave, I care not. But I warn you, do not forget where your duty must lie. Do not forget *you* are *mine*."

"In all ways," I promised, the words so practiced, so smooth now after these last four years, even if their sweetness made me sick. I caressed his bearded cheek, then let my hand slip down his chest, not taking my eyes from his. "As I have always been yours."

He grunted, his face flushed with the pleasure of my touch. His hand cupped my elbow, then slid up, his gaze shifting to my lips, my hair, my breasts. "See to your slave and speak with your brothers, then come to me. I wish to be reminded of the proof of your words."

I beamed at him with every scrap of charm and power I could muster, that he might be convinced of my love, my desire. "I will not be far behind."

And then I watched him go, that same dazzling smile fixed to my face, as if I could not believe my good fortune to be desired by such a man. That the men and women who milled in the megaron, the nobles and servants, might see my love. I even kept my smile when I turned to my brothers, who stared at me with pity in their eyes, while Aethra's lip curled in open disgust.

"Come," I said, as if I had only just remembered them. As if they were only a chore keeping me from the pleasure of my husband's company. Just as I had approached everything else I loved in the last four years, mastering the part I had been forced to play for all our sakes. "I would speak with you privately, all three."

"Out," I said, and the queen's megaron emptied without a word of protest, but for Leda, who always lingered. But Menelaus no longer relied upon her as a spy, since I had convinced him of my loyalty in our bed, and though she still held her position as high priestess, within these walls I was queen.

"I'm afraid I was forced to leave our most honored guest, Prince Paris of Troy, in his bath. If you would be so kind as to see him settled, Mother, I am certain my lord King Menelaus would be pleased. Prince Paris is to be given anything he desires, by the king's own order, and I know no maid who will refuse your command."

Leda pursed her lips, her eyes narrowing, but after only a heartbeat of hesitation, she left at last. Castor drifted toward the door, checking to be sure she had gone from the hall as well, and I let my false smile fail.

"What news, Aethra?" I asked at once, reaching for her hands. She grasped mine in return, though I feared her fingers were weaker now than they had been before. "Please tell me there is news. That it is good."

She closed her eyes, so wise, so brilliant, and it was only then, searching her for some sign of what had brought her, that I saw the sorrow carved into her face, the scratches of her nails upon her cheeks, and the roughly mended garments covering too-bony shoulders.

My heart seized. "Aethra?"

One of Theseus's sons, perhaps. Demophon or Acamas, lost in some accident. Or some ill tidings for Athens itself. It must be. It *had* to be. Theseus was crippled, but safe. Recovering, slowly but surely. He would be whole again one day.

"He fell," she said, tears slipping out from beneath her eyelids. "He fell, just as you warned. Betrayed by Lycomedes. Theseus is dead."

The words struck me like blows, and I stumbled back, tripping over a stray stool. "No."

But even as I spoke, I knew it was true. I had dreamed of it, after all. I had seen it coming.

Pollux caught me, guiding me to one of the long benches that lined the walls. I lifted my hands to my face, but he clamped down upon my wrists, holding them fast against my thighs. I stared at him through blurring eyes, seeing the mirror of my grief, the grief he would deny me now.

He shook his head. "If you mourn him openly, Menelaus will never believe the lie. Everything you've sacrificed, everything you've given up will be for nothing the moment he sees the marks upon your cheeks."

I gasped for breath, the sorrow so thick inside me, tightening around my heart, my lungs. If I could not wail, could not keen, could not tear myself apart to free it, this pain would turn me to stone.

"Helen," Pollux said, forcing me to look at him. "Helen, you must be strong. You cannot fall to pieces now. Not yet. Menelaus expects you still."

Menelaus. My tears slipped free, tracking hot down my cheeks. Menelaus, who had been so on edge these last weeks, so agitated, and who was so eager now to let me seduce the prince of Troy for his pathetic dreams of trade. Menelaus, who had come to find me in my nightmare and whispered Theseus's fate in my ear.

He'd arranged it all.

And he'd known. Knew of it, even now, and gloried in his success. That was why he had been so fearless in his demands, so unconcerned when Paris and my brothers arrived.

"He did this," I said. "He did this, and now I am expected to go to his bed? To play the part of his loyal, loving wife?"

Castor's hand fell heavy on my shoulder, and with it the balm of his gift. "The prince is here, Helen. You need pretend for only a short time longer, and you will be stolen away from here, from Menelaus. Or . . ." He squeezed my shoulder, and I felt his peace, his love. "Leave of your own accord, if you wish. Claim your fate and punish him for what he has done."

I hid my face in my hands, dug my fingers into my hair, my scalp, where Menelaus would not see the marks. To leave of my own free will, to abandon Sparta, my family, everything I loved. I had always had the choice, but I had never wanted it so dearly. All those men who would die, Troy's burning—a fitting sacrifice, a proper pyre for the hero I had loved.

The man I had ruined.

I stood, slipping out from beneath Castor's hand, touching Pollux's shoulder as I stepped away from them both. Aethra sat upon the stool that had tripped me, staring at her lap. I knelt before her, taking her hands, pressing my lips to her aged fingers. Was it any wonder she suddenly looked so old? So weak? She had lived so long for Theseus, and in some small part, for me.

"Wherever I go, whatever path I take, I would be honored to have you at my side," I told her.

She let out a breath, lifting her gaze to mine, fierce as any Fury sent by the gods. "There is only one way forward for me, Helen. Whatever choice you make, I know what burns in your heart. The same fire heats my blood as well, and it will be as I promised you after Tyndareus died. Our enemies will burn. Whether in the flames of this war, or those of our own making, they will burn until there is nothing left but ash and bone. And after that, I will find my peace among the dead."

I imagined Paris in my husband's place, for I would not sully Theseus's memory while I lay in the arms of his murderer, but I could not stomach the thought of giving my body to Menelaus after what I had just learned. Paris, however—from what I had learned of him through my nightmares, from what I had known of him in the moments we had spent together while he bathed—I did not think he would begrudge me this fantasy, this strange comfort.

So I imagined Paris's lips, Paris's hands, Paris's body beneath my own. I imagined it was Paris's pleasure I sought, alongside my own. I imagined Menelaus forced to listen as I found my release in the arms of another.

And after, while Menelaus slept the deep sleep of a man well satis-fied, I went in search of my prince. It would not do to neglect such an honored guest, after all, and Menelaus had made his wishes more than clear to me before. Whatever Paris desired, he would have.

He was not difficult to find, my strange shepherd prince. I had only to search out the largest clustering of idle maids, to listen for the gig-gling of young girls echoing through the halls. And it did not surprise me in the least to find him in the kitchens, smiling and flirting and charming even the normally cheerless cook. All of them so enraptured by his presence, his teasing and laughter, they did not even notice when I joined the small gathering of his admirers.

"Your bread is sweet as ambrosia, my lady," Paris said, pressing a kiss to the cook's gnarled hand, her knuckles thick with so many years of kneading dough. "My mouth waters for the thought of another taste, if you can spare even the smallest portion of a loaf!"

Melita's cheeks, already rosy from the heat of the cook fires, red-dened further. "Sparta is not so poor that we cannot afford to feed our guests as is right and proper. There's no need for a prince to come beg-ging for his meal!"

"Forgive me," Paris said. "You see, I was not raised as a prince but as a shepherd boy upon Mount Ida, and I fear I often forget myself."

"Well," Melita said, snapping her fingers for the bread. "A guest of King Menelaus surely has no call to be in the kitchens, no matter how honeyed his words. We'll have the evening meal run late if we don't get to it, and I'll not have the queen suffer for our own foolishness."

My fingers knotted in the fabric of my shawl, my own face flush-ing at her concern. In the last years, Menelaus had trusted me again with the running of the palace household, but it was true that he often looked for faults in my management. I hadn't realized how well the servants knew it, but I should have known. Menelaus did not possess a quiet anger, though since Tyndareus's death, at least he had not struck me.

"Ah," Paris said, his voice softening even as his smile faded. He inclined his head, accepting the loaf of bread she'd thrust into his hands. "Nor would I bring pain to your queen, my lady, and so I must beg your forgiveness a second time. If you or one of your young maids would only point me back upon my way—"

I cleared my throat then, and stepped forward to forestall an even greater disruption, for I could only imagine how many of Melita's maids would wish the honor, and there would be no small amount of ill will when one was chosen above the others.

"Forgive me for the disturbance, Melita, but I had heard the prince came this way, and I see I was not misled." I offered him nothing more than a polite smile, but I didn't miss the way his eyes warmed when they fell on me. "My lord Paris, you must allow me the honor of guiding you back where you belong."

I had thought I had known what I intended, that I had made up my mind to build Theseus's pyre as high and as hot as any fire had ever burned. But how could I turn my back upon my people so completely, people like Melita who did their all every day to protect me in return for the sacrifices I had made—even for Theseus's sake?

No. I had to find another way. I had to fight still to prevent this war, to serve my people as their queen. But it did not mean Menelaus would not suffer. It did not mean *he* could not burn.

"I hope you will accept my sincerest apology for abandoning you earlier," I said, clasping my hands lightly behind my back after we had left the kitchen far enough behind. I shouldn't have come to him without Clymene, at the least, and now that we were alone for the first time since his arrival, I felt . . . nervous.

All these years, I'd waited for this day. Dreaded its coming. But Paris was familiar, like an old friend returning home after years away. I wasn't certain if it was some trick of the gods, to make me all the more comfortable in his presence, or simply the result of seeing him so often in my nightmares, but Paris was no stranger to me.

"There's nothing to forgive," he said gently. "Flattered as I was to be served by your hands, I cannot begrudge you the rest of your duties as queen. Nor was I entirely unaware that you would not ordinarily have lowered yourself to such a task as your husband assigned you. I . . . I shouldn't have accepted such an honor. But a part of me had hoped we might speak privately."

I shook my head. "Menelaus might have desired me to wait upon your bath, but to have done so alone would have risked more than I dared."

"And now?" he asked.

I swallowed, my gaze trained upon the hall before us. "I should not have come alone to find you. Should Menelaus learn we were alone together, even in so innocent a fashion, it will end badly."

"For you?"

"For my brothers, most likely. Or my maid, Clymene. She is the king's cousin, but it will not stop him from doing her harm to punish me."

Paris glanced back toward the kitchens, then up ahead, before catching me by the elbow to stop me, his hand warm and calloused and prickling my skin with gooseflesh. "Helen, I must ask—do you remember me?"

I pressed my lips together, unsure how much I wished to admit. Was it better if he believed he must win me over? Had he dreamed of me, as I had dreamed of him? I did not dare ask.

He searched my face, released my elbow only to caress my cheek, his expression pleading. "I was the shepherd boy, Helen. The one you saved from Theseus's sword, all those years ago. Tell me, please, that you remember, because not one day has passed since that I did not think of you."

I stepped back, drawing his hand away, though my face had flushed, my whole body warming with his touch. "Does it matter what I remember? My duty will still be to Sparta, to my people, above all."

"And mine is to you," he said. "To your protection, your happiness."

"Perhaps when you were only a shepherd boy, that might have been so, but you are a prince of Troy now, Paris, just as I am queen of Sparta. We would both be fools to think that changed nothing."

"It does not change my feelings, my love and desire for you," he said, taking my hand. "I swore to keep your secret so long as it would aid you, but if your husband could dare threaten you, would punish you by harming those you love, it is clear to me that the future you ran from has found you, despite your efforts."

A laugh bubbled up from my throat, escaping sharp and short. He did not know how truly he had spoken. But how could he? He had dreamed only of a pretty girl. I had dreamed of fire and blood and death beyond reckoning.

"Swear to me, then, that you will never hurt those that I love. Swear to me that you will do no harm to my brothers, to my maids, my slaves, my very people."

"I swear it," he said, without even the smallest hesitation. "Anything and anyone that you love, I will love as well."

"And what of my enemies?" I asked, my heart racing.

His jaw tightened, but he did not flinch from my gaze. "You need only whisper their names, and I will see them breathe their last breaths."

"Menelaus." It was poison to speak it, but I did not care. The gods had cursed us both already, though Paris clearly did not know it yet. "If we are to have any future, Menelaus must die."

CHAPTER FIFTY-ONE

HELEN

I trust you have done everything within our power to see that Prince Paris is content," Menelaus said to me that night. We had returned to our rooms after the evening meal. Tomorrow Paris would have a proper banquet in his honor, and Menelaus had already promised him a seat at my side, but tonight I had seated my brothers beside me, and Paris at Menelaus's left hand.

Perhaps it was reckless to keep my brothers so near, but if my plan failed, then I would lose them utterly before long, and I saw no reason to waste even a moment of what time we had left.

"Everything but the satisfaction of his desire for me." I filled both our cups with wine, pretending a calm I didn't feel. Sitting beside Menelaus all evening had made my skin crawl. "Much as you might hope for Troy's friendship, I thought it best to deny him that particular honor."

"You do yourself few favors with teasing of that kind, Helen," Menelaus growled.

"I would not have teased him at all, had it been my choice," I said mildly, setting the pitcher aside. "I only pray you remember it."

"This is the influence of your brothers," he grumbled, shifting his gaze from mine. He took up his cup, swirling the wine inside. "Always when they return, you forget yourself, your place. Perhaps I should forbid their coming, exile them from Sparta absolutely."

"And how would you explain such a command to your people?" I asked, struggling now to keep my temper. "Castor and Pollux are beloved, Menelaus."

"Yes, and all of Achaea knows how well you've loved them," he snapped. "Which is all the more reason to keep them out."

"You cannot still hold those lies against us," I said, not bothering to hide my disgust. "Menestheus only sought to hurt me, to sow mistrust between us and weaken Sparta. Surely you must realize that by now."

"Menestheus spoke truth as well," Menelaus reminded me, his eyes narrowed. "Were it not for Menestheus, I have no doubt that you would still be lying, or worse yet, run off with that Athenian dog—aided in your escape by your brothers, no less. If I trust there is truth to his accusations, I have reason enough."

I bit back a curse and turned away. Four years I had spent humiliating myself to earn his trust and calm his temper. To keep my family safe. Four years, and he still nursed his wounded pride, blinded by his jealousy. Four years, and he still threatened everyone and everything I loved.

"You needn't worry my brothers will help me to run off with Theseus," I said, my voice low. "Not now that he is dead."

"I wondered how long it would be until that news reached you." Menelaus had the gall to laugh. "And long past time, too. If only Hades had never set him free, I would have one less reason to wish ill upon your brothers."

"Tell me, Menelaus, what offends you more? Is it that Pollux and Castor made Menestheus king of Athens when he had no true claim to the throne, or their wish to give Theseus back his crown and right the wrong they had done him once they realized their mistake?"

"It is their meddling in the affairs of any king that offends me," Menelaus said. "And I am not fool enough to think they would not meddle in mine as well, if an opportunity arose. They are a threat, Helen."

"They would not be a threat to you if you treated them as brothers. If you had not listened to Menestheus in those first months, but embraced them as my protectors and guards."

"And been humiliated?" He barked another laugh. "After all that I had already suffered at my own brother's hand? But let us not forget that it was you who sent them away. And to Thessaly, of all places! With that Lapith centaur filth."

My fingers tightened around my own cup, rage burning in my blood. Polypoetes was three times the man Menelaus was, and a thousand times more worthy of his crown. But I swallowed my defense of him, knowing if I uttered the words, Menelaus would be forced to act. He would not suffer an insult of that kind, and with my brothers in Sparta, beneath his roof—no.

I drank the wine instead, hoping it would dull my senses. Perhaps if I had enough, I would not notice when Menelaus took his pleasure. I should have mixed it with less water. Or added the sweet mead, to make it stronger. Give Menelaus enough of it, and he would be too soft to plant me. The more he spoke, the less I could endure it. Theseus's murderer—that was all he was now. All he would ever be.

"Send Castor and Pollux off again after tomorrow's banquet," Menelaus commanded, setting his emptied cup at my elbow. "I will not have them here, inspiring this disobedience in you."

"They promised Prince Paris they would remain to escort him back to Gytheio," I said, pouring myself more wine. I could not even look at the bed, too furious for sleep and too disgusted to pretend desire for my husband. "And the prince is fond of them, besides. Would you risk offending him by sending them away so suddenly?"

Menelaus grunted, his fingers coiling into my hair and his body so near I could feel his warmth. "If you do not curb your tongue and remember your place, Prince Paris will think me weak and unworthy, and all our efforts will be for nothing."

I could not bring myself to turn around, to welcome him as I knew he wanted, and I stared at the wine in my cup. Stared, because there was so little else I could do. "Have I not been dutiful and obedient these last four years? Has not every guest at our table witnessed our love and my devotion?"

"Then show me the same." He brushed my hair from my neck and pressed his lips to my skin. I shivered, true revulsion chilling my blood. "Grant me proof of it now."

I closed my eyes, holding myself still as his hand fumbled at my waist, loosening the belt I wore. I wanted to throw my wine in his face. To scream, to cry, to bash him over the head with the golden cup and curse him for everything he'd done.

Not yet. Paris needed time to arrange his death, and I could not have him doubting my loyalty, or I would never find my way free.

"Come, Helen," he urged. The flounced overskirt fell away once the belt no longer held it in place, and he hiked up the thin linen gown worn beneath, exposing me. He laughed, his breath hot against my ear as he drew me hard against his body. "You still owe me a son."

Obedient, dutiful, and devoted—that was what he wanted in exchange for allowing my brothers to remain. So when he bent me over the table, I didn't fight.

Menelaus invited Paris to go riding the following morning, leaving me to the work of organizing the banquet in his honor. In truth, there was little I needed to do but speak to Melita about the meal and arrange for seating within the megaron.

Pollux joined me in overseeing the slaves as they moved the furniture, both of us watching carefully to be sure benches and tables did not crash into the carefully painted plaster walls. Sparta's servants and slaves had always been treated well, in spite of Menelaus's temper, and like Melita in the kitchen, they were not unaware of what I might suffer should their carelessness cause noticeable damage.

"You are fortunate in some ways," Pollux said, his arms crossed over his chest as the steward directed the placement of the tables around the great central hearth of the megaron. "At least you have the loyalty and support of our people to protect you. Nestra suffers Agamemnon's rages entirely alone."

"Nestra would not be so poor in friends and allies if she would only swallow some measure of her bitterness and treat the men and women who surround her with kindness," I said.

"You know it was never easy for her, Helen, always set beside you. And it is harder still now, trapped in Mycenae with such a husband."

I sighed. "It isn't that I wish her ill, Pollux. Only that she has been, in some ways, the author of her own misery, and I cannot find the patience to pity her for it. Even when we were young, she believed she was the only one who suffered, the only one who struggled. There are so many things we might have shared, but she refused to see that perhaps she was not wholly alone, and it is the same still, now that we are older."

He gave a soft snort in response, whether for my lack of sympathy or for our sister's foibles, I was not certain. Truthfully, I did not see that there was anything to be done for Nestra—and even if there were, she would have been too spiteful to accept any help from my hand. Or if she did, it would be one more resentment, rising like a shield between us.

"Have you decided what you will do?" Pollux asked.

"I will not betray my people by bringing about this war, if that is what worries you," I said, for we stood far enough apart from the others to speak openly. "But nor will I forgive Theseus's murder. Or the threats still made against my brothers."

"We are strong, Helen," Pollux said gently. "And forewarned. Whatever threats he makes, they are only that. It is toothless talk, and even at its worst, we need only retreat north. Polypoetes would welcome us among the Lapiths should we need more protection than we are able to provide for ourselves."

I shook my head. "Forewarning has not served us so well as we would like."

"It could still," he said. "Only say the word, and Castor and I will see to the Trojan pup. If he does not live, he cannot steal you."

"But there will still be a war," I said, already seeing it too clearly in my mind. "And likely it would become an invasion of our own lands, instead of theirs. More of our people dead, Sparta itself burned to the ground. You cannot want that."

"Of course I don't," Pollux said, impatient now. He'd grown so grim so quickly, in these last years, and it broke my heart to know I was the reason. "But I never wanted to see my sisters used so poorly, either. By their husbands or the gods."

"You will not be forced to see it for much longer," I promised him. "And with any luck, Nestra's troubles will end as well, soon after."

Pollux's eyes narrowed. "Helen—"

"I've long hoped that I might find a way to make use of my stranger's passions, his determination to claim me as his own," I said, offering my brother a small smile. "And imagine Agamemnon setting sail to wage war against Troy, alone. Imagine if he destroys only himself beneath the walls of Troy."

"And what will the gods say to this plan of yours?" Pollux asked. "You deny them the war they seek, the blood and sacrifice they desire."

"They will have a war, and blood, and sacrifice. They will have Mycenae, and all the mercenaries Agamemnon has gathered to his side. The ruinous, impious men who ought to suffer for their sins. Why should they object at all?"

"You make it sound too easy, too clean. And after all they have done to ensure this future, your future, I do not think they will give it up so simply. To say nothing of the prince's desires. After he has cursed himself, betrayed sacred law for your sake, do you truly believe he will leave you behind?"

"It will not matter nearly so much if I stay or go," I said, nodding to the steward to send the servants back to their regular duties, now that the tables were arranged. "Sparta will have you and Castor, and all its men. I need not fear our destruction if I am stolen, and I trust you will not be fool enough to wage a war to win me back."

Pollux's lips pressed thin. "I would not want to leave you at the mercy of any man you did not choose, Helen."

"But you will," I said, meeting his eyes and holding his gaze. We were alone now in the megaron, and I dared to take his hand in mine. "You will do what you must to keep our people safe. To protect them, as I have fought so hard to do. You would not be so cruel as to steal all meaning from my sacrifice. Promise me."

His jaw tightened. "Forgive me if I pray it does not come to that."

"Promise me, Pollux," I insisted. For if he did not give me his word, I knew he would risk too much. "Promise me that you will not come looking for me again."

"Will you swear to tell me where you've gone in return?" he asked instead. "To send word so I will know you are safe and well cared for?"

"Wherever I go, I will send you word," I promised. I would hardly have reason to hide.

He let out a breath and drew me into his arms, tucking my head beneath his chin and holding me tight. "I swear I will not come for you unless you ask it of me, then. But I do not like this, Helen. I do not like this at all."

I wasn't certain I did, either, but if it meant my brothers lived, that Sparta was kept safe—I would ask for nothing else but that.

CHAPTER FIFTY-TWO

PARIS

A messenger arrived several days later, while Paris and Menelaus walked Sparta's outer walls. Paris had been pretending interest in the countryside, the fields and farms, the livestock and the people themselves, all the time wondering if he dared shove Menelaus from the rampart to be done with him altogether and claim Helen for his own.

Somehow he didn't think that was what Helen had in mind when she'd demanded Menelaus's death. So he clasped his hands lightly behind his back and smiled and nodded, resigning himself to more of Menelaus's boasting of Sparta's prosperity. As if it mattered to him at all.

"My lord king," the messenger called, interrupting Menelaus's talk of horseflesh.

Apparently Helen had two fine stallions of superior stock, but she'd given them to her brothers, preventing Menelaus from breeding them as effectively as he'd desired. An example of her foolishness, and how lost Sparta would be without his firm hand, Paris supposed. Or more likely an example of Helen's subtle defiance of a man she believed unworthy of the crown he wore. Paris had little trouble seeing why.

"Forgive me for the disruption, my lord," the messenger said, bowing low. "But I have news of your grandfather, Catreus."

"Go on, then," Menelaus said.

"Your grandfather has died at the hands of his son, as the gods foretold," the messenger said, not meeting the king's eye. "Your uncle begs the support of all his family, and that you, Menelaus, might see to Catreus's funeral rites."

Menelaus grunted in response, his gaze shifting from the messenger to Paris and back again. Paris held his breath. To see to his grandfather's rites, Menelaus must sail from Gytheio. It would be no effort at all to send one of his guards back to the port with a message for his men, and pathetically simple to arrange some accident to befall the king once he was at sea. He could even plant one of his own oarsmen upon Menelaus's ship to ensure that the king did not return. But he must sail. And he must not think for a moment that Paris wished him well away, or he'd never leave.

"Is that all?" Menelaus asked, gruff now. "Does he ask the same of my brother, in Mycenae?"

"No, my lord," the messenger said. "Your uncle spoke only of you, and he has since fled Rhodes, his sorrow too great."

"Then my uncle does not intend to claim his crown?" Menelaus asked.

The messenger shook his head. "His grief will not allow it."

"Surely the grandson of Catreus has a right to the throne," Paris said, for it was clear how Menelaus's thoughts turned. "Did not Athens once have some claim over that kingdom? Likely they will assert it once more, now that Crete has lost its king and its prince."

Menelaus's lip curled. "Theseus overreached, taking what he had no right to take, and I will not see Crete fall into the hands of Menestheus. Athens has taken enough from me already."

Paris gazed off into the distance, pretending disinterest. "Menelaus, son of Atreus and Aerope, king of Sparta and Crete."

"You will forgive my going?" Menelaus asked. "I would not wish to sour our friendship, but I see no other course. I cannot deny my grandfather the proper rites, nor see his people abandoned to Athenian greed."

"Of course," Paris said. "It is only right and honorable. No Trojan could find fault in such an act. You must go, and with the blessing of the gods."

"My queen will see to your comfort for as long as you wish to remain in Sparta," Menelaus said, speaking absently now. Paris could see in his eyes that he already planned his departure, eager for his new kingdom and crown. "Anything that you desire, you shall have."

"You are too generous, King Menelaus," Paris said gravely. "But I would not trespass upon your friendship by remaining."

"Nonsense," Menelaus said. "Stay. Enjoy our women and our wine. And when I return, we will speak of trade. With Crete in my power, I will have that much more to offer Troy as its friend and ally."

"Indeed," Paris agreed, smiling. "We will have much to discuss. But do not let me keep you now. Make what preparations you must, and claim your prize, King Menelaus. I promise you I will not feel neglected in the slightest."

Menelaus made his excuses and hurried off, taking the messenger with him.

Enjoy our women and our wine. Paris snorted to himself, watching Menelaus go.

If he only knew.

Helen had made it clear from the start that she would not risk any intimacies between them so long as her husband threatened those she loved, and Paris could not help but desire her all the more for it. He did not press her, not truly, for she would only have resented him if he'd tried, but nor did he relinquish any opportunity to stay by her side. Every moment was delicious torture, even the barest wisp of her scent driving him mad with need. But anticipation would bring its own rewards, of that he had no doubt.

"Paris, please," she pleaded, when he caught her by the hand, pulling her inside the small, dusty storeroom he'd found and marked for just such a purpose. "Menelaus is sure to be looking for me, with so much to arrange before his departure, and I cannot be found alone with you. Not now, of all times!"

"I will not keep you for long," he promised, caressing her cheek once the door had shut behind them. "But I needed to tell you. One of my guardsmen is even now upon the road to Gytheio, with a message for the men aboard my ship. Two of my oarsmen will present themselves to Menelaus's shipmaster come morning, a gesture of my goodwill for his journey. They will have orders to see that Menelaus does not return from Crete. Or even survive his trip there, if it can be managed. You will not see your husband again after he leaves this palace, I swear to you."

"Truly?" Her fingers tightened around his, a fierce light burning in her eyes, making her glow all the brighter.

She was so beautiful, even in shadow, and he could not help himself from pushing back the shawl that covered her hair, freeing the soft golden strands. How desperately he wanted to bury his hands in that bounty, to thread his fingers in her hair while he tasted her lips, her skin.

"We will be free, Helen," he said. "And I beg you not to leave me waiting, once he is gone. Come to me tomorrow night, and we shall both find satisfaction."

Her breath caught as he brushed his nose against the skin of her neck, his lips whispering along the line of her jaw. He nuzzled her ear and she shuddered, stepping abruptly back. "I must go. Before he realizes I am missing, I must go."

He sighed, releasing her only reluctant, when all he wanted was to pull her close. "If you do not come to me tomorrow night, I will find you. I will have you moaning with desire in his bed, and only regret that he will never know."

She drew the shawl up over her hair again, her brilliant green eyes dark with promise. "Perhaps the gods will inspire one of your men to whisper it in his ear while he breathes his last."

He laughed and let her go. Already she was his Helen in spirit, if not in body, and he longed for the day she would be wholly his. He had waited so long already. Years and years. But this final day was the hardest by far, to be so near to his goal and be forced to let her slip free.

It wasn't the first time he'd had to watch her walk away. Nor even the first time she had allowed him some small caress, or the teasing taste of her skin. But this time, it took all his strength not to follow her straight to her rooms, to her bed.

He ought to have thrown Menelaus from the wall while he had the chance.

The next day, Paris waited with Helen and her brothers by the palace gate, struggling to ignore her hand upon Menelaus's breast, her expression a study of longing as she whispered promises of love into her husband's ear. Always, she was the dutiful wife, filled with grief to see her king and husband go. Paris did not know how she managed it, that mask of adoration and desire, and he had wondered more than once how Menelaus had never noticed when it slipped.

He saw it when Menelaus wrapped her hair around his hand and claimed a kiss from her lips, just the slightest stiffening of her body before she gave in, the flash of disgust in her eyes when he released her at last.

"You will care for our guest and all his needs while I am away," he told her, not for the first time in Paris's hearing. "Anything that he desires, you shall grant him."

"Of course," she agreed, smiling tightly. "He will want for nothing, I promise you."

Menelaus clasped Paris by the hand then. "When I return, we will feast again, in celebration of our friendship."

"Your generosity knows no bounds, King Menelaus," Paris said. And he would take full advantage of Menelaus's thoughtless kindness, his greed for Trojan trade. Perhaps this very day, before the king of Sparta had even left his own lands, for Paris was not certain he had the patience to wait longer. Not with Helen vowing so faithfully that he would want for nothing in her husband's absence.

Once he had her in his arms, had found his way between her thighs, her promise would be fulfilled. Of that he had no doubt. He could not imagine wanting anything but the sweetness of her love, hard won and long awaited.

Menelaus grunted, his gaze resting for a moment upon Helen's brothers with clear dislike before he turned away, mounting his chariot and taking up the reins himself. He snapped them over the horses' flanks, and the team lurched forward, kicking up dust and grit as the wheels spun.

Paris watched until the gates were closed behind the king, but when he turned to share a smile with Helen, eager to revel in their new freedom, their love, she was already gone.

CHAPTER FIFTY-THREE

HELEN

If you do not come to me tomorrow night, I will find you.

I closed and barred my bedroom door, unsure of how I meant to proceed. Paris had not meant it as a threat, I knew, but his words felt like a noose around my neck, all the same. The same thick rope I had fought so hard to cut away, all these years.

"Here," Aethra said, pressing a cup of wine into my hands. "Drink."

I stared into the cup, pacing the length of the room without looking up. I could not risk inviting my brothers to my room, nor settling my jittering self in the queen's megaron, where Paris might intrude. I did not trust that a messenger would not be sent after Menelaus, reporting upon my actions after he departed, and I would not breed suspicion in his mind while he could still turn back. Only after he had set sail would I feel any kind of relief, any sense of freedom.

But Paris had not had to live my cautious life. He did not understand my patience—and why should he, when he believed me as eager for him as he was for me? When I had given him every encouragement in order to secure his loyalty and Menelaus's death.

"I fear he will not be refused," I said at last. "And if he fails—if Menelaus survives—I have doomed us all."

"If he fails, it is the will of the gods, Helen," Aethra said, watching me pace. "Fate taking its course, nothing more, and certainly no fault of yours."

"If Menelaus lives, it will mean war."

"And if war comes, at least we will have the satisfaction of seeing Menelaus and Agamemnon suffer. Theseus will have his pyre."

Theseus would have a pyre unlike any the world had ever seen. "But my brothers, my people . . ."

"It is a blessing that if this war begins, it will take men from nearly every corner of Achaea. There will be none left to threaten the women and children who remain behind," Aethra said. "As to your brothers, their lives are in the gods' hands. As they have been from the beginning. But Zeus loves his sons, Helen. Pollux will have his father's protection, of that you can be assured, and Pollux will always protect Castor."

I sat down upon the bed, dragging my gaze from the wine and meeting Aethra's eyes. "Must I go to him?"

She shook her head, kneeling before me. "He is not Menelaus, that you must fear reprisal. You need do nothing you do not wish to."

My eyes narrowed. "But?"

Aethra sighed, sitting back upon her heels. "Theseus would not want you to live your life alone, in grief and mourning. If there is any part of you that might find in him a true partner, perhaps . . . perhaps it is worth the gamble."

"No," I said, my heart aching. I had met the man who might have been my partner in Theseus's absence—the man I might have found some small contentment with, if not love. It was not Paris, no matter what desires he provoked. "To Paris, I am still a prize."

"Then give him nothing," Aethra said. "You've already given too much to waste more upon a boy who does not deserve you."

I steadied myself with more wine and considered having my evening meal in the privacy of my room, perhaps alone with my brothers, as I had not dared do in more than five long years. But why should I cage myself in my own palace, hide away like a slave seeking to avoid the eye of her master? No. Aethra was right. Paris was not Menelaus, and while I knew he had power of his own, I did not think he would use it.

"I had hoped we might speak sooner," Paris said, sitting down beside me when he found me at the head table in the megaron that night.

I would have rather been braced on either side by my brothers, but I could not slight our guest so openly before so much of Menelaus's assembly. As was always the way, those who had come for the feasting lingered, seeing to other business among themselves and with the palace. My days would be long, listening to petitions and seeing to their needs, but I welcomed the work. I'd been little more than an ornament on Menelaus's arm since Tyndareus's passing.

"I cannot neglect all my duties as queen, Prince Paris, even for you." I smiled politely, keeping my tone mild. "And in Menelaus's absence, I must act as king as well."

"Surely a burden you need not carry alone," Paris said. "After all, you have your brothers at your side, princes of Sparta. Is it not their duty to rule in your husband's place?"

"I fear my husband would take great exception if they tried," I said, picking at the roasted goat on my plate. "I would not have them risk themselves so soon."

"I see," he said, and I felt his eyes on me. "You doubt me, doubt even the gods, who have blessed us."

I let out a breath, unsure if I wanted to laugh or cry, but I turned to him all the same, that he might see the heartbreak I had kept hidden so long. "Your coming has been my curse, Paris of Troy. It is nightmare made flesh, seeing you here, knowing what comes after. You cannot imagine how long and hard I have fought to stop it all. If Aphrodite blesses you, it is only because she knows that Ares follows at your heels, ready to rain down fire and destruction over everything and everyone we hold dear."

He drew back, startled by the boldness of my speech, no doubt, for I had been careful until now to show him the woman he clearly wanted—affectionate and demure, blushing at her own desires and excited by his. In truth, there was little involving lust that made me blush. Not since I had given myself up to Menelaus.

"You cannot mean—" He stopped himself at the sharpness of my gaze, the disgust I did not hide, for I had been told too many times what I could or could not mean, and it did not endear him to me to see those words formed upon his lips. His jaw tightened, betrayal flashing across his features, but when he spoke again, he kept his voice low. "Aphrodite herself brought us together. She brought you to me, long ago, gave me my first taste of your lips. You did not want me then, I know, but your hero is dead now. He left you to this life, abandoned you to that accursed son of Atreus. *I* have freed you, Helen, not him. I traded nothing less than my honor for the promise of your love."

"And I traded mine for the safety of my people, my family, my love," I said. "Do you think I would betray them so easily? Theseus's body cannot even be cold, but you expect me to give myself up to you, to love you at all? Surely you cannot want so faithless a woman as your wife."

"Why should you be anything but faithless to a man undeserving of your love?" Paris asked. "You have known, as I have, that we were meant for one another. Fated, even, if what you say is true."

"Theseus was never undeserving," I snapped. "That you would speak of him in such a way, as something to be dismissed and forgotten, proves only that you know nothing at all."

Castor's hand closed about my forearm, reminding me of where we sat, and I turned from Paris, forcing my mouth into a placid smile. More than one of Menelaus's men was watching me, and I feared my voice had risen too loud.

"This is not the place, Helen," Castor murmured, his calm leaching up my arm. "Nor yet the time."

I closed my eyes, praying that Athena had seen fit to clog the ears of our assembly. After all, it was in defense of Theseus's honor that I'd spoken. Surely the goddess could not begrudge me that.

"Forgive me," I said to Paris, though I hardly meant it. "I am out of sorts."

He laughed, the sound more bitter than anything else. "If only I believed you."

But he let the matter drop, turning to speak to my mother on his other side.

"Are you certain it is wise to make your feelings so clear to him so soon?" Castor asked, eyeing Paris warily. "The dust has barely settled in your husband's wake."

"If I did not speak, I would have to spread my thighs," I said lowly, accepting the platter of bread from Castor's hands and serving myself. "Better that I take this risk."

My brother's gaze flicked back to me. "You need not fear going if he has done as he's promised."

I broke open the bread, avoiding his eyes. "Surely you must realize it is not fear that halts my steps."

"Theseus is gone, Helen," Castor said, pinching my elbow as if we were still children and he could not help but tease me. "I would not like to see you destroy yourself in grief, and nor would he."

"It isn't only that I grieve, Castor." I pressed my lips thin, hesitating. My brother was not wholly wrong to encourage me to marry again, though my greater concern was more for peace than personal joy. I did not like thinking of marriage so soon upon the heels of Theseus's death, but I could not remain unmarried for long if Menelaus did not survive his journey. Not without provoking some fool prince into marching on Sparta, thinking he would have me and my kingdom for his prize. "Perhaps you might send word to Thessaly."

"Ah," Castor said, his amusement evident even in so small a sound. "With news of this kind, he is likely to come south almost at once."

"There will be many who come," I said. "But perhaps it would be best if he were the first to arrive."

"You're certain this is what you want, Helen?"

"If he is willing to risk himself and his fortunes, better Polypoetes than anyone else." He, at least, would give me time to grieve, and share in my sorrow. "And so far north in Thessaly, perhaps I will be forgotten. Perhaps we will be safe."

"The messenger will leave this very night," Castor promised.

I nodded and said nothing more.

Paris would simply have to swallow his disappointment and return to Troy without the bride he had hoped for. Castor and Pollux would hardly allow him to take me by force, and with only one companion left within the palace walls, he could not be fool enough to try.

I stayed up late in the megaron, drinking with my brothers and Menelaus's men. Paris matched us drink for drink, laughing with his companion, teasing the serving girls and flattering my mother. I was glad of his good humor, and before I left the table, made certain to see that one of Menelaus's slaves was sent to his bed. Perhaps when he retired he might find some small satisfaction in her embrace, since I had denied him mine.

Pollux rose when I did, begging leave from the men, and for the first time in five years, we walked Sparta's halls without fear, arm in arm.

"You seem lighter already," Pollux said, studying me in the flickering lamplight. "Almost happy, even."

"Perhaps not happy yet," I said, smiling. "But not without hope of happiness, at least, once all of this is behind me. To have the freedom just to grieve is a great gift."

"Poor old Catreus could not have had better timing if he had planned his death for your benefit," Pollux said. "And if Menelaus means to secure his grandfather's throne, he could be gone for some weeks."

"If the gods are with us at all, he will drown in the sea," I said. And let him come face to face with Theseus's shade beneath the waves. "But you are not wrong. It will be months, likely, before we can say with any certainty that he will not return at all. My suitors will circle Sparta like so many vultures hoping for a feast."

"You hardly seem concerned, all the same." We climbed the stairs together, taking our time. Menelaus's chamber was joined to mine, on the second floor but outside the women's quarters, and I saw no reason not to take advantage of the alternate route if it meant remaining a few moments longer in my brother's company. "I fear the competition for your hand will be as fierce as it was before."

"But this time, we need not go to such lengths," I said. "Zeus had his choice, and now I will have mine. Before the rumor of Menelaus's death has spread, I will have a new husband and be well on my way from here. Let my suitors flock to Sparta if they wish, but they will not find the bride they seek. Only my faithful brothers, Sparta's honored and beloved princes, with news of my marriage on their lips."

"And what of your daughter?" Pollux asked. "Menelaus's heir."

I shrugged. In truth, I rarely considered her at all, but it hardly mattered. She wanted for nothing, and Menelaus spoiled her enough that she had no need of me. "Name yourselves her regents and let Leda and Clymene have the raising of her. Alcyoneus has already begun to tutor her as wisely as he did me, and if her uncles dote upon her in her father's place, all the better. You will raise her to be a fine queen without me, I'm certain."

"If her father is dead, she will need her mother, Helen," Pollux said, stopping with me outside Menelaus's door. "You cannot truly mean to abandon her so completely at so young an age?"

I sighed, slipping my arm from his. "Aethra spoke to you, didn't she?"

"Whether she spoke to me or not does not change the truth," he chided, leaning against the wall.

"The truth is that I cannot love her," I said. "And she is better off in the care of those who do. Whether it be Leda or Clymene or you—she was never my daughter, Pollux, and even if I had wanted her to be . . ." I shook my head. "I could not have been the wife Menelaus required and a mother as well. We all would have suffered for it, had I tried."

I left him then, slipping through Menelaus's empty room and into my own. Perhaps if I was fortunate, I would have a dreamless night.

CHAPTER FIFTY-FOUR

HELEN

"Helen, wake up."

My brother's voice and his hand upon my shoulder brought me awake. Pollux perched on the edge of the bed and leaned back as I sleepily struggled upright. Aethra stood beside him, wringing her hands in her skirt, her face alight. "What's happened?"

"It's Theseus," Aethra said. "Poseidon did not forsake him, Helen. He's come for us! But we must leave now. At once."

My breath caught, my heart seizing at her words, but I could not believe them. "Theseus?"

"He sent word from Gytheio," Pollux said. "He waits for you to meet him there. He means to sail for Egypt with the tide, and you with him."

I closed my eyes. Egypt. Theseus alive.

"He only waited for the moment of greatest opportunity to present itself," Aethra said. "And with Menelaus gone to Crete, there is no better time."

"No," I agreed, hope burning away the fog of sleep, sparks of it setting fire to my blood. Theseus was alive. Alive and safe and here! He had promised it. So long ago, when I had told him his fate, he had promised a fall into the sea would not take his life. He had promised he would only swim to safety, and I had dismissed it so easily, sure of his doom. But I had been wrong. I had never been so happy to be wrong. "It must be now, and best that we do not delay, or there will be Paris to contend with, in Menelaus's place."

"The horses are readied," Pollux said. "The Lapith stallions will make the best speed. But you must hurry."

I threw off the linens, surging from the bed. Theseus was alive. He'd come for me, after all this time—how could I have doubted him? I would never doubt him again. "Castor sent a messenger to Thessaly," I said. "To Polypoetes."

"And another will be sent with the dawn," Pollux promised.

I wrapped a simple linen chiton around my body, fastening it at my shoulders with silver pins. "We'll need gold, gifts for the pharaoh, trade goods—"

"Already loaded upon your chariot," Pollux said. "You would travel faster upon horseback, but I did not see how you would manage with so much to carry. You have a whole chest of gold and silver, and another again filled with skirts and gowns. Enough to guarantee your safety once you reach the pharaoh's court."

A shawl covered my hair, too bright and easy to see in the moonlight, all the more so with the circlet upon my brow, and I added several golden bracelets and armbands for good measure, sliding them up my pale arms before throwing myself into my brother's embrace. "Thank you, Pollux."

He laughed, pushing me away. "Thank me by going, and quickly. If you are caught upon the road, I do not see how you will ever manage to get away a second time."

Aethra was already out the door, waiting for me on the other side, but I could not help but press my hand to Pollux's cheek in one last caress, memorizing his face, even shadowed as it was. "You'll remember your promise, won't you?"

He squeezed my hand and let me go. "So long as you remember yours."

And then I fled.

Theseus had come, and I would not leave him waiting for even a moment longer than I must.

My brothers had taught me to ride as a girl, but it was Theseus who had taught me to drive a chariot, during those early days of our marriage in Athens. Theseus who had stood behind me, bracing my body with his own, his hands over mine upon the reins as I drove, first timidly, then with greater confidence and speed. As Aethra gripped the rim of the chariot at my side, jaw tight and legs spread for balance as we rattled along the road, I doubted Theseus had ever dreamed I would put his patient teachings to this particular use. Likely he had never imagined I would race a chariot through the night without him in the car to guide me.

Just as Polypoetes could not have imagined that I would use his horses to slip from his grasp a second time.

I snapped the reins, urging the horses faster, and pushed the thought away. I had promised Polypoetes nothing. And he would understand why I had gone, besides. Once he learned that Theseus lived, he would not question my actions at all.

A shame I could not say the same for Paris. I had sacrificed his honor for my own ends, and now I left him behind with nothing to show for his efforts. If Menelaus returned alive . . .

If Menelaus returned alive, it would not be Paris who was blamed. The thought loosened my hands upon the leather, slick with sweat from my palms, and the stallions lurched forward, making the chariot jump when it struck a rock I had not seen in the silver moonlight. I swore and caught the reins again, wrapping them tightly around my forearms to keep them from slipping, and slowed the horses from a gallop to a canter, then to a trot.

"What's the matter?" Aethra asked, now that she did not have to shout over the noise of the chariot and the horses. "Why have you slowed?"

I had left my brothers to face Menelaus's fury, if he returned alive and found me gone. And while I would shed no tears for Paris, I could not abandon my brothers so easily. Even for Theseus's sake.

"If Menelaus lives and returns to find me missing, Castor and Pollux ruling in my place, he will have them killed. That very night."

"They are not fool enough to remain in Sparta if Menelaus returns home," Aethra said. "And it was Pollux himself who sent you on your way. Castor who readied these horses. They knew the risks they took and did not hesitate for even a moment to see you made safe. Do not repay them by faltering now."

I urged the horses back to speed, but my heart still ached. If only I could know for certain that Menelaus was dead—but I could not trust in anything beyond the nightmares that haunted me still, and I did not truly believe the gods would free me so easily from my fate. Everything I had done had only bound me all the closer to the future they desired.

No. Some god among the Olympians had granted me these dreams for a purpose. To give me the power to stop this war. There was no other explanation for all I had suffered, and so near to freedom, to the safety and comfort of Theseus's arms, I needed to believe it. Menelaus would not return to Sparta, and Agamemnon would look for someone to blame for his death. The gods would have a lesser war, perhaps, but so many would be spared—Achaean and Trojan, both.

But in this moment, I held my fate, like the reins of the chariot, in my own hands. Perhaps the ride was wilder than I might have liked, and the horses difficult to tame, but it was I who drove, all the same. It was not a great comfort, but it was enough to keep me upon the road, giving the horses the freedom to speed us on our way.

Aethra was not wrong, after all. Castor and Pollux were not fools. My brothers had no shortage of friends, and if Menelaus returned, they would not linger long in Sparta.

One way or another, we would all make ourselves safe.

There were at least a dozen ships beached upon the sandy shore of Gytheio, and in the purple light of false dawn, exhausted from the long ride, we searched for some sign of Theseus among them.

My arms ached, my hands blistered from the rub of the leather reins against my palms, and though we drove slowly upon smooth sand, I still felt as though my teeth rattled in my jaw.

"We made good time," Aethra said, no doubt as tired as I was, though she had not fought the horses, as I had. Fast they might have been, but Polypoetes's stallions were determined brutes, eager to forge their own path rather than keep upon the road.

"Yes, but we can hardly go shouting his name from ship to ship." I drew the horses to a halt near a scraggly pine and let us all rest for a moment.

"His will be the ship readying itself to leave." Aethra nodded to the last in the line. "Pollux said he meant to sail with the dawn tide."

"He cannot be the only man hoping to catch the tide," I said. "And that sail—it does not look quite right for an Achaean ship."

"Why should his ship be Achaean?" Aethra asked. "He sails for Egypt, and the vessel itself matters little so long as it will not sink. Theseus is no longer king, that he can turn an Athenian ship to his service. He will make do with what he can find without drawing more attention to his presence than he must."

I snapped the reins lightly and guided the horses toward the ship. If we were wrong, there would be little we could do but drive hard away and hope they had no spears to throw after us. Gytheio was Spartan enough that I hoped we might find shelter and aid, should trouble greet us instead of Theseus, even if it was only out of loyalty to Menelaus's gold rather than love of me.

Aethra stepped from the chariot with a lightness that defied her age, and I pulled my shawl up over my hair, conscious of unseen eyes and the sounds of movement within the ship's hold. "Be careful," I warned her.

"If you hear my shout, you must leave me behind," Aethra said.

I pressed my lips together, refusing her terms with my silence, but Aethra paid me no mind. Likely she had not expected me to agree, and we hardly had time to argue now. She patted one of the stallions on its sweat-soaked shoulder and made for the ship while I wrapped and unwrapped the reins around my hands and arms, ignoring the stiffness of my fingers from gripping them so tight for so long. What we would do with the horses, I did not know. Perhaps take them on board with us, though I doubted Theseus would have feed and water to keep them. But to sell such fine stallions in Gytheio seemed foolish when they would serve us so much better as a guest-gift to secure the friendship and aid of a king.

Aethra had disappeared from sight aboard the ship, and the horses stamped and pawed, impatient as I was to learn our fates. Surely Theseus would have seen us by now. And I could not imagine why he would not come out to greet me—why he hid, still, inside.

A man leapt over the side of the ship, forgoing the plank. I tightened my grip upon the reins, but he carried no weapon, and against the lapping water, I thought I recognized the breadth of his shoulders—the easy grace of his movement.

"Theseus?"

He met the horses first, stroking their noses and necks with a calming hand and soft words. And then, his hand tight upon the halter, holding the horses firm, I saw him clearly at last. His shoulders not so broad as I had imagined, and certainly he did not stand as tall as I had hoped. I trembled with exhaustion, with disappointment so fierce, so painful, I could not breathe.

"I feared you would not come so far alone, but I ought to have known," Paris said, a bittersweet smile curving his lips. "There is nothing you would not risk for your hero, is there? And of course Aphrodite would know your heart, so bound by love for a man who left you to rot."

I shook my head, tugging at the reins. But my Lapith stallions, so well trained by Castor, would not break from the hand that held them. Or perhaps it was some trick of the gods to hold them steady. The same trick that had brought me here, delivering me into Paris's hands, when I longed for Theseus.

"He's dead, Helen," Paris said, and three more men vaulted from the deck, landing in the sand like so many lions, ready to ambush their prey. "And there is nothing left for you in Sparta. No threat to your people that your brothers cannot defeat. You need only take my hand, and the world both your husbands denied you can be yours. Freedom, Helen. Not a life spent in hiding, by your own choice or the will of another. But you sneer at me, at the gift I would give you, the sacrifices I've made for your sake, and I cannot help but wonder why."

I closed my eyes for a moment, swallowing back the sourness of defeat, the bitterness of sorrow. I had lost Theseus so many times, but never so cruelly as this. "Would you believe me if I told you that this freedom you offer me is false? You think it is some glorious gift, some beautiful offering you lay at my feet, but you do not see what comes after. War will follow us, snapping at our heels like fell wolves, and lapping at the blood that will drown your Trojan fields. We will not be free, Paris. We will cower behind the walls of Troy, trapped inside while good men die for the glory of nothing but the whim of fate."

"Aphrodite promised you would be mine," he said, giving up his grasp upon the horse's bridle to reach for me instead. One of the other men took his place, but I kept hold of the reins, biding my time. "The gods themselves have given us their blessing. How can any man stand against us?"

"Did Aphrodite promise you my love? Did she promise you we would have a peaceful, happy life?" I shook my head, remembering my own mistake when I had begged Poseidon for my child's life, for Theseus's safety, but forgotten to consider mine. "Only fools bargain with the gods; only fools trust in their promises, their gifts. Fools and children and lovers."

"Perhaps to your eyes I am all three," he said softly. "But I will not mistrust my goddess after she has given me so much. Or did you never wonder how a shepherd boy became a prince?"

"I wondered why the gods had punished me with nightmares of a burning city, of war and death and pain and rape. I wondered how I might escape such a fate. And when I thought of you, it was only to wonder how I might prevent your coming, how I might stop the ruin that played before my eyes night after night, day after day."

He laughed as if my words were nothing, just a woman's baseless fears. "And was there war when Theseus stole you from Sparta? When Telamon stole Hesione from Troy and made her his queen and bride? How many women did Heracles claim in his lifetime, and how many wars followed in his wake?"

"It does not matter what came before, Paris," I snapped. "Before the gods were not set upon this war. Before it was not a daughter of

Zeus who was stolen, a woman cursed to bring ruin upon men for the glory of her father!"

"Perhaps," he said. "But if it is the will of the gods, as you say, who am I to defy them?" He nodded to his men, behind me. "The queen of Sparta has been kind enough to bring us gifts. We will not do her the dishonor of refusing such a kindness. Put them in the hold."

"What of the horses, my lord?" one of the men asked.

Paris did not spare them even a glance. "The horses, too. We cannot leave them behind in Gytheio to tell your brothers where you've gone, can we?"

"Castor prepared them for the journey himself," I said.

"Beautiful, sweet Helen." Paris smiled, all politeness as he offered me his hand. "Are you so certain it was Pollux who came to your room? That your brothers had anything to do with this at all?"

I clenched my jaw, the realization as painful as a blow to the head. Of course. Of course it had not been Pollux sending me away in the middle of the night, unescorted upon the road. Aphrodite had blinded me so easily. Just a whisper of Theseus's name, and I came running to meet my doom.

"Send a message to Sparta," I begged him. "Send a message with these horses telling Pollux where I've gone. Tell him he must leave Sparta. That he and Castor cannot be found there when Menelaus returns home. Give me that much, and I will climb that ramp your willing hostage, I swear to you. I will give you everything you want."

"A willing hostage, or a willing bride, Helen?"

"Does it matter, so long as I am yours while I stand upon the deck?"

He considered me for a heartbeat, two, three, and then he turned to the man who held my horses so still. Lapith horses, so wild Polypoetes had feared they might do me harm if they were not tamed to my hand, and carefully so. But why should the gods let wild stallions stop them from having their way?

"See to it, then. We'll be well on our way long before they can arrange to follow. And let them have their horses back as well. We'll hardly have need of them when we reach Troy."

I placed my hand in Paris's then, before he could change his mind.

After all, I'd promised myself long ago that if I could not save myself, at least I would save them. Castor and Pollux would not die because of me.

Not yet.

CHAPTER
FIFTY-FIVE
HELEN

I stood alone at the prow of the ship, the morning breeze cool on my bare arms. Aethra had retreated below into the hold, but I could not stomach the darkness, or the memories that would cloud my thoughts. Unending days inside the basket, hiding from Theseus's men and listening to the scrabbling sounds of rats. I would not suffer it again.

If I threw myself into the wine-dark sea, would the war still follow? Was there anything left for me to do, any last desperate act I could take to stop this future, now that the gods had brought me here? I tugged the shawl from my hair and wrapped it around my shoulders instead.

I could murder Paris in his sleep, but his men would still bring me to Troy. If I drowned myself, Menelaus would not believe I was dead when he returned to Sparta to find me gone.

"I knew you would be pleased to go," Paris said, joining me again now that he'd seen to his oarsmen. He was not too proud, this prince of Troy, and the way he spoke to his men, laughing and teasing, listening to their complaints—he might have been a strong king when it was his time, if not for me.

"What makes you think I am pleased?" I asked, keeping my gaze steady upon the horizon. Sailing was not so miserable when I was not trapped inside a stifling tent or stored in a basket in the hold, but the rocking of the ship still unsettled me, my stomach sloshing as wildly as the waves.

"You look ahead," Paris said. "But a woman who did not want to go, who ached for her land and her people, for the love she had left behind—she would look back, desperate for even the barest smudge of that shore she'd been stolen from and eager for any sign of pursuit."

"I need not search for what I know will come," I said. "Menelaus will follow, of that you should have no doubt. And he will bring the rest of Achaea's princes with him, sending our armies crashing against your shores in a tidal wave of destruction. You doom your people by bringing me to Troy."

"What would you have me do?" he asked, his voice low and fierce. "What must I do to prove myself to you? Tell me what you would have me do, and I will do it, I swear. But you must let me try—you must give me some small opportunity to win your heart."

"Must?" I shook my head. "No, Paris. There is no *must*. Not anymore."

"You would live the rest of your life in sorrow, then?" he demanded. "Spiting me for acting in the service of the gods? For a war that is beyond our small power to stop? You could have happiness, Helen. We could have joy, you and I, if you would only give me the chance. Perhaps it will not last forever. Perhaps the war will come one day, and there will be sorrow, too. But should we not hold all the tighter to what pleasure we can find, should we not savor it all the more, knowing it might end?"

I wrapped my shawl tighter around my shoulders, gooseflesh prickling my skin. He did not understand that there would be no joy for me. That every small happiness I had found had been torn from my grasp so that I might stand here upon this ship for his pleasure. As his prize. I cursed myself for believing Pollux's words—or whoever had spoken them in his stolen form. I ought to have realized the gods would never give me such happiness as Theseus's return. But I had wanted it so badly. To believe we might have a life together, free at last, safe in Egypt . . .

Egypt.

"Perhaps there is some small hope," I said slowly, choosing my words more carefully than I ever had before. "Perhaps we might throw off pursuit, misdirect my husband's wrath and find some safety, borrow some small amount of time to . . . to know one another better."

Paris's eyes narrowed. "Another trick, Helen?"

I met his gaze, unflinching. For if I had mastered only one skill while living as Menelaus's wife, it was surely the telling of half-truths. "There is nothing I might do to stop this war, Paris. The gods have made that much clear."

He nodded once, accepting the truth of my position. He held me hostage, and willing or not, I had little recourse while we sailed. It was in both our interests to find some small amount of peace, to build trust. And he wanted to believe it was possible that we might, besides. "Then what do you suggest?"

"Let us sail not directly to Troy, but travel to Egypt first, instead. Menelaus would not dare wage war against the pharaoh, even if he discovers where we've gone, and should he travel to Troy directly in search of me, he will not find us there."

"And why should the pharaoh shelter us in Egypt for any length of time?" Paris asked. "What is to stop him from sending word to Menelaus and betraying our cause?"

"You are a prince of Troy, Paris," I reminded him. "And while I lived as Theseus's wife, I was Meryet, a princess of Egypt by some lesser wife. Do you think I would have dared to claim such a title without the blessing of Egypt's king? He was willing then to support me when I wished to escape Menelaus, and I believe he will do so again."

Paris let out a breath, considering my words, and I held mine, hoping, praying he would trust them. Because I had no doubt that the pharaoh would grant me his aid. Theseus would not have wanted me sent to Egypt if he had thought for a moment I would not be kept safe. And whatever agreement he had come to with the pharaoh before our marriage, through Pirithous and Demophon, it was time I made use of the protections implied.

"Lukios!" Paris called out to the master of the ship, turning back to his men at their oars. "Let us sail for Egypt first, before we return home to Troy."

I ducked my head, hiding my smile. In Egypt, granted sanctuary by the pharaoh and guarded by his gods, I would be beyond the reach of even Zeus, my father. And Paris—Paris would return home with empty hands, if I had my way.

Let the gods find a way to make their war without me.

"Are you certain of this, Helen?" Aethra asked me some days later, when we had our first glimpse of the lush river delta that marked the great Nile, and Egypt's heart. The reedy marshlands and sandy banks were evident even from a distance, and the delta itself was dotted with small vessels—fishermen, I supposed, plying their trade upon the waters.

I wished I had paid closer attention to Alcyoneus's geography lessons when I was a girl, but while I had loved learning the languages he could teach me, I'd never cared much for talk of rivers and mountains beyond Achaea. I had been meant for Sparta, after all, to remain in

Laconia all my life. Languages, I had realized, would serve me well as queen, but the only lands I had needed to know well were mine, and perhaps those belonging to my neighbors.

"Theseus meant for me to come here," I told her, my gaze still fixed upon the delta. We'd discussed it more than once since Paris had agreed to change our course, and by now these reassurances were old friends, though I was not sure either one of us believed them. Less so now that we faced the strangeness of this new land. For all that we shared the same sea, I saw little that felt familiar upon the horizon. "He meant for Egypt to be my refuge, and I will see that the pharaoh honors Theseus's memory by granting the protections he promised."

I reminded myself again that I must trust Theseus. Perhaps he did not live to guard me in body any longer, but that did not mean I was wholly without his protection. It did not mean I was alone.

"You have the tablet," I said. "The moment this ship touches shore in Pi-Ramesses, you will go to the palace and deliver it to the pharaoh. If his gods are with us—if Theseus's shade still lingers near—you will meet no trouble on the way. Use Theseus's name and mine. Shout that you are sent by Meryet of Athens if you must."

"If I had counseled you differently . . ." Her hand found mine, squeezing it tightly. "Will you forgive an old woman's foolish hope that her son might still live?"

"You were not the only woman blinded that night, Aethra," I said, touching my forehead to hers. "I believed it, too. Wanted it so desperately I would not have heard you, even if you had fought."

"He would be proud of you, Helen," she said. "His love for you—had I not seen it reflected back in your own eyes, I would have feared for him."

I blinked back tears, my throat thickening with grief. How Aethra could speak of pride after all she had seen me do, I did not know. "You speak as if we will never see one another again."

"I speak as a mother who wishes she did not have to leave her daughter behind," she said, brushing my hair from my face. "Whatever happens, remember who you are. Remember you were a queen of Athens as well as Sparta, and beloved by my son. Remember there is power in your beauty, though I know you are reluctant still to use it. Bring the pharaoh to his knees with desire, if you must, but make yourself free. All of this is for nothing if you do not find your way free."

"Helen?" Paris called, and I drew back, smothering my sorrow even as I memorized Aethra's words. For days I had slept beside him, pretending interest in the man who had brought me nothing but grief and fear for so many years. At least I did not have to behave as though I loved him. He would certainly have mistrusted it if I had.

But I left Aethra at the prow, walking past the oarsmen to join Paris at the bow of the ship. He preferred to have me there, upon his arm, where the men could see me while they rowed. To give them inspiration, he'd said, laughing, and I'd smiled along. He thought it was a gift, a kindness to me, because Menelaus had insisted I keep covered, had wanted me out of sight, that I would not tempt his men. He did not see that it was all the same—to set me upon display or hide me from their sight. It was still his choice, his preference, not mine.

"We'll be enfolded by the delta before nightfall," he said. "And reach Pi-Ramesses in two days, maybe three, so long as the winds are with us. I do not know how long the pharaoh will make us wait after that, but I hope it will not be more than another day before we're granted rooms within the palace."

"I look forward to spending my nights in a proper bed," I said, leaning against the rail.

"My bed," Paris said, coming to stand beside me. "Where I know you'll be safe."

I shook my head, not bothering to hide my irritation. "You're as paranoid as Menelaus."

"All the same," he said, and I let him fit me against his side. "In a strange land, and at the mercy of a strange king, I would rather be over-cautious than not. And besides, it will be no different than the nights we've spent camped on beaches, or sleeping upon the deck with your head pillowed on my shoulder."

"If custom demands we sleep apart, I will not insult the pharaoh by doing otherwise, and nor should you. Egypt is not Sparta or Salamis, where you need only fear offending the gods, for all the harm our small cities might do yours."

"That is hardly reassuring," Paris said, frowning. "If we must fear Egypt, perhaps we are better off finding another port in which to shelter from the storm of your husband's pursuit."

I sighed. "I only mean to say we should not give unnecessary offense, that is all. We will be safe in Egypt, Paris, I promise you."

"You've promised me many things, Helen," he reminded me, his lips against my ear. "Can you blame me, truly, for having reservations now?"

I shuddered, but fought the urge to shove him away, letting him believe it was desire, not disgust, that affected me. "Three more days," I said. "When we have a real bed, and it will not cause trouble among your men."

"Another promise?" he asked, his voice dry.

"Would you prefer to be thrown overboard while you slept?"

"I am not Menelaus that I must fear my own men." He stroked my hair, caressing my cheek, but his amber eyes did not soften with affection. There was something else in his gaze. Something harder. Mistrust, mixed with impatience and desire. He wanted me, it seemed, and he was tired of waiting. "You would do well to remember it."

I wasn't certain if it was a warning or a threat, but I wasn't interested in finding out. Three more days—I could only pray that Theseus had not been wrong to place his trust in Egypt's king.

CHAPTER
FIFTY-SIX
PARIS

He wanted to trust her.

Helen's hand in his, they were waved into the throne room of the pharaoh's grand palace. So bright with color and gold, it made Priam's palace in Troy seem poor and dull, a pathetic attempt to replicate the riches of a greater land. Everywhere he looked the walls were covered in images of men and women hunting birds with nets or carrying offerings to their pharaoh or their strange animal-headed gods. And the temples they had passed—the monuments! He had never seen works of stone so monstrous. Truly, Egypt's gods could not find fault in the honors they were given in these lands. They must want for nothing from their people.

Men and women, all dressed in white kilts and sheath dresses, filled the large open room and turned to stare at them as they followed their guide. Paris did not speak Egyptian, but he had no trouble imagining the content of their whispers when they looked upon Helen, her hair gleaming as golden as the sun, set off by the long, flowing white dress she'd insisted on trading for after they'd arrived.

The fabric of the gown was so sheer, it all but left her breasts bared, and Helen had even gone so far as to hire a woman from Pi-Ramesses to paint them with henna, the red-brown paste flaking off her body to leave a stain of patterns and designs upon her skin. Gold armbands and bangles, and a circlet set with a single striking emerald, completed her transformation from neglected wife to glorious and powerful queen.

"If I must seduce the pharaoh for our safety, I wish to be prepared," she'd said, when she'd appeared before him so provocatively dressed and adorned. "Of course, if the gods are with us, as you believe, it will not come to that."

Yes, he wanted to trust her. But when they entered the palace grounds and she began to speak in fluent Egyptian, a tongue he could not dream of understanding, and they were greeted almost immediately by her crone, Aethra, he was not so sure that he should. Paris had thought nothing of the fact that Helen had sent her out on some specious errand the day before, when they'd first arrived in Pi-Ramesses. It had never occurred to him that she might send her ahead to the palace as her own herald, and what requests she might have made of the pharaoh behind his back, he would have dearly liked to know.

Helen was far too relaxed, her smile too bright, too happy, after that. And his tension only grew as they stopped before the pharaoh's great golden throne, and a glance at his footstool revealed carvings of broken, conquered men and women under the pharaoh's sandaled feet. But for all his riches, the king himself looked . . . frail.

"Queen Helen of Sparta, daughter of Zeus the Thunderer; late wife and queen consort of Theseus, king of Athens and son of Poseidon Earth-Shaker," a man announced in Achaean, no doubt for their benefit, while a second man repeated him in Egyptian. "And Prince Paris of Troy, son of King Priam and Queen Hecuba."

Helen dropped into a graceful bow, not hesitating to humble herself before the pharaoh by touching her forehead to the floor, and Paris followed her example, if far more stiffly, speaking for both of them before Helen might. "It is an honor to stand in the presence of the king of Egypt."

The pharaoh grunted, his gaze locked upon Helen as she rose. The translator remained at his side, but the king of Egypt waved him away, leaning forward. His pectoral, a heavy breastplate in the shape of outspread wings fashioned of more gold and studded with blue lapis lazuli, glinted in the light. "So I meet at last my lost sister, Meryet."

Helen inclined her head. "I only wish our ruse might have lasted longer, Great King, that we would not meet under such unfortunate circumstances as these."

"It was not *our* ruse, Helen of Sparta," the pharaoh said, and Paris did not care for the way he studied them—as if they were only flies buzzing in his ear. "And why my father agreed to allow this masquerade, I still do not wholly understand. But the priests of Amun assure me that he had reason. They tell me that Amun has demanded your accommodation even now, though why our gods should wish to thwart yours, I cannot imagine. Is it your gold that speaks through my priests? Your beauty that has influenced them?"

Paris stiffened, but Helen laid a hand upon his arm, her nails biting into his skin, demanding he keep still and silent while she negotiated for their safety. A far less certain thing than she had led him to believe it would be. Had she known this pharaoh was not the man she had bargained with before? Her face gave him no clue at all, that queen's mask she had shown Menelaus firmly in place, and he wondered if he had ever truly seen it slip, or if she had only given him glimpses of what he wanted to see, all this time.

"Great King," she said respectfully, "I assure you that the little gold I have brought with me is nowhere near enough to buy me the support of your priests. Nor do I imagine your gods would leave them defenseless in the face of my beauty. If they have spoken, it is with your lord Amun's voice, not mine."

"You come before the Horus throne to beg my protection," the pharaoh said, sitting back again, his eyes narrowed and deeply shadowed. "But I cannot help but wonder, Helen of Sparta, daughter of Zeus, who will protect Egypt from you?"

Helen lifted her chin. "If your priests do not fear my coming, why should Pharaoh be concerned?"

The pharaoh's lip curled above his false beard, and his fingers tightened around the crook and flail—clearly symbols of his office—that until that moment had rested far more casually in his hands. Paris braced himself for a refusal, sure that Helen's words had insulted Egypt's king.

The pharaoh rose, speaking loudly to the room at large in his own tongue. Four of his royal guards stepped forward, and Paris had never wished so desperately for his sword. Helen had forced him to leave it behind, insisting they could not insult the pharaoh by bringing a blade into his throne room.

"Peace, Paris," Helen said. "They're only showing us to our rooms. Pharaoh has granted us quarters in the palace. He means to speak again to his priests and make sacrificial offerings to Amun himself, in the hopes that he might divine the will of his god directly. But the worst he will do is expel us from Egypt. Alcyoneus told me it is like our *xenia*, their *ma'at*. The pharaoh is above all, responsible for maintaining order and balance within his lands. So long as we do not threaten that order, do not introduce chaos to his court, we will be safe enough."

"So you say," Paris mumbled, allowing the guards to usher them from the throne room. It wasn't as though he had much of a choice.

But he couldn't trust her, even then. And he certainly did not trust the king of Egypt.

Paris paced his room. It was well appointed, no question, with brightly painted walls and fine linens upon the bed, but still a cage. They'd separated him from Helen, taking her away without a word of explanation. Of course she hadn't objected, either, only smiled, reminding him again that they must not insult the pharaoh or offend Egypt's traditions.

"You needn't worry about me," she'd said. "I'll be among the pharaoh's own women, and well cared for."

And how conveniently it served her, keeping her from his bed, from his arms, from his very presence. He should have seen through her pretty words, her excuses, night after night, day after day. He should have known not to follow where she led. To come to this place and rely upon alliances she had forged with Theseus.

Because it was Theseus she still loved. Theseus who was never far from her thoughts. Her hero was dead, and still she clung to the dream of that life, the dream of the peace she had thought she'd won in Athens. And the more time he spent in her company, the more he feared she would never look on him as anything but the man who had stolen it from her.

Paris shook his head, coming to stand before the window and staring out at the water, the sand, the golden temples and obelisks, piercing the sky. Aphrodite had promised him Helen. She had promised to give him everything he required to make her his. She would give him Helen's love, too. If he could trust in nothing else, he must trust in the goddess. He must believe in the promises she had made.

Whatever Helen had meant to accomplish, whatever hope she'd had of escape, it would come to nothing. The pharaoh had already made it clear he did not want her in his lands. Certainly he did not want the trouble that would follow on her heels. If Egypt craved order and balance, there was nothing and no one in this world who would upset it more easily than Helen of Sparta.

He had only to wait. And it would be just as Helen said. They would be expelled from Egypt, and this time, when they set sail, he would not listen to her honeyed words, her half-truths. They would sail for Troy, and within the circle of her high walls, Helen would learn to love him.

Aphrodite would make it so.

CHAPTER FIFTY-SEVEN

HELEN

You come to us at an unfortunate time, Helen of Sparta," a woman said, disturbing the quiet of the garden. It was built around a small pool filled with the Nile's water and covered in delicate flowers. White lilies and blue lotus blooms scented the air, and I could almost forget the uncertainty of my position in the warm afternoon sun, listening to the frogs just begin to stir and sing.

I could not deny that the wait—two days, already—made me anxious, even if I dared not show it. Certainly I could not speak of my situation to the other women. Better if the pharaoh's consorts ignored me, I supposed. Better if they forgot I was here at all. I could not afford to cause trouble for the pharaoh in his own home. What I learned of them and of their gossip, I learned from Aethra, who mingled among them, listening for any hint of the pharaoh's mind, that we might be prepared for his decision, whatever it might be. But even as distant as

I had been, I knew without even looking up that the woman who had seated herself on the stone bench nearby was Tausret, the pharaoh's great royal wife and queen of Egypt. Her voice, so full of authority, could not belong to any other.

I bowed low before her, answering in Egyptian, as I had been addressed, grateful I had been given opportunity to practice the tongue since our arrival. I did not understand everything, even so, but it would have to serve. "Forgive me, Great Lady, I did not see you."

She flicked her fingers, dismissing my apology, and folded her hands neatly in her lap, her gaze steady and searching on my face as I retook my seat. "Do you know what will happen when my husband passes from this world, Achaean?"

I lifted my eyebrows. "Pharaoh did not look unwell to me, my lady."

She sniffed in disgust. "And why should Pharaoh show weakness to his enemies?"

"Forgive me," I said again, ignoring her clear disdain. "But I have no wish to be Pharaoh's enemy."

"And yet you arrive here in the company of that Trojan prince," Tausret accused. "Upon a Hittite ship."

"Troy is Troy," I said. "Just as Sparta is Sparta, and Athens is Athens. King Priam can have no quarrel with Egypt, not so long as Egypt wishes to trade. Prince Paris will agree."

"Until Egypt steals his prize, perhaps," Tausret said coolly. "That is what you desire of us, is it not? And what then, Helen? Do you think your Prince Paris will be so pleased then? That he will not carry ill feelings back to Troy?"

I dropped my gaze, flushing. Egypt was so large, so powerful, I had not considered that they might feel threatened by a prince of Troy. But I had not thought of Troy as Hittite, either. Upon the mainlands of Achaea, our cities, our kingdoms were not so tightly woven. Perhaps Athens under Theseus had held the whole of Attica in alliance, but he had been an exception, not the rule. Agamemnon might aspire to something similar, yet an allied king would still rule his own land, and even the whole of the Peloponnese would be no more than a fly to Egypt's palm, should the pharaoh choose to swat us.

"If we allow Prince Paris to leave with you, we invite a different conflict. A united Achaean army raiding our shores, led by the men who might have claimed you for their own," Tausret said. "Or did you think us ignorant of the vows that were sworn?"

"Not even Agamemnon is foolish enough to attack Egypt," I said, certain of that much if nothing else. And how the pharaoh's wife had come to know so much of my past, I would have dearly liked to know. "Surely if you have spies in Achaea, they have told you that as well. But trade through the Hellespont has long been strangled by Troy. My abduction is simply the final insult, the excuse they require to wage their war. What has Egypt done to Mycenae? To Sparta? To Athens or Salamis or Pylos? What resentments can they possibly hold that would bring them here, so far from home?"

"You are as bold as you are beautiful," Tausret murmured, rising from the bench. "Perhaps if Pharaoh survives this illness, you might yet convince him of your cause. Pray the gods see fit to grant you the opportunity, for I promise you, the chaos that will follow his death will do you no favors at all."

"Seti's heir is barely more than a child," Aethra told me late that night. We'd retreated to the small room we shared after the evening meal, little more than two gilded beds and finely painted walls glorifying Egypt's great king, but it was not safe to speak freely until the hall of women had quieted, the rest of the pharaoh's consorts well on their way to sleep. "A boy named Siptah, though there is no small amount of discontent with the choice. Something about his mother's blood, perhaps, and the influence of his uncle. But Tausret's daughter by the pharaoh did not live to see her first blood, and the queen never bore him a son. You should see the way the women eye one another now, with Seti so ill, and all of them bowing and scraping before the great royal wife, knowing she'll be made regent until Siptah's grown."

I let out a breath. The pharaoh had not looked precisely strong, with deep shadows beneath his eyes that even kohl could not hide, but I had not imagined he could truly be so sick. "Tausret will not wish to shelter the most beautiful woman in the world. She is too sure of the risks, and I do not see how I can persuade her otherwise. A man I might convince through charm and seduction, but not the queen."

"The boy will be pharaoh, still, even if he does not rule alone."

But I shook my head. I would not condemn a child to a life of lust and longing that would never be satisfied. "Bad enough what became of Paris."

"Then you must place your faith in Amun, my dear, and pray he still takes an interest in your fate. For if you do not have the support of Egypt's gods, you will be on a ship, sailing to Troy, before long. I do not think poor Seti will survive the night."

And the pharaoh's death would come too close upon the heels of our arrival. That was what Tausret had not said, but I had heard the warning all the same. My presence might yet be construed as the blight upon the pharaoh's health, for he was not so much older than Menelaus or Agamemnon. Too young to sicken suddenly and die if not as punishment from the gods.

"Will the priests speak against me?"

"Egypt's gods will not be pleased if you meddle with their holy men," Aethra warned.

"Then it is as you say," I agreed. "We must hope Amun is still with us. But perhaps it would not hurt if I made some offering to their greatest god, hmm?"

Aethra sighed. "If Theseus only lived, and had come with us . . ."

"If Theseus had lived, I fear we would have faced the same challenges, only while less willing to do what must be done to overcome them."

"He would not want you to offer yourself up as a bribe."

"No," I said. "Nor would I have been willing. But if the price of peace and freedom is a life spent as consort to Amun, or even the falcon-headed god Horus, I will pay it."

After all, I had little left to lose in the trying.

I was not permitted to leave the palace, even to make an offering to the gods, but there was a small shrine in the palace itself, kept for the pharaoh's women, and Aethra brought me there at dawn. For all Alcyoneus's teaching, I knew nothing of Egyptian rituals and religious rites, and it was so early, it seemed even the priest who tended this altar had not risen yet. If there was a priest at all.

In Sparta, I might have made an animal sacrifice and offered the gods the blood of a bull, or even a horse, knowing what I asked for was no small matter. But I had no animals to sacrifice in Egypt, and I did not know what would please the god, besides. Instead I offered the bread and beer served us at every meal, and after a moment's hesitation, the golden cuff Theseus had placed on my arm the day we had been wed.

The walls of the shrine were painted with images of men and women carrying offerings to the god, including the great Pharaoh Ramesses and his queen, according to the carvings beneath. I traced the symbols within their oval seals, the names of the king and queen of Egypt set apart inside. Another image showed Ramesses standing before a seated Amun, with his goddess wife, Mut, and their son, Khonsu, at his side, speaking earnestly.

I was not a king of Egypt, or even a queen, to speak to them so, but I turned to the gilded statuette of Amun, the small votive figure one of many arrayed upon the altar, and bowed low as Alcyoneus had taught me, letting my forehead touch the floor in full obeisance. "Lord Amun, I beg your intercession on my behalf. Remember the protection you offered when your pharaoh accepted me in name as his daughter, and grant it now, through your servants on Earth, whoever they might be. Only tell me what I must do, and it will be done, but do not give me back to Paris, do not force me to continue on to Troy. If it is within your power to stop this war, I beg you, please, do not turn away."

Aethra rested a hand upon my shoulder. "Stealing you from your father's grasp is one thing, Helen, but I fear you ask the impossible of Egypt's great god. While you are in his lands, perhaps he might protect you, but those outside Egypt?" She shook her head. "Their lives belong to Zeus."

I closed my eyes and rose, sick with the truth of it, the knowledge that everything I had done, all that I had sacrificed, might yet be for nothing. "Then let Egypt's armies march, and Amun claim us all for his own."

CHAPTER
FIFTY-EIGHT
HELEN

The pharaoh did not live to see the sun set that night, and the hall of women was filled with the cries of his consorts and wives, weeping with grief and fear for what the future might bring. I understood only a little of their sobbing, but I did not envy them their lives, wholly dependent upon that of the pharaoh, knowing with his death they would have no true place, no matter how luxurious their retirement to distant estates. For the princesses and queens, perhaps it was different. They would always be daughters of the pharaoh and queens of Egypt and as such, accorded honor and respect, though perhaps not always within the palace of the new king.

It was a concern I had never had to face, as a daughter of Zeus and heir of Sparta—but not one I was wholly unfamiliar with. Had I truly been Meryet of Egypt as Theseus's wife, Theseus's fall would have resulted in a similar displacement, and I might have waited as these women did for word of my fate at the hands of his usurper, Menestheus.

As it was, my fears were of a different nature, though my fate was still held in young Siptah's hands, and reliant upon the grace of the queen regent, Tausret.

"The queen would speak with you," a young girl said, finding me with Aethra in the small garden the following morning. Likely she was one of the pharaoh's children, daughter of a lesser consort, and still young enough to wear her hair in a sidelock. "Alone."

I rose, but did not move to follow. "What the queen would say, the mother of Theseus will hear, regardless. Aethra will accompany me."

The girl wrinkled her nose, unsure of how to respond. "The queen said—"

"Then she will say it again when we arrive," I assured her. "She will know it was my stubbornness, not your failure, I promise you."

She shrugged and turned away, not bothering to look back to see if we followed. But she didn't lead us to the throne room, as I had expected. Rather, we found ourselves in the great royal wife's own apartment. The girl was dismissed, and the guarded doors were shut firmly behind us.

Tausret was not alone. Seated beside a table was a white-kilted man with gold and silver rings upon his fingers, and bracelets stacked upon his arms. Wealthy, then, and not bothering to hide it. But was it because he was so powerful he feared no one, or because he desired more than what he already had?

I offered the queen a shallow bow. "Queen Tausret, you have not met my companion, Aethra, consort of Poseidon Earth-Shaker and mother of Theseus, Hero of Attica and late king of Athens."

"A divine king's mother," the man murmured, leaning back. "What fascinating company you keep, my dear."

I ignored him, waiting for Tausret to acknowledge us. She had summoned me, after all, and I had no wish to give her cause to regret it. But after the briefest glance at Aethra, she turned her back on us, crossing to the window.

"The priests tell me if I send you from Egypt, it will offend the gods," she said, clasping her hands behind her back. The counterweight of her pectoral, meant to keep the heavy gold breastplate from sliding down her chest or dragging at her neck, bounced gently between her shoulder blades before it fell as still as the queen herself. "But if you remain, if Paris is sent home without his prize, there will be disruption of a different sort. Be it your husband's arrival to retrieve you with his foreign allies or offense given to a Hittite vassal when the balance of peace between our people teeters on a knife's edge."

"Had I known the trouble my arrival would cause you, I assure you, I would not have come," I said. "But now that I am here, it cannot be undone."

"Were it my choice alone, I would throw you to the crocodiles and be done with it all," Tausret said. "But young Siptah does not wish to let the famous Helen of Sparta leave his kingdom, alive or dead, without seeing her for himself."

I pressed my lips together, my stomach sinking. "With the greatest respect to the young pharaoh, I must respectfully refuse the honor. He is far too young and too impressionable, and I would not influence his desires."

"Ha!" The man rose, his dark eyes narrowing as he studied me. "Do you truly believe you have a choice? Pharaoh does not request, he commands, and we in Egypt must obey."

"Then I will leave," I said. "Place a ship at my disposal, and I will sail for Sparta with the tide. I will return myself to my own home, if you will but look away."

"And leave us with your Trojan prince, his men, his ship to be dealt with?" The man snorted. "Already he is resentful and angry, shouting to be let out of his room, to have you within his reach and beneath his eye."

"Surely there is one woman here who would be pleased to bed a prince! Even if he is only a Trojan. Send her in my place," I said. "He will learn to live with his disappointment before long."

"You underestimate your power if you think he will forget you so easily as that. Even our guards can speak of no one and nothing else, whispering of the beautiful woman they glimpsed once in the halls."

Tausret turned then, a fierce light in her eyes. "What if he believes it *is* her, Bay? Paris, first, and if he is deceived, then Pharaoh as well."

He shook his head, a crease forming between his brows. "And how do you propose we accomplish such a feat? You cannot simply produce another Helen from the clouds—there are no women so beautiful, even within the palace. Paris would not be fooled for a moment."

"Not out of the air, no." But Tausret smiled, her gaze shifting to me, appraising now. "We would need our best sculptor, of that there is no question. But if the gods are truly with us, as the priests believe . . ."

"You cannot be suggesting—" Bay swallowed the rest of his words at Tausret's glower. I would have smiled if it had not been my own fate in the balance, for it seemed Tausret shared my frustration with being told what she did or did not mean. "A *shabti* can only serve in the afterlife, not here. No matter how finely made."

"Similar to a *shabti*, or perhaps nearer to a *ka* statue, but truly neither. You could not have read the scrolls, but there is an account of a priest called Webaoner, who made a crocodile of wax, bringing it to life with his magic. Why not a woman out of clay?" Tausret said.

Bay made a strange noise deep in his throat. Whether it was frustration or agreement, I couldn't be certain. "You would truly trust in magic to solve our troubles now? And not just magic, but the priests, to see it done, to keep their council after, should it succeed."

"We rely upon the priests and their magic every day, every month, every season, every year, Chancellor," Tausret said. "Without them, without the help and protection of the gods, Egypt would starve, the spirits of our dead, every *ka*, would wander without hope of ever finding peace in the next life. I am not afraid to place my faith in them now. Indeed, what greater proof of my worthiness as queen regent? Even to sit upon the Horus throne itself."

The chancellor pinched the bridge of his nose. "You are certain it will work?"

Tausret offered a careless shrug. "If Amun truly wishes to preserve her, he will give the priests the power to see it done. They need only imbue the statue with just enough of her *ka* to fool the prince, and the Trojan will sail on, appeased. Siptah will have his harmless glimpse of the prize, and the true Helen can be returned home. *Ma'at* will be satisfied, and Egypt would be made safe."

I let out a breath, glancing at Aethra and seeing my own hope reflected in her eyes. With two of me, there would be no need for war. Even if the illusion did not last—if Paris only had his false bride for a year, for two, he would be satisfied. "If it can be done, Great Lady, I will honor Amun until the end of my days."

"I will go to the priests at once," Bay said, whatever doubts he might have had smoothed from his face now that it was clear the queen was resolved. He offered a bow and turned to go. "May Amun smile on us all."

I spent days in a small, dusty studio with an artist named Nebamun, sitting still, then standing, watching as he created my likeness in clay, sculpting carefully every dimple, every curve to match. At night I slept upon a makeshift bed in the corner of the room, that I might not be seen. Only Aethra, Tausret, and the strange chancellor Bay knew where to find me, bringing bread and beer, or the occasional fish or fowl for my meals.

From what Aethra had discovered, it seemed Bay was young Siptah's uncle, but that did not explain Tausret's trust in him, or his involvement. The admiring looks he gave the queen regent when he thought no one would notice, however, and the brush of her hand upon his arm when they passed one another in the small studio spoke much more eloquently.

"I could work for a year and never master her beauty, Chancellor," Nebamun told him, when he had at last admitted defeat. He refused altogether to call the work finished. "With so little time granted for the commission, this is how it must be."

Bay grunted, circling the sculpture, his gaze traveling back and forth between it and me. "Fortunately for you, Amun's own hand will finish the shaping. And we must trust in his power."

"Chancellor?"

"Cover it," Bay commanded, ignoring the man's curiosity. "And send it to the temple of Amun this very day. Time runs too short to allow an artist of your skill to chase perfection."

"As you wish, of course," Nebamun agreed.

"And me?" I asked.

Bay's smile was thin, for I was clearly a problem he wanted nothing more than to be rid of, a complication in the way of his courtship of the queen. "You will come with me."

I covered my hair with a shawl and followed him through the palace corridors, nearing the queen's rooms where I had been brought before. We stopped at an ostentatiously appointed apartment, and Bay glanced uneasily over his shoulder before he hurried me inside. The chest with my clothing, packed for me by Aethra in Sparta when we'd been woken in the night, sat beside an ebony table.

"If there is anything of yours you desire to keep, take it now. The rest must go with your *shabti* to Troy."

I dropped to my knees, throwing open the chest and plunging my hands into the sea of gowns and fabrics, my fingers searching for the cool metal of the circlet I'd worn as Theseus's queen, buried at the bottom in the hopes that it might be kept safe. I felt nothing of it, and began tossing the skirts and underdresses from the chest entirely, my heart constricting. Nothing else that I owned mattered, but the circlet—the circlet was all that I had left of Theseus now.

My fingers closed around the smooth gold at last, and I sat back upon my heels, relief flooding through my body. Even when I had given up everything else, thrown his cloak over the palace wall and banished him from my thoughts, I could not give up this circlet. I could not give up the memory of the life we had shared, however briefly, or the comfort of his love.

"Take the rest," I told him. "I need none of it."

He hesitated, standing still behind me, and I could feel his gaze, his curiosity. "They say ruin follows in your wake. That you use your beauty to drive men mad, and take delight in their torment."

"Yes," I agreed.

"But you refused to meet young Siptah."

"Yes," I said again.

"What is it that you truly want, Helen of Sparta?" he asked. "Why did you bring your troubles to our lands?"

"Men cannot fight the gods, Chancellor. Even the daughter of Zeus cannot thwart her father's will for long." I rose, careful of the clothes that littered the polished stone floor, and turned to meet his gaze. "But I hoped—desperately—that perhaps another god, another king among gods, might free me from my fate and deliver my people from their destruction."

"And if you fail?"

"As a queen of Sparta, I must serve my people first. I could not stand before them if I did not try." I pushed back the shawl and settled the circlet upon my head, my fingers brushing over the emerald, taking strength from its fire, from what seemed the whisper of Theseus's shade, always near. "But after this, there is nothing left. I have done everything in my power, and I can only hope and pray it will be enough."

"Enough to stop this future you fear?"

I shook my head, then covered my hair and the circlet. "Enough to survive it, if I've failed."

Bay brought me to the temple, cloaked and veiled, where Tausret waited with the priests of Amun and my clay *ka* sculpture. I held my breath while they said their prayers, sang their spells, and circled the lifeless form, sprinkling us all with the Nile's water, perfumes, and heady incense. The priests touched her mouth, her eyes, her nose, her ears, and then stepped back.

The room was dark but for the oil lamps flickering here and there around the clay. Whether it was to keep my interloping eyes from seeing sacred sights, or for the purpose of the ritual, I could not say, and I did not care. Whatever they required of me to bring my second self to life, I was more than willing to give. When one of the priests came to me, repeating the gestures and incantations, I did not flinch.

Once, I would have doubted. Before Theseus. Before the dreams. Before the gods had taken my unnamed daughter, a sacrifice of blood and body in a bargain they had betrayed. But now, when the thick fingers of my sculpted hand lengthened, smoothed, and twitched, and the red clay mass of my hair turned to delicate strands of gleaming gold, I only whispered a prayer of thanks and turned away.

"She must not see you," Tausret said, catching me by the arm as I passed. "She must believe her own lie, or the spell will be broken and she will turn to clay once more. Your spirit would be at risk, then. What is left of your *ka* will fly to the clay upon your death, should it be left whole, denying you the afterworld of your own people. And should she outlive you . . ."

"I will suffer the same again," I finished for her. Should she turn to clay while in Menelaus's hands or Paris's, I had no doubt the sculpture would be destroyed in a rage, my spirit made safe, and I had no intention of revealing myself to her eyes, causing both her destruction and my own. It was the chance she would survive beyond my uncertain life that might yet trouble me, but I could not quite bring myself to fear my untimely death. Certainly I would be no worse off than I had been before, if I woke to find myself in Menelaus's bed again, or Paris's, for that matter, instead of the afterlife. "I will face that struggle if and when it finds me. Only, if it is true she will take instruction from the priests, let her have happiness, too. Let her find it in Paris, for however long it will last—even Menelaus, after."

Tausret nodded, a flicker of sympathy in her eyes, and Bay guided me out.

"The lady Aethra will see to the needs of your strange *shabti*, serving her as she would you while she remains in Pi-Ramesses, but you will stay in my family's home, outside the palace, on the Nile's bank," Bay said. "You'll be safe from discovery there, so long as you remain inside. Once Paris has been sent on his way with his false bride, you'll have your ship and a crew to carry you home to Sparta, with the queen regent's compliments to your king. I cannot promise you won't arrive too late. Our spies say that your husband did not linger in Crete. That he has left Sparta again already, on embassy to Troy to bring you home."

"But he will not find me there," I said, far from surprised to hear that Menelaus had survived. It was as Pollux had said—the gods would not give up their war so easily. "Even if Paris sails tomorrow, Priam will not have me, and when Menelaus returns to Sparta empty-handed, he will find his wife where she belongs."

"Provided your gods will allow it," Bay said.

But that had always been the risk, and I could not let it worry me now. Amun had given us his blessing, his aid. Surely he would see this to the finish and return me home, even if Zeus had thwarted me before now.

"I owe Egypt a debt," I said. "We are nothing to Egypt's influence and wealth, I know, but if there is anything Sparta might provide—"

"Please," Bay said. "There is nothing we want more than to be rid of you and spared the trouble that will follow. We have acted only as we must to preserve *ma'at*." He inclined his head. "As you have as well, I think, loath as we might be to admit it."

From a man like Bay, I could imagine no higher compliment.

Two days later, hidden by shadow and the fluttering sheer curtains of the window, I watched as Paris and his Trojans floated by Bay's family home, a brilliant and beautiful Helen standing upon the ship's bow. She did not look ahead, her gaze trained upon the palace and the temples of Pi-Ramesses, her forehead creased in troubled lines I had only ever seen in reflection. I told myself I only imagined her unease, and the strange sense of a thread unspooling between us. Whatever magic the priests of Amun had wrought, whatever small piece of my so-called *ka* they had stolen to give the *shabti*-like woman life, I could not regret its loss.

I only wished her joy. Long years of happiness, undisturbed by dreams of war. Let her bask in Paris's love and adoration. Let her feel herself treasured rather than caged.

If I must be Helen of Sparta, let her find contentment as his Helen of Troy.

CHAPTER
FIFTY-NINE
HELEN

Tausret and Bay kept their word. My ship was readied, my crew assigned, and just four days after Paris had left Pi-Ramesses, Aethra and I were sent on our way.

"Not too close upon his heels," Bay had told me, when he'd brought Aethra to join me at his home. He had thawed in his manners considerably since the *shabti* had proven successful, though he spent his nights at the palace, in the apartment I'd seen briefly, near the queen regent's own. I thought perhaps it was Tausret's favors that accounted for the change more than anything else. "Better to give him the time to reach the sea. But you will have everything you require for the journey, and gifts of gold and silver to quiet your husband's temper, should it be needed. I chose the men myself, all happily married to beautiful wives, and honorable to a fault. They will see you safely home."

Now we sat on the deck, Aethra and I, counting sunning crocodiles and searching for the flaring nostrils of hippos beneath the brown water. The oarsmen had little to do while we floated up the Nile, and those who did not drowse were casting lots to pass the time, only a handful doing the work of steering and directing our course along the branches of the silty delta.

"Paris was suspicious at the start," Aethra was telling me, for I'd asked about my strange *shabti*, as Bay had called her, curious despite myself. "But one look in her eyes and you could see her innocence. When she told him she had missed his company and fought the queen for the right to return to his side, it was with such a ring of truth, he could not doubt her long."

"Will she love him?"

"I think she wants to love him. She was told she must. But—" The gaming men burst into laughter, and Aethra scowled over her shoulder at their noise. Perhaps to keep from looking at me.

"Aethra."

She sighed, smoothing a lock of hair behind my ear. "She is you, Helen. How, I do not begin to understand. But she is you, and I do not think there is any part of you that does not grieve, still, for the man you loved. She does not know what she grieves for, perhaps, not truly, but she knows she should. She knows there is more than what Paris can offer."

I nodded, watching a crocodile slither from the bank and glide through the water. "It's strange, isn't it? I never loved Hermione, never worried for her future or concerned myself with her happiness, but this clay creature—I want something better for her."

"You want something better for yourself," Aethra said gently. "And why should you not?"

I closed my eyes and lay back on the warm wood of the deck. "If I cannot save my people, my brothers, Theseus . . . If I fail in this, as I have everything else, perhaps I don't deserve it."

"Even a daughter of Zeus cannot unravel the tapestry of the Fates, Helen," Aethra said, brushing a hand across my forehead. "You have done all that you can, and bravely. Do not blame yourself for the stubbornness of the gods."

But the stubbornness of the gods had never stopped Heracles from succeeding, whatever the task he had set for himself, and I could not help but feel that if I had only chosen differently, somewhere, somehow . . .

I ought never to have let it get this far.

We stopped each night to rest, allowed the Nile to set our pace during the day, and so it was nearly three days later when we reached the mouth of the sea at the port of Per-Amun and found ourselves stalled.

"We've only to wait on the tide," Zaaset, the shipmaster, promised me, unconcerned. "It will give us time to be sure of our supplies, at the least."

And so we waited, mooring the ship and allowing the men to stretch their legs upon land before the real sailing began. Per-Amun had been little more than a fortress once, but like all points of trade, it had grown into a village, then a city in its own right, doing brisk business with the ships that sailed in and the caravans that passed it by. I watched the sky, keeping a wary eye on the dark clouds that roiled upon the horizon and the violent chopping of the sea beneath. The waves pummeled against the shore, even in the harbor, causing the men to grumble.

"Just a squall," Zaaset assured me, his sun- and sea-weathered face and careless shrug a reminder of his long experience. "You'll see, Lady. We'll be on our way in the morning, all the same."

But the morning came, and the seas were still high and rough, the wind blowing hard from the north with no sign of letting up. The shipmaster and the queen regent's seal secured us a room within the home of a minor city official, his young wife stiff and formal. Her husband was not so fine a quality as the men who served as my oarsmen, and he let his eyes roam. Had it not been for Aethra, steady at my side, I suspected his hands might have as well.

I hardly slept upon the straw mat, but Aethra's old bones required the finer bed, and it was more comfortable still than the deck or the hold. At least I did not toss and turn with the thought of rats gnawing on my toes.

One night, then two, then three days, with Zaaset's apologies, his confidence turning to a furrowed brow and dark looks cast at the horizon. The unseasonable weather delayed more than our journey, of course, and soon more ships had filled the harbor of the port city, and rough and weathered oarsmen were everywhere upon the streets.

"The seas have never been so rough this early in *akhet*," Zaaset confessed at last, after the fifth day. "There are some who say it will be an early winter, and many more looking to sell their cargo before it spoils in their holds."

I chewed the inside of my cheek, staring at the still-dark sky, which threatened a storm unlike anything these Egyptians had ever seen. Rain did not fall upon the desert, after all, not like it did in Achaea. Lightning flashed between the distant clouds, thunder drumming low and long, the whisper of my father's fury in my ears. I had stretched his patience too thin.

"Amun cannot let this go on," Aethra said, with far more certainty than I could summon. "He cannot allow Zeus and Poseidon to stall all trade with the East, trapping his people."

"Not all trade, nor all people," Zaaset said. He seemed to know every ship that passed us upon the river or came in from the sea, he had sailed for so long. I was glad Tausret had given him to us, for I could not imagine a more knowledgeable shipman, and never once had his gaze turned lingering or lustful. "From everything I have heard, it is only Per-Amun that is afflicted. And the ships coming in have done so easily enough. They say the clouds only threaten the shore, and it was only when they drew near that the seas became rough."

I said nothing. I had suspected from the start this was the work of my father, and Zaaset's words confirmed it. Paris had his Helen, and so long as Menelaus did not realize she was false, the gods would have their war. I had thought, hoped, that the *shabti* was Amun's way of shelter-ing me, but now I saw the truth. It was as Aethra had said when I had gone to pray: Amun could protect his people, but not those belonging to other gods in other lands. By coming here, I had forced him to take action—but for Egypt's sake, not mine.

"Tell the oarsmen we will remain in Per-Amun for the next seven-day," I said. "Keep guards upon the ship to protect our supplies and the queen's gifts, but give the others leave to entertain themselves, encour-age them to drink and game as they like, until they are useless for a crew even if the weather changes. Let us see what happens then."

For six days, the sea was calm, the dark clouds breaking into sunlight and blue skies. I took the long walk to the shore every morning, skirting the marshes to see it for myself. Zaaset acted as my guard and compan-ion so that Aethra might rest. She was strong enough still for many things, and spry for her years, but Theseus's death had aged her, and Poseidon's hand in turning the sea against us, I thought, troubled her more than she would admit. Always before now, it seemed, the Earth-Shaker had answered her prayers with kindness.

"Per-Amun has emptied again," Zaaset said. "The ships come and go without so much as a stiff wind rising against them."

"Of course," I murmured, more to myself than him.

Zaaset, used to my brooding by now, and never one to be put off by my distraction, cleared his throat. "Forgive me, Lady, but you do not seem pleased."

"Because the moment we have regathered our oarsmen and ready to leave, the sea and the sky will turn against us again," I said, grim.

"Because already I might be too late to protect my people and my family from wasting their lives in a foolish war."

"*Ma'at* demands our obedience to the gods, but you speak as if you would fight them."

"When the gods demand of me chaos, instead of order and justice, what else would you have me do?"

He grunted, but did not argue any further. In truth, there was little else to say. I would try again to sail for Sparta, but I had little hope of success. Even if we escaped to the sea, we would not get far. I imagined Poseidon's fist would smash our ship to splinters against the rocks, if he must. And Aethra—poor Aethra, to be struck down by the god she had loved, the father of her son.

It hurt me to think I had taken so much from her. Theseus first, and now Poseidon as well. I sighed and turned away, back toward Per-Amun.

I'd had my fill of the sea.

"Should I tell the men to make arrangements for their wives?" Zaaset asked, low-voiced. We had resolved to sail the following morning, regardless of the weather. Aethra had refused to be left behind, though I had made her the offer, and sat with us as we discussed our plans for the next day.

Zaaset had already made it clear he would do as I asked, but that did not mean he was blind to the risks we took, and I was glad of his practicality. Like Aethra, he was steady.

"I would not deny them that right," I agreed, though I recognized it might well be our undoing. If they feared the journey, we might board the ship before dawn and find it deserted, but more than anything, I was tired of holding the lives of men in my hands. "If we are fortunate, we will only be forced back."

Zaaset's expression in the lamplight was as grim as I imagined my own was, and none of us saw the purpose in speaking of what might happen if the gods wished to punish us for our hubris. Or *my* hubris, I supposed, for challenging them again.

"Poseidon will not drown me," Aethra said firmly. "Nor your men, so long as I am aboard. He is not so unfeeling as that."

"I cannot say the same for Zeus," I said. "And while he might love *you*, Poseidon has already made it clear he will not answer my prayers for aid."

Zaaset grunted. "No man goes out to sea with a certainty that he will return from the Great Green."

"You know this is different."

He shrugged as if it hardly mattered. "Chancellor Bay chose me for this journey, and the queen regent herself commanded me to see you safely from these lands. I will do my duty, and so will my men, for that is the will of *our* gods. What yours desire is no business of mine."

With that he rose, touching my shoulder as he passed, and leaving Aethra and me alone.

Our long-suffering hosts had taken themselves to their bed some time ago, and whether we succeeded or failed, I would not be returning to their home. Already I had seen the cracks forming in their marriage, the jealousy and the lust. When my host's gaze lingered too long, when I heard my name upon his lips in the night, shouted through the wall while he took satisfaction in his wife. I could only hope that if I left, they might have some chance to heal before whatever bond they had shared was utterly shattered. There was little else to be done.

"You need not risk yourself for my sake," I said to Aethra one more time. "Wait for the next ship traveling north, and I am certain Poseidon will smooth the way."

Aethra shook her head, taking my hands in hers. "This is what Theseus would have wanted."

And I knew so far as Aethra was concerned, that was all that mattered.

CHAPTER SIXTY

HELEN

Wind and waves and salt and spray, and the ship cracked open like an egg, spilling us and the pharaoh's gold like so much yolk.

The men shouted, reaching for me even as they struggled to keep their own heads above the water. But I did not fight. I could not fight any longer. The gods had struck me down, and I had doomed too many with me.

I closed my eyes and let myself sink into the sea. My *ka* would fly to my false clay body, and Zeus would have his war.

It was only right that I would be forced to watch.

CHAPTER SIXTY-ONE
THESEUS

In the water, his legs still had strength enough. He kicked hard, catching her by the hand, dragging her up. He did not need to look to know that his father had already seen to the others, washing them safely to the sandy shore. Poseidon would not risk taking lives that belonged to Amun-Ra. It was only Helen and Aethra whose fates he could command.

Theseus broke the surface of the water, calm now and quiet, and with Helen held firmly beneath one arm, he swam for Egypt's coast.

His father had driven a hard bargain. Neither Helen, nor he, would ever return home. But they would have one another. And even that much they never would have been granted if not for his mother.

His limbs brushed sand and rock soon enough, and he struggled to get his feet beneath him, to steady himself. Poseidon had not healed him wholly, could not when so much of his thigh had been torn from his leg. He would always have a limp, a weakness on his left side that he was not certain he would ever grow used to, but he was not so crippled he could not lift Helen into his arms and carry her from the sea.

She coughed and spluttered when he laid her down upon the sand, and Theseus took in the thirty other men given back to Egypt in a glance. A rush of water and the scrape of metal upon stone brought the heavy chests of gold and gifts tumbling up the beach, followed by the shattered hulk of the ship soon after. Everything that Poseidon had swallowed on Zeus's behalf, all of it returned where it belonged, to maintain the careful balance between the gods.

Theseus smoothed back Helen's golden hair, searching for signs of injury beyond the water she'd inhaled. Three more racking coughs, rolled half upon her side, and she had expelled it all.

"You're safe," he murmured, cradling her in his arms, her head tucked beneath his chin. "My brave, beautiful Helen. I promised you I would come, did I not? I swore upon the Styx to find you wherever you had gone, to keep you safe. And no man or god will tear me from your side again."

Her salty fingers touched his lips, his cheek, and then she stirred, struggling to free herself from his arms, to look at him, he presumed, for the moment he had given her the room, she only stared, wide-eyed and shaking.

"Theseus?" And then she jerked, fighting to rise, stumbling in the sand until he helped her up, steadied her with what was left of his strength. "Aethra!"

"Safe," he promised. "Just up the shore, I should think, where the rocks rise from the sand to form a shallow cave. Poseidon himself carried her from the waves. Likely he is with her still, and it will do us no favors to disturb them."

"And the rest of the men?" she asked.

"As you see." He jerked his chin, directing her gaze down the beach, toward the marshes and the sedge. "And be glad the priests insisted upon an Egyptian ship to take you north, crewed by the pharaoh's own men, or they would not have been half so fortunate, I fear."

"This is a dream," she said. "Or I am dead."

He laughed, gathering her in. "I am told we both have some years left, though I wonder if you will thank me for it. Would you have preferred Lethe's waters to my arms? To forget all that has passed, all that will come?"

She looked up at him then, again, and he saw the question upon her lips. Words shaped, but not voiced.

He shook his head. "The gods will have their Trojan war. Even if Poseidon had not tossed you back to these shores, by the time you arrived, there would have been no stopping it. Your father saw to that."

Her arms slipped around him, and she turned her face toward his chest, hiding her grief, her sorrow. He dropped his head, pressing a kiss to her tangled hair, and then lower, moving his lips against her ear.

"But your brothers live, as do my sons. We won that much, for what little comfort it might bring. And we won this. The rest of our lives, spent together, by Amun's grace and Poseidon's love for the mother of his son, who he could not stand to disappoint."

"All the others. All that death."

He held her more tightly, sharing her heartache. "Apollo should not have meddled with fate, nor burdened you with visions of what would come. He wanted to spare his city, his Troy. And he will do what he can, still, to save it."

She let out a breath. "I cannot fault him for fighting."

Theseus snorted. "Nor I, truly. But for involving you . . ."

"If he hadn't, I would not have begged your protection," she said gently. "I would not have turned to you for help, let you steal me away. We would not have had those years in Athens, Theseus. Known this love."

Likely, she was right, but he wondered—if she had not come to him, he would surely still have wanted her. They would never know, he supposed, what lengths he might have gone to. What might have been. And it served nothing to dwell upon it now.

"Come," he said. The men were stirring along the beach, waking from their shock and exhaustion. "Amun's priests have no doubt given the queen regent the news, but you would do well to write her, all the same. To ask her permission, formally, to remain. If she will have me, and it will calm her fears, tell her I am willing to serve in any capacity she might desire. Reassure her that we mean Egypt no harm."

"Should we not wait for Aethra?"

He narrowed his eyes, caught the barest whisper of girlish laughter over the sound of the waves. Of course she would be young again, in Poseidon's embrace. Theseus would not take the moment from her. "She will find us tomorrow."

And he and Helen had long years spent apart to make up for, besides.

EPILOGUE

There were nights, in those years that followed, that I still dreamed of the war through *her* eyes. Nightmares of blood and fire and grief, until Theseus shook me gently awake and soothed me with gentle words and soft kisses. He had not the power to banish them completely, though I did not realize the truth of it at first. Not until my bleeding did not come, and I confessed my terror to Theseus that we would have to trade another child for our love.

"You needn't fear, Helen," he'd said, taking me in his arms when he saw the tears in my eyes. "It is only Aegeus's blood left in my veins, not Poseidon's ichor. We've nothing to fear from another child."

And then he told me the rest. How he had traded his immortality for our life together, given up his power, his strength, his unnatural youth, even his strange sense of the tides and the sea. He had sacrificed it all that he might live to come to me.

"Heracles was made a god upon the pyre, and one day, perhaps, you will be remembered as a goddess of love and beauty, of fidelity and marriage. I will only be a king. A man who accomplished much, perhaps, but lost more. A man who died an ignoble death, when he was pushed off a cliff into the sea. But I care for none of that. My sons will know the truth, and we will grow old together. The rest hardly matters."

And so it was that we were watching our daughter splash and laugh in the surf—far safer than the Nile, with its crocodiles and hippopotamuses—when we saw the strange ship. Beaten and weathered, listing and half-sunk as it drifted toward Per-Amun.

I rose, shielding my eyes against the sun with one hand, my heart tripping at the sight. There was no question that it was Achaean, painted with great white eyes, and in that moment, I did not doubt who stood upon the bow. Golden hair blew in the wind, her arms wrapped tightly around a trim, helmeted man with a brilliant red beard and a sword upon his hip.

"Menelaus," Theseus said.

I watched my *shabti* for a moment longer, then turned away, calling to our daughter not to wade too deep.

The war had come and gone without me. I did not think Tausret, pharaoh now, after Siptah's death, would be pleased to see my *shabti* again, but I was free. Finally and at last, the fate I had fought was behind us.

After that day, I did not dream of death or war.

I dreamed of Helen in Sparta, hugging her daughter tightly with tears in her eyes, whispering words of love, of adoration, of fervent apology for ever leaving her behind.

Somehow, she was happy, and in Egypt with Theseus and the daughter I had never dreamed I could have, so was I.

ACKNOWLEDGMENTS

First and foremost, thanks so much to Stephanie Thornton for taking a look at the parts of this book that take place in Egypt and giving me some pointers on how to bring it to life. Thanks, too, to Wendy Sparrow for giving a quick read to my opening Helen chapters, to tell me if I was recapping effectively or not, and L. T. Host, Diana Paz, Rick Cook, Valerie Valdes, Kyra, and Zak Tringali, who not only read bits and pieces for me, but talked me through it when I was sure I was in over my head on this whole writing books thing.

Karen and Kevin, I don't even know what I would do without your support. Thanks for always listening to me, even when it's obscure writing or publishing gibberish. John, thanks for always being willing to test my knowledge as well as my storytelling. Drew the Third and Jamie, I can't tell you how glad I am to have you guys in my corner, pushing me to break out of my comfort zone and promote my author self, and Tom and Denise, thanks for your patience when I drop off the face of the earth in the midst of a draft and for being willing to pick right back up again when I resurface—with ideas and help in organizing a party to celebrate, no less!

And thanks so much to my agent, Michelle, without whom this book would not be in your hands, and my editor, Jodi, at Lake Union, for seeing Helen's potential and fighting so hard for her. It's been a particular pleasure during the editing process to work with Tegan, who knows her Greek myths and seemed to understand intuitively what I was working toward with both installments of Helen's story!

Last but not least, thanks so much to my family—extended and immediate—for all the support and love. Emilia, Mattias, Vitas, and especially Adam. Without Adam, I don't see how I could have made any of this a reality. I will thank you forever, and it still won't be enough!

DRAMATIS PERSONAE

Acamas: Youngest son of Theseus, by his second wife, Phaedra; prince of Athens

Aegeus: Previous king of Athens; one of Theseus's fathers, by Aethra; deceased

Aethra: Mother of Theseus; high priestess of Athens; consort of Poseidon and Aegeus; friend to Helen

Agamemnon: King of Mycenae; son of Atreus; older brother to Menelaus; close friend of Tyndareus and his family after spending several years in exile at Sparta as part of Tyndareus's household; husband of Clytemnestra, Helen's sister

Agelaus: Adopted father of Paris; shepherd of King Priam of Troy

Ajax the Great: Prince of Salamis; older half brother of Teucer; great-grandson of Zeus; one of Helen's suitors

Ajax the Lesser: Prince of Locris; one of Helen's suitors

Alcyoneus: Helen's Egyptian tutor; tutor to Hermione, Helen's daughter

Antilochus: Prince of Pylos; son of Nestor; one of Helen's suitors

Antiope: Theseus's first wife; former queen of the Amazons; devotee of Artemis; mother of Hippolytus, Theseus's first son; deceased

Aphrodite: Goddess of love and beauty; daughter of Zeus

Apollo: God of music, poetry, oracles, plague, medicine, and the sun; twin brother of Artemis; son of Zeus

Artemis: Goddess of the hunt, virgins, and the Amazons; twin sister of Apollo; daughter of Zeus

Athena: Goddess of wisdom and war; daughter of Zeus; patron goddess of Athens; appointed Theseus as her hero and champion in Attica

Bay: Chancellor of Egypt; uncle of the young pharaoh Siptah

Cassandra: Princess of Troy; daughter of Priam by Hecuba; sister of Hector, Paris, Deiphobus, and Polydorus (among others); twin sister of Helenus

Castor: Prince of Sparta; mortal twin brother of Pollux; son of Tyndareus by Leda; older brother to Helen and Clytemnestra

Clymene: Helen's maid in Sparta; cousin of Menelaus and Agamemnon

Clytemnestra: Princess of Sparta; mortal twin sister to Helen; daughter of Tyndareus by Leda; younger sister of Pollux and Castor; wife of King Agamemnon and Queen of Mycenae

Deiphobus: Prince of Troy; son of Priam by Hecuba; brother of Hector, Paris, Helenus, Cassandra, and Polydorus (among others)

Demophon: Prince and heir of Athens; son of Theseus by his second wife, Phaedra

Hades: God of the underworld and the dead; brother of Zeus; husband of Persephone

Hector: Prince and heir of Troy; son of Priam by Hecuba; brother of Paris, Deiphobus, Helenus, Cassandra, and Polydorus (among others), famed warrior

Hecuba: Queen of Troy; wife of Priam; mother of Hector, Paris, Deiphobus, Helenus, Cassandra, and Polydorus (among others)

Helen: Princess of Sparta; daughter of Zeus (in the form of a swan) by Leda; demigod twin sister of Clytemnestra; younger sister of Pollux and Castor; wife of King Theseus and former queen of Athens under the name Meryet of Egypt

Helenus: Prince of Troy; son of Priam by Hecuba; brother of Hector, Paris, Deiphobus, and Polydorus (among others); twin brother of Cassandra

Hesione: Queen of Salamis; wife of Telamon; mother of Teucer; stepmother of Ajax the Great; sister of King Priam of Troy

Hera: Queen of the gods; wife of Zeus; goddess of women and marriage

Heracles: Son of Zeus by Alcmene; hero; blessed with tremendous strength and ability; friend of Tyndareus; helped Tyndareus to reclaim the throne of Sparta; friend of Theseus

Hermes: God of shepherds, travelers, and thieves; messenger of the Olympian gods; father of Autolycus, who was the grandfather of Odysseus

Hippodamia: Former queen of the Lapiths; first wife of Pirithous; mother of Polypoetes; adopted daughter and kin to the centaurs; deceased

Hippolytus: Theseus's first son, by the Amazonian queen Antiope; friend of Polypoetes; devotee of Artemis; deceased

Idomeneus: Eventual prince of Crete; son of Deucalion; cousin of Menelaus and Agamemnon; one of Helen's suitors

Leda: Queen of Sparta; wife of Tyndareus; consort of Zeus (who came to her once in the form of her husband, and the second time in the form of a swan); mother of the twins Castor and Pollux, and Clytemnestra and Helen

Leonteus: friend and companion of Polypoetes; Lapith; one of Helen's suitors

Menelaus: Prince of Mycenae; younger brother of Agamemnon; son of Atreus; close friend of Tyndareus and his family after spending several years in exile at Sparta as part of Tyndareus's household; one of Helen's suitors

Menestheus: King of Athens; cousin of Theseus; former steward of Athens under Theseus; great-grandson of Erechtheus, founder of Athens; one of Helen's suitors

Minos: Former king of Crete; father of Ariadne and Phaedra; overthrown by Theseus

Nebamun: Egyptian sculptor

Nestor: Elderly king of Pylos; minor hero; father of Antilochus

Odysseus: King of Ithaca; suitor of Penelope

Oenone: Nymph living on Mount Ida; lover and consort of Paris; mother of Corythus by Paris

Paris: Adopted son of Agelaus; shepherd boy living in the lands surrounding Troy; an unwitting prince of Troy and son of King Priam by Hecuba; brother to Hector, Deiphobus, Helenus, Cassandra, and Polydorus (among others); father of Corythus by Oenone

Patroclus: Kin of King Peleus of Phthia; Myrmidon; one of Helen's suitors

Penelope: Cousin of Clytemnestra and Castor; niece of Tyndareus

Persephone: Queen of the underworld; wife of Hades; daughter of Zeus by Demeter; goddess of spring growth

Phaedra: Theseus's second wife; mother of Demophon and Acamas; daughter of Minos; sister of Ariadne

Pirithous: King of the Lapiths, in Thessaly; son of Zeus by Dia; father of Polypoetes by Hippodamia; cousin and friend to Theseus; presumed dead

Pollux: Prince of Sparta; son of Zeus by Leda; demigod twin brother to Castor; older brother to Helen and Clytemnestra

Polydorus: Prince of Troy; son of Priam by Hecuba; brother of Hector, Paris, Deiphobus, Helenus, and Cassandra (among others)

Polypoetes: Prince of the Lapiths, in Thessaly; son of Pirithous by Hippodamia; one of Helen's suitors

Poseidon: God of earth and sea, earthquakes, and horses; brother of Zeus; father of Theseus by Aethra

Priam: King of Troy; husband of Hecuba; father of Hector, Paris, Deiphobus, Helenus, Cassandra, and Polydorus (among others); brother of Hesione

Tausret: Great royal wife of Pharaoh Seti II and queen of Egypt; queen regent of Egypt during the reign of the young pharaoh Siptah

Telamon: King of Salamis; husband of Hesione; father of Teucer and the Great Ajax

Teucer: Younger brother of Ajax the Great; son of Telamon by Hesione; one of Helen's suitors

Theseus: Deposed king of Athens; Hero of Attica; son of both the god Poseidon and Aegeus, previous king of Athens, by Aethra; father of Hippolytus by Antiope; father of Demophon and Acamas by Phaedra; cousin and friend to Pirithous; husband of Helen when she lived as Meryet of Egypt in Athens

Tyndareus: King of Sparta; husband of Leda; father of Castor and Clytemnestra by Leda; adopted father of Pollux and Helen; uncle of Penelope; friend of Agamemnon and Menelaus; friend of Heracles

Zaaset: Egyptian shipmaster

Zeus: King of the gods; husband of Hera; father of Helen and Pollux by Leda, Heracles by Alcmene, Pirithous by Dia, Apollo, Artemis, Athena, Aphrodite, and Dionysus; brother of Poseidon; god of the sky, thunder and lightning, order and justice

AUTHOR'S NOTE

By now you've certainly noticed that this is not the traditional story of Helen of Troy. However, much like her abduction by Theseus, Helen's journey to Egypt, where she is replaced by a false Helen who is sent in her place back to Troy with Paris, is a documented lesser-known myth. *That* Helen spent the ten years of the Trojan War in Egypt, waiting desperately for Menelaus to swing by to claim her, and according to Euripides, under no small threat of a looming forced marriage to the pharaoh's son. After successfully retrieving the false Helen from Troy, Menelaus is shipwrecked on Egypt's shore, just after the pharaoh's death and just before Helen is imposed upon yet again. The false Helen on Menelaus's ship is whisked away by the gods and replaced by the dutiful, loyal, and faithful "true" Helen who was left behind.

As Dr. Bill Caraher, my ancient history professor at the University of North Dakota, once commented, the idea that Helen was not ever actually in Troy to be given up is in reality a more probable explanation for King Priam's unfathomable choice to wage a devastating war against the Greeks to protect his wayward son's stolen wife. Of course, we'll never actually know what happened, just as we will never actually know if Helen, Theseus, Paris, and Menelaus ever lived, and that puts us in a unique position to explore all the possibilities of what might have been. Helen might have been more than a passive victim. She might have been a player in her own game, as determined to avoid her fate as Paris and Menelaus were to win her. And in many of the threads of her story, Helen and Paris do stop in Egypt during their flight from Sparta. It then becomes a question of what happened while they were the pharaoh's guests.

By some accounts, the pharaoh takes possession of Helen upon their arrival and makes the executive decision to keep her safe until Menelaus can come to reclaim her, but the message sent to Menelaus gets lost somewhere along the way to Sparta. In other versions, Helen requests the pharaoh's help to escape Paris and return home. I chose to give her the most active role I could, to allow Helen to make her own choices as much as possible, rather than simply being carried off, willingly or otherwise.

Theseus's final return to Helen's side, however, doesn't exist in the myths. Not a single account suggests that Theseus ever made any effort to reclaim Helen after her brothers stole her back. Whether this is because he was trapped in the Underworld while her suitors assembled and throughout the entirety of her married life until she was carried off by Paris, or just because he wasn't interested by the time he escaped, isn't clear. (The timelines of Greek myths never are!) But it didn't seem fitting to me that he should be refused even the attempt. And while Theseus's fated end—a fall off a cliff—is a clear echo of his father's death in Athens, I never could reconcile myself to the fact that Theseus was robbed of his immortality *and* his final chance at love. Not when Heracles, by far the more bumbling, was deified and gifted with an Olympian bride. I hope you'll forgive my creative license in giving Theseus (and Helen!) the happily ever after he's been so long denied.

(And I absolutely wasn't going to leave Helen to Menelaus's dubious kindnesses for all eternity—Homer or no Homer.)

For this conclusion of Helen's story, I referred frequently to Robert Graves's *The Greek Myths*, particularly for references to Paris's early life. The only primary source I found for Paris's time spent arranging bull-fights and his adventure with Ares was the *Excidium Troiae*, a medieval manuscript (likely with earlier Roman roots) containing an account of the Trojan War. No matter how late the myth arrived, however, it certainly offers Paris's story a bit more shape outside of his abduction of Helen. His later adventures are rounded out by Ovid, who offers a fascinating character sketch of Paris in his *Heroides*: a man of bold and persuasive confidence, sure of himself and his suit, secure in the knowledge that no matter what excuses Helen offers, he'll win her in the end.

This different Paris is the one I wanted to capture, rather than the coward we're so used to seeing depicted during the events of the war itself. A boy who earned a greater name defending cattle and men from raiders, no matter what mistakes he made later, must have had some seed of courage and strength in his character, and I could hardly imagine Helen being persuaded to run away with a man who wasn't, at the very least, self-possessed! Part of my motivation in writing this book and including more of Paris's early life was to explore his character in ways that are often overlooked—as I did with Helen—including his run-in with Ares as a bull and his prior relationship with Oenone.

Helen and her brothers, along with Aethra and the other allies she meets along the way, spend a not insignificant amount of time debating whether her beauty is a gift and blessing of the gods, or a curse. Isocrates suggests that her beauty (and the war that follows because of it) is Zeus's way of showing his favor for Helen, raising her up above all his other children, because only beauty can overpower even the strongest man, and ensuring that she would be admired by all and fought over, to bring her the greatest renown. In essence, because of this gift of beauty, her song would be sung, her name remembered for all eternity. It was an argument that I found fascinating when I read it, and was eager to explore—it seemed only right that Helen should have the opportunity to voice her own opinion on the subject!

The Bronze Age is still so mysterious, and Homer's influence on early scholarship doesn't do a lot to make it clearer, but as in *Helen of Sparta*, I drew on the ideas of Dr. Dimitri Nakassis, and M. I. Finley's *The World of Odysseus*, creating a society in which kings held significant authority as the head of a centralized government but still required the goodwill of their assembly, their wealthy upper- and middle-class citizens, to maintain their power. This concept is clearly reflected in Theseus's own mythology, when upon his escape from the Underworld, he is rejected by the people of Athens and sent into exile, so it makes even more sense in the context of the story I chose to tell.

For anyone interested in the life of Tausret, queen regent and later pharaoh of Egypt, I recommend *Tausret: Forgotten Queen and Pharaoh of Egypt* by Richard H. Wilkinson, from Oxford University Press. I was also fortunate enough to draw on Stephanie Thornton's not inconsiderable knowledge of ancient Egypt, and if you haven't read her novel *Daughter of the Gods*, about another female pharaoh, Hatshepsut, you're missing out. (And it goes without saying that any errors in the Egyptology of this manuscript are mine, and mine alone!)

As much research as I did, please do forgive me my creative license in matching up my Greek myth to my Egyptian history. Pinpointing mythic events in the historical timeline is never an exact science, and mixing two different pantheons of gods, all with their own motivations, is always challenging to pull off. The decision to create the false Helen out of clay and bring her to life by the magic of Amun's priests, for instance, instead of allowing the Olympian gods to shape her out of clouds, seemed like a way to ground this element more firmly in history.

Magic is, by its very nature, fantastic, but the story Tausret tells Chancellor Bay of the magician who brought to life a crocodile he'd formed out of wax is a preserved Egyptian myth, and it seemed more likely that in Egyptian lands, Helen would have to operate under Egyptian rules, and under the authority of Egyptian gods and *their* magic.

My use of the word *shabti* in reference to the false Helen, however, is not entirely correct. *Shabti* usually refers exclusively to the figures placed in tombs to serve the spirits of the dead in their next life, and *shabti* generally are not animate outside of those terms. The *ka* statue might be a closer match in concept, meant as a resting place for the *ka* of a person after death, and this idea definitely colored the terms by which Helen's spirit would survive should her false self outlive her natural body. Neither was really an exact match, and ultimately, the simplicity of the word *shabti* over the expression "*ka* statue" won out for ease of use.

Myth and history don't always fit neatly together, and I can only hope that in the end, I created a story that allowed you, the reader, to imagine history as the ancient Greeks might have—happening in a world where gods and demigods engaged with their ancestors, where fantastic events and births were accepted facts, and where, just maybe, the most beautiful woman who ever lived had some small power over her own life and fate.

ABOUT THE AUTHOR

Amalia Carosella began as a biology major before taking Latin and falling in love with old heroes and older gods. After that, she couldn't stop writing about them, with the occasional break for more contemporary subjects. She graduated with a BA in classical studies as well as English from the University of North Dakota. A former bookseller and an avid reader, she is fascinated by the Age of Heroes and Bronze Age Greece, though anything Viking Age or earlier is likely to capture her attention. She maintains a blog relating to classical mythology and the Bronze Age at www.amaliacarosella.com and can also be found writing fantasy under the name Amalia Dillin at www.amaliadillin.com. Today, she lives with her husband in Upstate New York and dreams of the day she will own goats (and maybe even a horse, too).